"[A] feast of desert magic, palace intrigue, forbidden romance and veiled princesses making all their own hard choices ... For all the imaginative scope and fresh worldbuilding, the heart of Suri's series beats in the chests of its indomitable heroines. Their every struggle and sacrifice, triumph and fear, resonate more deeply than the fates of whole worlds in less personal fantasies"

Shelf Awareness

"Suri takes us back to Ambha with *Realm of Ash*, an equally lush and tender narrative ... *Realm of Ash* is about anger as allowed—and how anger gets things done. Which makes both books, I think, stories that we deeply, deeply need right now"

Strange Horizons

BY TASHA SURI

The Burning Kingdoms
The Jasmine Throne

The Books of Ambha
Empire of Sand
Realm of Ash

THE JASMINE THRONE

BOOK ONE OF
THE BURNING KINGDOMS

TASHA SURI

orbit

orbitbooks.net

ORBIT

First published in Great Britain in 2021 by Orbit

17

A CIP catalogue record for this book
is available from the British Library.

ISBN 978-0-356-51564-9

Papers used by Orbit are from well-managed forests
and other responsible sources.

MIX
Paper from
responsible sources
FSC® C104740

Printed and bound in Great Britain by Clays Ltd, Elcograf S.p.A.

An Hachette UK Company
www.hachette.co.uk

www.orbitbooks.net

For Carly.
You make the world good.

PROLOGUE

In the court of the imperial mahal, the pyre was being built.

The fragrance of the gardens drifted in through the high windows—sweet roses, and even sweeter imperial needle-flower, pale and fragile, growing in such thick profusion that it poured in through the lattice, its white petals unfurled against the sandstone walls. The priests flung petals on the pyre, murmuring prayers as the servants carried in wood and arranged it carefully, applying camphor and ghee, scattering drops of perfumed oil.

On his throne, Emperor Chandra murmured along with his priests. In his hands, he held a string of prayer stones, each an acorn seeded with the name of a mother of flame: Divyanshi, Ahamara, Nanvishi, Suhana, Meenakshi. As he recited, his courtiers—the kings of Parijatdvipa's city-states, their princely sons, their bravest warriors—recited along with him. Only the king of Alor and his brood of nameless sons were notably, pointedly, silent.

Emperor Chandra's sister was brought into the court.

Her ladies-in-waiting stood on either side of her. To her left, a nameless princess of Alor, commonly referred to only as Alori; to her right, a high-blooded lady, Narina, daughter of a notable mathematician from Srugna and a highborn Parijati mother. The ladies-in-waiting wore red, bloody and bridal. In their hair, they wore crowns of kindling, bound with thread to mimic stars. As they entered the room, the watching men bowed, pressing their faces to the floor, their palms flat on the marble. The women had been dressed with reverence, marked with blessed water, prayed over for a day and a night until dawn had touched the sky. They were as holy as women could be.

Chandra did not bow his head. He watched his sister.

She wore no crown. Her hair was loose—tangled, trailing across her shoulders. He had sent maids to prepare her, but she had denied them all, gnashing her teeth and weeping. He had sent her a sari of crimson, embroidered in the finest Dwarali gold, scented with needle-flower and perfume. She had refused it, choosing instead to wear palest mourning white. He had ordered the cooks to lace her food with opium, but she had refused to eat. She had not been blessed. She stood in the court, her head unadorned and her hair wild, like a living curse.

His sister was a fool and a petulant child. They would not be here, he reminded himself, if she had not proven herself thoroughly unwomanly. If she had not tried to ruin it all.

The head priest kissed the nameless princess upon the forehead. He did the same to Lady Narina. When he reached for Chandra's sister, she flinched, turning her cheek.

The priest stepped back. His gaze—and his voice—was tranquil.

"You may rise," he said. "Rise, and become mothers of flame."

His sister took her ladies' hands. She clasped them tight. They stood, the three of them, for a long moment, simply holding one another. Then his sister released them.

The ladies walked to the pyre and rose to its zenith. They kneeled.

His sister remained where she was. She stood with her head raised. A breeze blew needle-flower into her hair—white upon deepest black.

"Princess Malini," said the head priest. "You may rise."

She shook her head wordlessly.

Rise, Chandra thought. *I have been more merciful than you deserve, and we both know it.*

Rise, sister.

"It is your choice," the priest said. "We will not compel you. Will you forsake immortality, or will you rise?"

The offer was a straightforward one. But she did not move. She shook her head once more. She was weeping, silently, her face otherwise devoid of feeling.

The priest nodded.

"Then we begin," he said.

Chandra stood. The prayer stones clinked as he released them. Of course it had come to this.

He stepped down from his throne. He crossed the court, before a sea of bowing men. He took his sister by the shoulders, ever so gentle.

"Do not be afraid," he told her. "You are proving your purity. You are saving your name. Your honor. Now. *Rise.*"

One of the priests had lit a torch. The scent of burning and camphor filled the court. The priests began to sing, a low song that filled the air, swelled within it. They would not wait for his sister.

But there was still time. The pyre had not yet been lit.

As his sister shook her head once more, he grasped her by the skull, raising her face up.

He did not hold her tight. He did not harm her. He was not a monster.

"Remember," he said, voice low, nearly drowned out by the sonorous song, "that you have brought this upon yourself. Remember that you have betrayed your family and denied your name. If you do not rise... sister, remember that you have chosen to ruin yourself, and I have done all in my power to help you. Remember that."

The priest touched his torch to the pyre. The wood, slowly, began to burn.

Firelight reflected in her eyes. She looked at him with a face like a mirror: blank of feeling, reflecting nothing back at him but their shared dark eyes and serious brows. Their shared blood and shared bone.

"My brother," she said. "I will not forget."

1

PRIYA

Someone important must have been killed in the night.

Priya was sure of it the minute she heard the thud of hooves on the road behind her. She stepped to the roadside as a group of guards clad in Parijati white and gold raced past her on their horses, their sabers clinking against their embossed belts. She drew her pallu over her face—partly because they would expect such a gesture of respect from a common woman, and partly to avoid the risk that one of them would recognize her—and watched them through the gap between her fingers and the cloth.

When they were out of sight, she didn't run. But she did start walking very, very fast. The sky was already transforming from milky gray to the pearly blue of dawn, and she still had a long way to go.

The Old Bazaar was on the outskirts of the city. It was far enough from the regent's mahal that Priya had a vague hope it wouldn't have been shut yet. And today, she was lucky. As she arrived, breathless, sweat dampening the back of her blouse, she could see that the streets were still seething with people: parents tugging along small children; traders carrying large sacks of flour or rice on their heads; gaunt beggars, skirting the edges of the market with their alms bowls in hand; and women like Priya, plain ordinary women in even plainer saris, stubbornly shoving their way through the crowd in search of stalls with fresh vegetables and reasonable prices.

If anything, there seemed to be even *more* people at the bazaar than usual—and there was a distinct sour note of panic in the air. News of the patrols had clearly passed from household to household with its usual speed.

People were afraid.

Three months ago, an important Parijati merchant had been murdered in his bed, his throat slit, his body dumped in front of the temple of the mothers of flame just before the dawn prayers. For an entire two weeks after that, the regent's men had patrolled the streets on foot and on horseback, beating or arresting Ahiranyi suspected of rebellious activity and destroying any market stalls that had tried to remain open in defiance of the regent's strict orders.

The Parijatdvipan merchants had refused to supply Hiranaprastha with rice and grain in the weeks that followed. Ahiranyi had starved.

Now it looked as though it was happening again. It was natural for people to remember and fear; remember, and scramble to buy what supplies they could before the markets were forcibly closed once more.

Priya wondered who had been murdered this time, listening for any names as she dove into the mass of people, toward the green banner on staves in the distance that marked the apothecary's stall. She passed tables groaning under stacks of vegetables and sweet fruit, bolts of silky cloth and gracefully carved idols of the yaksa for family shrines, vats of golden oil and ghee. Even in the faint early-morning light, the market was vibrant with color and noise.

The press of people grew more painful.

She was nearly to the stall, caught in a sea of heaving, sweating bodies, when a man behind her cursed and pushed her out of the way. He shoved her hard with his full body weight, his palm heavy on her arm, unbalancing her entirely. Three people around her were knocked back. In the sudden release of pressure, she tumbled down onto the ground, feet skidding in the wet soil.

The bazaar was open to the air, and the dirt had been churned into a froth by feet and carts and the night's monsoon rainfall. She felt the wetness seep in through her sari, from hem to thigh, soaking through draped cotton to the petticoat underneath. The man who had shoved her stumbled into her; if she hadn't snatched her calf swiftly back, the pressure of his boot on her leg would have been agonizing. He glanced down at her—blank, dismissive, a faint sneer to his mouth—and looked away again.

Her mind went quiet.

In the silence, a single voice whispered, *You could make him regret that.*

There were gaps in Priya's childhood memories, spaces big enough to stick a fist through. But whenever pain was inflicted on her—the humiliation of a blow, a man's careless shove, a fellow servant's cruel laughter—she felt the knowledge of how to cause equal suffering unfurl in her mind. Ghostly whispers, in her brother's patient voice.

This is how you pinch a nerve hard enough to break a handhold. This is how you snap a bone. This is how you gouge an eye. Watch carefully, Priya. Just like this.

This is how you stab someone through the heart.

She carried a knife at her waist. It was a very good knife, practical, with a plain sheath and hilt, and she kept its edge finely honed for kitchen work. With nothing but her little knife and a careful slide of her finger and thumb, she could leave the insides of anything—vegetables, unskinned meat, fruits newly harvested from the regent's orchard—swiftly bared, the outer rind a smooth, coiled husk in her palm.

She looked back up at the man and carefully let the thought of her knife drift away. She unclenched her trembling fingers.

You're lucky, she thought, *that I am not what I was raised to be.*

The crowd behind her and in front of her was growing thicker. Priya couldn't even see the green banner of the apothecary's stall any longer. She rocked back on the balls of her feet, then rose swiftly. Without looking at the man again, she angled herself and slipped between two strangers in front of her, putting her small stature to good use and shoving her way to the front of the throng. A judicious application of her elbows and knees and some wriggling finally brought her near enough to the stall to see the apothecary's face, puckered with sweat and irritation.

The stall was a mess, vials turned on their sides, clay pots upended. The apothecary was packing away his wares as fast as he could. Behind her, around her, she could hear the rumbling noise of the crowd grow more tense.

"Please," she said loudly. "Uncle, *please*. If you've got any beads of sacred wood to spare, I'll buy them from you."

A stranger to her left snorted audibly. "You think he's got any left? Brother, if you do, I'll pay double whatever she offers."

"My grandmother's sick," a girl shouted, three people deep behind them. "So if you could help me out, uncle—"

Priya felt the wood of the stall begin to peel beneath the hard pressure of her nails.

"Please," she said, her voice pitched low to cut across the din.

But the apothecary's attention was raised toward the back of the crowd. Priya didn't have to turn her own head to know he'd caught sight of the white-and-gold uniforms of the regent's men, finally here to close the bazaar.

"I'm closed up," he shouted out. "There's nothing more for any of you. Get lost!" He slammed his hand down, then shoved the last of his wares away with a shake of his head.

The crowd began to disperse slowly. A few people stayed, still pleading for the apothecary's aid, but Priya didn't join them. She knew she would get nothing here.

She turned and threaded her way back out of the crowd, stopping only to buy a small bag of kachoris from a tired-eyed vendor. Her sodden petticoat stuck heavily to her legs. She plucked the cloth, pulling it from her thighs, and strode in the opposite direction of the soldiers.

On the farthest edge of the market, where the last of the stalls and well-trod ground met the main road leading to open farmland

and scattered villages beyond, was a dumping ground. The locals had built a brick wall around it, but that did nothing to contain the stench of it. Food sellers threw their stale oil and decayed produce here, and sometimes discarded any cooked food that couldn't be sold.

When Priya had been much younger she'd known this place well. She'd known exactly the nausea and euphoria that finding something near rotten but *edible* could send spiraling through a starving body. Even now, her stomach lurched strangely at the sight of the heap, the familiar, thick stench of it rising around her.

Today, there were six figures huddled against its walls in the meager shade. Five young boys and a girl of about fifteen—older than the rest.

Knowledge was shared between the children who lived alone in the city, the ones who drifted from market to market, sleeping on the verandas of kinder households. They whispered to each other the best spots for begging for alms or collecting scraps. They passed word of which stallholders would give them food out of pity, and which would beat them with a stick sooner than offer even an ounce of charity.

They told each other about Priya, too.

If you go to the Old Bazaar on the first morning after rest day, a maid will come and give you sacred wood, if you need it. She won't ask you for coin or favors. She'll just help. No, she really will. She won't ask for anything at all.

The girl looked up at Priya. Her left eyelid was speckled with faint motes of green, like algae on still water. She wore a thread around her throat, a single bead of wood strung upon it.

"Soldiers are out," the girl said by way of greeting. A few of the boys shifted restlessly, looking over her shoulder at the tumult of the market. Some wore shawls to hide the rot on their necks and arms—the veins of green, the budding of new roots under skin.

"They are. All over the city," Priya agreed.

"Did a merchant get his head chopped off again?"

Priya shook her head. "I know as much as you do."

The girl looked from Priya's face down to Priya's muddied sari, her hands empty apart from the sack of kachoris. There was a question in her gaze.

"I couldn't get any beads today," Priya confirmed. She watched the girl's expression crumple, though she valiantly tried to control it. Sympathy would do her no good, so Priya offered the pastries out instead. "You should go now. You don't want to get caught by the guards."

The children snatched the kachoris up, a few muttering their thanks, and scattered. The girl rubbed the bead at her throat with her knuckles as she went. Priya knew it would be cold under her hand—empty of magic.

If the girl didn't get hold of more sacred wood soon, then the next time Priya saw her, the left side of her face would likely be as green-dusted as her eyelid.

You can't save them all, she reminded herself. *You're no one. This is all you can do. This, and no more.*

Priya turned back to leave—and saw that one boy had hung back, waiting patiently for her to notice him. He was the kind of small that suggested malnourishment; his bones too sharp, his head too large for a body that hadn't yet grown to match it. He had his shawl over his hair, but she could still see his dark curls, and the deep green leaves growing between them. He'd wrapped his hands up in cloth.

"Do you really have nothing, ma'am?" he asked hesitantly.

"Really," Priya said. "If I had any sacred wood, I'd have given it to you."

"I thought maybe you lied," he said. "I thought, maybe you haven't got enough for more than one person, and you didn't want to make anyone feel bad. But there's only me now. So you can help me."

"I really am sorry," Priya said. She could hear yelling and footsteps echoing from the market, the crash of wood as stalls were closed up.

The boy looked like he was mustering up his courage. And sure enough, after a moment, he squared his shoulders and said, "If you can't get me any sacred wood, then can you get me a job?"

She blinked at him, surprised.

"I—I'm just a maidservant," she said. "I'm sorry, little brother, but—"

"You must work in a nice house, if you can help strays like us," he said quickly. "A big house with money to spare. Maybe your masters need a boy who works hard and doesn't make much trouble? That could be me."

"Most households won't take a boy who has the rot, no matter how hardworking he is," she pointed out gently, trying to lessen the blow of her words.

"I know," he said. His jaw was set, stubborn. "But I'm still asking."

Smart boy. She couldn't blame him for taking the chance. She was clearly soft enough to spend her own coin on sacred wood to help the rot-riven. Why wouldn't he push her for more?

"I'll do anything anyone needs me to do," he insisted. "Ma'am, I can clean latrines. I can cut wood. I can work land. My family is—they were—farmers. I'm not afraid of hard work."

"You haven't got anyone?" she asked. "None of the others look out for you?" She gestured in the vague direction the other children had vanished.

"I'm alone," he said simply. Then: "*Please.*"

A few people drifted past them, carefully skirting the boy. His wrapped hands, the shawl over his head—both revealed his rot-riven status just as well as anything they hid would have.

"Call me Priya," she said. "Not ma'am."

"Priya," he repeated obediently.

"You say you can work," she said. She looked at his hands. "How bad are they?"

"Not that bad."

"Show me," she said. "Give me your wrist."

"You don't mind touching me?" he asked. There was a slight waver of hesitation in his voice.

"Rot can't pass between people," she said. "Unless I pluck one of those leaves from your hair and eat it, I think I'll be fine."

That brought a smile to his face. There for a blink, like a flash of sun through parting clouds, then gone. He deftly unwrapped one of his hands. She took hold of his wrist and raised it up to the light.

There was a little bud, growing up under the skin.

It was pressing against the flesh of his fingertip, his finger a too-small shell for the thing trying to unfurl. She looked at the tracery of green visible through the thin skin at the back of his hand, the fine lace of it. The bud had deep roots.

She swallowed. Ah. Deep roots, deep rot. If he already had leaves in his hair, green spidering through his blood, she couldn't imagine that he had long left.

"Come with me," she said, and tugged him by the wrist, making him follow her. She walked along the road, eventually joining the flow of the crowd leaving the market behind.

"Where are we going?" he asked. He didn't try to pull away from her.

"I'm going to get you some sacred wood," she said determinedly, putting all thoughts of murders and soldiers and the work she needed to do out of her mind. She released him and strode ahead. He ran to keep up with her, dragging his dirty shawl tight around his thin frame. "And after that, we'll see what to do with you."

The grandest of the city's pleasure houses lined the edges of the river. It was early enough in the day that they were utterly quiet, their pink lanterns unlit. But they would be busy later. The brothels were always left well alone by the regent's men. Even in the height of the last boiling summer, before the monsoon had cracked the heat in two, when the rebel sympathizers had been singing anti-imperialist songs and a noble lord's chariot had been cornered and burned on the street directly outside his own haveli—the brothels had kept their lamps lit.

Too many of the pleasure houses belonged to highborn nobles for the regent to close them. Too many were patronized by visiting merchants and nobility from Parijatdvipa's other city-states— a source of income no one seemed to want to do without.

To the rest of Parijatdvipa, Ahiranya was a den of vice, good for pleasure and little else. It carried its bitter history, its status as the losing side of an ancient war, like a yoke. They called it a backward place, rife with political violence, and, in more recent years, with the rot: the strange disease that twisted plants and crops and infected the men and women who worked the fields and forests with flowers that sprouted through the skin and leaves that pushed through their eyes. As the rot grew, other sources of income in Ahiranya had dwindled. And unrest had surged and swelled until Priya feared it too would crack, with all the fury of a storm.

As Priya and the boy walked on, the pleasure houses grew less grand. Soon, there were no pleasure houses at all. Around her were cramped homes, small shops. Ahead of her lay the edge of the forest. Even in the morning light, it was shadowed, the trees a silent barrier of green.

Priya had never met anyone born and raised outside Ahiranya who was not disturbed by the quiet of the forest. She'd known maids raised in Alor or even neighboring Srugna who avoided the place entirely. "There should be noise," they'd mutter. "Birdsong. Or insects. It isn't natural."

But the heavy quiet was comforting to Priya. She was Ahiranyi to the bone. She liked the silence of it, broken only by the scuff of her own feet against the ground.

"Wait for me here," she told the boy. "I won't be long."

He nodded without saying a word. He was staring out at the forest when she left him, a faint breeze rustling the leaves of his hair.

Priya slipped down a narrow street where the ground was uneven with hidden tree roots, the dirt rising and falling in mounds beneath her feet. Ahead of her was a single dwelling. Beneath its pillared veranda crouched an older man.

He raised his head as she approached. At first he seemed to look right through her, as though he'd been expecting someone else entirely. Then his gaze focused. His eyes narrowed in recognition.

"You," he said.

"Gautam." She tilted her head in a gesture of respect. "How are you?"

"Busy," he said shortly. "Why are you here?"

"I need sacred wood. Just one bead."

"Should have gone to the bazaar, then," he said evenly. "I've supplied plenty of apothecaries. They can deal with you."

"I tried the Old Bazaar. No one has anything."

"If they don't, why do you think I will?"

Oh, come on now, she thought, irritated. But she said nothing. She waited until his nostrils flared as he huffed and rose up from the veranda, turning to the beaded curtain of the doorway. Tucked in the back of his tunic was a heavy hand sickle.

"Fine. Come in, then. The sooner we do this, the sooner you leave."

She drew the purse from her blouse before climbing up the steps and entering after him.

He led her to his workroom and bid her to stand by the table at its center. Cloth sacks lined the corners of the room. Small stoppered bottles—innumerable salves and tinctures and herbs harvested from the forest itself—sat in tidy rows on shelves. The air smelled of earth and damp.

He took her entire purse from her, opened the drawstring, and adjusted its weight in his palm. Then he clucked, tongue against teeth, and dropped it onto the table.

"This isn't enough."

"You—of course it's enough," Priya said. "That's all the money I have."

"That doesn't magically make it enough."

"That's what it cost me at the bazaar last time—"

"But you couldn't get anything at the bazaar," said Gautam. "And had you been able to, he would have charged you more. Supply is low, demand is high." He frowned at her sourly. "You think it's easy harvesting sacred wood?"

"Not at all," Priya said. *Be pleasant*, she reminded herself. *You need his help.*

"Last month I sent in four woodcutters. They came out after two days, thinking they'd been in there *two hours*. Between— that," he said, gesturing in the direction of the forest, "and the regent flinging his thugs all over the fucking city for who knows what reason, you think it's easy work?"

"No," Priya said. "I'm sorry."

But he wasn't done quite yet.

"I'm still waiting for the men I sent this week to come back," he went on. His fingers were tapping on the table's surface—a fast, irritated rhythm. "Who knows when that will be? I have plenty of reason to get the best price for the supplies I have. So I'll have a proper payment from you, girl, or you'll get nothing."

Before he could continue, she lifted her hand. She had a few bracelets on her wrists. Two were good-quality metal. She slipped them off, placing them on the table before him, alongside the purse.

"The money and these," she said. "That's all I have."

She thought he'd refuse her, just out of spite. But instead, he scooped up the bangles and the coin and pocketed them.

"That'll do. Now watch," he said. "I'll show you a trick."

He threw a cloth package down on the table. It was tied with a rope. He drew it open with one swift tug, letting the cloth fall to the sides.

Priya flinched back.

Inside lay the severed branch of a young tree. The bark had split, pale wood opening up into a red-brown wound. The sap that oozed from its surface was the color and consistency of blood.

"This came from the path leading to the grove my men usually harvest," he said. "They wanted to show me why they couldn't fulfill the regular quota. Rot as far as the eye could see, they told me." His own eyes were hooded. "You can look closer if you want."

"No, thank you," Priya said tightly.

"Sure?"

"You should burn it," she said. She was doing her best not to breathe the scent of it in too deeply. It had a stench like meat.

He snorted. "It has its uses." He walked away from her, rooting through his shelves. After a moment, he returned with another cloth-wrapped item, this one only as large as a fingertip. He unwrapped it, careful to keep from touching what it held. Priya could feel the heat rising from the wood within: a strange, pulsing warmth that rolled off its surface with the steadiness of a sunbeam.

Sacred wood.

She watched as Gautam held the shard close to the rot-struck branch, as the lesion on the branch paled, the redness fading. The stench of it eased a little, and Priya breathed gratefully.

"There," he said. "Now you know it is fresh. You'll get plenty of use from it."

"Thank you. That was a useful demonstration." She tried not to let her impatience show. What did he want—awe? Tears of gratitude? She had no time for any of it. "You should still burn the branch. If you touch it by mistake..."

"I know how to handle the rot. I send men into the forest every day," he said dismissively. "And what do you do? Sweep floors? I don't need your advice."

He thrust the shard of sacred wood out to her. "Take this. And leave."

She bit her tongue and held out her hand, the long end of her sari drawn over her palm. She rewrapped the sliver of wood up carefully, once, twice, tightening the fabric, tying it off with a neat knot. Gautam watched her.

"Whoever you're buying this for, the rot is still going to kill them," he said, when she was done. "This branch will die even if I wrap it in a whole shell of sacred wood. It will just die slower. My professional opinion for you, at no extra cost." He threw the cloth back over the infected branch with one careless flick of his fingers. "So don't come back here and waste your money again. I'll show you out."

He shepherded her to the door. She pushed through the beaded curtain, greedily inhaling the clean air, untainted by the smell of decay.

At the edge of the veranda there was a shrine alcove carved into the wall. Inside it were three idols sculpted from plain wood, with lustrous black eyes and hair of vines. Before them were three tiny clay lamps lit with cloth wicks set in pools of oil. Sacred numbers.

She remembered how perfectly she'd once been able to fit her whole body into that alcove. She'd slept in it one night, curled up tight. She'd been as small as the orphan boy, once.

"Do you still let beggars shelter on your veranda when it rains?" Priya asked, turning to look at Gautam where he stood, barring the entryway.

"Beggars are bad for business," he said. "And the ones I see these days don't have brothers I owe favors to. Are you leaving or not?"

Just the threat of pain can break someone. She briefly met Gautam's eyes. Something impatient and malicious lurked there. *A knife, used right, never has to draw blood.*

But ah, Priya didn't have it in her to even threaten this old bully. She stepped back.

What a big void there was, between the knowledge within her and the person she appeared to be, bowing her head in respect to a petty man who still saw her as a street beggar who'd risen too far, and hated her for it.

"Thank you, Gautam," she said. "I'll try not to trouble you again."

She'd have to carve the wood herself. She couldn't give the shard as it was to the boy. A whole shard of sacred wood held against skin—it would burn. But better that it burn her. She had no gloves, so she would have to work carefully, with her little knife and a piece of cloth to hold the worst of the pain at bay. Even now, she could feel the heat of the shard against her skin, soaking through the fabric that bound it.

The boy was waiting where she'd left him. He looked even smaller in the shadow of the forest, even more alone. He turned to watch her as she approached, his eyes wary, and a touch uncertain, as if he hadn't been sure of her return.

Her heart twisted a little. Meeting Gautam had brought her closer to the bones of her past than she'd been in a long, long time. She felt the tug of her frayed memories like a physical ache.

Her brother. Pain. The smell of smoke.

Don't look, Pri. Don't look. Just show me the way.

Show me—

No. There was no point remembering that.

It was only sensible, she told herself, to help him. She didn't want the image of him, standing before her, to haunt her. She didn't want to remember a starving child, abandoned and alone, roots growing through his hands, and think, *I left him to die. He asked me for help, and I left him.*

"You're in luck," she said lightly. "I work in the regent's mahal. And his wife has a very gentle heart when it comes to orphans. I should know. She took me in. She'll let you work for her if I ask nicely. I'm sure of it."

His eyes went wide, so much hope in his face that it was almost painful to look at him. So Priya made a point of looking away. The sky was bright, the air overly warm. She needed to get back.

"What's your name?" she asked.

"Rukh," he said. "My name is Rukh."

2

MALINI

The night before they were due to reach Ahiranya, Malini was not given her usual medicine. There was nothing in the wine Pramila handed her to drink before she slept—no aftertaste of cloying sugar that signaled she had been dosed with needle-flower.

"You will need to be alert when you meet the regent," Pramila told her. "Alert and polite, princess."

The words were a warning.

Malini did not know what to make of the new clarity of her mind. Her skin felt too tight over her bones. Her heart—finally allowed the freedom to grieve without the blanket of needle-flower to smother it—was a heavy throb in her chest. She felt as if her ribs ached with the weight of it. She crossed her arms around herself, and felt each indent, each hollow. Counted them.

After weeks muted by the needle-flower, the world was a painful ricochet of sensation. Everything was too loud, too hard, the light of the day too painful. The jolt of the carriage made her joints hurt. She was a sack of flesh and blood.

For once, she couldn't drown out Pramila's reading of the Book of Mothers. Pramila sat next to her in the carriage, stiffly upright, reciting with painstaking slowness. First, Divyanshi's childhood. Then, the crimes of the yaksa and their terrible devotees, the Ahiranyi. Then, the ancient war. Then, how it ended.

Then, the book closed, and turned. And reopened, and repeated over again.

It made her want to scream.

She kept her hands still and calm in her lap. Maintained the measure of her own breath.

She was an Imperial Princess of Parijatdvipa. Sister to the emperor. She had been named at the feet of a statue of Divyanshi haloed in flame and flowers. *Garland weaver*, they'd called her. *Malini*.

She had woven her first crown from roses shelled from their thorns, as her mother had taught her the words of the Book of Mothers with far more sweetness and verve than Pramila's dry voice could ever muster.

The mothers ended their lives willingly in holy fire. Their sacrifice was an old, deep magic that lit the weapons of their followers with flame and set the monstrous yaksa alight.

That was the point in the book when her mother had often pretended to wave a sword in front of her, bringing the tale some much-needed levity. Malini had always laughed.

Their sacrifice saved us all. If not for the mothers, there would be no empire.

If not for the mothers' sacrifice, the Age of Flowers would never have been brought to an end.

Sacrifice.

Malini looked out of the chariot at the land of Ahiranya. The air smelled wet and rich from rainfall. The thin curtain surrounding her concealed nearly everything, but through the gap that billowed with the movement of the wheels she could see the shadows of cramped buildings. Empty streets. Broken trees, splintered by axes, and the charred remains where some had been burned away entirely.

This was the nation that had almost conquered the entirety of the subcontinent in the Age of Flowers. This was what remained of a once great power: a dirt track so uneven that the chariot jolted violently every few seconds, a few shuttered stalls, and scorched earth.

And Malini had not seen a single brothel yet. She was oddly disappointed to realize that all those highborn boys who had boasted to her brothers about being able to bed a dozen women the moment you set foot in Ahiranya for the price of a single Parijati pearl had been grossly exaggerating.

"Princess Malini," said Pramila. Her mouth was thin. "You must listen. It is your brother's will."

"I always listen," Malini said evenly. "I know these tales. I was properly raised and taught."

"If you remembered your lessons, neither of us would be here."

No, thought Malini. *I would be dead.*

She turned back to Pramila, who still held the book open on her knees, the pages pinned flat by her fingers. Malini glanced down, identifying the page, and began her own recitation.

"*And Divyanshi turned to the men of Alor who served the nameless god above all others, and the men of Saketa who worshipped fire, and said to them, offer my son your sworn loyalty, your unbreakable vow, and his sons after him. Unite with my beloved homeland, in one dvipa, one empire, and my sisters and I will raze the yaksa from the earth with our honorable deaths.'*"

She paused, considering, then said, "If you turn to the next page, Lady Pramila, there's a very fine illustration of Divyanshi lighting her own pyre. I am told I look a little like her."

Pramila slammed the book shut.

"You're mocking me," she snapped. "Princess, do you have no shame? I am trying to *help* you."

"Lady Pramila," a voice called. Malini heard the clatter of horses' hooves as a figure drew nearer. "Is there anything amiss?"

Malini lowered her eyes. She saw Pramila's grip tighten on the book.

"Lord Santosh," said Pramila, voice like honey. "Nothing is amiss. I am merely instructing the princess."

Santosh hovered, clearly wanting to involve himself.

"We will reach the regent's mahal soon," he said, when Pramila remained silent. "Make sure the princess is prepared."

"Of course, my lord," Pramila murmured.

His horse drew away.

"See what happens when you misbehave?" Pramila said quietly. "You want him to report your childishness to your brother? Would you like to see more punishments rained down upon us?"

What more could her brother possibly do to her than he had?

"I still have other children," Pramila said. Her fingers were trembling faintly. "I would like to see them live. If I must *make* you behave . . ." She let the threat, half-formed, hang in the air.

Malini said nothing. Sometimes apologies only served to inflame Pramila's anger further. An apology, after all, could not right any wrongs. Could not bring back the dead.

"Double your dosage tonight, I think," Pramila announced, opening the book once more.

Malini turned her ear to Pramila. Heard the sound of the book cracking open; the rasp of fingers against the pages. The drone of Pramila's voice.

This is what a pure and holy woman of Parijat can accomplish, when she embraces immortality.

Malini counted the shadows of the soldiers through the curtain. Lord Santosh's figure was hunched over his horse, a parasol held over his head by an obedient lackey.

She thought of all the ways she would enjoy seeing her brother die.

3

PRIYA

Rukh stared at everything in the regent's mahal: the lattice walls cut into hollow roses and lotus flowers, the airy hallways broken up by white silk curtains, the bouquets of peacock feathers carved into the bases of the sandstone columns that held up the high, silver-tiled ceilings. He tried to dawdle and drink it all in, but Priya dragged him along mercilessly. She couldn't afford to give him the time to gawp. She was very, very late back, and although she'd warned the cook Billu that she was going to be late—bribed him with hashish she'd saved specifically for this occasion—there was only so far that she could stretch his goodwill.

She handed Rukh over to the care of Khalida, a sour-faced senior maidservant who agreed reluctantly to ask their mistress if the boy could do some menial work in her manse.

"I'll come back and see you later," Priya promised Rukh.

"If Lady Bhumika allows him to stay, you may collect him before the evening meal," Khalida replied, and Rukh bit his lip. Worry tinged his expression.

Priya bowed her head.

"Thank you, ma'am." To Rukh, she said, "Don't worry. Our lady won't say no."

Khalida frowned, but did not disagree. She knew just as well as Priya did how generous the regent's wife could be.

Priya left them both, went to the maids' dormitory, where she hastily daubed the worst of the mud and dirt from her frankly grimy sari, and headed to the kitchen. She tried to make up for her lateness by stopping at the stepwell on the way and collecting two brimming buckets of water. There was never a time when water was not useful in a busy palace kitchen, after all.

To her surprise, no one seemed to have noticed her absence. Although the large clay ovens were hot, and a few servants bustled in and out, the majority of the kitchen staff were huddled by the tea stove.

Mithunan, one of the younger guards, was standing by the stewing pot of tea, drinking from a clay cup held in one hand as he gesticulated wildly with the other. All the servants were listening to him intently.

"...only one advance rider," he was saying. "One horse. You could tell he'd come all the way from Parijat. His accent was pure court, and the watch captain said he was carrying the imperial token." Mithunan took a sip of tea. "I thought the captain would faint, he was so shocked."

Priya put the buckets down and drew closer.

Billu looked over at her. "Good to finally see you," he said dryly.

"What's going on?" she asked.

"The princess is arriving *today*," one of the maidservants said, in the kind of hushed and excited tone reserved for the best gossip.

"She wasn't meant to arrive for at least another week," Mithunan added with a shake of his head. "We weren't even told to look out for her on watch. But she hasn't got a retinue with her, the rider said, so she's moving fast."

"No retinue," Priya repeated. "Are you sure?"

Every royal from every city-state in Parijatdvipa traveled with a vast and mostly useless array of followers: servants, guards, entertainers, favored nobles. For the sister of the emperor to travel with anything less than a small army was an absurd concept.

Mithunan shrugged. "I only know what the rider told us," he said awkwardly. "But maybe the rules are different when—well, you know. In the circumstances." He cleared his throat. "Anyway. I was sent to bring some food back with me. We had a double shift and we might need to stay on for a third. The men are hungry."

"Where are the day shift guards?" Billu asked, already moving to pile a basket full of food.

"Out in the city," said Mithunan. "Captain said the regent wants everything safely shut down before the princess makes it here. Brother Billu, do you have any more tea? Or sugarcane? Anything to keep us all awake..."

Priya quietly slipped away as they continued talking, filching one paratha from the basket by the ovens as she went and stuffing it wholesale into her mouth. Sima would have called her a mannerless beast if she were here, but she wasn't, so Priya was free to be as uncouth as she liked.

She'd been wrong to assume someone had been murdered. There had been no throats cut or bodies laid outside temples. No rebel killings.

Just a princess, arriving early for her imprisonment.

After her work was done, Priya plucked Rukh from Khalida's care and guided him to the dormitory where the children slept. Once she'd found him a spare sleeping mat, she took him with her to her own dormitory, shared by eight other maids. Beneath the cover of the plain canopied veranda that surrounded it, ringed by fresh falling rain, she kneeled down, wrapped her hands in her pallu, and started carving the sacred wood down into a bead.

The burn of the wood through cloth was strong enough to make her swear. She bit down on her tongue for a moment, one pain to distract her from another, and kept on whittling, hands steady and sure. She could handle a lot more pain than this.

"Come and sit next to me," she said to Rukh, who was still standing in the rainfall, visibly overwhelmed by the direction his day had taken. He stepped onto the veranda. Kneeled down beside her. "Hand me one of those," she added, pointing to the small pile of ribbon and thread spooled on the ground next to her. He picked one up. She lowered the knife and took it from him.

"Is there anything else I can do?" he asked timidly, as she threaded the bead neatly onto the string.

"You could tell me how you're finding your new life so far," she said. "What work has Khalida set for you?"

"Cleaning latrines," he said. "It's fine. No, it's—really, really good. A bed and food is...is..." He trailed off with a helpless shake of his head.

"I know," she said. She really did. "Go on."

"I said I'd do anything and I will," Rukh said, all in a rush. "I'm very grateful, ma'am."

"I told you to call me Priya."

"Priya," he said obediently. "Thank you."

She didn't know what to do with his gratitude except ignore it, so she simply nodded and pressed the bead of wood against her own skin. The bead was small enough that instead of burning her, it merely warmed her wrist, its magic seeping through her flesh and into her nerves, her blood. She held the bead there for a moment, ensuring that it wouldn't be strong enough to harm Rukh but would still be strong enough to help him, and watched his face. He'd lowered his chin, gaze fixed on the raindrops splashing against soil. He still looked overwhelmed.

She remembered how she'd felt when she'd first come to the regent's mahal. She'd cried every night that first week, folding her sleeping mat over her face to muffle the sound of her own tears so she wouldn't wake the other girls.

"I'm going to tell you a story," she said to him lightly. He lifted his head and looked at her, curious. "Have you heard the one about the cunning yaksa who tricked a Srugani prince into marrying an Ahiranyi washerwoman?"

He shook his head.

"Well, give me your hand and I'll tell it to you."

She wound the thread around his wrist and began her tale.

"It was near the start of the Age of Flowers, before the Srugani and others like them understood how strong and clever the yaksa were . . ."

By the time Priya had rambled out what she could remember of that tale of masks and mistaken identities, a duel of honor and a washerwoman draped in a veil of white lilies and saffron, Rukh had started to relax, leaning back on the veranda and smiling a little as he fidgeted with the new bead of sacred wood on his wrist.

"Be careful with that," Priya told him. "It's not going to be easy to get more sacred wood. You know where it comes from?"

"The forest?"

"From the trees that grew when the yaksa all died," Priya said. "Sacred wood has some of their magic in it." She tapped the bead with her own fingertip. "No more yaksa means no new trees, which makes sacred wood costly. So treat it nicely, okay?"

"*There* you are," a woman's voice said. Priya and Rukh both turned their heads. The rain was fading again, but the woman standing at the edge of the veranda with her pallu drawn over her hair had been caught in the last dredges of the downpour, the cloth glimmering faintly with water. "Priya," she said. "Come with me. You're needed."

"Sima," Priya greeted her. She picked up the spools of ribbon, the knife, and the remains of the shard of sacred wood, and tidied them away. "Sima, this is Rukh."

"Hello, ma'am," he said guardedly.

"Nice to meet you, Rukh," said Sima. "You should head to the kitchen before you miss dinner."

"Go on," Priya agreed, as Rukh looked over at her for reassurance. "You can find your way to your own dormitory, can't you? The other boys should guide you from there."

He nodded. With a final mumbled thanks and the faintest smile in Priya's direction, he jumped from the veranda and ran off.

As soon as he was gone, Sima grabbed Priya by the arm and hauled her across the veranda, back toward the mahal proper. Her hand on Priya was strong, rain damp and faintly scented with soap from hours laundering clothes.

"So you *did* bring a stray home," Sima said to her. "I should have known it was true."

"Who told you?"

"Oh, one of the guards who let you in. I don't know," Sima said dismissively. "You're lucky Billu covered for you. You came back so late."

"If I'd known the markets were going to be shut, I wouldn't have bothered going out at all. I went to—help," Priya said. "You know what I do. But I couldn't do much. And then I found him. He was alone, Sima."

Priya saw a familiar mix of exasperation and affection flicker across Sima's face before her friend rolled her eyes and shook her head. "Speaking of market closures—you really do need to come with me." Sima let go of Priya's arm, twining her arm with Priya's with a conspiratorial air instead. "And we're going to need to rush."

"Why?"

"The princess is almost here," she said, as if Priya were a simpleton. "We're going to watch." She tugged Priya forward. "Come *on*. I had to bribe one of the guards with a whole flask of wine to get a good spot."

"I'm hungry," Priya protested.

"You can eat later," Sima said.

They went to a storeroom, high in the mahal, where a narrow barred window overlooked the marbled entrance courtyard. The window was only large enough for one of them to peer out of at a time. Priya looked first and saw the regent and his advisors, attendants with parasols standing beside them to keep at bay the ever-present threat of rain. Soldiers in Parijatdvipan white and gold were arrayed in a great crescent around them.

She drew back, letting Sima take her place.

"You should have kept some wine for us," Priya muttered, crouching on the floor.

Sima shook her head. "I'm not going to have time for drinking. I've got a new job. While you were off gallivanting around the city, Gauri was roping up girls to do chores in the princess's new dwelling. Sweeping up, cooking, the usual." Sima shot Priya a sidelong glance. "You should find her and volunteer too. We could finally work together again."

They hadn't shared chores since their first year in the mahal, when they were both still girls. Sima had left her village and her family and come to the mahal by choice, but she'd been overwhelmed by the size and bustle of the city. Priya had been like Rukh, of course: one of the pity cases taken in by the regent's wife, just another orphan abandoned, feral and angry and entirely alone. They'd clung to each other out of necessity at first. But they had soon built a friendship on the back of a shared affection for pretty girls, liquor, and nights spent gossiping in their dormitory, laughing with each other until one of the maidservants trying to sleep threw a shoe to shut them up.

"Is the coin good?" Priya asked.

"The coin is *very* good."

"I would have thought she'd have more volunteers than she could manage, then."

"Ah, no." Sima squinted through the bars. "Come over here. I can see horses."

Priya got up with a groan. When Sima didn't move, she nudged in close to her, pressing their faces together so they could both look.

The horses were beautiful, pure white and bridled in brilliant gold, drawing a chariot of silver and ivory bone. The inhabitants were hidden, shrouded above by a dark cloth canopy, surrounded by a wall of curtains. There were riders on either side of the chariot, but there was, indeed, no full retinue. Just a clutch of soldiers, bristling with weapons, and a nobleman who lowered himself from his horse and bowed perfunctorily to the regent.

"The princess," Sima said against her ear, as the curtain of the chariot parted and an older noblewoman alighted, "is being imprisoned in the Hirana."

There was a sudden white emptiness in Priya's skull.

"Gauri's struggling to get volunteers," Sima was saying. "There's me, of course. A few new girls who don't know better. That's all."

"But you *do* know better," Priya managed to say.

"I want the money," Sima said quietly. "I don't want to be a maid for the rest of my life. I didn't come to Hiranaprastha for that. And you…" Sima huffed out a breath, but Priya was so numb she didn't feel it, even though they were cheek to cheek. "I don't think you want to be here forever either."

"It's not a bad life," Priya said. "There are worse ones."

"That doesn't mean you can't want just a little bit more than you have," said Sima. "And what happened there—it was a long time ago, Pri."

"The Ahiranyi don't forget." Priya moved away from the window. Pressed her back to the wall and stared at the ceiling.

"Let the rebels remember," Sima said. "Let them write their poems and songs and take up arms. You and I, we should look after ourselves."

She didn't add *because no one else will*. That truth was ingrained in their marrow.

But.

The Hirana.

If Gautam had brought her close to the bones of her past, the Hirana was the grave where the broken pieces of her memory lay at uneasy rest.

It all tumbled over her then. The exhaustion. The void inside her. Rukh's bravado and loneliness, like a mirror flinging her own past before her. The thought of how easily a blade could part skin. The humiliation of being knocked over, dismissed, talked down to. *And what do you do? Sweep floors?*

She was meant to be so much more, once.

She couldn't be the person she'd been reared to be. But maybe, just maybe, she could allow herself to want a little more than what she had. Just a little.

It sparked up suddenly in her heart—a desire so small and yet so powerful that it welled up in her like hunger in a starving body. She couldn't let herself want her old gifts or old strength. But *this* she could want: enough coin to buy sacred wood without groveling before a man who hated her. Enough coin to make life a little *better*: for those children at the market, who had no one. For Rukh, who was her responsibility now. For herself.

Coin was power. And Priya was so tired of feeling powerless.

"I can see her," Sima gasped suddenly. "Ah—I can't see her face, but her sari is lovely."

"She's a princess. Of course her sari is lovely."

"Gray, though. I thought she'd wear something brighter."

"She's a prisoner."

"Who knows what imprisoned royalty get to wear? Stop sniping at me, Pri. Come and look."

Priya took Sima's place this time. A slim figure had just alighted from the chariot. Priya could see the edge of a hand still resting against the chariot's wall, the pearly fabric of the princess's sari moving slightly in the breeze.

"I'm going to find Gauri," she said, stepping back.

"Right now?" Sima asked, her forehead wrinkling in confusion.

Priya didn't want to wait. If she thought too long on how foolish this was, she would convince herself not to do it.

"Why not?" Priya said. "I need to ask her for a job. I'll come to the Hirana with you." She forced a smile. "You're right, Sima. It's time to take care of myself."

4

MALINI

They were greeted courteously by the regent, General Vikram. He had his young wife at his side—a pretty and doe-eyed Ahiranyi woman, who offered her a polite but timid smile, then retired to her own palace with apologies. Lady Bhumika was late into her pregnancy, and unable to keep up with the demands of entertaining guests.

Malini was not a guest, of course. She was not here by *choice*. But Lord Santosh—as disgustingly pleased to be in charge of her imprisonment as he had been on the day Chandra had placed the responsibility of her in his hands—insisted on a lavish meal. Advisors to the regent joined them, but to her relief Malini was given a place of honor at a remove from the rest of them.

Great platters were brought out. Perhaps General Vikram had been warned in advance that Lord Santosh, like Emperor Chandra, had a marked distaste for anything that was not inherently Parijati, because the meal resembled the food she would have eaten in the imperial mahal in Harsinghar. It was heavy with ghee and raisins and pistachios, saffron swirling fragrantly through pale dhal. She picked at it, struggling to make herself eat as the regent asked polite questions about the journey and Santosh responded. Ever since Malini had begun being dosed with needle-flower, her appetite had waned. She felt no hunger now.

She should have been weighing up the regent: his weaknesses, his beliefs, the likelihood that these things could be leveraged to turn his loyalties against Chandra. He could not possibly *like* her brother—no sensible man liked her brother, and General Vikram would not have held the regency for so long if he were lacking in intelligence—but her mind was still a tangle of knotted thoughts, made slow by the weeks of needle-flower.

She could only sit, and stare at her plate, and feel her own mind stumble drunkenly over what must be done. She would need to find a way to win over the maids of the household, now that she had no jewels or coin to bribe them for favors. She would need eyes and ears in the mahal.

"The princess does not yet know," Santosh said, sounding more gleeful than Malini liked, making her head rise, "where her prison cell is located. Would you like to do the honors, General Vikram?"

The regent's gaze flickered between them.

"Emperor Chandra has requested that you be housed in the Hirana, princess," he said.

Malini wished she could be surprised. But she was not. Dread and resignation pooled through her, rolling from her stomach through her limbs, until even her fingers felt numb.

"The Hirana," she repeated. "The Ahiranyi temple."

Pramila inhaled audibly. She had not known, then.

"The temple where the priests of Ahiranya set themselves alight on my father's orders," Malini said slowly, looking from Pramila's pinched face to the regent's unreadable one. "The temple where twenty-five children—"

"Yes," General Vikram said abruptly. He looked rather gray himself. He had, she remembered, been regent when her father had ordered those deaths.

"There is no other Hirana, princess," Santosh said with a mild chuckle. Oh, he was thrilled, wasn't he? "What better place," Santosh went on, "to contemplate your choices. To think about what awaits you."

General Vikram was looking away from her, his eyes fixed on the lattice window. As if by not acknowledging what lay before him, he could ignore her fate.

"Whatever my emperor brother wills," Malini said.

* * *

The Hirana was like nothing she had ever seen before.

It was a huge edifice, rising to a zenith where the temple proper sat. But there were no clear stairs up its height—no easy gradient of stones. Instead, it was as if someone had actually taken a pile of bodies—animal, mortal, yaksa—and stacked them upon each other to create a mountain of the dead. From a distance, to Malini's eyes, it looked grotesque.

It looked no better when she was guided to a rope and bid to climb it.

"You must be careful, princess," Commander Jeevan, the guide provided by the regent, told her calmly. "The Hirana is extremely dangerous. The surface is damaged in many places, and opens to deep pits. Do not release the rope. Follow my lead only."

The carvings upon the stone were uneven to walk on and distressingly lifelike. Malini looked at them as she climbed, clutching the rope tightly, Pramila huffing behind her. Snakes coiled, their teeth bared, mouths vast enough to act as a neat trap for an ankle; mortal bodies, etched out of stone, with hands upturned, fingers curled; yaksa, those ancient spirits that were part mortal and part nature, with eyes that oozed greenery, profuse vegetation escaping their mouths, their forms humanlike, but broken at the stomach, the heart, by thick, violent surges of leaves.

No wonder the world had feared Ahiranya once. Malini could imagine how the Hirana had looked in the Age of Flowers, when it had been lacquered in gold and the temple elders still held great power and the yaksa still walked the world. The figures below her, with hair of vines and razor teeth, skin like bark or crumbling soil, filled her with a visceral, instinctual wariness.

The Parijati soldiers that Santosh had brought with him to guard Malini climbed nervously. Santosh no longer looked gleeful. As they drew higher and the rain began to splinter the sky, his voice took on a distinctly whiny cast as he asked how long it would be before they reached the top.

"Not long, my lord," Commander Jeevan said, still calm. If he thought anything of their cowardice, he was sensible enough not to show it. "Maids have prepared the rooms for the princess in advance. I believe you'll be pleased."

Malini's prison was in the northern end of the Hirana. She was led through echoing, empty corridors—through a strange atrium opened all around to the sky—to a large chamber with a lattice wall hidden behind a faded curtain clearly intended to keep out the chill of the atrium. There was only one door. Another had clearly been sealed off—bricked shut to allow only one entrance and exit into the room. There was a single charpoy of woven bamboo for a bed. A trunk for her meager collection of clothing.

The walls were still stained black, the carvings in the room blasted and faded, worn by neglect and flame. Malini looked around. Raised her head to the ceiling, as the guards and Pramila and Santosh bustled around her, and realized, with horror, that this had to have been the room where Ahiranya's priests burned to death.

Of course it was. Damn her brother and the cruel, twisted nature of his mind. Of course he would lock her away far from all her support, all her alliances. Of course he would send her to a room in a decaying temple where dozens of children had died screaming in flame, simply for the crime of being too powerful, too *monstrous*—

"Yes," Santosh said. A heavy hand settled on her arm. Malini did not flinch. Did not hit him. She was proud and sickened by that in turns. "This will do. Emperor Chandra will be pleased."

After the guards had been placed at the entrance to the Hirana—after Commander Jeevan had left, guiding Santosh down with him—Malini lay back on the charpoy and Pramila opened the tiny bottle of medicine she wore at her throat. She poured two doses, as promised, into a carafe of wine. Placed it by Malini's side.

"Drink," she said.

Malini turned her face away. Closed her eyes.

"Not this again," Pramila sighed. "Drink, Princess Malini, or I will be forced to call the guards."

She would do it. She had done it before. Had them pin Malini's arms as Pramila wrenched back her head and pried open her mouth and forced the liquid in, watching Malini choke and splutter, all the while saying, *If only you were good—good as the emperor demands... No one wants to hurt you, princess, no one.*

Malini raised herself up onto her elbow and lifted the carafe. Drank.

Then she lay back down and waited for the drugged stupor to overtake her.

I cannot survive like this, she thought, already growing detached. The ash-marked ceiling stared back at her. *I cannot.*

"The regent has arranged maidservants to maintain the temple," Pramila murmured. Malini heard Pramila open the Book of Mothers once more, to begin Malini's lessons all over again. "You will not see them, though, princess. I've made sure of that."

Pramila knew Malini too well.

A draft made its way in from the strange atrium beyond, the one that was exposed to the elements, even at its roof where the sky peered through a vast opening cut into the stone. She shivered, curling up to ward off the cold.

Use what you have, Malini reminded herself. *Use anything and everything you have. What can you do? What do you have here that may save you?*

They were stealing her mind from her. They had denied her human company. She had nothing but herself. Nothing but the rage and grief that pulsed in her heart.

The darkness crept over her. She heard Pramila's voice, muted and distant. In the lightless world between sleep and waking, she tried to remember her old strength. Her old cunning. She wrapped her anger at Chandra around herself like new skin; as if she were a snake, sloughing off one body and making another.

She would force herself to survive. She would wait. And when an opportunity came to escape the Hirana—any opportunity—she would take it.

She promised herself this, and sank down deep, deep. Down into the memory of her heart sisters' screams as they burned.

5

ASHOK

When Ashok was ten years old, he entered the deathless waters for the first time.

That was the right age for the first immersion. He had lived at the temple since he was no more than a toddling child. He'd been selected and trained. Taught not to complain when seated in the sweltering heat of the midday sun or in the cold night's dark without a candle. He had learned how to cope with hunger, with the burn of an older temple sibling's hands twisting his skin. That was how the temple children of the Hirana were taught. How they learned about pain and strength and the need to excise weakness.

It had been a normal morning, until then. Elder Saroj had led him and the others through their prayers and chores, and watched as they had prepared gifts for pilgrims to take home with them: vials of deathless waters, broken from their source but still a beautiful, glowing blue in their bottles; sacred wood, whittled into tiny charms; tender fruits, their piths studded with spices carefully pressed into place by childish hands.

But after all that had been completed, instead of releasing them as usual, she had led them to the waters.

"Three journeys," she had said. "After three journeys through the waters, you will be elders like us. This is only your first journey. Don't forget: Those of you strong enough to survive must still work hard and grow even stronger. It is our responsibility to keep the faith, and to preserve the memory and traditions of Ahiranya's grand history. Even if the Parijatdvipan empire forgets what we once were, we do not forget."

Those of you strong enough to survive.

Ashok had not been worried. He'd known he was strong enough, because he had looked at the carvings of the temple elders from the Age of Flowers, those men and women who had conquered the subcontinent on the yaksa's behalf. Who had held terrible, incalculable power. He had looked and thought, *I am not going to be like* our *elders, holding only a shadow of power, a faint echo of what once was. I won't sit with the regent or bow to the emperor in Parijat.*

I am going to be like you.

He knew—the moment he emerged from the deathless waters for the first time, gasping for air to fill his lungs, somehow both hollow and full—that he had been right. Because in his head he saw the sangam. A place of myth. A world beyond the mortal realm where cosmic rivers met; where once, the temple elders had been able to walk. That day, years before the other children began to change and grow powerful, before the temple elders realized what the children had become—before everything and everyone burned—Ashok knew. The yaksa had heard him. Ahiranya's glory would return.

Now.

Now he stood in the confluence of rivers.

They met beneath his feet. River of soul; river of heart's flesh, red and deep; river of immortality, bubbling the green of life and the gold of the ageless.

Rivers of the living. Rivers of the dead.

He waded in deeper, the water rising to his ankles, his knees. He closed his eyes and held his breath, then released it, slow and even. He had done this before. He knew the way of it: how a breath unspooled could lead a man's mind from his flesh and deep into the grasp of the rivers. In Ahiranya's forest, his body sat cross-legged, back straight and eyes fast shut, breathing just so. In the confluence of rivers—the sangam, the holiest of sites—his soul made its way to the meeting place.

She waited for him, in the same swirling water, a mere shadow of a woman. She was trembling. She always trembled, now. Around her the river was an oil slick of violet.

"You're not well," he told her.

"Ashok," she murmured, lowering her head. "I'm well enough."

"Are you?"

"I've almost found the way," she said. "Almost. I'm sure."

"Tell me everything."

She wavered before him. The shadow of her was breaking— ink swirling into the river flow. She was not strong enough to be here. Every moment was a kind of agony.

"I can't remain long," she said. There was an apology in her voice, small and broken. "But I promise I—I'll save us. I *promise*."

He waded closer. He felt her then: her pain, her weakness, her love and loyalty. He held his hand out, a wisp of soul before him. Touched her cheek.

He thought of telling her to come home. He thought of telling her to return to her family, where she would be safe.

But if there was a hope—if there was a *chance*—

"I know what it means to be strong," she told him. "I know everything has a price."

So it did.

"Be strong, then," he murmured. "And I'll be here."

She faded away and he remained, the sangam winding around him.

6

PRIYA

It was only their fourth week climbing the Hirana when they faced disaster.

Priya was at the back of the line of maidservants, halfway through the climb, when she heard a scream that cut through the blackness, followed by the clang of a lantern striking the ground. She froze. Above her, the snaking line of lanterns wavered and went still, as their bearers froze along with her.

She sucked in a slow breath. She tasted rain, or blood, or something iron-sharp that somehow resembled both. She pressed the soles of her feet down onto the damp stone, grounding herself. In her left hand the guiding rope—slippery with water—stung her already abraded palm. Wet rope was an agony on raw skin, but Priya had only clung on tighter when the rain had begun to pour halfway through their ascent, soaking the rope along with their clothes and skin and supplies. It had stopped now, but only after turning the stone of the Hirana slick and dangerously smooth. It was no wonder someone had fallen.

Behind her Meena whispered, "What happened?"

Meena was the youngest maidservant who'd volunteered to take up this role, and she was a nervous thing at the best of times. The scream had shaken her. Priya could hear how shallow her breathing was now, a panicked in-out rhythm that made Priya's own lungs ache in sympathy.

"I don't know," lied Priya. She tried to sound calm, for Meena's sake. "Are you still holding on tight?"

"Yes."

"Good. I'm going to look."

"But—"

"Take the lantern." She handed their shared light to Meena, who grasped it with trembling fingers. "I won't be long."

Just like Priya had once known how to peel skin from bone, she'd known how to climb the Hirana. That was what the temple children had done, after all: led pilgrims seeking the blessings of the yaksa spirits up the Hirana's surface; guided the pilgrims up to the temple elders, who were the yaksa's chosen. There had been no rope then. Pilgrimage was a journey, after all, both spiritual and physical. It had a cost. Some faltered or failed. Some fell. The yaksa demanded strength from their worshippers, just as they had demanded it from their temple council.

Only the worthy could rise.

Priya had been worthy once.

Without the lantern in her hand, it was easier to move swiftly. She held the rope only loosely, darting up the Hirana as fast as she could. She and Meena had fallen behind the other maidservants—Meena's nervousness had slowed them both down—but Priya soon reached the point where the others stood, huddled so close their feet were almost touching.

The maidservant nearest to Priya was leaning out precariously, a hand twisting the guiding rope, the other holding her lantern as far out into the dark as she could.

In its light, Priya could see Sima.

Sima was trapped to the left of the guiding rope, slightly farther down the Hirana's surface: She must have tripped, slipping, her body sliding treacherously down the wet rock. Her arms were outstretched, every muscle in them defined. She had her fingers hooked into one of the fissures in the stone, knuckles white with the strain of holding her body up. The rest of her was invisible.

She'd fallen into a rift carved into the rock, a cleverly concealed gap hollowed out between a series of statues, shaped to follow the natural fall of shadow. From most angles, it would have been invisible. But now that Sima was caught in it, the trap was hard to miss. It held her like a mouth, toothless and grasping.

Priya had no idea how deep the rift was, but the thought of Sima losing her grip—of Sima being killed by the tumble that followed, or worse, being trapped alive down in the dark where no one could reach her—made Priya's stomach clench with nausea.

The leaning maidservant was yanked back by a rough hand.

"Don't lean out," Gauri, the head maidservant, said angrily. "I can't have you falling too. You," she shouted to a woman farther up, gesturing at her with her stick, "go and fetch a guard from the doors. Tell them a girl's slipped. Hurry!"

The woman began to climb. But she was too slow, on the wet ground, with the lamp and the rope in her hands. Too slow.

Sima was panting hard, the whites of her eyes visible in the flickering lantern-lit dark.

"I can't hold on," Sima wheezed.

"You can and you will," Gauri said. "You're a strong girl. Don't let go now."

But Sima was frightened, and her hands were surely as raw as Priya's, the stone glassy under her fingers. She would not be able to hold on until help came.

Priya looked down at the ground. At the stone, carved to resemble vines and leaves, melding with the green sprouting up through its cracked surface.

She'd known the Hirana once, and it had known her.

It knew her still.

She hadn't been sure the first night she'd climbed, when all she'd been able to concentrate on had been making her way up to the top without losing her nerve. But she was sure now. As she stood and forced herself to breathe—as the lanterns shook, and Sima's fingers slid the tiniest bit from their handhold—she felt the pulse of the wet stone beneath her feet, slithering as if the vines on its surface moved to cradle her. She had a feeling that if she pressed her ear to the Hirana she'd hear the stone heave, like the vertebrae of a great, sleeping beast.

She could step out. Let that spine carry her. All it would take was a leap of faith.

I shouldn't, Priya thought distantly. *Spirits, I really shouldn't.*

But this was Sima. Her friend.

She kneeled down. The yellow lantern light threw shadows over her bare feet. The stone beneath her was black, its surface fissured like a cracked egg, leaking lichen and moss from the yolk. She touched her fingertips to the green; felt the warmth of it beneath the rainwater.

"Ground protect me," she murmured. Then she stood once more and stepped away from the guiding rope, out to the left and into the darkness.

She heard shocked cries above her—heard Gauri yell her name—but Priya did not lift her head. She kept on moving. Slow, careful, cursing herself in her head.

She did not want to do this. She would regret doing this.

She wanted to do this. She wanted to know if she *could.*

She could hear Sima's panicked breath.

There were raised carvings, on this step: serpents coiled into heaps, a cobra with its mouth parted and its teeth pointed up. She felt the sharp edge against her skin. Froze.

She heard a voice in her head. Not her brother's this time. Low, cultured. Amused.

An elder.

You and the Hirana have a special bond, don't you, small one? The memory of hands on her shoulders. A figure looming over her, robed in a sheath of white cotton, beads of sacred wood cascading from their hair. *But don't forget it's built to trick your eyes. So don't trust your eyes.*

She swore internally. Closed her eyes, as if her temple elders were still alive and there to be obeyed, to approve of her. She moved her foot farther to the left, trusting her skin. Roughness gave way to soft vines, tangled together. Beneath them the stone was solid.

One step. Another. Another. She tested the ground. Broken, here. Solid, here. She could hear Gauri still shouting, voice hoarse. The stone dipped, sudden and sharp, and Priya stopped once more, curling her toes against the ground. Sima's breath was close now, very close, so Priya opened her eyes.

Sima lay on the ground before her. The whites of her eyes were bright in the dark.

Priya drew back her feet and kneeled on the ground where it was rough enough to hold her steady. Then she lay on her stomach. Held out her hand.

"You can climb now," she said. "If you use me. But you'll have to let go of the rock and take hold of me. Can you do that for me, Sima?"

"I…" Sima stopped. Her bloodless fingers twitched. "I… don't think I can."

"You can," Priya said steadily.

"I'll drag you down too. We'll both die."

"You won't," Priya said, although she wasn't entirely sure. "Come on now, Sima."

"The ghosts are going to take me," whispered Sima. "I know it."

"If there's any justice, the spirits of the temple elders and temple children are with the yaksa, somewhere far away from the Hirana," Priya said quietly. "And if there isn't, well. I don't think those ghosts would want good Ahiranyi lives, when there are plenty of Parijati above us for the taking."

"Priya," Sima bit out. "Don't. You'll—"

"Get in trouble? You can tell me off properly when we're both safe. I promise I'll listen."

Sima let out a whimper that might have been an attempt at a laugh. She squeezed her eyes shut. "Priya. I'm scared."

"You don't have to be scared. I'm right here." Priya pressed her upper arms down onto the stone, dragging herself a little closer. Just enough that she could touch her hand to Sima's. She could feel Sima's fingers shaking. "The worthy are always safe on the

Hirana," Priya said. "That's what they used to tell pilgrims. And you're worthy, Sima. I've decided it. So you're going to be fine."

Sima's grip faltered. Her body jolted, and Priya scrambled for her, heart racing. Sima's hand clamped back against stone a moment later.

"Priya!" Her voice was reedy with terror.

"Take my hand," Priya said. "Come."

After a long, fraught moment, Sima did. She clasped Priya's hand in a painful, wrenching grip. She choked out a sob, then a scream, and dragged herself up, up. Her nails dug into Priya's skin. Priya gritted her own teeth, hooking her foot against rock, and prayed they'd both survive.

Finally, Sima was free from the hollow. Gasping, they both climbed to their feet. Above them, the other maidservants were silent—afraid, perhaps, that a single noise would make them fall.

Deep breath in. Out.

"Hold my arms," Priya said finally. Now that she had Sima, the panic had finally caught up with her. She could feel it singing in her blood, in the hot sting of the nail marks on her arms. "I'll guide you back to the rope."

It took time. But eventually they climbed back to the others and gripped the guiding rope. Sima collapsed to her knees, crying; another maidservant murmured to her and placed a hand on her head.

Priya felt a sharp rap against her shoulder. She turned to see Gauri. The older woman's face was bloodless white. Eyes unblinking.

"You fool," she said. "Both of you. Stop blubbering, Sima. We're late."

Sima hiccupped something incomprehensible in response. But she rose to her feet. The maidservants began moving once more. Gauri gave Priya one last look—terrified and furious and too thoughtful by far—then turned away.

"I can keep carrying the lantern, if you want," Meena said. She stood behind Priya, trembling like a leaf.

Priya curled and uncurled her hands. Her whole body ached.

"No need," she said. "Thank you for carrying it, Meena. But I'm fine now. Here, let me take it from you."

Two guards waited at the gates to check each of the women carefully for weapons. They examined Gauri's stick, as they always did, before handing it back to her with a nod of respect. They were both soldiers who'd traveled with the princess from Parijat, and they looked at the rest of the maidservants coolly, dismissively.

Priya looked at them in return. She missed her little knife.

"She's waiting," said one. Then he added, "I heard a girl fell. Sorry for your loss."

Gauri's jaw tightened, just slightly.

"We were lucky not to lose her, spirits be thanked," she said. "I sent one of mine to ask for your help. Did she not request that you come?"

His expression was remote. He shrugged.

"We were told not to move. But all's well, I suppose, if the girl's alive."

"All's well," Gauri agreed. But she did not look happy.

Priya couldn't help but think that if one of their own, like Mithunan, had been guarding the princess—or even the regent's own personal retinue of cold-eyed men—they would have come to save Sima. Or at least would've tried.

The guards opened the gates. The maidservant who had gone ahead was waiting for them, face marked with tears. When she saw Sima her expression brightened—but the brisk tap of approaching footsteps dimmed it once more, and she lowered her head.

The princess's attendant appeared in the entrance hall.

Lady Pramila was a Parijati noblewoman, tall and severe. She was always clad in a sari embroidered with white jasmine flowers as a mark of her highborn blood, a thick shawl wrapped around her head and shoulders. Around her waist she wore a belt, and upon it she wore a set of keys and a knife sheath. For all her noble blood and the fineness of her sari, she was no more than a jailer, and every single servant—Priya included—already hated and feared her.

"There are only three hours before dawn," Pramila said coolly.

"The rain delayed us, my lady," Gauri replied. "The monsoon is—that is to say, it is difficult to climb in this weather. We almost lost a girl."

Pramila shrugged as if to say, *That is no concern of mine.*

"She lies asleep in the northern chamber, as always," she said. "Make sure you're gone by daylight. If your work is not done by then, so be it."

"My lady."

"The next time you're late," said Pramila, "I will need to inform the regent of my displeasure."

Gauri bowed her head deferentially. Priya and the others did the same. As soon as Pramila was gone, disappearing into her study, Gauri turned to them.

"We'll start in the kitchens," she said. "Quickly, now. And if you tarry, I promise to beat each and every one of you blue."

Priya kindled the kitchen fire, fanning it into steady flames. She chopped onions and peeled vegetables, setting them aside to be cooked. That finished, she moved to one of the temple corridors commonly used by the guards and began to scrub the floor clean of their muddy footprints.

"Priya." Priya raised her head, startled. Sima was looking down at her, arms crossed in front of her. "I—I wanted to say thank you."

"You don't need to."

Sima nodded. Her face was drawn. There was a question in the tilt of her head, in the curve of her mouth.

"I've never seen you like that before," Sima said.

"Like what?"

"Brave. I suppose."

"Hey now," Priya said, "I'm very brave. Who was the one who

caught the lizard that got into our dormitory when all the other girls were screaming? Me."

"What you said," Sima replied. "When you were—when you saved me. I…" She hesitated. "Did you…?"

Priya waited. She wondered what Sima would ask. *Were you a pilgrim once?* That would be fine. Priya could lie convincingly, if Sima asked her that. But if she asked, *Were you a temple child?* How could Priya lie, then, when even being on the Hirana made her past feel so close, her skin too tight to hold it in?

Ah, spirits, Priya hoped Sima wouldn't ask.

Finally, Sima said, "Gauri wants you to find Meena."

"What?"

"Meena's missing," Sima said. "Hiding, I expect. I think she was very frightened."

"She was," Priya agreed. Sighing, she dropped her rag in the bucket. "I'll go and find her."

"I'll finish your work," said Sima. "And, Pri, if you need anything…"

"Yes?"

Sima kneeled down, taking up the sodden cloth.

"Then talk to me," she said. "I owe you. That's all."

Priya made an effort to find Meena. Truly she did. But if the girl was crying in a corner somewhere, she'd likely turn up in her own time. After peering into a few small cloister rooms, once used to house the effigies of spirits—now empty and gathering dust—Priya discarded the task and took the opportunity to head where she'd wanted to go all along.

Beyond the cloister rooms, Lady Pramila's study, the kitchen, the latrine, and the bathing room—not far from the living quarters that once belonged to the old temple elders—lay the triveni.

The triveni was a room open to the air, held up by huge pillars carved to resemble yaksa. They grasped the ceiling with vast arms. Three branches of the temple were accessible through the triveni: the forbidden northern chamber where the princess slumbered, and those to the west and the south. Between them were swathes of the sky, the sunrise entering unimpeded from the east. If one was unwary, they could step directly out onto the Hirana's outer surface—and straight into all its dangers.

Priya was not unwary. She crossed the triveni's surface, which was covered in deep, sweeping grooves intended to resemble water on a shore. She came to the plinth at the room's center. Above the plinth was the roof, a circle carved in the center like a window to the sky. The plinth's surface was wet, its pale stone rain-washed and glimmering.

As she had so many times before, she murmured a prayer and pressed her hands to the plinth's surface. She lowered her head.

She remembered there had been fat cushions on the floor once, for the temple elders to sit upon comfortably. And there had been chandeliers hung from the ceiling, laden with candles. She remembered running between the cushions, a hand dragging her back from the edge, and another cuffing her around the ear. *Behave or you'll fall, you silly child.*

She remembered the rasp of silk against the ground; a crown mask of varnished wood, glinting in the light. Her brother's voice. The laughter of her other siblings, mingled together. That, and no more.

A noise broke her reflection: a crash, overloud, splintering the air. She raised her head with a jerk.

"Meena?"

The noise had come from the corridor ahead of her. The northern chamber. If the fool girl had gone toward the prisoner's room...

Priya lifted her hands from the plinth and slipped into the corridor, which was dark, one mere torch guttering in its sconce. On the walls were stone reliefs of the yaksa at war, conquering the world with swords of thorn in the gnarled wood of their hands. The paint had peeled and faded long ago, but the images were still clear. The mythical temple elders of old stood by the side of the yaksa, staring at her through crown masks, featureless apart from their open chests, which were hollowed out, three streams of water pouring from them onto a battlefield of corpses.

Forcing herself not to hesitate—not to linger and stare, drinking in the stories with her eyes—Priya slipped past them, bare feet silent on the ground.

She paused suddenly. The floor was damp, and not with rain. The ceiling and walls were enclosed here. She kneeled. Touched the liquid and raised her fingers to her face. Wine.

Close—very close—came the sound of muffled sobs.

Priya turned her head.

The wall to her right was latticed, with perforations wrought into the shape of flowers. Through it, Priya saw cloth, heavy silk curtains wavering as if in a wind, partially torn from their hooks. A metal pitcher upon the ground, the source of the spilled wine. She leaned closer . . .

And met a woman's eyes.

For a moment, Priya didn't know where she was. She was in her own past. She was staring at another temple daughter, sprawled on the floor before her. She was staring at her own ghosts made flesh.

Wide dark eyes. The whites bloodshot with weeping. The eyebrows were thick and arched, the skin a pale teak. The sobbing eased, and Priya could hear the woman's breath: a staccato rhythm, rattling and sore.

It was the breath that brought Priya back to herself. Left her back in her own skin, shaking on her knees.

The prisoner. She was staring at the prisoner. The emperor's sister. The *princess*.

There should have been no way for this to happen. The prisoner should have been sleeping.

But the lattice wall—this lattice wall—was in a corridor that no maidservant should rightly have entered. No one had thought to block the lattice with more than a simple curtain; no one had thought this could occur.

Look away, thought Priya. *Look away*.

She should have lowered her gaze. She should have bowed.

Instead she stared, unblinking, into those eyes. She stared, and held her own breath inside herself, a tight kernel that threatened to burst against her ribs. She was like a bird, pinned by the wing. Flight was beyond her.

The prisoner gazed back in return. She was lying on the floor, propped up on her elbows, her hair a wild, dark curtain around her. The wine had stained her pale sari wound-red. Still holding Priya's eyes, she leaned forward.

"Are you real?" Low voice, kept carefully soft, to avoid notice, and rough from weeping. "Speak. I need to be sure."

Priya's mouth parted. No sound escaped her lips. She wanted to ask the same in return.

The prisoner swallowed. Priya heard the click of her throat; saw the tilt of her head, as she regarded Priya with an expression that Priya could not hope to understand.

"Real, then." Her eyes were rimmed in red. "Good."

"Please," Priya whispered again. "Forgive me. Princess."

She scrambled to her feet. Bowed, head low, hands clasped before her. And then she turned and fled.

She heard nothing behind her. Only the absence of weeping. Only the princess's hoarse breath, fading into the silent void of the night.

She raced back to the triveni.

At the center of the room, on the low plinth, sat Meena. Her back was to Priya, but she turned when Priya approached. Blinked at her. There were tear tracks on her cheeks.

"Priya?"

"You shouldn't be here."

"I was just tidying," said Meena, which was such an obvious lie that Priya could only stare at her, openmouthed, for a moment.

"Get down."

"I was just..."

"Get down from there," she repeated. And then, because her tongue and her heart were traitorous sometimes, she said, "That isn't for you."

Meena climbed down. She crossed her arms before her, look-ing all the world like a guilty child.

"Do you know how near you are to the princess's chambers?" Priya asked, shaken, her racing heart making her voice suddenly tremble. "Do you know the trouble we could be in, if the princess were to hear us? Or spirits forbid, Lady Pramila found us here? We have one job: We come here in the dark, we clean and pre-pare the food, and we leave before first light. We do not disturb the prisoner. We don't allow her to know we exist. Those are the regent's orders, and we obey, you understand?"

"I—I'm sorry," Meena said shakily. "Please don't tell Gauri."

"I won't." She gripped Meena's arm. "Think of the extra coin you'll get for this job and behave next time, okay? Think of your future. Now come on. We're going back to work."

They left the triveni behind.

7

PRIYA

It was early morning by the time the maidservants made it down from the Hirana and back into the mahal. Billu had a plate of food warm and ready for them, and they divided the roti and pickles between themselves. Gauri excused herself quickly, claiming she needed her rest.

"We should rest too," said Sima, dabbing her roti through the leftover fragrant oil and brine. Priya opened her mouth and Sima raised a finger up to stop her. "*Don't* speak until you've finished eating, Pri, please."

Priya rolled her eyes and swallowed down her mouthful of food with a swig of water, then said, "I'm not tired yet."

"What are you going to do?"

"I'm going to the orchard," she said. "Billu," she called, and the cook turned from the humongous pile of onions he was hacking his way through. "I'm heading over to the orchard, so if you want me to carry anything to the boys...?"

"You should be going to sleep," scolded Billu, but he gave her some parathas to carry with her, and a big flask of tea, the steam carrying the warm perfume of cardamom. "Tell them there's a little onion sabzi left, if they're quick," he said. "But I won't send it with you. Too messy."

The few people with rot in the household had been assigned the task of clearing the blighted acres of the regent's orchard, alongside the servants who usually managed the care of the regent's trees. The rot-riven were, after all, already marked—they couldn't be infected again. Or that was the logic used, at least.

For days they had been working from first light, hacking down the branches and piling them into a bonfire. Priya followed the smoke and found them clearing an old, old tree. It was vast, thick-trunked with deep, sprawling roots that were half-visible, now that the soil around the base had been cleared away. The roots had been pared open so that the interior would begin to dry out and catch alight more easily.

The men working wore cloth wrapped around their mouths to stop them from breathing in the worst of the smoke, but Priya wasn't half as prepared. She drew her pallu over her mouth as she balanced the food and the flask against her hip, taking shallow breaths and trying not to think of all the things the smell of smoke always made her think of. Her brother's arms around her. Blood. The Hirana.

The princess, staring at her with bloodshot eyes, dark as pitch. *Are you real?*

She forced the thought back and peered through the haze until she caught sight of a familiar small figure, staggering under an enormous pile of wood.

"Rukh!" Priya called.

He looked over the stack, and his eyes creased with a smile when he saw her. He excitedly flung the wood onto the bonfire.

"I've brought everyone food," she yelled out, and there were relieved noises from the other men as they lowered their machetes.

There were vats of salted water set nearby, and all the workers poured pitchers of it over their own hands before they began to eat, to cleanse their skin. Salt, some thought, helped keep the rot at bay.

"How is life as a servant going?" Priya asked Rukh, after she had parceled out the food and passed the flask of tea to the nearest man, who murmured his thanks.

"The food is great," Rukh said, wiping his wet hands on

his tunic. His eyes were fixed on the parathas. He grabbed one quickly.

Priya wanted to interrogate him a little more. She'd only seen him now and then since leaving him in Khalida's care, usually in the times when he came to eat in the kitchens in the early morning, along with the rest of the servants. Once or twice, he'd come to sit with her after dinner and let her tell him yaksa tales. That was all. But he was tucking into the food with such joyful vigor that she hated to interrupt him, so she sighed and said, "Give me your hand." She took hold of his wrist. "You can eat with the other one."

"It's a lot better," he said, through a mouthful of food. "Doesn't hurt as much."

"Don't talk with your mouth full."

He pushed the rest of the paratha into his mouth, cheeks stuffed, and nodded quickly. She bent her head to hide her grin, inspecting his fingers. The bead hung snug at his wrist on a strong thread.

She felt a wave of relief. His rot was no better, but it was no worse, the skin still puckered around the growth beneath it, but unbroken. The bead of sacred wood was working its magic.

"When the bead goes cold, come to me straight away," she said. "Before it gets worse, Rukh. Not after."

"Okay," he said mildly. "I promise," he added, under her stern look.

"You should probably join them," she said, gesturing over at the others. "I've got to go to bed anyway." She resisted the urge to ruffle his shorn hair. He wouldn't appreciate that in front of others.

"In a second," he said. He rocked back on his heels a little, eyes lowered. "Priya. Will you..." He hesitated. "Will you do me another favor?"

"Another favor?" she asked, incredulous. "You mean besides getting you a job? You do have some cheek." She paused. "Well, it depends what it is."

"Please. Don't go up the Hirana this week."

That... was not what she'd expected. "At all this week?"

"All week," he confirmed. He swallowed. "Please."

It was such an absurd request that she could only laugh. When he raised his head, she arched an eyebrow at him.

"How will I keep a job if I don't work, hm? You think the regent keeps on women who don't pull their own weight?"

"Say you're sick. They won't make you climb if you're sick, and you said his wife is kind, she wouldn't let him send you off," Rukh pressed on, determined. "Please, Priya. Everyone says that place is haunted. And after what happened with you and Sima..."

"Sima was the one who fell," Priya pointed out. "Not me. And you're not asking her to fake illness, are you?"

"She's not you," said Rukh. "You're the one who spends your money on sacred wood for children with rot. No one else wasted that on us. You're the one who gave me this chance. Not her, or anyone else." His expression was solemn, filled with an earnestness that was both childish and somehow too mature for that sharp, small face to contain. "Priya, just. Please. Just for a week. Until the rains die down?"

"You'll have a place here no matter what happens to me," she said. Maybe he needed to hear that—needed to be sure. "But I have no plans to get hurt. If I have a choice, I'll be around to help you, you understand? Some things we can't control, Rukh. We both know what the world is like. As long as I can help, I will. But I can't help if I don't work."

"You still shouldn't go," Rukh said mulishly. And as he glanced down, Priya recognized what he was trying to hide.

Guilt.

"Is there some other reason you don't want me climbing?" she asked carefully.

Rukh said nothing. Then, awkwardly, he muttered, "Because you matter to me."

"That's very sweet," she said. "Why else?"

"I've told you the truth." He sounded wounded, but Priya wasn't convinced.

"Don't mistake my being softhearted for being a fool," Priya said levelly. "You're not good at hiding your feelings."

"It's not safe," he repeated.

"Come now," Priya coaxed. "What have you heard? Have the maids been making up tales of dangerous and evil spirits? Surely you know better than to listen to them."

Rukh shook his head. "Never mind. I'm going to eat now."

"Rukh." She was fairly certain that it wasn't ghost stories that had him biting his lip and tugging that thread around his wrist. But she wasn't sure how to get the truth out of him.

"You should listen to me," he said, frustrated. He took a step back. Another. "You should trust me. I trusted you."

"That's not how trust works," she told him, baffled.

When she tried to follow him, he began to run, pelting his way into the trees. One of the men yelled after him, warning him to come back or he'd get a beating later. But he didn't reappear.

Eventually she gave up waiting for him to return and went to the dormitory instead, flinging herself down on her mat, exasperated and exhausted, staring at the ceiling until she finally, begrudgingly, fell asleep.

When she woke it was evening, the air velvety with dying warmth, and Sima was sitting cross-legged on the bedroll beside her own, undressed, her shoulders still damp from bathing. Sima was sewing up her sari blouse, the sleeve torn clean in two.

"What a mess," Priya murmured.

"I ripped it when I fell," Sima said. "Why didn't you rest earlier?"

"I was looking for Rukh."

Sima gave a faint snort. "Of course you were."

"What does *that* mean?"

"Nothing. He was looking for you, too," she said lightly. "Did you do something to make him angry?"

"Why do you say that?"

"He doesn't want you to earn a living, apparently. He asked

me to give you this." Sima fished into her bedroll; pulled something out in her fist. "He said he'll take it back if you return it to him after sunset."

"He was *here*? When I was waiting for him in the orchard?" She let out a groan. "Hand it over."

Sima dropped the bead of sacred wood, still threaded on string, into Priya's palm.

"*Fool* boy," Priya cursed. "He knows he needs to wear it constantly." She clutched the bead tighter, the heat of it radiating against her skin.

"My fall must have scared him," said Sima.

"It did." Priya exhaled, frustrated. "But I told him I can look after myself. I saved you, after all."

Sima shook her head. Drew on her sari blouse over her damp shoulders, brushing her hair back from her neck. "That won't stop him from worrying," said Sima. "He's trying to protect you."

"He's a child," said Priya. "Doesn't he know it's his elders' job to protect him, not the other way around?"

"Why would he know that?" Sima asked bluntly.

Sima was right, of course. He'd had no one, before Priya had brought him to the mahal. If his family had been farmers, they'd probably died of starvation when their crops had grown rot-riven, leaving him alone. He likely came to Hiranaprastha without anyone to care for him.

"Besides," Sima went on, "most of us, we see children with rot that bad, and we look away. There's no point crying over something you can't fix."

"Even a sick child?"

"Especially, maybe," Sima muttered, smoothing down the sleeves of her blouse. "There's so many of them, you'd never stop. Priya, you're kind to care about him. Kind for all the little things you do out in the city, but you're going to break your heart over that boy when he dies. And he *will* die."

"My heart is fine," Priya said, a little stiffly. "You don't have to worry about me."

After an uncomfortable silence, Sima spoke again, more gently. "Give him a few days. He'll stop worrying. I'll tell Gauri you're not well."

Priya uncurled her fingers and stared down at the bead. A few days. That made sense. But Rukh had asked her not to climb the Hirana for a single week. If he was worried about her safety, why set a time length at all? Why not ask her to give up the job entirely?

Something wasn't right. She'd known that, when Rukh had made his request. But the certainty had only grown stronger.

I need to speak to Bhumika, she thought. Dread coiled in her belly. *I need to do it now.*

"How long until sunset?" she asked.

"Not long."

If only he'd been honest with her. She hadn't known he had any guile in him.

"I'll simply have to worry him, then," Priya said. She lifted the thread up and looped it over her own wrist. "I'll return it to him in the morning."

She made her way swiftly down the servants' corridors, the mazelike routes created so they could travel through the palace without crossing paths with the nobility. Eventually, she emerged into the central garden of the mahal and began to walk toward the rose palace.

Lady Bhumika was a woman who valued privacy and beauty, and her quarters reflected that. Instead of living in the grand opulence of the mahal, she maintained her closest household in the rose palace: a manse within the rose garden that lay at the heart of the grounds. Its doors were surrounded by fronds of flowers: sheaves of white and burgundy, pink and glorious red.

Usually the doors of the rose palace were flung open, the sumptuous carpet of the living room crowded with visiting high-born women who sat under a ceiling inlaid with a starburst of emeralds cut to resemble leaves, listening to music and drinking wine, laughing and playing the kind of frivolous games of politics that Priya had little patience for.

But today the doors were shut, the air painfully quiet, and there were only two people at the entrance. The sour-faced senior maidservant, Khalida, was speaking to another woman. The other woman was carrying a case at her side. It was open at the top, and even from a distance Priya could see its contents. Vials. Calipers. She was a physician.

Priya stopped in her tracks as both women caught sight of her.

"Girl," Khalida said. "What are you doing here?"

"I've come to clean my lady's chambers, ma'am," Priya said, bowing her head in respect, keeping her voice demure.

"Not today," Khalida said. "Our lady is unwell. She doesn't have time for you. Go away now."

At another time, Priya would have pushed or bribed or cajoled Khalida into allowing her entrance. But time was running short before dusk and the physician was still standing by, looking between them. Priya knew there would be no bending of the rules around a stranger. So instead she bowed her head again. "Ma'am."

She turned and walked away. As she did so, she heard the physician's voice rise in a question, and Khalida's voice respond.

"...one of our lady's strays. Barefoot beggars, all of them. She can't stand to see an orphan go hungry. But they do like to whine for scraps."

I hope a rat eats your hair, Khalida, Priya thought sourly.

A stray. It wasn't untrue, not really. But that only made the words sting all the more.

It was a night of miracles. Priya made it to the base of the Hirana with time to spare, and Gauri did not say anything, which meant the princess had not mentioned Priya's mistake to Lady Pramila. Thankfully, there had been no rain for hours, so the Hirana's surface had baked dry in the day's sun. And despite Meena's insipid trembling, she too turned up at dusk, scampering behind the others with a pack of firewood strapped to her back.

"Let me carry that for you," Priya offered. But Meena shook her head.

"Oh no, I can do it. Only—will you carry the lantern?"

Priya agreed, and they began their climb. The moon was full, fat and gleaming, its silver light almost as strong as lantern-glow. At the Hirana's summit, the guards checked them for weapons, allowing them entry, and Pramila greeted them with her usual frosty instructions before they went to work.

Priya was sweeping the floor clean of cooking fire ash when Gauri grabbed her by the arm.

"Come," Gauri snapped. "Meena's gone missing again. Find her and bring her to me. I can understand her being afraid yesterday. But twice in a row—it's too much."

"Ma'am," Priya said deferentially. She put her broom aside and walked off.

"Tell her if she does this again she won't have a job. Do you hear me, Priya? Tell her that!"

Priya headed straight for the triveni, but there was no sign of Meena on the plinth, or anywhere else.

The air was clear and cold, and Priya was alone with nothing but her own memories, the lines upon the floor, and the knowledge that the prisoner lay at the other end of the triveni, one corridor away.

She had tried not to think of the princess. But she couldn't help it.

Those eyes. She pictured them and something nameless flooded through her. For a moment, she'd felt as if she were staring into a dark mirror. Her past reflected back at her and made into something new.

Priya knew what everyone knew about the princess, and only that. Emperor Chandra had ordered his sister to rise to the pyre alongside her handmaidens, to sacrifice themselves as the mothers of flame had done, so long ago. But the princess had refused the honor. And now she was here.

You almost burned too, Priya thought as she stared at the corridor. *Just like me.*

That voice. The rasp of it. That mouth, shaping words in the semidark.

Are you real?

Stop being a damn fool, Priya told herself.

But she found herself crossing the triveni again, barely paying attention to the velvet night sky around her, or the figures of the yaksa carved into the great pillars holding the ceiling up above her. She moved as though the dark corridor ahead of her and the lattice wall that lay within it were a light and she were a particularly stupid moth.

"Priya." A small voice. "Stop."

The voice came from behind her. Priya turned.

Meena was behind her. In one crooked arm, she was cradling a small pile of firewood. Her face was strangely pale.

"I need your help," said Meena.

"What's happened?" Priya asked, alarmed. "Are you injured?"

"No."

"Is anyone else?" When Meena shook her head, Priya said, "Then what is it?" When Meena remained silent a heartbeat too long, Priya pressed on. "Let's go back to the kitchens. I'll ask Sima to brew you a cup of tea. Something to calm your nerves—"

"I know what you are," Meena said, the end of her words a quiver.

Priya's words died abruptly.

"I knew it the moment you saved Sima. When you moved— you moved like you'd walked on the Hirana before, like the ground *knew* you." Meena swallowed, visibly. Then she said, "You're a temple daughter. Or you were, once."

"You're mistaken," Priya said.

"How many times did you pass through the waters before the council died? Are you once-born? Twice-born?"

"Meena," Priya said gently. "You're addled. Go to the kitchens, now."

"I'm not," Meena said firmly. "I'm very sure. I know you're a temple child. You were raised here, in this temple. Raised to rule our faith. And then the regent burned you all, didn't he? You and your elders. But you survived, somehow. Hiding in plain sight. You're not the first I've met. *He* told me what to look for. I *know*."

Meena crossed the triveni. She took hold of Priya's arm. Her grip was like iron.

"Look at this," Meena said, voice firm, fierce. So Priya looked.

In Meena's left hand, half-concealed beneath the drape of her sari, was the shape that Priya had thought was kindling.

It was a mask. It must have been hidden among the bundle Meena had been carrying on her back. The guards would not have noticed it when they checked the maidservants for weapons. It was, after all, not a weapon. It was no more than wood, deep and dark, bent and carved into crescents that stretched from a central hollow. But it was beautiful, and familiar, and every inch of it was carved from the boughs of sacred trees. Close to it now, Priya could feel the warmth of it, rich as a bloodied heartbeat.

A crown mask.

The bead of wood at her wrist didn't hold even a shadow of such power.

Priya flinched, despite herself.

"You recognize it," Meena said, and her shaky voice was full of triumph.

"I don't know what you mean."

"Please, Priya. You do. I know you do." Meena took a step closer. "You can help me find the deathless waters. You have to. We need their strength to free ourselves from an empire that has always hated us, from rulers that want us to roll over like dogs for the crime of being better than them." Her grip tightened on the mask. "They've stolen so much from us. Our language. Our elders. They deemed our culture filthy, they let us *starve*. We need the waters, Priya, we all do, before it's too late."

"You're hurting my arm," Priya said steadily. "Let go of me. And we'll return to work and forget any of this happened."

"Aren't you listening to me?" Meena's face was a picture of despair. "This mad emperor will burn us all. We need to be strong. We need to be what we once were."

"I am listening to you," Priya said levelly. "And I think we should return to work. I think you want something from me that I can't give you."

There was a sound, beyond the triveni, as two maidservants passed, chattering to one another. Priya stiffened, utterly silent. *Do not come in here*, she thought. *By soil and sky, please, do not.*

They passed. Their voices faded.

Meena was watching her, intent as an animal gazing upon prey. But she trembled, and trembled, as if her own instincts terrified her.

"Show me the way to the deathless waters," Meena said in a quicksilver whisper. "Just tell me how to reach the waters, simply tell me, and I'll leave here. I'll cause no trouble."

"What do you mean, 'trouble'?" Priya asked.

Meena swallowed. Her gaze was unflinching.

"Being strong means being ruthless," said Meena. "I know that. And I am—not afraid. To do what needs to be done."

"Strong," Priya repeated. Oh, she remembered what strong had meant, when she was a girl. "Do you mean that you'll torture me? The other maidservants? Do you mean that you'll kill them, to force me to show you the way?" When Meena remained silent, Priya smiled at her—a fierce, hard smile. "There would be no point, anyway. I don't know the way."

"Don't lie to me," Meena said, voice suddenly high and thin as if she could not control it. Her grip tightened. Ah, that hurt. "I've asked the others. You've lived in the regent's mahal since you were a girl. If anyone knows the way, it's you."

"Meena," Priya said, in the calmest voice she could muster, even as her heart raced, "if I had the power of the deathless waters at my fingertips, do you truly believe I'd be toiling in the regent's household? Wouldn't I be more than a maidservant? Think sensibly."

"I think you are a coward," said Meena, suddenly viperous. "I think you're willing to lick the regent's boots, and you disgust me. You're nothing like *him*."

Priya could not ask her who *he* was—could not say a word—

because Meena released her and clasped her face instead. She dug sharp nails into Priya's jaw; tightened her hand like a vise. For a small woman, she was strong. There was a feverish light in her eyes.

"Tell me the truth."

Priya felt Meena's hand dig in tighter and tighter.

She forced words out through a mouth pressed tight by Meena's grip.

"Meena. *Stop.*"

Meena's nails dug in harder.

When Meena did not stop, Priya did the only sensible thing she could and stomped down on the other woman's foot. Heel first, the full weight of her body behind it. Meena gave a shriek, her grip slipping, and Priya grabbed the hand still latched to her face. She dug her own nails into Meena's wrist and wrenched herself free.

She could have yelled for help, then. But Meena was panting before her, a crown mask clutched in her hands, and she had called Priya a temple daughter. Fear left Priya's lungs airless. She thought of her brother, his eyes terror-wide in yellow firelight. She thought of darkness, and water, and his voice in her ears.

Don't cry. Oh, Pri, don't cry. Just show me the way.

Meena raised the mask.

"Meena," Priya said sharply. "Meena, do not do it. *Do not.*"

"I'll risk anything. I'll do anything," Meena said, voice taut with fear and despair—and something else too. Something poisonous. "I have no choice. I can't go back without an answer. So tell me now. *Please.*"

"I'm being honest with you. *I don't know.*"

In the silence that followed, Priya heard a distant roar of thunder.

"This was your choice," said Meena. Her lower lip was trembling. "I hope you know that."

She placed the mask over her face.

Priya stood still, cold except for the place where the bead

warmed her wrist. She watched the crown mask press against Meena's skin. In the spaces between the bands of wood, she watched Meena's skin flush instantly, suffused with heat. Meena gave a gasp and raised her head; in the dim light her face was like a lamp, glowing from a deep light within as the strength of the sacred wood poured through her.

Meena took a step forward. Then she froze. A pained hiss escaped her, through tightly clenched teeth.

"Take it off," Priya said urgently. "Meena, right now, while you still can."

But Meena did not take it off. She breathed in and out, in and out, hunched forward with pain. When she raised her head, the skin between the bands of wood was mottled, pinched. The wood stood out against it, having taken on the pearly, varnished sheen of bones boiled clean of flesh.

Meena had chosen her path—chosen to fling herself into the hands of death. Priya would not do the same.

She ran.

She didn't make it very far—barely even turned her body toward the door of the triveni—before she felt a blow to her back that knocked the air from her lungs and threw her to the floor. Her hands slammed into stone. Pain jarred through her. She heaved herself onto her knees, struggling to get back to her feet.

Meena shoved her back down with the efficient application of an elbow to the spine. Priya twisted onto her side, thinking of shoving Meena's weight off her, or—no. That would fail. Slight as Meena was, she had a mask of sacred wood on her, and Priya could feel the new strength of Meena's hands already as she pinned Priya down against the stone, panting behind her mask, her eyes wild.

Instead Priya grasped for Meena's throat, trying to cut off her air long enough for Priya to slip out from under her. She managed to get her hands on Meena's skin, digging her nails into the tendons there—even as Meena ground her knuckles into Priya's shoulders, her knee into her stomach. Priya gritted her teeth, tightened her hand, and—

Meena pinned her hands to the floor.

"*Stay*," commanded Meena, and Priya tried to wrench her hands free, tried to twist to the side, but Meena simply tightened her grip until Priya's hands felt as if they were on fire, the bones of her wrists grinding painfully.

"You feel it, don't you?" said Meena. She pressed her hands down harder and Priya gasped. "I've tasted the deathless waters. I have its gifts."

"Then you shouldn't need me," Priya forced out, turning her cheek down against the stone, letting her body go limp. She tried to look as if she'd given up the fight. Let Meena believe she'd won. After all, in that moment—her hands pinning Priya's shoulders, grinding her bones down, knees in Priya's gut—she *was* the victor.

Meena had realized it too. And that knowledge seemed to soften her. She leaned down closer—close enough for Priya to smell her skin: the rotten, cooked smoke of it.

"I've only had a taste," Meena confessed. "And not from the source. Only—a mouthful from a vial. No more. And it's not..." Her grip spasmed. Her skin was burning hot. "It's not enough."

Priya tried to twist free again. She could not.

"Tell me the way," Meena said heavily. "I don't have long."

"The mask is killing you, Meena."

"It's making me as strong as I need to be." Her words were confident enough. But Meena's eyes were red, and barely blinked. She knew what she was becoming. "The deathless waters are killing me with hunger. The mask is killing me with power. And I—don't care." There was a hitch in her voice. "But I need answers. For the sake of Ahiranya, and the others like me who want to save it. I need to know the way."

"I don't know the way, you idiot. You—sniveling *child*. You called me a temple daughter. You know what I am. Did you never think to question my motives for coming here, as I should have questioned yours?" Priya craned her neck, lifting her head one bare, painful increment. "I can hardly remember anything. Oh, I passed through the waters, I *am* once-born, but when I watched my siblings and elders burn, I lost everything. I'm damaged goods. My mind—" Priya cut herself off, afraid she would do something ridiculous like laugh at the dying woman above her who seemed liable to break Priya's wrists. "I can't help you. I've been trying to remember myself—I came here and I thought, *I'll try.* But now perhaps I never will because of your foolhardiness. The only people who can show you the way now are all dead."

"No." Meena's voice trembled like a flame. Her eyes were wild. "No, no!"

Meena's grip had eased, just a little. She was distracted. Priya took her chance.

She slammed her own head against Meena's, hard enough for her skull to rattle and her skin to burn from the heat of the sacred wood. In the moment it took for Meena to recover from the shock of it, Priya managed to reach one hand up and wrench at the mask.

She scrabbled with ugly, clumsy scrapes of her fingernails, worming her fingers between the blazing heat of the wood and the mottled char of Meena's flesh. She felt something smooth beneath her fingertips, slick and overwarm. She realized with horror that Meena's skin, around the sockets of her eyes, had burned clean down to tissue and bone. Meena gave a terrible shriek that rose and rose into a howl that echoed across the triveni, its columns and its absences, cutting through the crash of the rain that had begun to fall.

Priya shoved her backward. Climbed to her own feet. Her fingertips were blistered. Meena was still writhing on the floor, but Priya could hear footsteps in the corridor—could see Gauri and Sima in the doorway, suddenly, frozen and openmouthed.

"Get out of here!" Priya yelled. "Go!"

"Tell me," Meena said raggedly, rising to her feet. "One of you. Please."

When Sima saw Meena's face she shrieked and clapped her hands over her mouth. She took a step back.

"Meena," Priya tried instead. "Stop. They know nothing, Meena. Stop!"

But Meena was not listening. She moved with the frenzied focus of someone on the knife edge of death and desperation, crossing the floor and grabbing Gauri by the shoulder. Gauri screamed as she was jerked into the room and thrown against a pillar by Meena's desperate hands. The older maidservant's stick clattered to the ground. She scrabbled uselessly as Meena held her and gasped in, out, in, out, asking nothing, the whites of Meena's eyes red with blood.

Gauri whimpered. Slumped forward.

With a furious shout, Priya leapt onto Meena's back. She wrenched Meena's head to an angle, forcing her fingers back under the edges of the loosened mask. When Meena did not even flinch—soil and sky, had she lost all sense of pain?—Priya shoved her forward hard, crushing Gauri against the pillar as she slammed Meena's head against stone again, and again, and again. Then she released Meena, who crumpled, just a little.

"Run," she barked at Gauri, and the older maidservant stumbled, and fell, then rose to her feet again as Sima grabbed her by the arms and dragged her away.

"Guards!" Sima was yelling. "Guards, help! *Help!*"

Meena gasped again—a long, thin exhalation that stretched into a hollow rasp. She turned, lightning-quick. Grasped Priya by the throat. Lifted.

Priya's feet were not touching the ground. Her lungs ached and burned and she could not—she could not move her hands, though she tried to raise them. Her control was failing. Her body felt as if it were swathed in cotton.

Her lungs ached. Her vision was going black. But the dark was rich and textured, rippling like a lightless river. As Meena's hand tightened an increment further, Priya felt the dark cleave open.

She felt water at her feet; three rivers joined around her ankles, swirling over her flesh. In the dizzying dark, she saw her brother's shadow, kneeling, inked in red by the veins beneath her eyelids. She felt old memories clamor like bells, each one chiming against the next: an older temple sister testing her tolerance for pain, dipping her hand in hotter and hotter water, as the elders watched; little Nandi, her temple brother, helping her lay flowers and fruit in a shrine alcove, and filching one juicy segment of fibrous golden mango; pilgrims falling prone before the masked elders, begging for a memento of Ahiranya's old glory. All things she'd lost. Pieces of herself.

Around her she could hear the Hirana singing, waiting, breathing for her. All she had to do. All she had to do . . .

Her eyes snapped open.

She clenched her hands around Meena's wrist as the lines on the triveni's surface flowed and shifted, throwing Meena briefly off-balance, allowing Priya to break her choke hold and slam a closed fist into Meena's stomach. When Meena doubled forward, Priya punched her again, sending her stumbling across the floor.

Priya was once-born, she *was*, and the small tangle of memory she'd regained was enough to make the Hirana move with her, its stone constantly changing beneath Meena's feet like receding waves, throwing her back, back, to the triveni's edge where it lay open to the sky. As Meena stumbled, Priya paused to grab Gauri's stick up from the ground. Only seconds had passed, but it felt as if ages had slipped away with her breath.

"You don't know what strength means," she murmured. Her voice was hoarse, but it was steady. She was glad of that. "You don't. But I learned. I know what it means to carry the waters."

She held Gauri's stick out before her. Touched the tip of it to Meena's chest. Keeping her eyes on Meena's, she said, "Keep on moving."

Finally. *Finally.* The Hirana was speaking to her once more. The response the Hirana had given her when she was on its surface had been the rumblings of a thing asleep. This was a wakeful voice. Just a whisper, a nudge, but it was enough.

Meena moved. She took slow, reluctant footsteps back, back, as Priya nudged her with the stick toward the edge of the triveni's surface, where it melded into the Hirana's pockmarked, death-riddled stone. Meena stopped when her heels touched upon the edge.

They stared at one another. The rain fell.

"Please," Meena whispered.

"Who is he?" Priya's hands were damp with sweat and rain. She could hear shouting, somewhere, drawing closer. "Who was the temple son who gave you a taste of the deathless waters? Who condemned you to die?"

Priya could not see Meena's expression through the mask. But she felt it, when Meena broke free from her shocked stupor; when Meena shoved forward, Gauri's stick bending between them, a fierce cry escaping her throat as she tried once more to get her hands around Priya's throat.

Priya dropped the stick and grabbed Meena by the front of her blouse. The rage that took her then was all-consuming. How *dare* she.

"The Hirana won't spare you," she said savagely. "You're not worthy."

And then she shoved Meena hard with both hands.

Meena fell without another sound.

Priya stood frozen, her hands still outstretched before her. She sucked in a breath. Another. The sheer rage that had taken her left her abruptly. Her hands began to shake.

Oh, spirits. What had she done? What had just *happened*? Her heart was still racing, but she couldn't feel her limbs.

She lowered her hands. Turned.

The prisoner stood in the entrance of the northern chamber. Watching her.

The prisoner—the princess—was taller than Priya had thought she would be. And thinner. It was absurd, to think that now, when Priya's life was finished; when she had murdered another woman in front of the emperor's sister and spoken of the deathless waters. But the princess was tall and gaunt, and although her eyes were still red, she stood utterly still, unblinking, her mouth a smooth, unreadable line. She looked entirely unafraid.

Had the princess seen what she'd done? Heard what she'd said? The princess didn't look as if she thought Priya would kill her, and wildly for a moment, Priya wondered if she should. No one could know what she was. But she was shaking, she couldn't, she didn't want to.

The guards rushed in, the maidservants at their back. Pramila strode after them, a naked blade in her hands.

"Princess Malini!"

Priya's vision was still singed black. She could not think. She could not breathe. Ah, spirits above and below, Priya knew what they all saw, and how damning it was: the walls marked with blood. Priya, a lowly maidservant, bleeding. The princess. The princess...

"Pramila," the princess gasped. Priya watched in numb surprise as the princess's face crumpled with tears, her cheeks suddenly blotchy. The princess grabbed ineffectually at the edges of her shawl, as if trying to draw it up to her face, to protect herself from the eyes of the male guards, who stood and gawped, their weapons drawn. But she dropped the shawl, over and over again. Her hand was shaking. Then her teeth began to chatter, as if shock had overcome her. The princess leaned back against the door. "Pramila, ah!"

Lady Pramila dropped the blade and raced to her side, clasping the princess by the arms. "You there," she snapped at one guard. "Restrain that servant. Now."

A guard strode across the room, grabbing Priya brutally by the arm. Priya bit the inside of her cheek. She did not look at Gauri or Sima. She would not show how afraid she was.

"She saved my life," the princess gasped. She was looking at Pramila, blinking rapidly, her expression terrified and open. "That maid—she saved me. There was an assassin and she risked herself for my sake and I—ah, Pramila, I cannot breathe! I cannot breathe!"

The princess collapsed in Lady Pramila's arms. For all her thinness, her weight dragged Pramila down with her. And Priya could only stare openmouthed as everyone rushed to help the princess. As the guard's hand loosened upon her arm, softened by the lie.

8

ASHOK

The sound of the rain drew Ashok back into his skin. He heard it drum with a hundred thousand fingertips against the soil. He heard it beat a low, hollow song against the wood that surrounded him. He breathed deep and slow, a breath that was like the winding and unwinding of a coil of rope, and knew that it had been raining for some time, and that it was not the sound of the rain alone that had brought him back. He could feel a strange pain along the vertebrae of his spine; there was a heaviness in his throat and his eyes, a threat of grief he wouldn't allow himself to fulfill. No tears. A man did not weep.

But Meena was dead.

He had felt her go, in the sangam, the space that lay beyond flesh. He had felt the painful blood-heat of the mask upon her face, melting her skin to sap, and the slide of her body to death. The loss of her lay upon his shoulders.

He had trained her: taught her how to scrap with other children with her nails and her teeth, how to handle a blade and throw a punch and sever a man's artery just so. He'd taught her what the Parijati had leached from Ahiranya's bones. He'd instilled in her the knowledge that freedom for Ahiranya was worth any price.

Then he had given her a vial of water and let her choose. As if a choice, carefully bred into your nature by grief and training and hardship, was any choice at all.

What a waste of a good weapon.

He exhaled and leaned forward, pressing his chin to his neck to ease the vise of tension still clamped upon his spine.

Although the rain was still fierce, Ashok was dry. He had chosen his spot well. He sat, cross-legged, in the hollowed heart of a dead tree, a great husk of a thing with its innards scraped clean. Around him, in a clearing still black and ash marked from the burning of rot-riven trees, there was no similar cover. His brothers and sisters were camped in a nearby copse gently shaded by great leaves large enough to blot out the worst of the rain. They were invisible to him, from here, and he to them.

He was glad of the privacy. He pressed his knuckles to his eyes, left then right, and rose to his feet. He stooped to leave the shelter of the tree, then stepped out into the falling rain, which was clear and sweet and shockingly cold.

For all Meena's failures, there was a poetry in her death that moved him. He was best at war—the kiss of a blade against a throat held more eloquence to him than a verse—but he had sat in pleasure houses, listening to the poets spin tales about the brave rebels, weaving them into the rich epics of the Age of Flowers. Interspersed between forbidden recitations of the Birch Bark Mantras, they twined together the actions of Ashok's masked band with the legendary strength of the ancient temple elders. They spoke passionately of how the mothers of flame had cruelly erased Ahiranya's bright future. The most skilled poets set grown men weeping with rage and passion.

He wondered what they would make of Meena's death—a rebellion upon the Hirana, a failed fight against a cruel regent.

He would have to let the story slip.

If his grief had undone him after all, at the thought of the tale of her, the tragedy of it—if his eyes stung with tears for an impetuous soldier who had chosen her death unflinching—then he refused to acknowledge it. Let the rain take what he did not want. Let it hollow him. He was a leader of men and women, a temple son tested and twice-lived. And he had felt someone else in the sangam: a presence like a blade, focused and clean and pure, that had turned its cold hands on him, and seen him, through the river of heart and flesh.

Plans. There were always plans to be made or undone, and no time to mourn.

Kritika waited under the cover of the vast leaves, the long end of her sari draped over her hair. Ashok did not know how long she had been watching for him.

"What passes?" she asked.

"Meena won't be returning to us," Ashok replied. "She's dead."

Kritika sucked in a sharp breath. Her mouth, her eyes, her very bones seemed to pull tighter.

"She acted rashly," said Ashok.

"How?" Kritika dabbed her tear-wet cheeks ineffectually with her fingertips. "What did she do?"

Ashok shook his head. The sangam did not show him everything. It could not. Within its liminal space, he had the capacity to feel a great deal: memory, emotion, fragments of thought. But Meena had not been twice-born—had barely been once-born, thanks to the deathless waters she'd consumed from the vial. And she had reached for him only in the moment when she had begun to fall from the Hirana, when death had been an inevitability. All he had felt from her had been impressions, as muddied as light through monsoon rain. Pain, molten flesh. The flash of piercing eyes. The claws of gravity at her back. The bitter thread of words unspoken upon her tongue.

Ashok. Please—

forgive me.

He told Kritika none of it. Instead he rolled his shoulders, his spine all grief knots, and said, "She wore the mask."

"I thought that was only for emergencies. Do you think she was discovered? Attacked?"

"We'll know soon enough. Tell Ganam to pack up and move the main camp." The rebel movement against Parijatdvipan rule was disparate, made up of multiple limbs that did not all obey the same master. But if the rebellion had a heart, then Ashok considered it to be his people. They were the ones willing to commit violence, and they were good enough at it to move swiftly, masked and lethal, murdering advisors and merchants and imperial loyalists, slowly eroding the struts holding up the empire's bones. Sometimes he called the main camp his own temple council, half joking. But he had seen the way it made their eyes light up. He thought often now of what a useful yoke a tale could be.

And his people *were* a council of a kind, canny enough to help him maintain his own network of spies and allies, across the highborn households of Parijatdvipa. Even the regent's household, which was irritatingly difficult to infiltrate.

Speaking of. He did not think Meena had been interrogated. But he could not be sure. Better to be cautious than see more of their number dead. "You should go to the mahal. See if there's anything more to be learned about her death."

Kritika swallowed. Inclined her head. She turned to walk away, and Ashok halted her, placing a hand upon her shoulder. "I grieve her too," he said.

"I know." Kritika lowered her eyes. "I don't doubt you," she added, in a rising tone that denoted respect. "But..."

She trailed off. Ashok looked at her face—how drawn it was, the way even the wrinkles upon it seemed like bands of pain—and said, "Tell me."

"Sarita is ailing," Kritika said reluctantly. "And Bhavan is—not long for this world."

Two more. Two more weapons, trained and lost.

"Then we need to find the deathless waters all the more urgently, for all our sakes." He pressed his knuckles to his forehead. "Wait a moment, Kritika," he said. "Let me think for a time."

Cost and gain. Sacrifice and success. He had lost Meena, lost a mask made of sacred wood, lost a pair of eyes in the general's mahal and feet upon the Hirana for approximately nothing. This mission had all been sacrifice and cost, with no success or gain to balance its disasters. He had failed.

But as a boy, he'd had truths bred into his bones by loyalty to a higher vision, a vision that was pitiless in its demands. He turned to those truths now. They stared back at him in return, unblinking, all-knowing.

All failure was born from weakness. This was truth. He had known better than to send Meena on a task that required both patience and cunning. She was—*she had been*—too rash and too fierce, too openhearted. And she had known she was dying. She had known they were all dying. Desperation had undone her. And as her leader, he should have known it would.

But Ashok had wanted her to succeed. He had wanted it because she had reminded him of another girl and another time, of hopes sacrificed, and he had thought, *If Meena is even a shadow of her...*

He lowered his hand. Kritika waited, quiet and watchful. "I have been a fool," he said finally.

Sentimentality had its place when it served a function; when it helped achieve the greater ideal of an Ahiranya free and powerful, as it had once been. But his love—no. The blood tenderness of it was nothing but weakness.

Love had led him astray and wasted Meena's life. Even now, his weak nature quailed at the thought of doing what was necessary. Even now, he thought of a night long ago, when he had kneeled under the wavering light of lanterns, his hands upon bird-bone-thin shoulders. His sister's shoulders.

He remembered telling her a lie. *Wait here*, he'd said. *And I'll come back for you. I promise.*

She'd looked at him with such trust. He'd never forgotten that look.

"There is a maidservant in the regent's household. A woman named Priya. Tell our newest addition to bring her to me. The resistance has need of her."

He had tried to save her once. He had let her go. He had

set loyal eyes on her now and again, and through them, he had watched as she had grown up without him. He'd believed he could let her live free of the purpose that held him constantly by the throat. But he could not be weak any longer. He had felt her in the sangam. She had been there when Meena had died. There was strength in her now—so much power, more than she had possessed in all the years he'd kept watch on her—and he could use her.

If only he had made this decision sooner. If only he had told Meena to reach out to her, to ally with her. But no matter. There was still a way forward. He could still turn his sister's gifts to his own ends.

Ahiranya was worth any price. Even her.

9

VIKRAM

Late nights were often a requirement of Vikram's role as regent of Ahiranya, and they were at times a pleasure. Other times they were a burden. Sometimes, like tonight, they were both.

Tonight, Vikram was playing the diplomat, entertaining one of the low princes of Saketa, Prince Prem, who had been merrily holed up in a brothel in a neighborhood of disrepute, drinking and whoring with a few of his men and a handful of disreputable noble cousins. According to the complex rules of Saketan blood lineage, Prem was considered a first cousin of the high prince who ruled his city-state, and was therefore of similar status to Vikram. Despite his role as regent of Ahiranya, Vikram did not possess a jot of highborn blood. Everything he'd earned under the last emperor, Sikander, he had earned in his own right as a general of Parijatdvipa.

Another low prince or city-state royal might have demanded more obsequiousness from Vikram than he would have enjoyed providing, but Prince Prem was a genial, frivolous lecher and no trouble at all, requiring nothing but the typical courtesies. He'd visited Vikram a few times since his arrival, and had largely been pleasant if rather unedifying company. He held his liquor well and had brought an excellent Saketan vintage with him on every visit. He played pachisa with the grace required not to irritate, his moves measured and his repartee witty.

It would have been a pleasant evening, much like the ones that had come before it, if not for the presence of Lord Santosh. The man had refused to play pachisa. "I know the other nations of Parijatdvipa like it," he'd sneered. "But in Parijat we are more refined." He hadn't touched Prem's Saketan wine, or the array of Ahiranyi liquors arranged in beautiful colored casks upon the table for the delectation of guests, instead demanding that a proper Parijati liquor be brought for him. This, he did not share.

As he drank, he interrogated Vikram about Ahiranya's rebellions, which had grown notably bloodier since Emperor Chandra's coronation. He commented on the high number of Ahiranyi servants in the mahal—"If this were *my* mahal, General Vikram, I would fill it with *our* countryfolk"—and asked question after barbed question about the routines of the guards, based on the observations his own men, scattered through Vikram's forces, had fed back to him.

After an hour of Santosh's attention, Vikram's patience was wearing thin, and Prince Prem was attacking his wine with worrying enthusiasm, a false smile fixed to his mouth. And still, Santosh continued.

This is the man Emperor Chandra sends to sniff around my regency, Vikram thought with hysterical despair. *This buffoon. I should let him have it. Either he will destroy Ahiranya within a year, or it will destroy him.*

But Vikram would not, and could not, give up his regency so easily. For years, he had held this fractious nation together, paying every necessary price to see it survive under his rule. Until Emperor Chandra commanded his removal, he would fake ignorance of Santosh's purpose and do his best to maintain everything he had.

That Emperor Chandra liked Lord Santosh well enough to allow him to prod at Vikram's authority did not reflect well on the emperor. Chandra was nothing like his elder brother, Aditya, who had at least had the semblance of a good ruler: a suitable coterie of friends and advisors, drawn from across the nations of

Parijatdvipa, and therefore the full support of the empire's city-states. And a sense of honor that would have stopped him from indulging in anything too ambitious.

A shame that he'd found a new faith and left his duties behind.

"Tell us about Parijat," cut in Prem. "How is it in the capital? Is Harsinghar as beautiful as I remember it?"

"Harsinghar is always the most beautiful of cities," said Santosh seriously. "The palace is being redecorated."

"How so?" Vikram asked. He did not have any particular interest in architecture, but he would feign an interest if he had to.

"Statues are going to be built for the new mothers in the imperial court, so they may be thanked and worshipped for Parijatdvipa's glory," Santosh said proudly, as if he'd had a hand in it.

Smiling at such a pronouncement was difficult. Vikram wore prayer stones and prayed to the mothers, lighting candles for them morning and evening in the family shrine. He did not know how to find any common ground between Emperor Chandra's version of faith and his own. But smile he did.

"Fascinating," said Prem, sounding suitably awed. "And how will they fit that many statues in the court? Is it being expanded?"

A beat of silence. Vikram reached for his own wine and drank.

"The statues will be for the mothers Narina and Alori alone," Santosh said. "The other women were given a gift—were purified—but they lacked the qualities to be true mothers of flame."

Not highborn, Vikram translated. But he said nothing and did not allow himself to feel revulsion. It would have been hypocritical, after all he himself had done.

"Ah, my mistake," Prem said blithely.

Santosh gave him a tight, displeased smile, then looked at Vikram. "Anyway, General Vikram," he began. "I wanted to discuss your advisors. Your Lord Iskar is from Parijat—"

"Ah, Santosh," Prem protested. "I'm here to drink and have fun, not to talk politics. Shall we converse about something else?"

"I can see you have little concern for important business,"

Santosh said, with no subtlety whatsoever to disguise his disdain, which made sense, Vikram supposed wearily. Subtlety was cultivated out of necessity, by people who knew that power needed to be treated with care—who understood how easily it could be stolen or taken. Santosh had the emperor's ear, and the emperor's crude belief in the supremacy of Parijat and Parijati blood. He had no need for such things as subtlety. "But I am at the forefront of imperial politics, Prince Prem, and I can't simply act as you do."

"You're at the forefront of politics, and Emperor Chandra sent you here?" Prem's forehead creased with puzzlement, even as he continued to smile. It gave his expression a rather mocking edge. "You're very far from Parijat here, Santosh! Besides, it isn't politics that brings people to Ahiranya." He grinned as he lifted his wine. "It's pleasure. The brothels are *very* fine."

Santosh's expression was slightly concerning, his sneer taking on an edge of cruelty. So Vikram intervened, saying, "Lord Santosh graciously accompanied Princess Malini on Emperor Chandra's behalf. A great honor that he fulfilled admirably."

Prem's smile twitched slightly, but even he seemed to see the sense in avoiding commenting upon the princess. Santosh purposefully turned, excluding Prem from the conversation. To Vikram he said, "Speaking of Princess Malini and her—contemplation—there are things you and I must discuss, General Vikram. Just as Emperor Chandra is keen to see his sister reflect on her choices, he would like his most difficult nation to learn to be more biddable. I have many suggestions to make on his behalf. I know the emperor's mind on this matter extremely well. We spoke of Ahiranya often."

Vikram did not allow his anger to show on his face, but Prem seemed to have no such control. The prince's eyes had already narrowed at Santosh's slight against him—the slight of a mere highborn lord of Parijat against a Saketan of royal blood—and Santosh's casual boast of closeness with the emperor had only served to goad him.

"You're right, you're right, what interest do I have in politics?"

Prem announced, overloud. "It was my uncle who always cared for politics—and he was removed from his treasury position by the emperor only a month ago, wasn't he? Or was it three months? Numbers aren't my strong suit as they were his, but I do remember that when he complained he was executed. Put to death, just like that," he said brightly. "A real scandal."

"Prince Prem," Vikram murmured, but there was no stopping the man.

"I can't rightly remember who took his place—ah." A click of his fingers. "One of your cousins, I think. Congratulations."

Vikram lowered his own glass. "Lord Prem," he said. "You are inebriated, I think."

Santosh's jaw was trembling with fury.

"You drunk sot," he said, in a tone that suggested he would be using far worse words—or perhaps his blade—if not for the disparity in their status. "When Emperor Chandra finishes cleaning up the imperial court and this forsaken hole of a country, I'll be sure to direct him to Saketa. You need to be reminded of your place."

Prem lurched to his feet. Vikram rose more sedately to his own.

"Let me escort you out for some air, Prince Prem." Without waiting for a response, Vikram took the man by the shoulders and led him from the room.

Prem did seem unsteady on his feet. One of Vikram's servants in the hall beyond gave him a questioning look, asking without words whether Vikram would like the prince taken off his hands and gently escorted to a room to convalesce. Vikram did not respond to it. No matter how things had changed, Prem was important enough to receive his full attention. The last thing he wanted was an angry letter from the high prince's scribes, on top of everything else.

"Sorry, sorry," said Prem.

"No need, my lord."

"How long is *he* staying?"

"As long as Emperor Chandra wills," said Vikram. "And you?"

"As long as my coin allows," Prem replied with a laugh. "I'd hoped we'd be able to talk alone. The last time I came we played an excellent game of pachisa. I'd like to do that again."

"You're always welcome," Vikram assured him, slapping his back with fake joviality. *You should be careful,* he considered saying. The prince was young. An older man's advice could not harm him. Things weren't as they once were. A man who did not recognize that would not live long.

"You know that his rudeness to me and to you will not be the end of it, General Vikram," Prem said, placing an arm loosely around Vikram's shoulder. As if they were friends. "We should certainly meet again, you and I, even if not for games or wine. You may be Parijati but not the sort, I think, that will do well in this new age."

Dangerous talk, bordering on treasonous. Vikram said nothing.

Prem leaned in, voice lowered, eyes intent. He was, perhaps, not as drunk as Vikram had believed.

"I am saying, General Vikram, that Emperor Chandra is changing Parijatdvipa." His breath was sweet with aniseed. "He thinks that because the mothers forged his line and the city-states remember their debt, we'll kiss the hand of any inbred Parijati he favors. But we Saketans don't forget that he's not the only scion of the mothers with a right to that throne. And I don't think you forget either, General Vikram. There is another way."

The prince would not be the first to think—or say—it. And Vikram was almost tempted to agree. Almost. He knew Prem had something to offer—some bargain to make, some information to exchange.

But Vikram had not achieved his status by taking unnecessary risks.

His last meeting with the freshly enthroned Emperor Chandra, just after Emperor Sikander's death, was seared upon his brain. Back then, the new emperor had not yet begun to remove non-Parijati advisors from their posts—had not ordered the execution of old, venerated Dwarali war ministers or Saketan treasurers, or burned a noble lady of Srugani descent and a princess of Alor. He *had* burned a famed courtesan and all her attendant women, but popular rumor suggested she had been a favorite of Emperor Sikander, and Chandra had been well-known for his virulent distaste for impurity in women. It had struck some of the nobility as cruel—but they overlooked it as the type of blood and tumult that was to be expected when a new emperor rose to power.

They hadn't yet begun to understand the horrible depths or the commitment of Chandra's faith.

Chandra had been genial, welcoming. He had smiled at Vikram, thin-lipped, accepting his bow with grace. Offered him a Parijati sherbet made of sugarcane and crushed flowers, handed to Vikram by a lovely maidservant. Chandra had exchanged pleasantries. Light conversation.

Then he'd said, *Tell me how you did it, General Vikram. Tell me how the temple council burned. Tell me how they killed the children.*

Vikram would never forget the look on the emperor's face.

Despite his years of service, he had believed that people were not innately cruel. Everyone Vikram had ever had a hand in killing—even the temple children—he had killed out of necessity. But Chandra…Chandra listened to every excruciating detail, with a light in his eyes and a smile on his mouth. And everything he had done since that first meeting had been a confirmation of that first smile, that first flash of teeth that had sent a foreboding chill down Vikram's spine.

I have use for a man like you, he'd said.

Those words. The pleasure in them.

Vikram had understood that a man like that should not be crossed.

Prem must have seen that his expression had grown suddenly shuttered, because the smile died upon his face.

"General Vikram," he said. "Perhaps I've overstepped."

"Yes," said Vikram. "I fear indeed you have."

It was almost a relief when a guard barreled down the corridor. A young, green one, followed by the commander of Vikram's personal guard.

"The princess," said Commander Jeevan. "The conches have been sounded."

"It has been a pleasure, Prince Prem," Vikram said. "Perhaps we will meet again soon."

Prem agreed politely enough. But they both knew Vikram had rejected whatever overture he had been offering.

Vikram would not meet with the Saketan prince again.

Vikram climbed the Hirana slowly, laboriously. He was too old for such exertion and most miserably of all, the rain refused to relent. The servant at his back was holding a parasol above his head that was pitifully ineffectual against the downpour. Every time the surface of the Hirana dipped, the man wavered, the parasol teetering and tilting in his grip.

At least Jeevan was with him: a solid, reliable presence, watching his back, bow and arrow in hand.

The only small pleasure was that Santosh had not accompanied him. The man had tried, but he was clearly terrified of the Hirana, and the liquor had made him too unsteady on his feet. He'd clambered up for two minutes then relented and returned to the ground. He'd sent one of his own Parijati guards in his stead, who followed behind Jeevan, clutching the guiding rope as if his life depended upon it.

Vikram did not bother to fear the Hirana. When the temple elders still lived, it had been the regent's responsibility to supervise the temple council. Every month, he had been guided up the Hirana by one of their youngest temple children and had eaten with the elders. He hadn't thought much of them, those relics of a long-gone age—a time when Ahiranya had still been powerful—playing their symbolic role. But still, he had found them quaintly fascinating. They had been friendly to him, even shown him the little tricks of magic they could still perform, shifting the Hirana's surface subtly to their will.

He was not afraid of the Hirana. But he was afraid of the consequences of this night.

An assassin. A Parijati princess, howling and weeping, insensible with terror. If not for the intervention of one maidservant—a thing of pure chance—the emperor's sister would be dead, and Vikram's own death sentence would have been sealed.

He reached the Hirana's summit, and the guards at the door bowed to him. Their commander opened the gates and led him in.

"She's here, my lord," the guard said in a low voice. "Lady Pramila hasn't left her side."

They entered a cloister room, an outcropping from the western corridor of the Hirana. Princess Malini, only sister of Emperor Chandra, king of kings, master of the empire of Parijatdvipa, was kneeling on the floor, vomiting into a bucket.

"Take it away," the princess gasped, shoving the bucket one-handed, even as she gripped its edge precariously for balance. "Please."

"And have you ruin the floor?" Her jailer's voice was grim. "No. Keep it close, there's a girl."

"General Vikram begs your indulgence, princess," said the guard, bowing his head once more, drawing back into the hallway. He left Vikram alone with the women.

The princess lifted her head, her face gray, eyes wet.

Before her brother had sent her to be imprisoned, isolated, upon the Hirana—*where she may contemplate her decisions and the state of her soul, as I have contemplated it, in a place befitting of her fate*, the emperor had written—Vikram had seen the princess once, on a visit to the imperial mahal in Parijat itself. She'd been a genial and pretty thing, wrapped in fine silks. Royal daughters did not wear crowns. Instead they wore imperial symbols: jasmine flowers, yellow and white, twined into a halo; marigolds and roses, gold and carnelian, fresh and still touched with dew, bound to the roots and ends of a heavy braid.

The woman he looked upon now did not resemble the flower-wreathed princess of Parijat. She did not even look very much like the princess who had arrived nearly a month ago at his mahal. That girl had been quiet and dour but healthy enough, tall and shapely with severe dark eyes and a wary turn of the mouth.

This woman was thin and dirty, panting hysterically, skin mottled with tears, eyes sunken and red-rimmed.

Mothers of flame protect him, he should have concerned himself far more closely with her welfare than he had, emperor's orders be damned.

"Princess," he said, speaking in Dvipan—the formal language of court, and a royal daughter's mother tongue. "Were you injured?"

"Merely frightened, my lord," her jailer said quickly.

Vikram looked at the princess, wavering where she knelt, her face flushed with suffering.

"She requires a physician," he said.

"She does not, my lord," said Pramila. "She has a frail constitution. She merely needs rest. Medicine, and rest."

Vikram was not convinced. Far from it. How could he be, when the princess continued to tremble, her hair as loose and wild about her as a priest's, her body all gaunt ugliness?

"Princess Malini," he said once more. "Tell me how you fare."

He saw the princess swallow. Saw her raise her chin. "An assassin tried to take my life, General," the princess croaked out, in a voice that wavered like flame. "My imperial brother and master would never have allowed such a thing in his household."

Ah.

He was conscious of the eyes upon him. The guards that surrounded him, barring Jeevan, were all Santosh's men and not his own. And Santosh had plenty of reason to report any and all of Vikram's failures back to the emperor.

Emperor Chandra clearly did not care, overmuch, for the princess's well-being. He would not have sent her here if he did. But nonetheless she was royal blood, sequestered in Vikram's care.

If she had died at an assassin's hands imprisoned in Ahiranya, if Vikram had failed to keep her safe, and allowed imperial blood to be spilled on his lands...

Well. Emperor Chandra was not known for his generosity. Vikram again remembered the hunger in his eyes, when he'd asked about the temple children burning. It was not a hunger Vikram could trust.

"I vow to you, daughter of flowers, that every effort will be made to keep you safe as a pearl," Vikram said.

She shook her head. "It is not enough, General. How can it be enough? Oh, mothers of flame, protect me. I cannot survive here, alone and unloved!"

"Princess," hissed Pramila. "No. Silence, now."

"I..." Her face crumpled. "I have nothing here. No attendants. No ladies. No guards that I can trust. I was gently raised, General. I am sure I will die like this."

"Princess," he said. He kneeled, then, before her. His knees ached. "Your brother has ordered that you be kept in solitude. In contemplation. I cannot give you the court you once possessed. It would be treason."

"One attendant would be enough to put my heart at ease," whispered the princess. "General, the woman who saved my life—can I not have her? She is only a maidservant. No doubt she knows nothing beyond obedience. I doubt she even speaks a civilized tongue. It would be as if you provided me a—a loyal hound. She would not disrupt my contemplation. But perhaps I would feel...safe."

It was not an unreasonable request.

One maidservant. Well. Surely the emperor would not be wrathful if Vikram provided the princess one simple Ahiranyi girl to sweep her floors and help her sleep at night. Surely Lord Santosh would not object to this measure if Vikram framed it as a way of calming a frightened girl. One maidservant was a small price to pay, to keep the princess biddable. Even now, looking into his eyes, her breath was calming. New color flushed her cheeks.

"What," Vikram said carefully, graciously, "can I, a humble servant to your family, do but attempt to ease your pain? You will have the maidservant. I promise it, princess."

After Vikram had spoken to the Hirana guards, the weeping princess, and his closest advisors—and even comforted his wife, who had woken when the conches sounded and begged for news of her precious servants immediately upon his return—he went to his own private chambers, stood upon his shaded balcony, and stared into the distance for a long moment, gripping the wood of the balustrade so tightly it creaked in the vise of his hands. A servant, standing in attendance by the door, asked him tentatively if he wanted to change his garb. His tunic and dhoti, both a silk so dark a blue they were almost black, had grown sodden, darkened with rain and sweat by the journey up and down the Hirana.

"No," Vikram said shortly. "Arrange a bath for when I return."

He did not want fresh clothing for this task.

The servant murmured an acknowledgment and withdrew. Vikram left the veranda, returning to the cool interior of the mahal, and made his way deeper and deeper into the building, and deeper still, beyond gates and guards, down to a dark staircase protected by barred doors and men alike.

Santosh was waiting for him there. Vikram had hoped the man had gone to bed. But one of Santosh's men must have informed him of Vikram's location.

Beneath the mahal, in the prison cells, a priest awaited them.

"General," the priest said. "Come. She is prepared."

Santosh bowed his head. For once, he was quiet. In the presence of a priest of the mothers, he finally showed proper respect.

The priest had pale eyes, green-brown, and a mark of ash upon his forehead and his chin. He was a true Parijati priest, and accordingly, he had arranged the assassin on a slab of stone, swathed her in white cloth, and marked her skin with resinous perfume. He had put right the worst of her fall: All her limbs were where they should have been, which Vikram gathered had not been the case when the guards had first found her, at the foot of the Hirana. A garland of flowers, half-wilted from the heat, was piled at her feet.

Priests showed respect to the dead, whether they deserved it or not. And Parijati priests showed special respect to women who had passed on. It was their way.

In the lantern light of the cell, Vikram looked at the body. At the face.

He turned away quickly. Not quickly enough.

No amount of drink would blot out the image of that skull. No fall had pulverized it. It looked as if it had...melted.

"The mask she wore has power in it," the priest said tranquilly. He held his hand before him, and Vikram saw that the skin was burned. "Take it with this cloth, if you wish to look upon it," the priest added, holding the mask toward him. "Carefully."

Vikram held the mask of wood, stained with blood and gristle, in the glove of perfumed cloth the priest had offered him. He looked at the eyeholes, the gape of a mouth. He could feel the heat of the thing through the cloth, warmer than flesh.

"You call it power," he murmured.

"Yes."

"The rot?"

The priest shook his head. "The woman's body is clean of impurities."

"What is this, then?" Santosh asked. Vikram startled. He had forgotten that Santosh was there. The Parijati lord's face was gray. "Some kind of Ahiranyi witchcraft? I thought their cursed power died with their yaksa."

"No," Vikram replied, shaking his head. "Likely just a product of the forest. The wood there has always been—unusual."

Even before the rot, he thought.

With weariness, he realized so much had gone wrong during his reign. The rot had begun. The temple children had grown more powerful. They and their elders had burned. The rebel unrest had swelled unceasingly, rising as the rot spread hunger and death and displaced villagers from their ancestral homes. And now...this.

"There will need to be justice," Santosh demanded. "Witchcraft—whatever it may be, it is a *crime*. These Ahiranyi think they can bring back the Age of Flowers. They need to be punished. They must learn that Emperor Chandra is not weak."

Vikram nodded. "Rebels will be interrogated and executed," he said. The rebels who were likely behind this would be nigh on impossible to capture. The most violent of them, masked and therefore faceless, were too good at vanishing into the forest, where no sensible man would follow. But the poets and singers, who recited forbidden Ahiranyi poetry in bazaars and daubed mantras on walls, who offered visions of a free Ahiranya—they would be an easier target. A suitable scapegoat.

Even as he spoke, he knew it would not be enough. And sure enough, Santosh's mouth firmed. He shook his head.

"They owe us more, General Vikram," said Santosh. "They owe the emperor a sacrifice."

What would be enough justice—enough blood, enough death, enough suffering—for an emperor who sought to burn his own sister to death?

What must I do to ensure that my rule survives this night's work?

Vikram thought, grimly, of his young Ahiranyi wife, her placid eyes, her foolish, kindhearted nature and the child in her belly. His wife—who collected orphans and rot victims with a kind of mania—who had perhaps brought the assassin into their home, however unwitting...

She wouldn't be happy with what he had to do. But she would accept it. She had no other choice.

He looked at the bones of the assassin on the stone slab before him, the open husk of her face, the bare vulnerability of the jawbone devoid of meat. The room was filled with the stink of death, despite the garlands and perfume.

Vikram lowered the mask down upon the table.

"Have her last rites," he said. "With all due reverence. Scatter the ashes. She has no family to take them."

The priest inclined his head. He understood the ways of the dead.

"With all due reverence," Santosh repeated.

"Would the emperor object to such?" Vikram asked.

"Ah, no," said Santosh. "No. Emperor Chandra would be pleased to see the proper religious order respected. To see a rebel purified, at the last."

Santosh had made something that Vikram intended as an honorable act into a vengeance. And indeed, perhaps it was. The Ahiranyi preferred to bury their dead, after all. A rebel would not want to burn.

"It will be the first purification of many," said Santosh. He no longer looked drunk or boastful. Only intent. In his face, Vikram saw a shadow of the glinting, brittle evil of the emperor. "We will make Ahiranya pure, General Vikram. In Parijat's service."

10

RAO

Rao didn't know when the imperial soldiers began marching through Hiranaprastha. He was in a brothel, his back to the wall and a half-empty bottle of arrack in his fist. There was a courtesan twirling at the center of the room as men watched in semi-inebriated rapture. The courtesan was dancing beautifully, every turn of her belled ankles a bright, melodious chime. But this was a small and decrepit pleasure house that had barely anything in common with the large pink and turquoise palaces lining the city's glittering river. It was painfully cramped, the alcohol cheap and the hall so crowded that men were packed shoulder to shoulder. It was so crowded, in fact, that the man to Rao's left had lodged his elbow into Rao's side and kept it there for the last half hour. Rao's ribs ached.

He wished he'd been drinking the arrack and not simply emptying it out piecemeal into his sharp-elbowed neighbor's cup. He wished the dancer would finish and the poet would hurry up and begin his salon. But although the poet had entered some time ago, his acolytes had been arriving in straggling batches, their expressions hunted.

The three women who usually attended him had crept by, ushered through the room by a man who glared at anyone who gave them too long a glance. A few men in heavy shawls, dripping from rain, had turned up and pushed through the crowd to the corridor that led to the cramped back rooms of the brothel. But there were no young scribes yet—no men with tonsured hair and bound manuscripts under their arms, fingers stained with ink, ready to copy the poet's words.

The poet wouldn't begin until they were all here. He never did.

So Rao waited. And pretended to drink. And watched the courtesan spin.

Rao only knew something was amiss when the brothel madam entered the hall and waved one bracelet-laden arm at the musicians, ordering them silent. The music ended in an abrupt, discordant stumble of reed flutes and cymbals, as one musician after the other raised his hands awkwardly before him at her urging.

The courtesan whirled to a stop with a smooth turn of her heels against the emerald-tiled floor. The folds of her skirt rustled to stillness. Her braid looped itself artfully around her throat. Without missing a beat—even though there was no longer any rhythm to guide her—she clasped her hands before her and bowed, ending the dance.

Rao could only be quietly impressed. To perform with grace before a crowd of drunk old lechers was a hard enough task. To end a six-stage Ahiranyi traditional dance in its third step was even harder, for a woman who valued her art. And this woman—who had danced in the hall three nights in a row, each night swirling her way through a blatantly seditious piece intended to venerate the yaksa spirits seasoned with *just* enough flashes of hip and ankle to please the customers—clearly valued her art very highly indeed.

"I'm afraid that is all for tonight, my lords," the madam said apologetically, as her girls crossed the room and drew heavy brocade curtains across the perforated screen walls of the hall. The sounds of the city were immediately blotted out. The faint sweetness of the night breeze was replaced by the scent of sweating men, pipe smoke, perfumed oil, and lantern fumes. "The soldiers are walking again tonight."

There was a startled murmur from the crowd. The soldiers never closed the brothels. The pleasure houses were the reason Parijatdvipans came to Ahiranya at all. It had always been considered more licentious than any other part of the empire. The Ahiranyi did not guard their women's purity as carefully. In the past they had even allowed their men to marry men, and their women to marry women. When Rao had still been a boy, he and his friends—other young nobles of Parijatdvipa's city-states, all of them—had managed to get hold of a contraband copy of the banned Ahiranyi religious poetry, the Birch Bark Mantras. They'd laughed and joked, mocking the text and each other to hide their embarrassment as they read explicit tales of lewdness alongside tracts where the yaksa conquered nation after nation, bathing them in blood.

It was only since his arrival in Ahiranya, where passages from the Birch Bark Mantras were painted on walls and recited by poets who used the brothels as cover to disseminate their politics, that he had come to understand that what he and his friends had blushed over as lewdness was a source of faith and defiance to the Ahiranyi, who joined stories of seductive beings of flower and flesh, of two men lying together, and of world-conquering glory on the same lyrical breath.

The rumblings of discontent that had started to echo through the crowd died quickly, as confusion gave way to caution and fear. Men clambered to their feet. Began to leave. If the brothel was closing, then something terrible had happened. Better to be somewhere safe than wait to hear from the soldiers directly what had occurred.

Rao remained where he was for a moment. The brothel madam stood, watching the men go. She looked calm enough, but as the curtains were closing he'd seen the tightness around her eyes. The sweat dotting her upper lip.

She was afraid.

Maybe the fact that she allowed her girls to dance subversively and rented her rooms to Ahiranyi poets was enough of a reason for her to be frightened. But Rao had a feeling that the fear on her face was too real, too *immediate* to simply be abstract.

He should have left then. But Rao was one of the nameless faith, and he understood the sacred power of instinct—the way a body's knowing could be a gift from the nameless, a prophecy written in the thud of the heart or the ice of fear winding down a spine. He felt it then: a kind of foreboding. Not quite fear. Not quite curiosity.

There was knowledge here, if he was willing to take it.

He stood. Instead of leaving the brothel, he crossed the room and entered the corridor leading to the poet's salon.

There was no one else in the corridor to watch him, but he made a point of swaying as he walked anyway. An ungainly, drunken sway. He knew he smelled of tobacco and the opium pipe, of wine—his jacket was open, his hair loose. He had no marks of status: no chakrams like bracelets on his arms or neck-laces of pearl around his throat, no fine blue Aloran turban, no brace of daggers on a belt at his hips. He wore instead a plain necklace of prayer stones, fruit pits polished and joined with darts of silver, the kind all Parijati men wore. And that was what he was. Not a nameless prince of Alor, prophecy-born, but a Parijati highborn, rich and doltish and deep into his cups.

He stopped, slumping to the ground. Closed his eyes.

Listened.

Soldiers in the room, and women weeping, and men murmur-ing in low voices. The soldiers were asking questions and one of the men—not the poet, Rao knew his voice—was arguing. "We're scholars, sirs, and artists. We're not rebels, we only discuss ideas."

"No one said you were rebels," the soldier replied, which made one of the women start weeping more fiercely.

The poet and his followers *were* rebels, though, of a kind. In this room, he'd heard them speak of secession and resistance through the medium of Parijati poetry—the metaphor of rose and thorn, of poisonous oleander, of fires and honey, turning Parijat's own language against itself.

He thought of the lies—and truths—he'd had to pay to learn their secrets. The discontent among Ahiranya's highborn. The threads of unease that united them, and their merchants and warriors and potters and healers. The way the mishandling of the rot, the deaths of farmers, the banning and debasement of Ahiranyi language and literature, had all culminated in the work of an unknown number of masked, armed rebels who murdered Parijatdvipan officials and merchants with pointed viciousness, and a much vaster number of poets and singers who spread the image of a free Ahiranya.

The poet and his followers were not the masked rebels of Ahiranya's forest. But they were part of the soul of the resistance against Parijatdvipa, bound to highborn funders, and Rao had hoped they would have use to him.

Now, unfortunately, their use was gone.

A noise. Rao raised his head.

"You there," said the soldier. He wore Parijat's white and gold, with the regent's mark on his turban. His booted footsteps were heavy. "What are you doing here?"

Rao hadn't heard him approach. Perhaps he'd drunk slightly more of the arrack than he thought he had.

"L-looking for the way out," Rao slurred. "Sir."

He could see the soldier weighing up his options: leave the drunken sot he'd found in the hallway to be thrown out by one of the brothel's capable guards, or drag him into the salon to be interrogated alongside the poet and his acolytes? Rao saw the soldier's interest in him waver. Rao was a drunk fool, there was nothing of note about him—he'd made sure of that—and how likely was a Parijati man to be involved in the Ahiranyi resistance? He would vomit, perhaps, or cry. Much better to leave him.

Rao gave a drunken hiccup and tried to straighten up. The soldier rolled his eyes, muttered something unsavory under his breath, and turned to go.

Behind them, in the salon, a woman screamed. One of the men began to shout, then went abruptly silent, as a thud echoed down the corridor. Thud of flesh, of metal, of blood.

The soldier reached reflexively for his own sword. He looked at Rao once more. The shock of the noise had made Rao straighten up, his spine iron, his eyes wide. He was holding himself far too steady.

The soldier's eyes narrowed.

"You," he said. "Get up."

Rao swallowed. Searched for the slur his voice needed. "What—"

He had no more time to dissemble. The soldier grabbed him by his arm, wrenching him up so suddenly that if Rao hadn't been naturally light on his feet the movement would have dislocated his shoulder. The soldier dragged him through the corridor and into the salon.

He was flung to the floor. He just about managed to get his hands under him before his nose cracked down on stone. Scrambling up, he was shoved back down by the boot of the same soldier who'd found him.

A dozen sets of eyes turned on him: a handful of the regent's imperial soldiers, dressed in Parijatdvipan white and gold, sabers at their belts; a huddle of terrified women, holding one another; a few men still in their shawls, one slumped to the ground, his throat cut, his blood pooling on the floor.

And the poet, Baldev. He was an older man, heavyset as only the wealthy could afford to be, with a square jaw and nose that was a firm, aquiline blade. That noble face of his was a rictus of fury, and of fear.

"I found this one outside," the soldier who'd dragged Rao in said gruffly.

"One of yours, is he?" This was asked of Baldev, by another soldier.

Baldev looked at Rao.

Rao thought of the way he had eked a space out for himself at these salons, slowly coaxing one of Baldev's followers into extending him an invitation. He thought of the questions he'd asked Baldev, once the poet's mistrust had thawed somewhat and he'd begrudgingly come to believe that Rao was not a man with ill intentions and was merely what he'd claimed to be: a Parijati man with a scholar's bent, high ideals, and a desire to see Ahiranya free.

He thought of what Baldev had revealed to him. The secret half shared after the last salon.

I know someone who may be able to help you.

"I do not know this man," Baldev said, looking Rao up and down with visible scorn.

"Are you sure of that?"

"I do not consort with men who are not of my own people," said Baldev. His voice was sonorous, a rumbling velvet made for poetry and politics. Now, it was weighty with deliberate distaste for the drunk Parijati man sprawled upon the floor—and for the soldiers surrounding him. "This house is full of depraved Parijati lechers like him. By all means, arrest them all. I would be glad to see my land free of them. He is no acolyte of mine."

The women, the men, all studiously avoided looking his way. He returned the favor and stared at the floor.

"Fine," said another soldier. He spoke softly, but the cuff of silver on his upper arm marked him as the commander. His eyes were unblinking. "I have a few simple questions for you, poet. Answer with innocence, and you may go."

"A riddle, is it?" Rao glanced up and saw that Baldev's smile was mirthless. It was only the puckered tightness of that smile that told Rao he was afraid at all.

As he should have been. Beneath the knife edge of adrenaline, beneath the watchful patience that long years of court and weapons training had inculcated into him, Rao was afraid too.

"Did you have any involvement with the attack on the regent's mahal?" the commander asked.

"No," said Baldev.

"The night the conch sounded—you were here?" The commander's voice was mild.

Silence. Perhaps the reality of what lay before Baldev was sinking in.

"Yes," Baldev said finally. "We were here. My acolytes and I."

"Preaching a rebel political ideology," the soldier prompted.

Baldev said nothing.

The commander took a single step forward, hands clasped behind him.

"Do you have many women come to your...lectures?" The commander's gaze slid to the women huddled together, shaking faintly with fear. "Speak. Or I'll gut another man."

"No. Not many women."

"Are you sure, poet?"

"Women of repute don't often enter pleasure houses."

"We hear Ahiranyi women don't worry much for their reputation," said one of the other soldiers. Another next to him laughed. Those two, Rao noticed, did not wear exactly the same uniforms as the rest. They did not have the regent's mark on their turbans, and the man's common-speech Zaban did not have the lilting Ahiranyi accent. "What are these women, then? Whores?"

"Hold your tongue," their commander said evenly.

"Sorry, Commander Jeevan," the man said. He did not sound particularly repentant.

"Speak," the commander said to the poet.

"Maidservants," the poet said stiffly. "Nursemaids. Respectable enough."

"You'll have no trouble remembering one particular woman, then: small, young. No taller than that one over there." He gestured at one of the women, who let out a small exhale—of terror and anger both—without raising her gaze. "Dark skin. You know her?"

"That could be any number of women."

"She called herself Meena."

"No," said Baldev. "I don't know this woman."

"Until recently," the commander continued, "she was a maid at the regent's mahal. She tried to kill his guest. A messy business. Luckily she was stopped." A pause. "We wondered," he said, "where a woman may go to learn such things. A maid. And here you are, poet."

Rao could almost hear the argument forming on Baldev's lips: What use could it be, to a man like him, to attack a guest of the regent?

Then Baldev remembered that the emperor's sister was prisoner in the regent's care. Rao could see him remembering it: the sudden grayness that came over the poet's face.

Nothing he said would save him.

"We found a few scribes writing material they shouldn't have," the commander continued. "Outright heresy, hidden in Ahiranyi script."

"Where are they?" one bold woman asked. Her voice shook.

"They've been taken to the execution grounds already."

"Spare the women, at least," Baldev whispered. In all his evening lectures, his recitations, his voice had never sounded so small.

"The women are the problem," the commander drawled.

"What will you do to them?" the poet asked. His voice shook. Then firmed. "We have heard what Emperor Chandra does to women. Please—"

"A better death than unclean women deserve," one of the two Parijati soldiers said loudly. "You Ahiranyi don't know how lucky you are."

The commander's mouth thinned. Then he turned his attention to his men. Made a gesture.

Round them up.

It was too much. One of the Ahiranyi men who'd been kneeling in the blood of his compatriot gave a yell and threw himself forward. There was a hiss of steel, shouting—a burst of fresh blood, as chaos descended and the women shot for the door.

There seemed, in that moment, no reason *not* to intervene. Whatever the soldiers believed Rao to be, they were going to kill him too. So he turned, shoving one of the soldiers off-balance with an apparently careless scramble of his own hands and knees against the stone. In the tumult of bodies and weapons, it was a miracle that Rao was not crushed or stabbed. When he felt a boot in his ribs he took it as his due. His head met the floor. Stars burst behind his eyes.

Without a weapon, there was nothing to be done but to allow his weight to roll, and to grab another soldier's leg. He groaned. Behind him, around him, the men were yelling. One threw a book. Sheaves of poetry burst against the floor.

One of the women was out the door and down the hall, a soldier running after her. Rao remained where he was on the floor.

He bit out a curse when a knife landed in the ground by his head. He looked up and saw the poet Baldev staring down at him, face bloodied, a bruise blooming over his eye.

Baldev spat in his face.

"Parijati scum," he snarled. It was an ugly expression, entirely at odds with the reasoned, intellectual manner he'd taken in the past. "You're all Parijati scum!"

Baldev punched wildly at the nearest guard—and then he was flung to the floor, pinned, and Rao was left where he was.

The soldier above him—one of the men not wearing the regent's mark who had stared at his commander with barely concealed disdain—looked down at Rao, for the first time with a sense of kinship.

"He shouldn't have done that," the soldier said gruffly. "Once you get under the surface, they're all brutes."

Rao said nothing. His ribs hurt. His face was hot with blood.

If he'd had a sword, he could have taken the man's head.

The soldier offered his hand. Rao took it.

"Sir," said the soldier to his commander.

"Let him go, then," the commander said, in that same bored drawl. "I think we can agree he's only what he seems to be."

Still, the soldier hesitated.

"I—I can pay," Rao stammered out, hating himself a little for the ruse of it. He fumbled. Dragged the Parijati prayer stones, those piths joined by links of silver, from the neck of his tunic. "I—I can—"

Finally, that seemed to be enough.

"Go," said the soldier. "Run, you drunken bastard. You'll know better than to interfere with imperial business next time, won't you?"

"Yes, sir," said Rao.

A better man would have fought valiantly for those weeping women, those men. The poet. A better man would not have been in this room—in this brothel at all.

But Rao was not a better man. He was only a man with a purpose, and his work was not yet done.

He stumbled to the door.

The poet was not looking at him. The poet had saved his life.

Rao left him to his death.

He woke to the sight of Lata leaning over him, her forehead creased into a fan of lines. Above her the ceiling was covered in carvings of roses and iris blossoms. He was back in the palace of illusions, then. Distantly, he could hear faint strains of music. But the rooms he'd rented in *this* fine pleasure house, an establishment with pink lanterns at the door, were as large as a king's, and well-insulated from the noise below.

"Stay still," Lata said. "I'm cleaning your wounds. Your ribs are bruised."

"At least tell me you didn't take off my dhoti," Rao said thinly.

He meant it as a joke, but Lata said, "No. I let Prem do it. Stop trying to raise your head."

Rao ignored her and looked up. Prem, low prince of Saketa, stood at the end of the divan. He smiled, his eyes crinkling.

"Hello, Rao," Prem said. "You're a mess."

Rao huffed out a weak laugh and lowered himself back down.

"I don't suppose you had any luck convincing the regent to help us, then," said Rao.

"You're lucky I didn't," said Prem. "If I hadn't returned early, you'd be dead on the street."

"I told your men where I'd gone for a reason."

"You should have taken them with you."

"That would have made me a little too conspicuous, I think."

"You're right," said Prem. "You shouldn't have gone out at all."

"It was important," Rao said. *And not the first time*, he added silently. If Prem's men hadn't told him what Rao had been up to, then Rao wasn't going to.

Prem reached leisurely for his pipe, which had been hidden under the folds of his voluminous shawl: a wool thing of deep, deep blue that draped over his fingers and was tightly knotted around his throat.

"We're staying in a perfectly good brothel, and you go to a cheap shack instead. Sometimes I don't understand you, Rao."

"I went for the poet. A man named Baldev."

"What did he have that you needed?"

"Information about Ahiranya's rebels," Rao admitted.

"I don't see why rebels would want to help our cause," Prem said. But he was listening, his eyes a faint glitter in the lantern light.

"They wouldn't. I didn't tell him our cause. I told him a lie. I told him I wanted knowledge." He took a slow, shallow breath, feeling the ache of his own ribs, his own lungs. "And I gained it."

Prem puffed his pipe.

"The poet," Rao said after a moment, "the last time I went to his salon, he admitted to me that he and his sympathizers have the support and protection of a powerful figure in Ahiranya. He told me…"

I cannot give you a name. Some things are too precious. And some things, I am not privy to.

Are you not?

A faint smile.

I am not an important man.

The poet had hesitated. Had met Rao's eyes as the two of them sat in the back room of the brothel, dawn light creeping in through the window. And Rao had stared back, earnest, wide-eyed, a rich and foolish man with a good heart. Those were always the best lies, the ones set over real bones.

Come back and we'll talk, boy.

"There are sympathizers to Ahiranyi secession from the empire at every echelon of the country's government," Rao said eventually. "I didn't have a chance to obtain a name. The soldiers came before I'd finished with him."

"Oh, the soldiers. That, I know."

"The poet saved me," murmured Rao, thinking of Baldev's fury. The knife that hadn't even grazed him, for all the anger with which it had been slammed into the floor. "He didn't have to."

"Ah." Prem took another puff of his pipe. Released a breath of smoke. "And why did he do that?"

Rao rose to a seated position with difficulty. "I earned his trust."

"How?"

"I told him I'd read the teachings of Sunata." There was a pause, a silence that stretched until Rao said ruefully, "You don't know who Sunata is."

"Not all of us like books as much as you."

"Sunata was a sage." Sages were wise men and women with no affiliation to any faith or creed. "Sunata's teachings underpin— never mind." Rao shook his head. Winced. He'd forgotten for a moment that his body was a pummeled bag of bruises. "He wrote that there is no meaning in the universe: no fate, no high blood, no rights of kings over land. Everything is emptiness. The world only has meaning when we give it meaning."

"He sounds astute," murmured Lata, still applying a paste of spices with unnecessary firmness to Rao's bruised ribs.

"I don't understand," said Prem. "Make it simpler, Rao, there's a friend."

"People who follow his teachings reject all kings, all royalty, all empires. They believe in . . . self-determinism. I suppose that's the closest explanation."

"Ah," said Prem again. "I expect his teachings aren't popular with kings, then? The high prince wouldn't much approve of that."

"His books were burned in Parijat," said Rao. "And in Alor. In Saketa—"

"So, everywhere," said Prem.

"Not among sages," said Lata. But of course, Lata was a sage herself, and they would never burn books. It was anathema to their calling.

"Have you read him, then?"

"No," said Lata. "I don't care for that brand of philosophy, particularly."

"I'd hoped that we could use what the rebels have," said Rao. "I hoped . . . well. It doesn't matter now."

"The rebels are masked brutes," Prem said. "They want to tear down Parijatdvipan rule, Rao. They want the good old days of the Age of Flowers back." His lip curled, a little. No scion of a city-state of Parijatdvipa thought of the Age of Flowers, the era before the mothers defeated the yaksa, with anything resembling nostalgia. "Even if the rebels have the support of highborn Ahiranyi in kicking the rest of us out—what did you want to achieve? We're hardly here to help the Ahiranyi get their freedom from imperial rule."

"A way to get *her* out."

Prem exhaled again. "Always that."

"Of course," said Rao. "Of course."

Prem did not call Rao a fool. Not over this. Perhaps he pitied Rao too much to do it. Instead he said, "I'm sorry. I know how much she means to you."

As always, embarrassment curdled in Rao's stomach at the thought that Prem—that anyone—misunderstood the situation.

"But you've done all you can," Prem was saying. "And so have I. The regent won't see me again." Another curl of smoke. "A shame, really. Emperor Chandra will replace that one soon enough. And Lord Santosh is a damn idiot. He'll just be Chandra's puppet— setting a new bunch of poor girls on fire and harping on about the purity of Parijati culture, as if the rest of us are as low as the Ahiranyi and need to be led."

But there were other people in Ahiranya who could prove useful, Rao thought. Nobility who were not as likely to lose their positions as the regent. Ahiranyi highborn, who were perhaps funding rebels—rebels who could be utilized to support a coup against Chandra and see Princess Malini freed.

"You shouldn't smoke in here," Lata said, the familiar disapproval of her voice almost a balm. "Go outside, Prem."

"Is he such an invalid?"

"No," said Lata. "But I don't like the scent of it. Go."

"As the sage orders," Prem said, inclining his head with a smile. He turned to go, wreathed in smoke. He lowered the pipe. Looked back.

"Rao," he said. "You know Aditya needs us. You know Parijat-dvipa needs us to make sure the right brother sits on the throne. Emperor Aditya. Imagine that."

Rao said nothing. He had imagined it. But it was Aditya's fault that that vision hadn't yet come to pass.

"Just . . ." Prem exhaled. "I'm going to him. As soon as the festival falls. You should come with me. He'll need you. You've done all you can to save her. And so have I."

"Have we?" Rao said.

"Yes," Prem said. He smiled again, something sad in the uptick of his mouth. "We have."

Rao wanted to argue, and he knew Prem was ready to respond in kind, but Lata interjected.

"Prince Prem," she said. "Let my patient rest."

Silence. Then, "I'll be back later, Rao."

Rao lay back and closed his eyes as Lata moved around the room, murmuring to herself about clean linens and boiled water.

He thought of Malini, up in that prison. So close, but too far for any of them to reach her.

He thought of the letter she'd written to him. A hasty, tear-stained scrawl, not in court Dvipan, not even in the shared common Parijatdvipan tongue of Zaban, but in the modern, city Aloran his sister had taught her. The letter had been delivered by a handmaiden with haunted eyes. She'd been bribed with Malini's last scrap of gold. Her mother's wedding bangles.

The letter had ash upon it. Salt and ash.

Chandra is sending me to Ahiranya.

And there, underlined, a quiet desperation in the curve of every letter:

Save me.

Lata kneeled down beside him. He opened his eyes. She looked pinched and tired.

"Will you leave, then?" Lata asked quietly.

"What do you think?"

She said nothing for a moment.

"I think we need to bandage your ribs," she said finally. "Hold still. This will hurt."

"Don't worry," Rao said, swallowing. The roses stared back down at him, so red upon the ceiling that they resembled spatters of blood. "I'm very good at following orders."

11

PRIYA

There were prison cells beneath the mahal. Priya had never had reason to consider that reality before. But she had good reason to now.

The guards had been gentle enough with her. They'd allowed her to make her own way down the Hirana's surface—by necessity, more than anything else, she suspected—then bound her hands and guided her beyond the general's orchards, the near-overflowing stepwell, and into a separate iron-gated staircase that led down into the bowels of the mahal. They had locked her into a cell, bid her to sit and rest until she was called upon, and then left her.

There was only one window in her cell: a high slat, covered in a filigree of bars, that seemed to let in barely any light but allowed the rainwater in freely. It had stopped raining finally, *finally*, but the water still poured through the slat in a slow, steady stream, as everything the soil couldn't swallow up rolled down the sloping earth and into Priya's chamber.

She wondered if the design of it—the slope, the window, the water pooling unavoidably at her feet—was intentional. After an hour of standing in the murky chill, too numb with shock to do anything more, she decided grimly that it probably was. She edged her way to the farthest corner of the space. Sat, curling forward, her head upon her knees.

The minute she sat on the ground, her body began to shudder. She couldn't control it. She clutched her own palms to her elbows, struggling to control her breath, and felt a wild kind of panic tighten her chest.

She'd wanted to remember, hadn't she? Oh, she could admit that to herself now. She'd wanted more than fragments of memory. Well, she'd achieved her wish. More than achieved it. For a moment, as she'd fought Meena, she'd been the Priya who was a temple child. She had seen the sangam in her mind.

And she'd killed a woman.

Meena had been trying to kill her, of course. But that didn't make her feel any less shaken now.

As a child, she'd learned how to inflict and handle pain. All temple children of the Hirana had been taught to be strong in the same way, so that they would stand a chance of surviving the process of becoming an elder. Three journeys, through magical deathless waters. Three journeys that could leave them dead by drowning. Or other, worse ways.

Priya had sunk beneath the waters once. Only once. And she'd come out with gifts. The ability to manipulate the Hirana. The skill of slipping into the sangam.

She hadn't done that since she was a girl. She hadn't been able to.

She looked down at her hands. She'd wanted coin. Wanted power. Maybe, in her secret heart of hearts, she'd even wanted her rightful gifts. But now she stared at her trembling fingers and wondered if her wants were wise. Wondered if her memories had splintered to save her from a greater pain.

Eventually, despite the cold and the water, she dozed. The heat began to filter in, as the sun rose, and she slept uneasily, dreaming that the water beneath her feet was hissing and writhing, that eyes watched her from the dark.

When she woke she saw that someone had brought food. She ate it, then curled up once more. Slept, and dreamt of the water again. Her brother's shadow in the liquid dark.

Hours passed.

The door clanged open. She thought more food was being brought for her. Instead, she felt a hand upon her arm.

"Come," said the guard. He was armed to the teeth, but his voice was gentle enough, and his grip, too. "Lady Bhumika wants you."

Within Lady Bhumika's chambers in the rose palace, there were profusions of flowers set in ornate vases upon the windows. Cut lilies floated like pale clouds on pools of water, shifting as if a breeze nudged them about with light hands.

Lady Bhumika herself sat on a divan of amethyst silk. She did not recline, despite the profusion of pillows behind her. She sat tall, one hand resting on the swell of her belly. A maidservant stood at her side, fanning her. When Priya entered the room and bowed low, Lady Bhumika did not smile. Her eyes were rimmed with shadow.

"All is well, child," she said, in a soft voice. "My husband has asked me to make arrangements for you. You need not be afraid."

"My lady," Priya said, and bowed her head once more demurely.

Bhumika had a reputation as a kind mistress. Ever since her marriage she had taken the rot-riven and orphaned into her household. All her guards, her servants, were her chosen, and fiercely loyal for it. So when she said, "Leave us alone, now," it was no surprise that her maidservant lowered the fan and her guards bowed their heads in acknowledgment, all departing in swift silence.

The doors closed with an audible thud. Priya raised her head.

After a moment, Bhumika spoke.

"Tell me what happened." The softness of her voice fell away, leaving only iron behind, and they were no longer maidservant and mistress.

They were temple daughter and temple daughter. Sisters, although Priya did not often allow herself to think in those terms. She didn't like to look too closely at what sisterhood meant, a decade since their siblings had burned.

"Meena attacked me on the Hirana," Priya said. "She knew what I was. She wanted me to show her the way to the deathless waters. And when I told her I couldn't, she tried to hurt me." Images of the fight flickered through her mind. They were too fresh to even feel like memories, yet. Her heart still raced. Her skin still itched with magic. "She had a crown mask."

Bhumika's right eye gave a rather expressive twitch. "Then? What happened?"

"She put on the mask. She hurt Gauri and tried to hurt Sima. And I—I threw her from the Hirana."

"Did you say anything to reveal yourself?"

Priya said nothing.

"Priya."

"Only to her." She did not mention the princess. She did not know what the princess had heard, after all. Still, her words felt like a lie, one that curdled to bitter terror on her tongue.

"How could you have been such an idiot? Have I taught you nothing?"

"She was going to kill me. What was I meant to do? Hug her?"

Bhumika rolled her eyes. "Spirits, Priya. You could have said nothing. You could have cried out for help. I know there are plenty of guards up there."

"And let *them* speak to her? She already knew what I—was. Am." Priya raised her head. "Killing her was the only thing I could do to protect us. It would be worse if I'd admitted what I was and still let her live, wouldn't it?"

"Obviously, yes," Bhumika said tersely. "And how did she know what you are anyway?"

Priya shrugged. Ah, she knew that would only inflame Bhumika's usually well-hidden temper further, but she was feeling rather ill-tempered herself. She'd been attacked. She had *killed* someone, and no matter how many times she told herself that it was something she'd been reared for, and tried to convince herself that she'd had no other choice, it had shaken her. And it angered her that she felt anything at all—that she wasn't *strong* enough to feel nothing.

It was easier to be furious at Bhumika than to be angry at herself.

"Have you told anyone else about your past?" Bhumika asked.

"I'm not a fool."

There was a long silence. Bhumika stared at her unblinking. Finally, mulishly, Priya added, "No."

Bhumika's eyes narrowed. She drummed the fingers of her left hand upon her knee. "First you saved Sima, and now—"

"You'd rather I'd let Sima die?"

"To protect yourself? Yes," snapped Bhumika. "Have you considered that saving Sima might be exactly what revealed you to the rebel?"

Bhumika was right, of course. That was how Meena had figured her out. She'd seen Priya confidently climb the Hirana, as the temple children once had.

"I can't do as much as you can, twice-born," said Priya.

"Don't call me that."

"Fine. Anyway, you know, Bhumika—I can't even do as much as a once-born like me should be able to. Walking on the Hirana, saving Sima—it was a risk, but it wasn't more than any brave woman could do or would do. Even if I weren't what I am," Priya went on, "I would have risked myself for Sima."

A once-born should have been able to enter the sangam at will. Should have been able to manipulate the surface of the Hirana with ease. Should have felt nature, all its glowing, breathing power, wherever she went.

She'd had all that, as a little girl. Before the night of the fire had broken something in her.

The twice-born like Bhumika had been stronger still. And the thrice-born . . .

Well. There were none of them left, now.

"I think," Priya said slowly, "that you're just determined to be angry with me. I have done nothing wrong. I didn't ask to be attacked by a rebel searching for the deathless waters. And I have done everything I can to protect myself. And you."

"You could have died. Do you understand that?"

"I do."

"You could have been accused of being an assassin. Or a rebel. Or both."

"I'm truly not a fool," Priya snapped. "I don't know how often I have to tell you. I know."

Sometimes she hated Bhumika. She could not help it. There was something about her temple sister that made her blood burn and poison rise to her tongue. Bhumika was all falsehood: meek to the world, fire in her heart. Bhumika liked fine sweets and fine saris and fine music. She had never, ever scrubbed a floor. And Bhumika had married the regent. That, Priya would never be able to comprehend, for all that Bhumika had saved countless lives in her role as his gentlehearted wife.

When Priya's brother had abandoned her on Gautam's doorstep, it had been Bhumika who had saved her. Bhumika, who had arrived in her mahogany palanquin and taken Priya into her household and ensured that Priya had food and shelter and the opportunity to live anew.

I can't give you power. I can't give you what we lost. I can't even give you a family, Bhumika had told her. *But I can give you a job. And that will have to be enough for you.*

"Thank you for getting me out of the prisons," Priya forced herself to say, tempering her tone. "I appreciate it."

"Well, you don't have me to thank," said Bhumika. "It was the princess who interceded on your behalf. She told Vikram that you saved her life. She begged to have you as her own maidservant. *Begged.* And what could he do, but agree?"

"*What?*" Priya croaked out.

"There's lemon water on the table by the window," Bhumika said, gesturing vaguely to the left of the room. "Pour yourself a glass, and pour me one too."

Priya did. Her hands did not even shake. But Bhumika's voice was kinder when Priya handed her the glass. Spirits knew what Priya's expression must have held, to blunt the edge of her ire.

"The general is in a difficult position," said Bhumika. "The princess is . . . not her brother's favorite individual. But she is still imperial blood, and if she dies here—by assassin or by sickness or some ill chance—then the general and his household will be punished. All of us will be punished." Bhumika's hand moved a little, where it rested on her stomach. "The princess must be kept in solitude. The emperor ordered it, and he must be obeyed. But her isolation means that Vikram cannot see her regularly either. She cannot be watched, or protected, as well as any of us would like." A pause. "The general is inclined to give her what little he is able to."

"You're telling me," Priya said slowly, "that you can't save me from this task."

"I've never been able to make you do anything, Priya. You could walk away, if you like. I think you of all people would find a way to survive, somehow. But if you stay, and become the princess's maidservant, you could do us all a great deal of good," said Bhumika. "The general was concerned when he beheld the princess. She is sick, and weak, and she cried a great deal. He doesn't believe she is entirely well, or that the servant sent with her by the emperor is entirely—attentive. From what I saw of her when she arrived, I am inclined to agree. I can't place any loyal guards on her doors. Lord Santosh has too many spies in the household for me to rearrange things quietly." Her mouth twisted. "There's only you, Priya."

"You want me to watch her," Priya said. "Spy on her. Keep her safe."

"It would be helpful if you could keep her alive without exposing either of us, yes."

Priya's stomach felt leaden. "I'll do my best," she managed.

"Drink your water. You look terrible."

"I've been sitting in a cell all day. Of course I look terrible."

Drink.

Priya drank. Bhumika watched her as she did so, her own glass untouched, her gaze too knowing by far.

"I know you want to find the deathless waters," Bhumika said finally. "No—don't lie to me, Pri," she went on, when Priya gave her an incredulous look. "Lie to yourself if you like, but I *know* you. And I know you think if you find the waters, you'll find yourself. But, Priya, you remember as well as I do the price the waters can demand. I do not want to see you die for this. And if you choose to help me instead, if you watch the princess and her jailer, if you give me information—you may save many more lives than you can imagine."

"Save your husband, you mean," Priya said. She regretted the words even as she spoke them; but it was too late, there was no undoing them. And it was not exactly untrue, was it? It was General Vikram who had the most to lose from the emperor's ire. People like Priya had already lost everything.

"I see. And what do you think will happen to this household if he dies, exactly? No, don't answer me," Bhumika said, when Priya's mouth parted. "Judge me all you like, Pri, I don't care what you think of me, or anyone else. Call me a whore and a traitor if you wish, I simply don't care. All I want is to ensure an outcome where as many of us as possible survive. So, will you watch over the princess or not?"

"If the regent has ordered it . . ."

"Don't think of the regent. *I'm* asking you. Will you do it?"

Priya looked into Bhumika's eyes. "You would trust me?" Priya asked.

"It seems so," said Bhumika mildly.

But still, Bhumika looked at Priya with wary, guarded eyes, the way she always looked at Priya—as if Priya were about to run off a cliff, or push someone off one; as if Priya were unpredictable.

Priya thought of the princess's dark eyes, bloodshot with weeping. She thought of the princess watching her after Meena fell to her death. Thought of the lack of terror in that blank face. The smooth, steady gaze.

"I'll do it," she said.

Bhumika exhaled. "Good." She drank her own water in one

swift gulp. Lowered the glass. "Go and bathe. Rest. I'll make the arrangements."

Priya turned. Hesitated. "Bhumika..."

"What?"

"Meena. The assassin." Voice halting. "She told me she'd drunk the deathless waters from a vial. And that the power was killing her. She told me a temple child gave her the waters. I know now, we're not alone after all. We're not the last."

Silence.

"Bhumika," Priya prompted.

"Leave me alone," Bhumika said tiredly. "I've got enough to worry about already."

"You can't mean that."

Bhumika shook her head. "Can't I? If there's a temple child out there cruel enough to peddle deathless water—*bottled*, what folly—and send children to die on their behalf, then we do not need to find them. They're dangerous. And we have enough danger to contend with, Priya."

"I suppose we do," Priya said.

"You suppose correctly. Now go and clean yourself up. You smell awful."

Priya turned to go. Bhumika's voice stopped her.

"The boy you brought, Priya."

Priya turned back, alarmed. "He's fine? He's doing fine, isn't he?"

"I've heard nothing, so I must assume he is," said Bhumika. "But please don't bring any more strays home. I know I have a benevolent reputation, but I can only get away with so much before I'll have to explain myself to my husband."

Priya said nothing. What was there to say?

"I know how you help rot sufferers in the city," Bhumika went on. "You could have asked me for aid with them, you know."

Bhumika had just pointed out exactly why Priya had not asked. But Priya didn't mention the regent. Instead she said, "I shouldn't have had to ask."

"I can't do everything," Bhumika said. "Unfortunately."

Priya registered just how exhausted Bhumika looked then, and felt a pang at the thought of all the tasks Bhumika was struggling with. But before she could say a word, Bhumika was speaking once more.

"I'll arrange a supply of sacred wood for those that I can. In the city—and within the mahal."

"And for Rukh? He'll need more than the rest. More often."

A pause. "He's dying, Priya. It would be a waste to give him additional help."

Priya swallowed. "I brought him here," she said. "And now I won't be here to help him."

"Your soft heart," Bhumika said. And Priya did not know if it was an insult or not. She only knew that Bhumika turned her head away, to the roses upon the windows that were rustling in the breeze, and said, "Just go. I'll do what I can. That's all I promise you."

Priya left Bhumika and walked toward the servants' chambers. Bhumika had not sent a guard to escort her, and Priya was glad of that. She needed time alone.

It was darkening to evening, but Priya did not suppose she would be needed or wanted at the Hirana tonight. In the fading light, she could see that the hem of her sari was stained with water and mud, and blood, too. The realization made her wince. It would be no end of trouble to remove it.

It was easier to think of the stains on her hem than it was to think of anything else.

"Priya," whispered a voice.

She turned.

Rukh stood under the shade thrown by one vast carved column, his hands in fists at his sides. He looked slight and out of place, and even from here, she could see that his wrists were painted in the shadows of underskin leaves.

Rukh, who had warned her not to climb the Hirana. She gazed at him steadily—his guilty, familiar face, his skin flushed with green—and touched a single fingertip to the bead of sacred wood at her wrist.

"What have you done, Rukh?"

"I'm so sorry," he said. "I really am. But I...I didn't talk to you, ask for your help, for work, just because I needed it. Even though I did—I did need it. I was told to talk to you and try to get into the mahal. I was ordered." He swallowed. "And now I need you to come with me. Out of the mahal. Please?"

Told. Ordered. Who had ordered him?

A chill ran through her. She could guess.

Slowly, she shook her head. Before she could speak, Rukh darted forward. He grabbed her hand.

"I told them you wouldn't come," he said earnestly. "That you wouldn't forgive me. That you're not as weak as they think. And maybe...maybe you shouldn't come. But they promised me they won't hurt you, Priya, and I believe them. They asked me to make sure you weren't hurt, so you'll be safe. Or I wouldn't—I couldn't—" There were tears of frustration in his eyes.

"Rukh." Her free hand hovered over his head before she lightly smoothed his hair. "Calm down. Speak slowly. You're not making any sense."

He furled and unfurled his fingers around her wrist. He said nothing for a long moment, and Priya sighed.

"I'm hungry," Priya said. "And tired, and I've been told reliably that I smell awful. I just want to sleep, Rukh. I don't have any desire to play these games."

"If you don't come," he whispered, "I don't know what they'll do to me."

"Who?"

"You know."

"I'd like you to tell me," she said.

He held her wrist, still. His fingers were light enough on her that she could have broken free with no trouble at all. She didn't.

"The rebels," he sniffed, his head hanging before he looked up at her. "The rebels in the forest."

She looked into his eyes for a long moment.

She'd thought she knew exactly what he was. She'd thought he was a little like she'd once been—starving, hurt, alone. She'd pitied him.

The pity hadn't changed. But as she looked at him, she let her assumptions about him fall away. He was more than a *little* like the child she'd once been. He had his own secrets. His own obligations. She knew exactly how that felt.

It worried her. Worry for him.

He's in danger, she thought. *He still needs me.*

"Steal me something from the kitchens," said Priya finally. "And then I'll come with you."

12

PRIYA

The Parijati placed many names for Ahiranya's great forest upon their maps. They segmented it, delineating it with fine lines, affixing labels on all the parts where humans were able to survive, where time did not move strangely and the rot hadn't infiltrated: the burnt fields of the east; the thick tranches of ancient mangrove, where marsh villages on their water-stilts flourished, to the west. Name after name, each painstakingly transliterated between Parijati and all the disparate scripts and tongues of Parijatdvipa. Only the Ahiranyi language was not included.

The Ahiranyi tongue had been erased, of course—reduced to a scattering of phrases and words that the people of Ahiranya sprinkled through common-tongue Zaban. But Priya, who'd once been taught traditional Ahiranyi as a temple daughter, knew that the Ahiranyi had never had names for the forest. Ahiranya *was* the forest. The woodland was as unnamable as each breath of air, as indivisible as water. It was the cities and villages they named, the mountains they charted. The woods, they left alone.

But that did not mean Priya did not recognize the place Rukh had led her to. They had snuck from the mahal out into the surrounding city of Hiranaprastha. They had made their way through a city shuttered and gutter-lanterned, to the place where the trees melded with the houses, and small alcove temples to the yaksa hung above them in branches, affixed high among the leaves by flat boards hammered between the trunks. They had walked along narrow paths delineated by ribbon and flag, carefully carved though the forest by travelers between Hiranaprastha and smaller villages.

But soon they veered away from the ribbon markers, nothing to guide them but their shared lantern and minute etchings on the bark, the symbol language used by hunters and woodcutters. And then Priya looked up, and realized they were in the bower of bones.

The bower of bones was an ancient place—both a grave and an entrance to an old, old trail carved by yaksa hands. There were places in Ahiranya where time moved differently; this path was the strongest of them and the most well-marked. The seeker's path, some called it, because it led to the neighboring nation of Srugna, and Srugna's great monasteries to the nameless god, where priests meditated on the secrets of the cosmos and worshipped their god above all other immortal beings.

But it was a cursed place too. Local villagers and woodcutters in search of sacred wood to harvest claimed to have heard whispers among the graves. They found footsteps in the dew-wet soil, at sunrise, and the bodies of rot-riven animals on the ground. It was as if the creatures had come to the bower to die. Or been left there, some said, by ghostly hands.

When the flesh rotted away, those ghosts returned to finish their work. Above Priya and Rukh hung the bones of the animal dead, strung up on ribbons of red and yellow. They gleamed yellow-white in the light of the lantern. As the wind rustled the leaves, trapped rainwater fell in a cold shimmer, and the bones chimed against one another with the click of chattering teeth.

"Well," Priya said mildly. "What a pleasant spot for a meeting."

"I don't usually meet them here. But..." He shrugged, his expression guarded. "I was told to, this time."

Meena had worn a crown mask. She'd drunk deathless water broken from the source, and fought viciously, so Priya already knew these rebels were the hardest kind—the ones who used murder as their method of resistance.

She'd heard the gossip and stories of the rebels who wore masks. When the merchant had been killed, people had spoken of seeing a masked figure leaving his haveli. She thought of that now—of rebels who struck fast and vicious—as she glanced down at Rukh.

He looked miserable; his arms were wrapped tightly around himself. She felt anger curdle in her, at the thought of them using a starving boy, a dying boy, turning his heart to their ends. It wasn't right.

She raised the lantern higher, the dark night staring back at her between fronds of leaves and bone.

"What usually happens, when you meet the rebels?" she asked.

"I give them information," he said. "Before they sent me to you, I told them whatever I heard in the markets. They used to give me food."

Not much food, she thought.

"No sacred wood?"

Rukh shrugged.

"Okay," Priya said levelly. "What did they want you to do in the mahal?"

He said nothing.

"Come on," she coaxed. "Surely you can tell me now."

"Just to be their eyes and ears," he muttered. "To watch you. And—anything else interesting. Anything they could use. That's all."

She nodded. "Are any other servants doing the same?" she asked, and he immediately frowned.

"A few, I guess," he said after a moment. "I don't know. There might be more of us hidden."

"Us?"

"Rebels," he said.

"You're not a proper rebel," Priya said immediately.

"I *am*," he insisted.

"Meena was a rebel," she said. "She knew how to kill. You don't."

"How do you know?" Rukh asked. There was a mulish set to his chin.

She looked down from his sharp little face to his clenched fists. With his hands as they were, prickling with threat of new green growth, she wondered if he would be able to handle a knife, even if he was given one. Knives required delicacy.

"You don't," she said simply. "Whatever she is to them, you're not that."

"You don't know everything about me," Rukh muttered.

"Clearly not," said Priya.

There was no sign of anyone around them. No villagers, no hunters, no rebels. Priya supposed she and Rukh would just have to wait. She lowered the lantern to the ground. Then she straightened.

He stared at her. She stared at him.

"You're not the only one allowed to believe in things," Rukh said in a low voice. Priya was disturbingly reminded of the tone she'd taken with Bhumika. "I'm allowed to want the world to be better. I'm allowed to want to help make that happen."

Ah, soil and sky, she needed to learn how to talk to her temple sister with more authority and less petulance, when they were alone. If this was how it made Bhumika feel when Priya spoke to her, then it was a wonder they ever managed a civilized conversation.

"I didn't say anything, Rukh," Priya said evenly. She made herself stay calm. The calm was an armor that she wrapped around herself, as she stood on ground laden with the dead, and listened to the wind, and thought of the decisions Rukh must have made to bring himself here, only a boy but beholden to killers. Only a boy, and she had not seen the signs that the rebels had set their claws into him. She had not *known*. Her evenness sounded like steel, because it was. "But I think you should try to believe in things that won't get either of us killed in the future."

"They won't hurt you," said Rukh. "I told you. I promised. They asked me to make sure you wouldn't climb the Hirana. That you'd be safe."

"They asked you to do that?"

He nodded.

"Why?"

"I don't know. I thought you'd know," he said.

She couldn't think of that yet. There would be answers soon enough, probably. So instead she said, "If I had listened to you—if I had remained in the mahal and let the others climb on their own—Meena probably would have tried to kill someone else." She thought of Sima's scream, of Gauri's body crashing against the pillar.

"I didn't know she would hurt anyone," he whispered.

She gave him a look. "You don't protect people," she said, "you don't tell them not to go somewhere, unless they're at risk of getting hurt if they *do* go. So you knew, Rukh. Don't lie to yourself. You know what these rebels do."

He turned his head away.

"They're trying to do something important," he insisted. But his voice was thin.

Priya sighed. She could not help it. "Are people you fear so much truly worth your loyalty?"

"They're worth my loyalty *because* I'm afraid of them," he said. "They are here to fight the empire. I've seen General Vikram. I've seen his soldiers. If they're not stronger than that..." Rukh's words trailed away.

"Being able to frighten children isn't strength, Rukh."

"They don't just frighten *me*," he scoffed. "You saw the streets. They frighten the regent. He wouldn't send all of his men out otherwise. That's what real power is."

If only she had Bhumika's eloquence, or her keen, instinctual understanding of Parijatdvipa's thorny games of power.

"Power doesn't have to be the way the regent and your rebels make it be," Priya said eventually, making do with her own artless words, her own simple knowledge of the way the world worked. "Power can be looking after people. Keeping them safe, instead of putting them into danger."

He gave her a suspicious look. "Are you saying you're powerful?"

She laughed reflexively. "No, Rukh."

What power did she have? What had she really done to change

anything at all in Ahiranya? She'd been thinking of Bhumika, not herself.

The idea of her having any power...

For a moment on the Hirana, she'd had it. She'd learned the limits of that quickly, in the cell and in Bhumika's chambers. And in the moment she'd killed Meena, it had felt like weakness too; a quicksand of rage inside her.

"Don't be stupid," she added, after a moment. "I'm not strong, Rukh."

"You tried to protect me and the other kids," he said. "Tried to make sure we wouldn't die of rot, at least. You gave me a home. That sounds like what you just said."

It was a child's logic, a child's conviction. Still, Priya turned her face away from him. The way he saw her was far, far from the way she saw herself, and she didn't know how to respond.

The wind rasped through the bones once more.

"Did you really kill Meena?" Rukh asked hesitantly, lowering his arms.

"I told you I did."

"Did you... Did you mean to?"

Priya began to speak. Stopped, the words settling upon her tongue. She held her breath, momentarily. Listening.

The silence around them was no longer empty. It was watchful. Priya felt the hairs on the back of her neck rise. She turned.

A man stood on the graves. The bower threw shadows across him. But his face...

He wore a mask. Not a crown mask, wrought of sacred wood, but one made of normal mahogany, carved with a ferocious curl to the mouth and eye sockets wide enough to reveal thick eyebrows and eyes the deep brown of turned soil.

Rukh stepped forward, coming to stand at her side. He moved as if to speak, and the man raised his hand, quelling him to silence.

"Please," said the man courteously. "Tell me. Why did you kill her?" His voice was gentle, his mask mocking.

"Will you harm Rukh, to make me speak?"

"No," he said. "Rukh is one of mine."

"Will you harm me?"

"That," the man said, "depends upon you."

Priya heard Rukh swallow convulsively beside her. She raised her head and squared her shoulders, standing firm and tall. She pressed her teeth together. Remained silent.

The man took a step forward. She watched the movement of his feet—smooth, winding motions. He felt the earth without looking upon it, trusting instinct. He moved with almost utter silence. No wonder the wind and the rattle of the bones had masked his approach.

"You won't answer me?"

That, Priya thought, was self-evident.

"Kneel," said the man. "Lower your head. Kneel. You will obey, and you *will* speak."

She could not see the man's mouth. But she was sure—almost sure—that he was smiling.

A memory rolled over her. Childhood duels. An older boy, still skinny but taller every day, grinning at her. *Kneel,* he'd said. *And obey. Say I'm better than you. You know you're not going to win, Pri. May as well do it now.*

And she'd ground her own teeth together, smaller, more stubborn, ready to prove herself, and she'd said—

"We'll see about that," she murmured.

She took a step forward of her own, and another, moving the way temple children moved—a dance upon the dirt, a thing bred into the muscle and bone. She angled herself away from Rukh, hoping he would have the sense to remain where he was.

Those eyes through the mask. That particular shade of brown. The hope in her...

She was almost, *almost* sure.

She would not kneel. She would not speak until she wanted to speak—until she had the answers she hungered for.

She didn't wait for him to attack. She darted at him instead. He braced himself, and she feinted to the right. He turned swiftly, following her in that same loop of furious motion, but she moved again, sliding beneath his arm.

She faced him and the two of them circled, winding around one another like predator and prey. Priya knew what she was: muscular, but narrow-boned and slight in comparison to his breadth. She would only win by cunning.

When she was in range, she reached for the kitchen knife tucked in the waist of her sari, drew the blade from its makeshift sheath as he turned toward her, and raised it. His gaze sharpened, and she heard his breath quicken.

With lightning speed, he grasped her wrist, tightening his grip to force her fingers open and the knife to drop. But it was too late. She'd already raised it to the side of his head, and slashed through the first threads of the three-twined rope binding the mask to his skull.

With her other hand, she wrenched the mask. There was no stickiness of melting flesh—no painful heat burning her already singed and sore fingertips. She felt nothing but wood grain and skin. She looked at his face.

He flung her back and she fell to the ground. He pinned her— hand to each wrist—and she was reminded of her childhood, and of Meena, and the smell of burning flesh all at once, a dizzying skein of tangled memory. It was as if time had folded, creasing through the middle, as paper does.

"When I was a girl," she gasped out, "you used to test me just like this."

"And you never won," he said.

"I was younger and smaller and weaker, and that hasn't changed," Priya told him. "But my intent wasn't to win. I wanted to know if you were...you."

His grip loosened.

"Priya," he said. "You're stronger than you used to be."

"Ashok," she said.

Brother. Bones above her, and his face beneath them, carved to shadow by the moonlight. Her voice cracked. "I thought you were sick. I thought you'd *died*."

"I *was* sick," he said quietly. "And I thought I would die too." His eyes traced her face, and she thought perhaps he felt as she did—flayed by feeling, overwhelmed by the weight of time. "It's a long tale."

She swallowed. Her throat felt tight, and her wrists ached.

"Will you let me up?"

He released her. The mask lay on the ground between them.

Rukh was watching them, bright and wan all at once. He looked at Priya as if everything suddenly made sense. He looked at her as if he finally saw her for exactly what she was.

She told him to walk away. She told him to wait in the distance, beyond the bower of bones. She couldn't think. Her mind was a narrow point of focus, all of it honed upon her brother—her living, breathing, infuriating brother.

Her brother gave him a nod, and Rukh went. And then her brother told her his tale.

They had both been hungry all the time, when they had lived on the streets of Hiranaprastha. She remembered that. But Ashok had caught an illness—not rot, something far more prosaic—that had made his lungs rattle and made him spit blood. He'd grown weaker, his magic fading with his body's strength. And Priya had still been his responsibility, small and hungry, her magic splintered along with her memories. The power that had condemned their siblings had been beyond both of them.

He'd worried about feeding her. She'd woken him, sweating, shaking, from nightmares he'd had of what would become of her after his death. And then one night, when his hands were drenched with blood and Priya slept curled against his side, he had made his decision.

"I went to Bhumika and asked her to take you in," he said.

"You abandoned me," Priya murmured.

"I let you go."

Was that agreement or correction? She didn't know.

"You did not have to simply leave me," she said. "You could have told me the truth."

"Ah, no. I thought I was finished. I thought I'd leave you at that old bastard Gautam's for Bhumika to save you, and go into the forest, and die a good Ahiranyi death." A faint, bitter smile curled his mouth. "And I couldn't say good-bye to you. I couldn't stand the thought. I was weak."

"But you didn't die."

"No."

"And still, you never came back for me."

She wouldn't weep or clutch at him like a child. He'd have no patience for such emotion. He never had.

"I was found by a woman," he said. "She took me in and nursed me. She told me she knew what I was. 'I remember your face,' she said. 'I was a pilgrim many a time, to the Hirana. I remember all your faces. And I have a gift for you.'

"She gave me vials of deathless water. She fed me the waters. She saved my life, and she gave me a mission. A purpose. With her, I finally learned the use of what we are," he said, light in his eyes. "The elders trained us to be strong. Then the waters gave us gifts the likes of which our elders hadn't seen for generations."

He moved his hand above the ground. Priya watched the grass move, bending as if under a physical touch.

"We are like the temple elders of the Age of Flowers, Priya. Those thrice-born who conquered swathes of the subcontinent. I realized—surely we have strength enough to take Ahiranya back as our own? Surely we *must*? Parijatdvipa refused us the right to our own rulers. The empire calls us depraved even as it takes its pleasure from us, and profits from it. They let the rot kill us and do nothing, because our lives hold no value to them. This emperor…" Ashok's lip curled. "This emperor is a monster. But even before he rose to power, I realized all this. My purpose. My task. And you, Priya—you were just a child."

"Weak," she said. "You thought I was *weak*."

"You were a child," he said again, which wasn't disagreement.

She looked at his face. His strong, hale face.

"You drink from the vials," she whispered. "Even now."

He nodded once, slowly.

"The water keeps me alive. And it makes me strong."

"The waters must be taken from the source," Priya retorted. "Ashok, you *know* that. Remember what happened to pilgrims who tried to drink from the vials? To rise you need source water, rich with magic—not something bottled and made small and—and *faded*. And to feed it to others—" She thought of Meena, her stomach roiling.

"The three journeys through the deathless waters aren't without danger either," he cut in calmly. "Plenty of temple children died in those trials."

That isn't the same, she wanted to say, but didn't.

"I drink to be strong enough to see the people who wanted to burn us—who debase us—removed from our country. And those who choose to drink with me do the same. It's a calculated risk," he told her, more gently, perhaps in response to the look of horror on her face. "We only have to survive long enough to find the deathless waters and pass through them. No more."

"You won't," said Priya. "You can't. The way is too well hidden."

"It takes time," said Ashok. "And access to the Hirana that I do not have. I sent Meena for the task, but..." He trailed off. "I cared deeply for Meena," he said. "I wish you hadn't killed her."

"As do I, brother. I also wish she hadn't tried to kill me," Priya shot back. "That was your handiwork. I had no desire to harm her. But better her than me."

"Yes," he agreed simply. He looked at her—a long, assessing look. "I should never have kept you from my work. You're not like Bhumika, to play at weakness. You have always been made of stronger stuff. Priya...sister. You're not a child anymore. And you're more powerful than you were as a girl. You can help me now, if you're willing. Will you help? Will you find me the way to the deathless waters? You have access to the Hirana. Access and time—and more patience, I think, than Meena possessed."

She had more access than he knew.

"Why not ask Bhumika? Why not try to find the way yourself?"

"There are too many guards for me to get near the Hirana," Ashok said. "And Bhumika would sense my presence. She has no interest in helping me."

His tone was suddenly cold, at the mention of their shared sister. But then his expression smoothed once more.

"I wanted you to be safe. Meena should never have touched you," said Ashok, in a voice intended to weaken her anger, to crack her resolve like the fragile shell around a yolk.

"She should never have touched anyone," Priya retorted. "But that is what your rebels do, isn't it? Kill."

"For a purpose."

"Parijatdvipa kills for a purpose."

"An unjust purpose, and you know that well enough." He sounded eminently reasonable. She could not make him flinch, it seemed. "They want to maintain their empire, and they know that there is a greatness in us that they must suppress. They belittle us. They control us. They let us die of rot."

"The rot," said Priya, "is hardly the general's fault."

"Is it not? Some of us believe the rot is Ahiranya rising up in protest against imperial mastery."

Priya crossed her arms. "That's utter foolishness, brother."

"Is it really?" Ashok said, an otherworldly light in his eyes. "Why else did the deathless waters begin to grant us gifts? Generations of temple children passed through the waters unchanged and then— us." He held his hands before him, palms open. "Suddenly we had the mythic powers of the yaksa in us. Power in our voices, in our skin, in our souls. Suddenly the rot arrives. You think all of it without purpose? You think there was no grander significance to all of this?"

"And what good have those gifts done us?" Priya snapped. "I barely have any power at all."

"But you've regained the strength you once had," he said. "You're almost what you were meant to be." *Imagine what more we could gain together*, his voice implied.

She said nothing to that, a stubborn silence. She knew the Hirana had strengthened her. She'd felt it, when she'd lain on its rock and reached a hand to Sima. She'd felt it when she'd sent Meena toppling to her death. She'd sought that strength out.

And yet.

"I watched the thrice-born burn, just the same as you did," Priya told him finally. "Their gifts couldn't save them. Nor their strength."

"We won't make their mistakes," said Ashok. "We won't trust wrongly."

"I shouldn't trust you," she replied. But she felt elated and furious and very close to tears. She couldn't distrust him. She didn't know how.

His expression softened. He reached out a hand—held it between them both, like a question—then touched his knuckles to her cheek.

"You've grown so much," he said wonderingly.

"Time has that impact, generally."

"Your nose is crooked. Did it use to be?"

She took his hand, lifting it away. He released her.

"You must believe me, Pri. I've worried for you," he said, serious once more. "I've watched out for you, through other people's eyes." He didn't look at Rukh. "Though it would have been easier for me to do if you hadn't been in the regent's household."

"I only ended up there because of you."

"I thought you'd leave Bhumika's service once you were older," he said. "She should not have kept you on as a mere maidservant."

"I'm not a child anymore, Ashok," Priya said steadily. "I may have ended up in the regent's household because of you and Bhumika, but neither of you controls my decisions now. I'm a woman grown. If I had chosen to, I could be a married woman and a mother."

He snorted. "You were never inclined to be a married woman."

"If only I lived in the Age of Flowers after all," she said dryly, not allowing herself to feel any bitterness. "Then I could have married a woman like the ancients used to. But I could still have chosen to make a home with a nice girl, marriage or no marriage," Priya added with a shrug. "I chose to stay at the mahal."

"Why?"

Priya began to speak, but Ashok was already talking once more.

"You stayed, Priya, because you can't forget what we should have been any more than I can. You feel the injustice of what was stolen from you. You may not want to see Ahiranya free the way I do, but you want what's rightfully yours. And mine." He leaned closer. "Please, Pri," he said. "Help me. Help us both."

It was as though she were no longer standing on the mossy ground of the forest, a grown woman with her hands in fists at her sides. Instead, she was a child drenched in soot and blood. Her head was against the crook of his shoulder as he ran, struggling to hold her, as he whispered, *Don't look, Pri, don't look, don't look.*

Just show me the way—

"We need the deathless waters." His voice was a midnight wind. "Will you find the way for us, Priya? Will you help me take back what was stolen?"

She thought of Bhumika, pregnant and wed to a murderer, using everything she had to give a handful of orphans a modicum of life, and Ahiranya a modicum of stability.

She thought of Rukh, who had thrown his lot in with rebels, who had rot-riven hands and no future to speak of.

She thought of the Hirana. A heartbeat beneath her feet.

Maybe wanting more than what she had was selfish. Maybe it was a mistake. But she thought of all she had suffered, and all Ahiranya had suffered, and felt the kernel of anger in her chest bloom open.

"Yes," she said. "Brother. I suppose I will."

MALINI

It was early morning when the maidservant arrived. Malini was lying on her charpoy, curled up on her side, the room tilting and swooping lazily around her, when Pramila unlocked the door and entered.

"You're a very lucky girl," Pramila was saying. "Your new tasks won't be terribly onerous, and when you leave my service, you'll have much finer skills. You'll perhaps even rise in the regent's household. Won't that be nice?"

"Yes, my lady." The voice that replied was low and warm, with the lilting inflection of an Ahiranyi speaker of Zaban. Malini closed her eyes, glad her back was turned, and readied herself.

She'd seen this maidservant twice. Once, when she'd flung the dosed wine across the floor with numb hands, too addled by needle-flower to do anything but crawl and sob and peer at the face through the lattice and wonder, hysterically, if she had dreamt it all up.

The second time, she'd watched the maidservant murder a woman.

She could not remember the maidservant's face. Only her arms, and the rippling shift of muscle in them as she'd fought. Only the way she had straightened, shoulders back, the wind against her black hair. She could only remember the maidservant turning and—looking at her. The shock in those eyes.

She could remember thinking—even as she wondered if the maidservant would kill her, even as her mind bent and twisted and examined the things she'd seen and heard—*I can use this one. I can use her.*

She had fought to have this opportunity, feigning a collapse in the presence of Pramila and the guards that had left a very real bruise on her hip; crying like a hysterical child before the regent. All of it, in order to have this: a maidservant who was not Santosh or Pramila or Chandra's creature, a maidservant who was likely *not* simply a maidservant, standing before her within the walls of this blighted prison.

"Princess," said Pramila. Her voice was clipped, almost blade-hard, at Malini's back. "I have your new maid. Here, as you begged for. Aren't you pleased? Won't you greet us properly?"

Malini took in a steadying breath and rose up onto her elbows. Then sat up straight. Turned, setting her bare feet on the stone floor. The room tipped alarmingly around her, then settled.

"The one who saved my life," Malini said slowly, taking her time over the words so that she could also take her time looking the woman over. "I remember."

The maidservant stood in a spill of light coming through a high window, half her body illuminated, half in shadow. She was in a slightly finer sari than the one she'd been wearing when Malini last saw her. Someone must have dressed her up for this meeting. Swathed in burnt umber, her hair bound back in a neat braid, the maidservant was not beautiful or charming or even particularly ugly. There was something forgettable about her: about the way she stood, with her head slightly forward and her shoulders curved, the plainness of her clothing, her slight height. If Malini had not seen her on the triveni—had not seen her through a lattice in the dark—she would have looked right through her.

"The one you demanded from the general, yes," Pramila said. "*Bow* to her, girl."

The maidservant gave a start, as if she'd forgotten Pramila entirely, then bowed. She touched her fingertips to the floor.

Then she rose, and whether by accident or design, her eyes met Malini's.

In the spill of sunlight, her eyes were warm brown, her lashes more gold than black.

"Come closer," said Malini. "Please."

The maidservant did. She crossed the floor, leaving Lady Pramila behind.

"What is your name?"

"Priya, princess."

"I am Malini. But you must call me your lady, not princess. You are my household now."

Priya had likely never had any reason to know the intricacies of titles in an imperial woman's household, but she said, "Yes, my lady," obediently enough anyway.

"How did you come to work in the regent's household, Priya?"

"I am an orphan, my lady," Priya said. "The regent kindly took me in when I was a young girl."

"How good of him."

"I am grateful for the regent's kindness," Priya said. Her voice was subservient but her eyes—her eyes were still fixed on Malini's, as if mesmerized. Her lips were slightly parted.

"And I am so grateful that you're here, Priya," Malini said, never letting her eyes waver from Priya's own in return. The way the maidservant looked at her—it made her *wonder*. "I have been so afraid. I struggle to eat or sleep. With your protection perhaps I will be more at ease."

"I hope so, my lady," Priya said.

Pramila had told Malini tersely, when Malini had expressed a desire for information, that the other maidservants would still come to do the bulk of the work of feeding the guards and carrying supplies and cleaning once a week at night, when they would not be able to disturb Malini's contemplation, but the new maid would take care of Pramila's and Malini's comforts. Their baths. Their meals. "If we're lucky, she'll know how to dress and braid hair," said Pramila, in a tone that suggested she did not expect a girl who swept floors to know anything of the sort, but she lived in eternal hope.

"I would love it dearly if you could tell me stories, Priya," Malini said earnestly, leaning forward, clasping her fingers before her. "Would you be willing to do that? And guard me when I sleep? I think it would help me a great deal."

Priya nodded mutely.

I would not know what you are if I hadn't seen you, Malini marveled. *If you hadn't moved as you did on the Hirana.*

I do not think you are used to being seen, are you, Priya?

It made something warm settle in her stomach, that thought. That she had recognized the value of this woman when others hadn't. That somehow, however unwitting, when she had found that Pramila had failed to lock her room and stumbled out into the corridor and seen the maidservant on the triveni, she had witnessed a woman full of raw potential. Someone powerful who looked at her and looked at her, as if Malini—sick, unkempt, her curls in a snarl and her mind liquid—had the sun inside her.

Someone she could use to set herself free.

She hoped. Oh, mothers. She hoped.

"The maid will have plenty of other duties to attend to," Pramila said from the door. "She won't be able to sit at your heels all day, princess. Remember that."

"The general gave her to me," said Malini. "To ensure my health, and my ease."

Pramila snorted. "And what tales can she tell you, princess? She's likely not even literate. Are you, girl?"

"I am an Ahiranyi maid," Priya said, which was not exactly agreement. "And no more."

Malini smiled at her, the barest lift of the corners of her lips, and saw the maidservant's eyes widen a little.

Surely, they both knew that was a lie.

"My nursemaid told me Ahiranyi folktales," Malini said. "And my brothers and I thought they were fascinating. You know those, don't you, Priya?"

"I do, my lady. There is a—a child I tell such tales to sometimes, in the mahal." She added, "I would be happy to share them with you."

Malini had seen this one kill a woman without hesitation and with seemingly no remorse—seen her move with shocking agility and brute strength. But there it was, clear in her words. A soft heart.

"Thank you," Malini said, and smiled. "I would like that very much, Priya."

14

PRIYA

Priya had been upon the Hirana not even a week, and she felt as if she would go mad.

Without anyone to help her launder the clothes and sweep the floors, lug the water and build fires—not to mention feed the entire household, including the door guards—she was overwhelmed. Although Pramila clearly thought a weekly visit from the other maidservants was enough, it was most assuredly not. And Priya was beginning to feel like a prisoner herself.

Pramila was always watching, always sour-faced and oozing resentment. At night, she ensured that the guards locked the northern chamber with Priya and Malini inside. At dawn, it was unlocked once more, so Priya could attend to her duties all over again.

Malini merely... slept. And woke, sometimes, to watch Priya with her unnerving dark eyes, before requesting small favors: a glass of water, a little attar to freshen her pillows, a wet muslin for her head to ease the day's heat.

She did not ask for tales. She did not ask about what Priya had done to Meena that night on the Hirana. The questions she did not ask were like a quiet sword at Priya's throat.

Every evening, before the door was locked, Pramila would visit Malini and lecture her about the mothers of flame. She would recite many passages from a thick book that she held upon her lap. Malini would listen without a word. Then Pramila would give her wine, which Malini obediently drank before falling into a stupor of sleep.

Once, when Priya was keeping herself busy folding Malini's clean saris, Priya heard Pramila talk about the temple elders and children. She found her hands were suddenly frozen; unable to make herself move, she listened.

"...and the children chose to follow the elders and burn. An honorable death even for the impure," Pramila said pointedly.

"The children didn't burn willingly," Malini murmured. She was lying on her back, her hands clasped over her stomach, eyes open and fixed on the ceiling. The ceiling that was blackened by a corona of soot from the night Priya's family had died. "How could children choose to burn?"

Pramila sighed, as if this was a tired argument, one they had worn out between them.

"The lesson," Pramila said, "is that burning is holy. It puts an end to any human failings. It is a gift."

They didn't notice her or think of her, even when the cloth slipped from her trembling hands.

When the weekly visit of the other maidservants finally occurred, she was not allowed to sneak away to meet Sima or Gauri. She paced the northern chamber, not looking at the princess, not listening for her friends walking beyond the walls. And then, begrudgingly, she slept, wrapped in her shawl on a straw mat by the door.

She spent the time thinking of Bhumika, flint-eyed and heavy with child, desperately trying to hold her frayed household together. She thought of Ashok, who was alive—who had asked her to save him, and save them all, by doing exactly what she wanted to do anyway.

She thought of Rukh, the child she'd taken responsibility for and left, who wanted to help make a better world.

She pressed her ear to the straw mat and imagined she could hear them: the waters, strange and deep and powerful, moving somewhere beneath her. Just out of reach.

Patience. She needed patience. Her connection to the Hirana was growing. Now, when she walked across the stone, she felt it warm like sun-drenched earth beneath her feet. The carvings on the walls of the northern chamber had begun to move. Subtly, spirits be thanked—no more than a slight change in the shapes of eyes or mouths, or the position of yaksa hands, venom-tipped fingers turning upward or curled palms opening. The flowers around them had bloomed new petals, curled like licks of flame. Any more, and even Princess Malini or Pramila would likely have noticed, eventually.

Once, as a girl, she'd been told she had a special bond to the Hirana. She could have found the way to the deathless waters with her eyes closed—with nothing but instinct. As her bond to the Hirana grew, that instinct would return . . .

She hoped.

The maidservants had brought grain and firewood and oil. They'd left the Hirana sparkling clean, and hidden beneath a pan, they'd left Priya her own message: thumbprints, hastily imprinted on a scrap of white cloth.

Priya swallowed a lump in her throat. For those who couldn't write, this was the only kind of memento they could leave for a loved one going far from home.

The maidservants had cooked breakfast for the princess: slow-simmered kichadi flecked with cumin, and thick parathas with yoghurt and sugar and raisin-studded malai. But by the time Malini woke in the late morning, sluggish and barely aware of what lay around her, the parathas were stiff, the kichadi cold, the malai congealed. Pramila barely touched her food either. It was as if the both of them were gnawed by something that left no room for hunger. So it was the guards who ate the most, with Priya keeping a choice piece for herself.

The water Priya warmed every dawn was barely ever used by the princess. It was Pramila who used it, perfunctorily bathing, allowing Priya to comb her hair, snapping at her when she caught a tangle or bound it back too tightly. Malini simply slept dirty, tangle-haired. And Priya...watched, and obeyed, and felt her contempt for Pramila grow.

She was not certain if Pramila neglected Malini on purpose, or if she considered the matter of feeding, bathing, and caring for the princess the work of attendants and therefore below her dignity. But she suspected it was the former. The woman demanded her fire be lit and her food be warm but cared nothing for Malini's well-being, beyond ensuring that she listened to sanctimonious tales and drank her evening wine.

She marveled at the uselessness of highborn women, her scorn for the lot of them curdling in her. Priya had been a girl of status once, but temple children were plucked from villages and settlements across Ahiranya and then tested, day in and day out, for their strength and resilience and cunning. If Priya had refused to start a fire as a girl, she would have been boxed around the ears for laziness. In her childhood, idleness was weakness to be unlearned.

Thank the spirits, there would be a holy day soon, and for a time she would be free.

"Of course you're not leaving."

"All servants have a day's ease," Priya said. "My lady," she added, after a beat. It wouldn't do to anger Pramila *too* much. Not when she needed something from her.

"You stay here," Pramila said slowly, as though Priya were stupid. "You serve an imperial scion now, girl. Don't you understand? Your local customs don't apply."

Priya was fairly sure servants in other parts of Parijatdvipa also had days of rest, but what good would it do to say so, when Lady Pramila was looking at her as if she were an idiot, her mind clearly already set?

"I...I have other duties."

"Not anymore. Your duties are here," Pramila said. "Now bring me dinner and a cup of tea. There's a girl."

Priya bowed her head, murmuring an acknowledgment. She

warmed some food, brewed a pan of tea laden with spices and bamboo cane, her hands trembling with banked fury.

She poured the tea. Prepared a plate. Returned to Pramila's side and arranged the meal. Lowering her eyes demurely, she said, "If I may speak to my fellow maids, perhaps..."

"Yes, yes," Pramila said, waving a hand in dismissal. She took a key from her belt. Tossed it to Priya. "Keep it, girl. I have another. Do whatever is needful. But do not allow the princess to wander, you understand?"

"I do, ma'am," said Priya. "Thank you."

There was a small triumph in that at least: She had permission to talk with the others, and also had evidence that Pramila no longer felt the need to watch her. Her false meekness had set her free—left her invisible and given her a way out of Malini's cell.

Priya was beyond suspicion again. She could explore the Hirana once more.

She sought out Sima, grabbing her outside the eastern chamber. Sima whirled when she felt a hand on her arm. Then her eyes widened, and she flung her arms around Priya, drawing her into a bone-crushing hug.

"That's a lot of emotion," Priya said, lightly teasing. "I'd almost think you missed me."

"Of course I've missed you. Do you know how boring it is without you? None of the other girls gossip about anything, they're owl-headed idiots, the lot of them." Sima sniffed. "But look at you. Your sari—"

"I was ordered to wear it."

"Well, it's rather nice. I wouldn't say no to a new sari." As neatly as she had mended the rip in the sleeve from her fall, it was still visible—a faint, puckering scar in the fabric. "Why haven't you spoken to any of us? I looked for you. Gauri asked the jailer about you, but was told you were busy and to stop asking questions."

"I have duties at night that keep me busy," said Priya. "Not that I like it. I've missed you too. You have to tell me everything I've missed. Everything, okay?"

Sima laughed.

"Of course. Where should I start?"

"Tell me about Gauri first," said Priya. "And Billu, if you like. And—"

And Rukh, she almost said. But then she paused. The words withered on her tongue, unspoken.

Of course. Rukh.

"And?" Sima asked.

Priya shook her head.

"Go on," she told her. "Start with them. And you. I want to know what you've been doing without me, too."

Thankfully, Sima began to talk without any further prompting. And Priya listened, and thought of the problem of Rukh. Rukh, and his rot, and his loyalties.

Rukh was loyal to the rebels. Rukh was a spy. Trapped here in the Hirana, with no day of ease, Priya couldn't watch him. Couldn't protect him from himself.

Priya knew it was her duty to tell Bhumika about him. She *knew*. But she wasn't going to.

The certainty of that seeped through her. Settled into her bones.

There was only so much a single servant boy could learn about the workings of the mahal. He was no trained spy. He was no assassin. He was just a child. He was young and idealistic and dying and alone, and she wouldn't—couldn't—be the one to send him back out into the city with nothing. And Bhumika *would* send him away if she knew the truth, of that Priya was sure.

For a boy with rot, with hunger, with no family . . . it would be a death sentence.

"I need a favor," she said to Sima, when Sima eventually went quiet.

"Tell me."

"Rukh," she said, and Sima sighed, as if she'd guessed what was coming. "I—can you make sure he's all right? He's still so new to the mahal, he doesn't really know how anything works.

And can you check that he has enough sacred wood? If Lady Bhumika has provided any...? I know it's a lot to ask."

"I told you I'd help you any way you need, didn't I? I'll try."

"If he behaves oddly, or you're worried, could you—send me a message somehow? Leave me a note when you visit?" Priya cursed inwardly. There was no way for her to say anything close to *If he betrays the household, let me know* with subtlety.

Sima gave her a measuring look, as if Priya's words had struck her oddly. But she nodded anyway. "You know I will," she said.

This time it was Priya who hugged her, so fierce that Sima protested, laughing, that she couldn't breathe. So Priya drew back and said reluctantly, "I should go. The princess will be waking soon. I need to be ready."

"You're safe?" Sima blurted out. "And—well?"

"I'm just fine," Priya said.

"And the princess...?"

"She isn't a difficult mistress."

"But still more mistress than you want, I expect," Sima said, with the faintest, bitterest smile. She reached for Priya again. Clasped her hand, then let it go. "Take care, Priya. And...talk to me again. Assure me that you're well."

Priya shook her head. She felt all the banked fury in her, the itch that wanted nothing more than to fling off the responsibilities of the deathless waters and the ailing princess and return to the comforting weight of her normal life. Part of her wanted desperately to leave with Sima, to escape the trap she'd made for herself.

But the rest of her wanted to see this through.

"And what will you do if I'm not well, in the end?" Priya asked.

"Nothing," Sima said. "I could do nothing. But I'd still want to know. That's what friends want."

Dawn came, and the maidservants left. As the first gray light filtered over her charpoy, the princess arose. She gave a groan and placed her face in her hands. Then she raised her head. Her hands trembled. The whites of her eyes were veined red.

"Priya," she said. "I wish to bathe."

Priya was used to gentle, strange requests from the princess when she was half asleep. But Malini was wide awake now, standing, her voice a firm command.

Surely it would break no laws to do this simple task, but still Priya touched the hard-earned key on her waist chain. Pramila, she hoped, would not yet be awake.

"I'll warm the water, my lady," Priya said, moving around the room to collect a drying cloth, soap, a comb.

"No. I need cold water. Now, please." She held out one arm, sandalwood pale, beckoning Priya closer.

Priya approached her, and Malini laced her arm with Priya's, leaning her frail weight against Priya's smaller frame. Priya should not have been able to support her as easily as she did, but then, Priya was all muscle and sinew where Malini was all fragile bones and barely a scrap of flesh on her.

Priya looked at the hand on her arm. The seawater color of Malini's veins through her soft skin.

Priya thought, absurdly, of the bower. The clink of white bones in wind.

They walked slowly together from the northern chamber across the triveni. Priya expected Pramila to appear at any moment, but thankfully there was no sign of her as they left the open air and entered a dark corridor. The maids had snuffed out the lamps along the wall on their departure, preserving the oil and the wicks for future use.

"You must forgive me for being such terrible company," said Malini. "Once, I was wonderful company. But I am not entirely as I used to be."

Malini's eyes suddenly met Priya's, and Priya nearly stumbled. It was like the moment when their gazes had first locked through the lattice—a jolt that hummed through her. Priya did not know if she would ever get used to the strangeness of being seen, really seen, by someone who had power over her.

"I have terrible dreams," Malini said, as if in apology. Her voice, in the semidark, was like the brush of a wing against Priya's ear. "Every time I sleep, I dream them. I dream of the imperial mahal. I dream of my favorite attendants. I dream of..." A hitch in her breath. "Of what my brother did."

A pause. Her breath, quiet as the tread of a tiger's paw.

Priya looked away from her. "This way, my lady," she said, guiding Malini into the bathing chamber.

Without waiting for Priya to undress her, ignoring Priya's vague attempt at a protest, the princess sat down on the low stool set on the floor. She brushed her tangled hair back from her face with an impatient hand as Priya dragged over a full bucket of now lukewarm water the maids had left.

"Cold, I said."

"My lady—"

"Please," said Malini.

Priya went to the kitchens—there was water there, stored for cleaning—and brought a kitchen bucket full to the bathing room. She set it on the ground, took the long-handled ladle, and dipped it into the water.

"Hand me the ladle," Malini said.

Priya didn't argue. Malini took it from her and poured the cold water straight over her own head. There was a splash as the water met the stone floor, a hiss from between Malini's gritted teeth. Her hair was dripping, her sari soaked.

Priya looked away and made a show of seeking out the comb she'd tucked into the waist of her sari, and the soap too. She'd forgotten the drying cloth, and marveled silently at the absurdity of her own life.

"Shall I wash your hair?"

Malini was silent for a long moment, head bowed. Then she dipped the ladle once more in the water and poured it over her head.

"Yes," she said finally, water trailing rivulets down her face. "If you like."

Priya stepped behind her and squatted down, hooking her sari between her knees to stop it from getting wet.

Lightly she took Malini's long hair in her hands. It was thick and dark and utterly, horribly snarled. Priya didn't dare to think how long it had been since someone had brushed it. Malini certainly hadn't done so—oh, these highborn women—and Pramila would hardly have tried. Still, Priya carded her fingers gingerly through its length, trying to ease the lightest of the knots with nothing but her damp hands.

"I'll need to use oil," said Priya carefully, "to get out the worst of your knots. I can't do much more as it is."

"My maids in Parijat used jasmine oil," said Malini. "My mother's favorite, though I never cared for it."

Malini didn't even wince when Priya caught at one snarl with her fingernail; didn't react when Priya murmured an apology and reached for the ladle, pouring more water over Malini's hair before she began to lightly scrub a thin lather of soap into it, washing it clean.

Beneath the weight of her hair, Malini's bare neck was pale, her shoulders through the wet cloth all birdlike bones. There was an old scar on her neck—a faint tracery of silver, curved like a sickle moon.

"May I tell you a secret, Priya?"

If Sima had said that to her, she would have leaned in, conspiratorial; would have laughed or grinned, and said, *You can tell me whatever you like*—light, casual words. But she could not be casual with the princess. She thought of all the questions the princess had asked her, when she'd first arrived. The steady, patient stream of them, measuring Priya.

Priya scrambled for the right words, wishing she had Bhumika's quick mind and silver tongue.

"I am your loyal servant, my lady," she said hurriedly, filling the silence. "You can tell me whatever you wish."

Malini was silent for a time, as Priya untangled her hair, as the water dripped to the floor.

"Do you know," Malini said, "why Pramila tells me tales of the mothers of flame?"

Because your brother wants you to burn, thought Priya. She understood that.

"I don't know, my lady," Priya said. It seemed like the safest answer.

"Because my brother wants me to be pure and honorable like them. Because he thinks the only way a woman can truly serve the empire, the only way a woman can be good, is through the sacrifice of her life." She lowered her head a little, looking down at her hands. "I worship the mothers, Priya. I should want to be one of them. The burning is, after all, the lot of only the bravest and noblest of women. But I was—afraid." Her voice cracked, a little. "I did not want to burn, Priya. And now every morning I wake from dreams of flame and believe I am on fire."

Priya swallowed, hands stilling. Malini's words—they were too much.

Once, the temple children had burned.

She understood a little how Malini felt, in that moment. Priya stood behind her, hands still entangled in her hair, thinking of bodies writhing and screaming and burning, and found that nothing tethered her to her skin but the cold drip of water, the damp coil of a curl of hair around her thumb.

"He sent me here so I would think of all those who burned and sacrificed themselves. Willingly and unwillingly. A good burning and a bad one." Malini swallowed audibly. "But they are all the same. And all I can see when I sleep are my women, and now children, and fire..."

Malini's voice faded. She raised her head.

"I do not usually talk like this," she said. "I'm sorry."

"Please don't apologize, my lady," Priya murmured.

"I would not sleep at all, I think," Malini said slowly, "would not rest, if not for my medicine. And now for you."

"I did not know you took any medicine," Priya said dumbly.

"A dose is placed in my wine, by Pramila," said Malini. "Something made of flowers. Needle-flower, perhaps. I know nothing more."

"Medicine brewed from flowers," Priya said slowly. "I see." A hard dread coiled in her stomach. It could not be. And yet...

The apothecary sold exactly such a thing in the Old Bazaar. Gautam had tiny husk-sized casks of it, a yellow thread of warning wrapped round the stopper of each bottle. A medicine brewed from needle-flower. A little could dampen pain. A little more could give bliss.

A little more than that could kill.

Sometimes it was given to the sick in measured doses over time to ease pain, but prolonged exposure could cause a sickness all of its own—a wasting of the mind and flesh that ended inevitably in death, or something horrifically close to it.

Did Pramila want the princess dead, or did she simply want to weaken her?

It was not a matter of whether Pramila wanted Malini dead, of course. It was a matter of whether the *emperor* did, and what would become of Bhumika's carefully carved-out sanctuary if he achieved his goal, thus ensuring that General Vikram failed to protect Malini as he'd sworn to do.

Priya looked at Malini's back then, without worry or shame, but with a clinical kind of fury, at the sharpness of her bones, the translucence of her skin. Oh, she knew the fragility of a mortal body—its resilience could only be stretched so far. Even if the emperor did not want his sister dead—and what was Priya meant to know of an emperor's intent?—Malini could die so easily. She thought of vulnerable lungs, the stuttering pulse of that mortal heart.

"How often do you take your medicine, my lady?" Priya asked calmly.

"Every evening," said Malini. "And sometimes during the day, if Pramila decides I am unduly—restless. Why?"

She craned her neck, looking back at Priya.

Malini did not look unknowing or even curious. There was a challenge in the arch of her brows.

"That is a great deal of medicine," said Priya. "But—I am not a physician. I am only a maidservant. What do I know? My lady."

"It is not my choice, whether I take the medicine or not," Malini said. "You understand, of course. It is Pramila's choice, and I must obey."

Finally, Malini turned away. Priya fumbled for the ladle. Cleansed Malini's hair, then set it down. Took hold of the soap and kneeled before Malini, perfunctorily scrubbing Malini's arms and her feet, exposed by damp cloth. She did no more than that—she did not think Malini would care for more. It was the cold she hungered for, not the cleansing.

Priya raised her gaze when she lowered Malini's left foot to the ground. She could not tell if Malini had been crying, not through those already red eyes, the water on her face. But Malini's jaw was trembling faintly, her hands curled upon her lap into fists.

"Whenever you want to bathe in cold water, you just need to ask," said Priya. "I'll arrange it."

The trembling eased, a little. Malini's smile was weak but pointed—a lash of white teeth against the gray of her face.

"Thank you," said Malini. "That is—kind of you, Priya."

Priya swallowed. Lowered her head. She ground her own teeth together, forcing herself not to ask the razor-winged question racing about her skull.

What do you want from me?

And even more dangerous.

What do I want from you?

15

BHUMIKA

Even Bhumika's most loyal guards protested when she called for a palanquin to be arranged.

"Your health, my lady," they said. "The child…"

"Is inside me," Bhumika said, "and has no plans to go anywhere yet."

One said tentatively, "If General Vikram hears of this…"

"He won't be pleased," Bhumika admitted, huffing as she donned her strongest, lined boots, with some difficulty. The girth of her belly was ever interfering with her daily business. "But why would he hear of this? Fetch my shawl, please."

One of her girls brought over the shawl and arranged it neatly around Bhumika's shoulders.

"We," one hesitating guard said, "would hate to see more conflict between you and the master."

"Perhaps I should take a war chariot instead of a palanquin," mused Bhumika. She smiled, to show she was joking. Mildly, she added, "We're going now."

Only a handful of Lord Santosh's men had remained in the household to act as spies, and she avoided their notice simply by ensuring that her departure did not cross over with any of their guard shifts in the vicinity of the stables or the mahal gates. With the assistance of her own men and women, she had learned to track their patterns—the watches they took, the duties they demanded be assigned to them, the questions they asked.

She had met Santosh only once, when he'd first arrived at the mahal. It hadn't taken her long to understand what he was: a pompous man, petty and small-minded, and hungry for power. She hadn't thought much of him.

Santosh liked to think he was keeping a close eye on her husband. He had not yet realized that his spies were being watched in return, and he likely wouldn't. He lacked the sense to be wary of maidservants. Like many of his ilk, he looked right through them.

Bhumika's husband had allowed the markets to reopen after the raid on the brothel, albeit reluctantly, out of necessity. People needed to buy food, after all. The streets of Hiranaprastha were still relatively quiet, but people could not put aside all their daily cares because of rebel activity or the general's soldiers patrolling, even if they wanted to.

Through the net of the palanquin's sliding doors, Bhumika watched the bustling food stalls pass, tables laden with pans of hot oil for frying freshwater fish, pakoras and samosas, even Srugani-style rice dumplings with carefully pleated edges.

As a girl, Bhumika had loved the bustle of Hiranaprastha, the constant motion and energy of the city. She had never been able to enjoy it directly—as a noble daughter, she had been sheltered, only able to watch the city through a palanquin screen as she did now—but she had preserved the image of it in her mind like a miniature portrait. Noise. Life. Her own quiet body, hidden and protected, watching it all.

The world beyond the palanquin screen had changed since her girlhood. Although the sound and motion remained, the edges of the portrait had frayed. There were more beggars now. The buildings were poorer, drabber. Color had leached out of Hiranaprastha. And Bhumika was no longer just a quiet body, consuming the city with her eyes alone.

She was carried from the bustling center, out beyond the

quieter markets, the pottery district where she had once bought exquisite blue vessels for her rose cuttings, over a stretch of overgrown fields and barren hills dotted with houses, toward the burnt, flattened field where imperial traitors were put to death. Here, there were only a few homes—a scattering of dwellings for the men and women who guarded the jail and then cleared away the dead. Behind those houses loomed the high walls that encircled the field. Forbidding walls of wood and stone, rimmed with jagged points of glass. In the morning sun, they shimmered like the dome of a crown.

She rapped the side of the palanquin—three raps, an easy way to alert the bearers to slow their pace. A moment later, she saw a figure exit one of the dwellings—an ancient woman with thick white hair piled upon her head in a neat, knotted bun, dressed in a plain gray sari with a brown shawl thrown loosely around her shoulders. The woman bowed her head. Waited.

Bhumika's palanquin bearers lowered her to the ground. Bhumika alighted, ignoring the twinges of her body as she bent and stood, her spine and hips burdened with the uneasy ache of the child in her belly. She thanked the servant who offered her an arm, taking it gratefully so that she could rise to her feet with some modicum of dignity.

"Are you sure this is best?" Her servant was frowning.

"Yes," Bhumika said. "Entirely."

She had not cultivated servants and followers who obeyed without question. But sometimes she tired of all the hesitation, the concern. It had grown so much worse since... well.

She touched her fingertips to her stomach, then tucked them away once more beneath her shawl. The old woman nodded at her in greeting.

"It's begun," said the woman. "We can watch from the east."

She guided Bhumika and her servant to a staircase that led to a tower overlooking the execution grounds. Within the walls was a macabre theater of death. There was a watching crowd—a thick throng of men standing shoulder to shoulder, with the wealthiest watchers seated above them, in high stalls—and soldiers stationed in the opposing watchtowers, ready with arrows.

At the center of the grounds were the elephants. Parijati war elephants were enormous, heavy-tusked, and small-eyed. Bhumika had never liked elephants, and these were blinkered and whip-flayed, their tusks already wet with gore. One unfortunate scribe—recognizable by his tonsured head—was being forced down to a plinth of rock, his head pressed to the surface as the mahout led the elephant close and urged it to raise its leg. And lower it.

The noise of the scribe's screams and the wet splinter of his skull were only partially masked by the yells of the crowd. Bhumika watched and listened and did not wince. In some ways, she was a temple daughter, still.

"He views from above," said the old woman, "with a few of his men. See." She raised a finger, pointing at a figure in one of the high stalls. And yes, there sat Bhumika's husband, calmly observing as the champions of Ahiranyi independence were executed. She could see Vikram's advisors around him, and Santosh at his side, in a position of honor the man did not deserve.

She had learned more of Santosh's nature, from the girl who had served wine on the night Vikram had entertained Santosh and a Saketan prince; from the older woman who swept all the guest rooms, including Santosh's own. They had spoken to Khalida, who had spoken to Bhumika, and confirmed that her low opinion of Santosh was entirely correct. He was not a clever man, but he was a driven and ambitious one. He would require watching.

The mahout led the elephant away. There was a pause. Bhumika fanned her face with a hand and wondered at the delay. The execution groundskeepers ran out in groups, lugging straw and firewood with them, and giant buckets of a viscous liquid that they poured over the wood as it was laid. Bhumika leaned forward to get a closer look, but she could not be sure what it was. Oil? Ghee?

There was another roar, as more rebels were finally brought out. These figures were not hooded, their faces bare to the crowd. From their short stature, their figures, Bhumika knew they were the women. Maidservants.

Someone had dressed them up like brides.

A ripple of noise ran through the crowd, an uneasy shift that moved the press of bodies like a physical tremor through muscle.

Bhumika's whole body revolted in an instant, a wave of revulsion sweeping through her. She pressed her own hand to her mouth to hold back the nausea.

She could not afford to be sick or horrified. Later, perhaps. But not here, and not now. *So Emperor Chandra intends to purify our women*, she thought, with forced detachment. *How generous of him, to murder us thus.*

The women were forced to climb the pyre. Their hands were tied.

One of the men brought forward a torch.

Bhumika did not look away from them. It was important to remind herself of what was at stake: how easily the tensions in Ahiranya could bubble over, how delicate the balance she had struggled to cultivate alongside her husband truly was.

The air smelled of rancid smoke. The crowd was screaming.

She forced herself to think.

Her husband would not return home for some time. His advisors were with him. Lord Iskar's haveli was nearest. They would go there. There would be drinking, and rounds of catur, and in the midst of all the gambling and games of strategy and dice would be the business of politics. She knew the way of it, for men like them.

And Lord Iskar, of course, would be keen to cultivate Lord Santosh's favor, now that it was eminently clear that Ahiranya would be the place where Emperor Chandra tested his particular brand of faith, and where Santosh would, perhaps, soon be regent.

So she waited, hands clasped in front of her as the arena emptied. She waited and breathed with shallow, steady care, mindful of her roiling stomach and the sick, cooked smell of the smoke.

She waited until she heard the creak of the stairs, and the old woman said, "My lady."

Then she turned and watched as the mahout touched his hands together in a gesture of respect. He still smelled of blood and the beast. He raised his eyes.

"Lady Bhumika," he said.

"How are your girls, Rishi?"

"Well, well. I have a son, now."

"My congratulations. And your wife's health?"

"Well. She's well."

"Thank you for indulging in pleasantries with me," Bhumika said. She gave him a smile. She saw some of the tension in his shoulders ease. "And thank you for coming to speak with me."

The mahout inclined his head again. "I owe your family a debt, my lady. I don't forget."

"And I am grateful for your loyalty," she replied sincerely. "Now please. Tell me. They were tortured?"

"Yes."

"The women too?"

He nodded silently.

"What did they say?"

"They admitted they have support from Ahiranyi highborn. Funding for dissemination of their poetry."

"Did they offer any names?"

"No," said the mahout. "No names. They had none to give."

Good.

Patronage of Ahiranyi rebellion—even in the form of art— was a crime, and not one Bhumika could admit involvement in.

"And their connection," she said tentatively, "with the rebels."

"The rebels wore masks," said the mahout. "They knew no more than that."

She shouldn't have felt relief at that. But she did.

"Thank you," she said again.

Her servant stepped forward, holding out a small drawstring purse of coin.

"For your help," said Bhumika, as the mahout took the purse with murmured gratitude. "And when your son is ready for an apprenticeship . . ."

"My lady," he said. He bowed deeply and departed swiftly, the old woman following him down. Now only Bhumika and her servant remained, above an execution ground hazy with smoke, its ground stained dark with blood.

"Shall we return to the mahal, my lady?"

"No," she said. "Take me to my uncle's home."

The Sonali family haveli was built in traditional Ahiranyi style. Modest by grand Parijati standards, it was nothing but exquisite to Bhumika's eyes.

The Parijati loved their airy, expansive mansions, rich in pale marble and sandstone and high columns. Ahiranyi architecture was modest, almost quaint by comparison. The Sonali haveli was largely open to the sky, divided into parts only by delicate wefts of lattice screens, decorated in leaf and flower motifs carved into wood. Only the bedrooms were covered, closed off from the open air by curtains of light purple silk.

She entered the central courtyard, where a water well played melodic, liquid music. One of the maidservants had conducted morning prayers: There was a small platter of flowers floating in the well.

"Lady Bhumika," one maidservant said in greeting. "He's awake."

"Wonderful," she said. "Show me to him."

Her uncle's room faced the courtyard, allowing in the fresh scent of water and the faint warmth of the sunshine. She knew he loved listening to the patter of monsoon rain on the courtyard stone; the deeper echo of it as it met the water of the well. He'd been ill for many years, and such small comforts were precious to him.

She rapped lightly on the doorframe as she entered. She was greeted by the sweet scent of red lilies, arranged in blue lacquer pots around the windows, the walls.

"Uncle," she greeted him, kneeling by his divan. "It's me."

"Ah," he said, voice creaking. "It is you." A smile curled his mouth.

He looked older. Thinner. There were lines of pain around his mouth. A bad day, then. She would try not to demand great conversation from him on this occasion. She'd only visited him a bare handful of weeks ago, but time was creeping over him with steady cruelty.

"I hear your husband has had trouble."

"Where did you hear that, uncle?"

"You're not the only one with loyal eyes and ears." He tsked. "A messy business. He should have shown mercy."

"He did what the emperor wanted," Bhumika murmured, although she agreed with all her heart.

"We should not do what powerful people tell us, simply because they tell us," he rasped. "You know that."

He covered her hand with his own. His fingers trembled. "Are we alone?"

She raised her head. The servant who had led her in was gone.

"Yes," she said.

"Do you remember when they came for you?" he asked.

"I remember," she said. But he was caught up in the memory, and her response was not enough.

"You were so small," he murmured. "And so alone. I did not want them to take you. There are plenty of children who can learn to serve on the council, I told them. But my girl is a Sonali. She stays with her family."

"It wasn't so terrible," she lied. "They treated me well."

He shook his head. But he did not argue.

"You're a good girl, Bhumika," he breathed. "You've made a good marriage. Ensured that our nobility have standing. You are not what the elders would have made you, and I am glad of that. Glad we saved you, your aunt and I."

Priya had survived the massacre of the temple children by chance. She wore the scars of that night, still, in her nature and her memory.

Bhumika had not been there.

Her family had never wanted her to be a temple child. She and her male cousin had been the last of their family line, after her parents had perished of a fever. And then her cousin had died too, of a wasting illness, and Bhumika had been the only one left. Her uncle had brought her home for the funeral. After the burial, the sharing of food and song, he had asked her to remain at home. He and her aunt had argued—about heresy, about what the temple council would do if they didn't return Bhumika, about how they *had* to return her—but her uncle had prevailed.

When the other children had died, Bhumika had been in this house. Drinking tea. Listening to birds beyond the window lattice. Playing the part of a good Ahiranyi highborn girl, instead of the temple-blessed creature she truly was.

She had tried to use her survival for good. When the regent—older and grim, with the blood of her siblings upon his hands—had courted her, she'd smiled at him. Kissed him. She'd wed him. She carried his child. And in return, she'd gained the power to protect those displaced or orphaned by the rot, and the influence and means to fund her fellow Ahiranyi. Small things. But better than nothing.

And still, she sat in the quiet sickroom, with her uncle's hand in her own, and thought only of the gore beneath an elephant's foot, the screams over a pyre. Blood, flesh. Soil.

Fire.

She leaned forward and kissed her uncle's forehead, beneath the weak wisps of white hair that still haloed his head.

"Everything I am, I have achieved because of you," she said. "Now sleep. Please. You need your rest."

She went to the household prayer room.

She had nowhere to pray in her husband's household. He worshipped the mothers of flame, kept his Parijati ways, and she...

She was his wife.

Uncle Govind did not maintain the prayer room, particularly. For form's sake, there were candles lit, and the finely wrought statues of yaksa were dusted clean and polished to an oily glow by the careful hands of servants. But there were no new offerings at their feet—no fruit, no shell of coconut, no flowers—just empty platters.

She sat down on the floor mat. Sat as straight and neat as she could, her legs crossed. Closed her eyes. Breathed. And breathed. Winding deeper, and deeper.

The sangam unfolded around her.

She opened her eyes. Waited. She knew it was only a matter of time until he came to her.

The waters moved around the shadow of her, deep and strange.

She had loved the sangam as a girl, when she'd first entered it. Loved its beauty and its strangeness. Loved its power.

Now she refused to look at it. She simply said his name.

"Ashok. Come."

She moved forward, the water's weight rippling around her. Stars burst and withered above her. And there was Ashok. He too was shadow. When he moved the shadow of him grew dappled, blurring for a moment, then settling, light breaking through a canopy of leaves.

She wondered how she looked to him.

"Bhumika," he said. "It's been a long time."

"I don't care for this place."

"And you don't care for me," he said. "I know. So let's not play your usual games of pleasantries. Tell me. Did you watch them die?"

"I did."

"Was it brutal?"

"Executions are always brutal," said Bhumika. "Anything else would defeat the point."

"I knew they were going to burn the women," he said. "Does that surprise you?"

"I know you have your spies," she said. "Just as I have my own."

"Nothing like you have, but we make do. You have an executioner, don't you?" he said. "But I have a man who sweeps up the temple to the mothers of flame. Apparently not all the priests are supportive of the emperor's interest in purification. They're worried the rebels may burn down their temple in return."

"Should they be worried?"

His shadowy mouth curved into a grin. "Who knows," he replied. Then his smile faded. "You know, of course, that your husband is a fool."

Bhumika did not entirely disagree. But Ashok's words were an attack on her, not Vikram: on her choices, on her sacrifices, on the life of a Parijati highborn wife that she wore, a mask of her own.

"He had to retaliate. The emperor required decisive action." Or so Vikram had told her, his brow a furrow of irritation, when Bhumika had questioned his decision to kill the rebels by crushing. If she had known about the burning...

Ah, too late now.

A statement needs to be made, he'd said. *You can't understand, my dove. You have a soft heart.*

"So he puts poets and maidservants to death? Does your husband know he killed the very people you fund from your family purse?" When Bhumika did not deign to reply, Ashok laughed. "I told you he's a fool."

"You were the one who set a false maidservant in my household," Bhumika said tightly. "You were the one who made him and his ilk consider this necessary. You knew your actions would have consequences."

"I need the waters." His voice lowered. Liquid dark. "Surely you understand that."

Of course she did. She felt the pull of the waters every single day. She felt the yearning in her, the gravity of it tugging at her blood. If the power of it could have unspooled her veins from her body, it would have. She understood why Priya climbed the Hirana. She understood why the sangam haunted her own dreams.

"I need them more than you know," he told her.

"You've been consuming the waters," said Bhumika. It was a knot in her chest, that knowledge. "Broken from the source. I understand exactly how much you need them. A desperation of your own making, I think."

He said nothing. That was answer enough.

"Why?" she asked, hating how it hurt still to think of him one day dying. As if she owed him anything at all.

"I've been consuming the vials for a long time," Ashok said quietly. "And it keeps me strong. Keeps me alive. Now my new family—my soldiers, my fellow warriors—consume it too. They may not be twice-born like me. They know the vials will kill them. But they do it anyway, because like me they know that we must be free."

He stepped closer to her.

"We've taken back forest settlements. We've placed people carefully where we needed them. In merchants' houses. In high-born havelis. We've gained patrons. You're not the only noble funding rebellion, Bhumika." He leaned closer. "We're learning every point of vulnerability, every place to strike so that the bones of the empire crumble around us."

"All those plans will mean nothing when you're dead and the rest of us are left to clean up the blood you've spilled," said Bhumika.

"I won't die," Ashok said. "None of us will die. We'll find the waters. We'll live. Reinstate the temple council. If we bring back even a shadow of the Age of Flowers, it will be worth it."

"Oh, Ashok. This won't end as you hope."

"We have Priya now."

Even in the sangam, even in a place where they were dappled shadow, Bhumika's face must have revealed something of what she felt, because Ashok said, "I sought her out."

"Your damn rebel maid almost killed her."

"I apologized."

"Ah. That's fine, then," Bhumika replied scathingly. "As for having her—if you think you have any control of her, then you don't know her at all."

"I do have her. She told me how much she's missed me. How she loves me still." There was something like true sorrow in his voice. True feeling. "She didn't know I lived."

Bhumika didn't say, *She ran away a dozen times seeking you, and a dozen times my guards brought her back. She wept for you and if she'd known you lived, she would never have rested, she would never have given up on you—*

Instead she said, "She doesn't know the way either. Leave her be."

"But she'll find it. I know she will. Of all of us—she was always the one who could find it. She has a gift."

A gift. Yes.

"Decisive action," Ashok mused, when Bhumika did not reply. It took Bhumika a moment to realize he was repeating her own words regarding Vikram. "I think I need to perform some decisive action of my own. Those poor maidservants and scribes deserve justice. And I don't think you're inclined to provide it." His shadowy hands clenched, with the creak of trees bending to the wind. "And now my followers and I have the strength we need to put the world right."

"Whatever you're planning to do, don't. Ashok. This will only escalate." She had terrible visions of the emperor's soldiers swarming over the country. Trees felled, people burned, blood in the soil. Their history and their present obliterated. What little they'd saved, of resistance and art, of their culture, lost.

"Parijatdvipa is the rot that must be torn from Ahiranya," he said. "The empire only rose because it crushed us. It doesn't deserve to keep us under its boot any longer."

"And what will you replace it with, exactly? Your plucky band of rebels?"

"When we have power, we won't be called rebels anymore."

"Of course. Apologies, Elder Ashok," she said, her tone mocking. "And who will your new council trade with? Who will sell them the rice and cloth we need to survive?"

"We're a rich nation, Bhumika."

"I'm in a much better position to know our wealth than you are. We have forest, yes, trees that could be felled and wood that could be sold, the most profitable short-term route, for all that if Parijat-dvipa were to trade with us at all, their terms would be less than favorable. But our people's culture relies on the forest not being cut down. And our fields and forest are riven with rot. Perhaps you've noticed." When he was silent, she said, "Ashok, we need allies."

"And we'll have them," he said calmly. "When we're free. That matters more than anything. It's worth any price."

"You think I don't want a different world than this?" she asked. "You think I want the ruler of our country to be an outsider, beholden to an emperor's whims? You think I *want* our siblings dead? You don't understand that I'm trying to protect what remains of us—of our Ahiranya. I'm fighting for survival, and you—you're choosing to gamble what little we have on a hope that may obliterate us."

"Don't pretty up your whoring," he said, with a savagery that made her pause and then laugh, furious.

"There it is," she said. "There's the brother I know. The vicious bastard who once beat me blue to impress our elders. To prove himself strongest. You think being called a whore shames me? You think you haven't bartered your body for your own ends? What do you think pouring death down your throat *is*?"

"Don't worry," he said. "I won't hurt you again. You're not as strong as you once were. You wouldn't survive it."

He placed a hand against her chest.

"But your husband," he said. "And those Parijati highborn. Well."

"Ashok."

He shoved her down.

She returned to herself. Shaking, she rose carefully to her feet.

The floor of the courtyard was being swept clean of dust. She crossed it. Made her way to her palanquin.

"Home," she said to her guards. They lifted the palanquin and obeyed.

*   *   *

Her husband had returned. He was in her quarters, in her rose palace, finishing lunch when she arrived.

"You took the palanquin," Vikram said, rinsing his hands clean in rose-scented water.

"I went to visit my uncle," said Bhumika.

"How is his health?"

She shook her head. Walked over to him, brushing a fingertip lightly against the back of his hand in greeting. "I am going to pray for him. Incense for the mothers. And I will burn jasmine."

Vikram made a hum of approval. Or perhaps it was sympathy.

"I have a new maid," said Bhumika lightly, taking the glass of lemon water a servant proffered. "Oh, don't look at me that way, my love. This one is trustworthy. She's from my uncle's own household."

One girl had escaped the soldiers at the brothel. Only one. It was only right that Bhumika protect her.

"You don't have the sense to know who to trust," he said.

There was a hardness to his tone. So Bhumika lowered her eyes, chastised.

"My soft heart makes a fool of me," she said.

"This one should be interviewed by someone trustworthy," he said, as water was brought to him as well, a sheen of condensation upon the metal cup. "I'll have Commander Jeevan speak to her."

Bhumika nodded.

Vikram hesitated.

"Lord Santosh," he began. Then went quiet. "Emperor Chandra is ordering women burned."

She said nothing.

"This is not the way of the mothers of flame," he said. "This Chandra...if the older brother ruled, if he hadn't left his family and faith, it would not be so. But some men dream of times long dead, and times that never existed, and they're willing to tear the present apart entirely to get them.

"I am glad you did not see it," he added, and she wondered for a moment if he was testing her. If he knew. But no. He had never suspected her of anything, her poor, unknowing husband.

"Oh, Vikram," she said quietly. "I am sorry."

He sighed, and said, "You have nothing to apologize for." He drank deeply, then lowered his cup. "Now. Come here. Tell me about your day."

When Vikram was gone, Bhumika retired to her room. Khalida came in not long after, a pot of flowers balanced against her hip. Her expression was tight.

"Lady Pramila won't release her," said Khalida. "The maid Gauri told me. She won't give your girl a day's ease. What do you want to do?"

"Nothing," said Bhumika. Here, through her window, she could see the edges of the Hirana, framed in sunlight.

"I can insist on your behalf that household rules around the treatment of servants are adhered to."

"That doesn't matter," said Bhumika. "I'll find a way to talk to Priya regardless."

She knew the Hirana's power. She knew how it was already changing Priya. She had a hunch, a suspicion, and she would know soon enough if it was correct.

"What are you holding?" Bhumika asked. "A gift, is it?"

"Jasmine from Parijat itself," said Khalida, placing the pot on the window by Bhumika. "General Vikram sent it to you. It's a gift."

"How kind of him," Bhumika said, and saw Khalida's lips quirk at the sweetness of her voice.

It was not a container fit for jasmine flower, and the fragrant blooms would die soon enough.

"Is he here?"

Khalida knew she wasn't speaking of her husband.

"Yes."

"Tell him to enter."

As she waited, Bhumika brushed her fingers over the flowers; felt the deep, river rush of the deathless waters within her. She watched the small blossoms wither and fold in on themselves beneath her touch. There was no reason not to kill them, if they would not survive anyway.

"Lady Bhumika."

A man's voice. A man's shadow on the marble, as he bowed behind her.

She turned.

In her years of marriage, Bhumika had made sure of one thing, at least: Vikram was master of his mahal, but the first loyalty of the majority of maids and children, the soldiers and serving men, those who cooked the food and set the fires, and held arrows and swords against the dark, was to her.

She—the regent's kindly wife, his vapid dove—had saved them. She had given them work and a home. And she demanded nothing in return.

Not yet, anyway. Not until now.

She did not speak of the executions. She did not speak of Ashok. "You may be needed, soon enough," she said. "And I am sorry for it, but I must ask for your loyalty. I must ask for your service. I must ask for what you promised me."

There were resources you should use sparingly. Resources too precious to be wasted. There were resources you must test before the time truly comes when they will be needed.

This was his test. He raised his eyes. On his arm, the cuff of metal marking his status gleamed the faded silver of a scar.

"My lady," he said. "You have it. Always."

16

PRIYA

Now that she knew Malini dreamt of fire, Priya began to dream of water. Clear, cool, rippling. Rivers winding beneath her feet, hissing like snakes.

When Meena had strangled her, she'd had a hallucination a little like this: of water coiling about her ankles. Of her brother limned in red, liquid-shadowed, more water than skin. In the moments after, she'd been able to use gifts that had long been inaccessible to her.

Her time on the Hirana had already changed her, but now it was shifting and molding her dreams. She woke once in the night and saw that the ground had changed beneath her; the imprints of flowers were all over the stone. As she blinked, confused, they faded.

That night she woke again, as she so often did—pitch-dark around her, no sound of other maidservants at work to break the stillness—and realized something was different. She could hear a new noise. Not the rush of water that slithered through her dreams. Not Malini's breath, slowed by her medicine and deepened by sleep.

Weeping.

She stood up. She crossed the dark room to the side of the princess's bed. Malini was curled up on her side, face twisted into a rictus, her shoulders bent to a sharp angle behind her, raised like wings. She was still deep asleep—the drugged wine had seen to that—but a ferocious nightmare had its claws in her.

Priya kneeled down on the charpoy beside her. Lightly shook her shoulder, then a little harder, and harder still when Malini remained curled tight as a thing of shell.

"My lady," she whispered. Then more firmly: "Princess Malini. Wake up. Wake *up*, princess."

Malini gave a jolt. Moved, with the sudden speed of a viper.

The grip that latched onto Priya's wrist was vicious. Malini's nails dug into her skin, all cruel points untempered by hesitation or fear. Her eyes snapped open, but they were unseeing, looking through Priya as if her flesh were glass.

Priya instinctually closed her left hand around Malini's, trapping the vise of Malini's hand in a vise of her own. She knew exactly what to do: how to tighten her grip just so, to make Malini's hand spasm and release her, or twist the princess's wrist until the bone gave way with a snap.

"Please, my lady," she said instead, keeping her own breath steady to hold back the pain. She knew how to do this, too. "It's only me."

For a long moment the cruelty of Malini's grip did not falter. Then, slowly, awareness returned to her eyes. She released Priya abruptly—but Priya was still holding her. Priya uncurled her own fingers calmly, carefully. When Malini remained frozen, Priya lowered her arm for her and said, "You were having a nightmare."

"I think I'm going to be sick," Malini said faintly, and turned to the side, covering her mouth.

Priya leapt up, looking for a basin, but Malini was not sick. She merely remained on her side for a long moment, head lowered, hand over her mouth. Then she raised her head and said, "Sometimes—my medicine..."

"There is no need to explain, my lady."

"I was dreaming again." Priya watched Malini twist the fabric of her sari into knots in her hands. "I am...not myself."

Priya wished then that she could go and speak to a healer, or even to Gautam. They would be able to tell her exactly what dangers to watch for as exposure to needle-flower became full-blown poisoning: the cadence of breath, the significance of sleep paralysis and venomous dreams, the dangers that could be read in the pulse or the near translucence of Malini's flesh.

But she had no one to speak to. She could only watch as Malini deteriorated.

She thought of how she would comfort Sima, or even Rukh, and could not imagine giving Malini the kind of casual, easy intimacy she'd give either of them. She considered placing a hand against Malini's back, but—no. She couldn't.

"Do you wish to bathe, my lady?" Priya asked abruptly.

"It's not remotely near morning," Malini said in a flat voice. "I can't leave this room."

"You can," Priya said. "Leave, that is. If you'd like to. My lady."

She had the key to the room bound to her waist chain. She unhooked it, holding it to the faint light.

Malini looked at it. Looked away, her face in profile.

"I do not want to bathe," said Malini. But she didn't lie back on her bedding once more, or demand water or food. She did nothing but sit hunched over, her hands curled like claws. Staring at nothing.

"A walk, then," Priya offered. "A little exercise would perhaps do you good."

"Do me good—would it really?" Malini's hands curled a little tighter. "I do not think walking will cure what ails me."

There was no bitterness in Malini's voice. Only resignation.

"Walk with me regardless," Priya said, "and I will tell you a tale of the yaksa."

Malini finally raised her eyes. Deep, dark. Considering.

She rose to her feet.

"Pramila will be angry," said Malini, once they had left the room and begun walking down the corridor.

"We can return to your room if you wish, my lady," Priya said. She wasn't surprised when Malini shook her head. Malini was leaning upon Priya's arm, clinging on as if Priya were the spine holding her frail body up. But her expression was clearer—more focused than it had been since the moment they were formally introduced to one another, lady to maidservant.

The wind was blowing across the triveni—one hard, buffeting wind that raced down the three open, empty corridors of the Hirana with the hollow roar of a beast. Priya, dressed in her new sari with no shawl to draw over her shoulders, was beginning to regret her decision to coax Malini from the dark, sick quiet of her jail. She'd have actually preferred the sticky heat of a monsoon-laden night to this strange, unseasonable weather.

"We'll walk around," Priya said. "Once or twice. And then we'll return to your room, if you like." *Before the guard patrol next passes through the triveni, ideally.*

"Did I hurt you?" Malini asked abruptly.

"What?"

"Your arm. Did I hurt it?"

"A little, my lady," Priya admitted.

Malini took hold of Priya's right wrist, raising it to the spill of moonlight. Her mouth thinned.

"I don't bruise easily," Priya told her. But Malini did not let go. She looked at Priya's hand as if she could read it—read every callus and whorl, every line upon Priya's palm—like language.

And Priya watched Malini in turn because—well, she could admit it to *herself*, at least—because she simply wanted to look at her. Looking at Malini felt like a forbidden thrill, but somehow less frightening than meeting her eyes, which was too . . . equalizing. Intimate.

Oh, Priya knew an infatuation when she was in the middle of one.

"You're strong," Malini observed. "I felt the grip of your hand on me. But you didn't even try to stop me."

"I didn't want to hurt you."

"How odd," Malini said. Her voice was soft. Finally, she released Priya's arm.

"I did not mean to harm you either," said Malini. "I do not like acting without intent."

Priya shook her head. "I'll be more careful if I need to wake you in the future," said Priya.

She hooked Malini's arm into her own once more and began guiding her around the edge of the triveni.

"Now," Priya said. "A tale of the yaksa."

She told Malini a simple tale. A story told to children, of a young man, a woodcutter, who was born under ill stars. If he fell in love, his beloved would share his cursed luck. Any man or woman he married would die an early death.

"So he avoided other people," Priya said. "And his family worried about him all the time. And then he told them he'd found someone to marry after all."

"Who?" Malini asked.

"A tree."

"A *tree?*"

"That," Priya said, "is exactly how his family responded. They weren't impressed, I promise you. But he garlanded the tree like it was a bride to him, and he told it tales and gave it offerings of flowers and secrets, and one day the tree transformed into a beautiful man. It had been a yaksa all along. The yaksa built the woodcutter a mahal of banyan and banana leaf, and they lived together happily. Now, when children are born ill-starred, we give them a first marriage to a tree, so the yaksa will watch over them, and their second, mortal marriage will be sweet."

Malini gave Priya an odd, unreadable look.

"Men can fall in love with men, in Ahiranya?"

Oh. Priya swallowed. She'd made a mistake. A simple, innocent Ahiranyi tale was far less so to people who were...not Ahiranyi.

Surely Malini had heard the stories people told about the lasciviousness of the Ahiranyi: their willingness to sell pleasure, the looseness of their women, the fact that they were willing to sleep with their own sex? And surely, like all Parijati, she abhorred it.

"I'm sorry, my lady," Priya said. "A silly maidservant like me, I should have known better." She bowed her head in apology. "Please forgive me."

She felt Malini's hands on her shoulders. Suddenly they were facing one another.

"Please," said Malini. "I'd like to hear your answer."

"I suppose they can do so anywhere, my lady."

Malini shook her head. "It isn't done, in Parijat." The tone of her voice did not suggest she would welcome questions, so Priya asked none.

Instead, Priya said with false lightness, "Well, men can only marry women now. One of the first regents did away with the way things used to be here."

"And there are such tales," Malini said, "about women too?" There was something hesitant in her voice.

"Yes," said Priya. She swallowed again. She knew exactly why her throat felt dry. "What other tales shall I tell you about the yaksa, my lady?"

"Everything," Malini said immediately. "Anything. I was told tales by my nursemaid, but they were clearly sanitized, made palatable for good Parijati children. I want to know a tale no one would ever tell me." She paused, considering, then said, "Can you tell me a tale from the Birch Bark Mantras?"

"Those tales are forbidden, my lady," Priya said, even though she had memorized them by rote as a girl, and still remembered fragments of each poem, ragged ghosts of verse.

"Tell me where the yaksa came from, then," said Malini. "That must be innocent enough."

It probably wasn't. But Priya didn't say so.

As she guided Malini over a dip in the floor, she glanced down. The floor, marked by grooves like waves. Like water.

Those waves had moved, too. They were not where she'd left them, yesterday.

"The yaksa come from the same place everything comes from," Priya said slowly. "From the rivers."

"Rivers?"

"The cosmic rivers from which universes are born," Priya said. "Rivers that flow from the yolk of the World Egg. Rivers of heart's flesh and heart's blood; rivers of immortality; rivers of the soul. The yaksa were born in these rivers as fish, and swam through them until they found the world on the shore. They entered our world from there, but it was the youngest of them, Mani Ara, who came to Ahiranya, and made it her home."

"What is the World Egg?"

"The egg that the world was born from."

"And where," Malini murmured, with a faint tilt of her head, "did the World Egg come from? The World Peafowl?"

Priya made a valiant effort not to roll her eyes. "How do the Parijati believe the world was born, my lady?"

"From fire," she said. "We believe another world burned, and out of it came our own. From ash and flame."

"And where did that other world come from? My lady," Priya added, with barbed deference. "From another burning world, perhaps?"

"It's burning worlds all the way down," Malini said, voice dry, a curl of amusement shaping her mouth. "You've made your point, Priya."

Priya's face felt annoyingly warm. She was glad she was far darker than Malini and didn't show her wounds and hungers as easily on her skin. She looked away.

"My nursemaid told me of one river," Malini said. Her voice was low. "A magical river, hidden beneath Ahiranya's surface. A river called the deathless waters. Perhaps you know of it."

It took everything in Priya not to stiffen. She had been lulled into a false sense of security by the brush of Malini's hand on her arm, by shared tales. The cold knot that twisted to life in her belly was all the more shocking for it.

"You heard me speak of them to Meena," Priya said quietly. "To the rebel. Didn't you?"

Malini did not deny it. Instead she said, "I know it worried my father. The children developing strange gifts in Ahiranya. He spoke of it with my mother. He said something had to be done."

Her father. Emperor Sikander.

"My lady," Priya said quietly, tamping down on the little twist of rage in her heart. "Why did you bring me here? Why did you lie about me, and claim I saved your life?"

There. She'd said it. She'd faced the reality, finally, that she'd made a terrible error when she'd revealed herself before Meena, before Malini, and hidden the truth from Bhumika.

"I don't know why that rebel was here," Malini said finally. "She did, perhaps, want to kill me. But when I saw you, Priya…"

Her voice faltered.

"You're strong," she said finally. "And I will ask you no questions about your strength but…I very much need a friend, in this place. A friend who understands how it feels to lose and grieve people you love. A friend who can keep me safe from my fears. And I—I hope that you will be the friend I need."

A friend. As if they could be friends.

Malini's touch was so light. The princess felt fragile and looked fragile. *How can you be this soft?* Priya thought helplessly. *How can you know what I am and look at me with eyes like that? How can you be so stupidly trusting?*

"You don't make friends," Priya said, speaking through the lump in her throat with some difficulty, "by speaking of their dead."

"No," Malini said with a faraway look. "I suppose you don't."

"I liked it better," Priya managed to say, "when you spoke of peafowls. You can do more of that if you like."

Malini shook her head once more, a low sound of amusement escaping her. It wasn't quite a laugh, but it was the closest she'd come since Priya had met her. And Priya, not knowing how to feel, guided Malini once more around the triveni, watching as the wind whipped about Malini's hair—and stopped abruptly.

Pramila stood in the western hall, watching them. Her jaw was tight. Her expression was furious.

"You," Pramila said, "are not allowed to leave your cell."

Her voice wavered like a flame. For a second, Priya thought she was weeping. And then she realized that the waver was not tears but anger, a storm of it that Pramila couldn't quite modulate. Pramila crossed the room, trembling with the force of her feelings.

At Priya's side, Malini said nothing.

"I knew you'd find a way to use the maid," said Pramila. "And here you are. Did you pay her? Bribe her?"

"I was not feeling well," Malini said thinly. "I needed air."

"Give me your key," Pramila said to Priya. She said it abruptly, holding her hand before her.

"No," Malini said. "Don't give it to her, Priya."

Priya had already unhooked the key. She had no opportunity to return it to her waist before Pramila seized it from her.

"It is such a small thing," Malini said, in a voice close to tears, "to leave my room, and feel the air upon my face. If you would only allow me a little kindness, *please*."

"Do not beg," Pramila said, disgust in her voice. "Every time you weep and you beg—I know it's all a lie, I know what you are—"

"I only beg because you keep me penned up like an animal. Do you think my brother wants me to die locked in a small room in a foreign land?"

"No, this isn't the way I think he wants you to die. You know exactly what he expects."

"Do you really want me to suffer as she did, Pramila?" Malini asked. Her voice was velvet. An entreaty. But Pramila flinched as if it had been a blow.

Pramila hissed, eyes harsh with rage, and without pause raised her hand to hit Priya—not Malini—around the face. It was not going to be a perfunctory blow of chastisement, Priya saw that immediately. Pramila's hand was curled into a beringed fist, a hard knot of knuckles and metal rings that would leave Priya bloody, and Priya only had a second to feel a kind of breathless fury rush through her, at the ugliness of being used as a proxy for Malini, before she raised her own hand to knock Pramila's arm away.

She didn't have the chance. Malini slammed into Priya, grasping her wrists with her cold hands, and placed herself squarely between Pramila's fist and Priya's face. Priya felt a thud and a blinding pain as Pramila's hand caught Malini around the ear, and Malini's skull cracked against her own. Priya couldn't move, couldn't fight—Malini was holding her, her nails digging in as they had when Priya had woken her from a nightmare, a pressure like a needle-edged vise.

"No," Malini said. Her voice cracked a little. "No, you mustn't."

Priya could barely see, through the shield of Malini's body bent against her own, through all her loose dark hair, made even wilder than usual by the wind. But she felt Malini's breath on her skin, and knew the words were meant for her.

She froze, then. Malini did not let go.

"Prin-princess," Pramila said haltingly. "Are you hur—"

"You may hit me again if you like," Malini said. "But you will not hit Priya. She has no part in our business." She remained hunched over Priya. "Go on, Pramila. Do as you will."

"Oh! Oh. You think I won't strike you properly?" Pramila gave an ugly laugh, and through the curtain of Malini's hair Priya could see snatches of her face: her wet, furious eyes, and the sneer on her lips. "You think I wouldn't dare risk harming you, when you're here alone with me? You *deserve* to be struck."

"I am still the emperor's flesh and blood," Malini said, voice thin but steady. "Still a princess of Parijat. Strike me, if you will, but do not forget that my brother sent me here with a purpose."

"Fulfill your purpose then," Pramila ground out. "Accept your fate, so that I no longer need to look at you."

Malini said nothing to that, and Pramila's expression flickered—spasmed with something dark that lay far beyond hate. Then she calmed. Reined in her fury. She straightened her shoulders. Smoothed the pleats of her sari.

"More medicine, I think," Pramila announced. "You're over-wrought, Princess Malini."

Malini's exhale was a shudder. Almost soundless.

"Now," Pramila said. "Move. Princess."

For a long moment, Malini remained where she was, folded over Priya, holding her wrists in that painful grip. Then, finally, she released Priya and moved away.

Priya lowered her head. Waited.

Pramila raised her hand. Malini made a sound, faint as falling leaves.

Pramila struck Priya, unimpeded. This time the blow wasn't fueled by rage. This was a deliberate act designed to remind Priya of her place, and Malini of her own, but it did not make the cut of the rings any less painful, the blood in Priya's mouth any less nauseating.

"Fool girl," Pramila said. "Take the princess to her room. *Now.* I'll be along in a moment."

It wasn't long before Pramila stormed in, carrying the carafe.

"Drink it," she said, slamming the wine down at Malini's side.

Malini tried to pick up the vessel, but her hands were trembling. Their brief walk—when she had been so lucid—had exhausted her. Before she could drop it, Priya crossed the room. As she drew closer Pramila flinched—or moved to strike her, it wasn't entirely clear—but Priya looked at her, and the older woman went still. Priya saw a flicker of shame pass over Pramila's face, at the sight of Priya's bruised, red lip. The rage had passed through her, after all, and now they were all still here. Pramila. Malini. And Priya, who did not matter at all. Who wore a split lip and a red cheek as a reminder of Pramila's shame.

I will need to take control of this task from Pramila, Priya thought. *I will need to ensure that the princess isn't poisoned anymore, or she will die.*

Priya leaned down and took the carafe from Malini. She poured out a measure and placed it in Malini's hands.

"Carefully now, my lady," she said. "Here."

She helped Malini raise the cup to her lips. Helped her drink.

If Pramila hit her again she was not sure she would be able to control herself, or that she would want to. She pressed her teeth over her tongue, distracting herself from the throb of her cheek.

Still kneeling before Malini, she offered the carafe back to Pramila, eyes demurely lowered.

If she hurts me again, I will break her fingers. Her wrist. I'll give her face a bare-handed blow. I won't stand it. I won't. I—

Pramila took the carafe and swept from the room without another word. A moment later Priya heard the click of the lock. With no key herself any longer, she knew that she and Malini were prisoners until morning.

She exhaled, some terrible tension unfurling from her shoulders.

"You are not good at allowing your pride to be debased, are you?" Malini murmured.

"My lady, I am a maidservant," Priya reminded her. "I have no pride to debase."

A small smile crossed Malini's lips.

"Ah, that is a lie you think you need to tell a highborn lady, is it not? But I know you have pride. We all do. You may 'lady' me, and 'ma'am' at your seniors, but I can see the iron in you."

Malini raised a hand, brushing her knuckles against the swelling of Priya's cheek. Her fingers trembled, still. Priya could feel the sting of the touch. It burned through her blood, sang, and she thought, *Oh.*

Oh no.

This was more than simple fascination. This was attraction and it was . . . not remotely convenient.

"Sometimes you must allow your pride and virtues to fall away in order to win the war," said Malini.

Priya's breath stuttered, just a little. "Thank you," she managed to say. "For protecting me."

"Don't thank me. I didn't save you for your sake. I did it for mine. If she had angered you truly enough, you would have hurt her. And then you would have been sent away, and I would be alone again." Malini was already beginning to sway. She exhaled, then closed her eyes and lay back.

"Will you stay near, when I sleep?" Malini had turned her face away. "Just—you may lie down here if you like."

Priya swallowed. Did she . . . ? But no.

There were things they didn't do in Parijat.

And there are things, Priya told herself firmly, *that I will not do, because I am not that much of an owl-brained fool.*

"I'll sit by you, my lady," she said. "Until you fall asleep."

Malini did not argue. She clearly did not have the energy to. She lay still, eyes closed. Her face was going to bruise. Malini's skin was like paper.

Breath. Pulse. The color of her gums, her nails. Priya did not need to see any of those things to know that Malini was dying by steady increments.

She needed a way to keep Malini alive. And she needed the Hirana's strength. *Patience*, Ashok had told her. Patience and time were key. But patience could only get her so far. And she'd never had a surfeit of it to begin with.

She would take control of the dosages of poison. She'd prove herself biddable and easy to ignore once more, so that Pramila would hand her the responsibility, never questioning her motives. She'd keep the princess alive—for the sake of Bhumika and the household, and also because it was right.

And not because she wanted to. Not because of that at all.

17

PRIYA

At first, she thought it was another dream.

The water at her feet. Winding of liquid, sleek as rope. The memory of her brother's red-limned shadow.

Then she felt the magic of the yaksa singing through her. Salt in her veins.

She remembered the cosmic rivers. The World Egg.

(The World Peafowl. No. She wasn't going to think of that.)

She looked around and—through the haze of dreaming, through sleep—forced herself to *see*.

Dark water beneath her. Water of a river. Three rivers, meeting and winding: a river of a red so deep it was nearly black, pulsing around her, ugly with life. A river of green flecked with gold, rolling like grass in a howl of wind; a river of darkness. Lightless, a rippling void.

She felt the rivers beneath her feet. The rivers winding through her skull. This was no dream.

This was—

"Priya." Bhumika's voice. She sounded relieved. "You're finally here."

Bhumika stood before her, waist deep in water. She was a shadow, darkness against the water; the river around her glowed faintly rose—shimmering with the red-limned light of her.

"The sangam," Priya said, awed. "I haven't seen it properly in so long."

"The Hirana's influence," Bhumika murmured. Then she said, "What do you mean, properly?"

"When Meena strangled me, I thought I saw a glimpse of it. But not like this."

"Well," Bhumika murmured, displeased. "You didn't tell me that when we talked of it, of course."

Priya shrugged. "It didn't seem important."

Bhumika let out a sigh. Priya looked away from her, taking the sangam in.

The rivers wound beneath her, but above her they were mirrored, blanketed with stars. The cosmic rivers were a folded, creased flower—dozens of worlds pressed together, bound by the movement of water.

"At least this saves us meeting in person," Bhumika said, watching as Priya turned all about—as she waded a circle through the water, three rivers roiling around her knees. "Tell me about the princess."

"She's sick."

"I knew that, Priya."

"Pramila is poisoning her with powdered needle-flower, dosed via wine," added Priya. "I'm not sure if she intends to kill her or not, but—"

"It amounts to the same," finished Bhumika. "You don't think the emperor intends to finish her, then?"

Bhumika had feared that General Vikram and his household were one of the emperor's targets—that he sought to remove his sister and the general in one fell, economical swoop. But Priya was not so sure now. She waded deeper, drawing closer to Bhumika, the cosmic confluence rising to her waist.

"No," she said. "Not by poison. I think—I'm almost sure—he wants her to burn. But if she continues to refuse, perhaps he thinks the poison will have to do. Death by needle-flower would be . . . it would be a bad death." She pushed the thought away. "Do you know what she did to anger him, Bhumika? *Why* he wants her to burn?"

"No, that I don't know. Perhaps nothing, Priya." Bhumika sounded suddenly weary. "There were women burned in the city today—imperial justice, apparently."

"*What?* Did General Vikram order it?"

"One of the emperor's men—never mind. It isn't important. All you need to know is that the emperor takes pleasure in the burning. It gives him something of value. Serves him some kind of purpose—of control, or faith, I don't know."

Priya moved even closer, and through the strangeness of the sangam felt the echo of what Bhumika had seen: the burning women. The screams.

She stumbled. "That's what the emperor wants?" she managed to say.

"Apparently so."

The water glowed around them.

There had always been a distance between Priya and her elder temple sister. A gap that couldn't be bridged by words. They had not been close, when the temple elders still lived and Priya was just a small girl. And from the moment Bhumika had taken Priya in, she'd made it clear they could not be family. The kinship between them had become something sharp and sour that bound them together regardless. It made honest words hard.

But something about this place—the strangeness of it, the river-ink of Bhumika before her, and the echo of Bhumika's horror—loosened Priya's tongue. Let the words flow free.

"I haven't been able to come here in so long. Is that what it's like to be twice-born?" she murmured. "To be able to enter the sangam and simply be—more than human?"

"We're entirely human," said Bhumika, "no matter what we can do."

Priya laughed. Looked around pointedly, at the rivers knotted about them like compass roses. "You think *this* is human?"

"I think this is an aberration. A problem. And not something we should indulge in."

"Then why are you here?" Priya challenged.

"Because I need to be," snapped Bhumika. "Because so many things are falling apart. Because so many things are terribly wrong in Ahiranya, and I need to use every tool in my limited arsenal."

"Do you meet Ashok here?" Priya asked bluntly. When Bhumika was silent she added, "I know he's alive."

"You should have told me you saw him," Bhumika replied.

"You should have told me he was *alive.*"

"He didn't want you to know."

"Oh, you were lying to me out of respect for him. I see."

"I never lied to you."

"Don't play silly games, Bhumika. You knew I believed he was dead, and you let me go on believing it. That was a choice to hide the truth from me. That's as good as a lie."

If Bhumika had been less shadow and more skin, she probably would have looked ashamed.

"He's dangerous, Priya," Bhumika said finally. "And I did exactly what I thought was necessary, for the child you were when he abandoned you."

"But I'm not a child anymore."

"Ah, Priya. Nothing is so simple."

"No," said Priya. "And I'm not asking for you to simplify the complexities of your life, Bhumika. I know my limits." She sounded bitter, she knew. She didn't really care. "But I can only act with the knowledge I have. The knowledge I deserve. So I am going to continue seeking the deathless waters. Because he needs them, and so do I."

"Ashok wants to inflict chaos."

"He wants to build a new world," Priya said defensively, even though she'd said much the same to him, when they'd stood beneath the bower of bones. "A free Ahiranya."

"No," said Bhumika. "He wants a return to the old Ahiranya. He's chasing a dream, a mirage, of a time when Ahiranya was isolated and alone and strong. How many hundreds upon hundreds of years ago was that?" Bhumika's voice was all scorn. "He wants a world that can't be forged without blood and death and sacrifice. In that way, he's no different from the emperor."

"Ahiranya is dying. Literally rotting."

"But that doesn't change our duty," Bhumika said, "our need to keep it whole. If we are temple children still, then I can't allow myself to forget that. And neither can you."

"Ashok," Priya said deliberately, "was the last person to treat me like family."

One beat. Two.

"Well," Bhumika said in a controlled voice. "If that's how you feel, then that's how you feel."

"Bhumika, I am *literally* your servant."

"And what else could you be? My long-lost sibling, perhaps? A distant cousin? I could hardly adopt you, could I? Being the general's wife—using the general—requires certain sacrifices. It always has."

Even in shadow—even in the sangam—Bhumika's hand drifted without conscious thought to her waist. Priya felt oddly ashamed. She looked away.

Why are we always so ugly to one another?

"Anyway," Priya said abruptly. "I want to end her poisoning and stop the needle-flower entirely. But I'm not the one who gives her the wine."

Bhumika drummed her fingers lightly. "Could you make yourself that person?"

"Pramila doesn't think much of servants." Priya crossed her arms. "And she certainly doesn't think much of me."

"But she needs you," said Bhumika.

"She needs much more than me. But yes."

Bhumika nodded, as if she'd come to some decision.

"Keep the princess alive," Bhumika said. "Just a little longer. That's all I ask of you, Priya. What you do with Ashok…" She shook her head. "Just do this for me. That's all."

Then Bhumika reached out, both hands before her, and violently shoved Priya down under the water.

*   *   *

Priya woke with a gasp.

Malini lay deep asleep on the charpoy beside her. The sun was beginning to rise. And Priya would have almost—almost—believed it was just a dream, if not for the memory of the flint of Bhumika's eyes. The magic singing and coiling in her blood.

The lines upon the floor, which had moved into a mimicry of stars.

18

MALINI

Malini knew she was growing sicker. It was becoming more difficult to make herself speak. Quiet was simpler, easier. The needle-flower was a dark pool, enfolding her, pressing down upon her tongue.

Days passed. She had asked Priya to stay near her, to lie down beside her if she liked, and Priya had taken the request to heart. Often Priya sat by her and told her stories: more about the yaksa, but also silly, frivolous tales that she'd clearly dredged up from her childhood. Once, she told Malini about an elephant who asked its mice friends to save it from a hunter by biting through the ropes binding it.

"Do mice and elephants speak the same language?" Malini asked, when Priya was halfway into the story.

"Don't pick holes," Priya scolded. "Does everything really have to make perfect sense, my lady? It's a tale for children."

"I think it's a fair question," Malini said. She knew her voice was thin, reedy with exhaustion, but she managed a laugh when Priya gave her a mock frown. "Now, imagine if you were the size of an elephant and I were the size of a mouse. Would we really be able to have a conversation?"

"Well, you'd be too frightened to tell me how foolish my stories are, at least," Priya said.

But as Malini grew sicker, the stories petered out. More often than not, Malini woke from nightmares to find Priya dozing on the floor beside her charpoy, head pillowed on her arms and her body curled on its side.

One night, she felt the charpoy shift; heard the creak of the frame behind her curved back.

Malini's breath stuttered out of her. "Priya?" she whispered.

"I'm here."

Malini turned over.

"I'm not dreaming?"

"No," said Priya. "No, my lady."

"That's good." Malini's voice was a little hoarse. She curled her fingers against the weave of bamboo and saw Priya's fingers mirror her own, a half breath of distance between Priya's knuckles and her own. Malini could barely make out her face. In the night's gloom, Priya's skin looked ghostly dark, her mouth and jaw in shadow.

Perhaps it was the needle-flower that made Malini feel as if Priya would vanish at any moment, unspooling like the coil of smoke from a candle flame. Malini wanted to reach out and feel her skin; the reassurance of solid fingers and smooth nails, the dip and swell of knuckles, all of it real and proof of life.

But she didn't. She stayed still and listened to Priya's breath; watched the whites of Priya's eyes, as Priya watched her in turn.

"Why does Lady Pramila hate you, my lady?" Priya asked suddenly.

"Did Pramila say something to you today?"

Priya shook her head. "No, my lady."

"Jailers always hate their prisoners," Malini said.

"The way she responds to you is not simply how a jailer responds to a prisoner, I think."

"Is it not?" Malini frowned. "I thought it was. After all, power makes everyone monstrous. At least a little."

Priya's mouth turned down at the corners. She looked— worried, perhaps. That was good.

"Please, my lady," she said. "I want to help."

Malini wanted Priya's pity. She wanted to bind Priya to her. She *needed* an ally. She had already been vulnerable in front of Priya, drawing her in, making a confidante of her. Now she would have to do so again. But ah, it was a hard thing to do: Making herself speak through the weight of needle-flower. Pouring out words. All of it was hard, and hurt.

There was a long moment of silence, as Malini drew on her reserves of strength and shifted, rising to her elbows. She stared at Priya through her curtain of hair, wishing she could read her better, wishing that her own mind were less swaddled by poison.

"Her daughter was my friend," said Malini. "My lady-in-waiting. She rose to the pyre—both my ladies did so—and I refused. Pramila can't forgive that. Part of her sincerely believes it was an honor for her daughter. An ascent to immortality. And part of her knows the truth: that the pyre was my punishment. That her daughter died, burning and in agony, because of me. And I continue living despite all my errors, and her daughter does not. Neither of those are things she can forgive."

Priya swallowed visibly, shifting to mirror Malini's position. "Why did he wish to remove you?" Priya asked. "Your brother."

There were many things Malini could have said. *I betrayed him. I tried to remove him from his throne. I saw him too clearly, and he hated me for it.* But those were not truths that would help her now. What truth would?

Malini brushed her hair back and met Priya's eyes.

"Because I am not pure."

Priya's eyes widened, just slightly.

Ask me, Malini thought, not looking away from Priya's gaze, *what makes me impure. If you're brave enough, ask me.*

But Priya did not.

"I am sorry, my lady," she said instead.

"Pramila wants me to die on the pyre," Malini said in return. "Sometimes she will sit by my sickbed and tell me how blissful immortality will be. And—sometimes—she will ask me to imagine how it would feel to burn. And I did. And I do, Priya. I do, and I do, and I do."

When Priya startled, beginning to reach out as Malini's voice wavered, Malini warded her away with a hand. "No," she went on. "I'm—I don't want to be comforted." Suddenly she was shaking, grief and anger rushing through her, and she did not want to be touched. That would be too much. Too much, when her skin already felt overfull with feeling. A shallow breath. Her hands lowered. "Pramila thinks I'll choose it. The pyre. The burning. But perhaps it will not come to that. If I grow any weaker, it will not."

"No," said Priya. "I suppose not."

"So now you know," said Malini. "I would ask you to forgive me for telling you my hurts, but I regret nothing I've done. I want you to know that, Priya."

There. A real truth, unvarnished and laid bare.

Malini had peeled her heart open and poured her heart's blood out before Priya, given her everything ugly and tender, metal and sweet about her past. And Priya...

Priya did not touch her, but she kept her hand near Malini's own. She kept her eyes on Malini. Steady and sure.

"I've told you many a time, my lady," said Priya. "I'm only a maidservant. You don't need to even think of apologizing to me."

"But I do think of it, Priya," said Malini. "That's all."

Pramila came to visit her during the day. Malini only knew it because she woke warm from the heat of the midday sun, and because Priya's voice had startled her out of her slumber, lifting her from the deep pool of drugged sleep to the shallows of almost wakefulness, where the room tipped lazily around her but she could still *think*. Still hear, as Pramila settled herself on the edge of the charpoy with a creak of wood.

"She's resting, my lady," Priya was saying. Malini kept her eyes closed, her breathing steady. "I can try to wake her if you wish, but she sleeps soundly."

Pramila made a noise of acknowledgment. Cleared her throat.

"Your face," Pramila said. "Does it pain you?"

There was a pause.

"No, my lady," Priya replied.

"I should not have hit you," Pramila said stiffly. "I have never beaten any of my maids before. It is beneath me. But here, in this place..." She drummed her fingers upon something solid. The Book of Mothers, perhaps. "The princess makes me forget myself."

Malini would not open her eyes. She would not. It was enough to hear their voices.

"You think you love her a little, perhaps," Pramila continued. "She is a dazzling mistress, for one as lowly and uncouth as you. But she uses everyone, girl. Even me. Why do you think I keep the guards away from her? It's more than piety alone. They'd be taken in by her pretty face and sweet words. She's a manipulative child. No matter what she says, remember you're no more than dirt beneath her feet. Remember that the next time she asks you for a small favor." Her voice lowered. "Remember that, the next time she provokes my ire."

"Ma'am. I do not admire her," Priya said, voice halting. "I only—I need to keep this position, ma'am. I have people to care for, who are reliant on me. I cannot lose my standing or my income."

"Despite what the princess may say to you, I am the one who decides if you remain or not," Pramila said, an approving note in her voice. "You've been a good worker, apart from one unfortunate lapse. You need not fear anything as long as you remember who it is more...prudent...to obey."

"Oh, thank you," Priya said. "Thank you so much, Lady Pramila."

Malini heard the sound of Priya's footsteps against the floor, drawing closer.

"Please allow me to help you more, Lady Pramila. May I... I could light incense in your study in the evenings, to sweeten the air. Or, I could make your favorite meals, if we have the ingredients? And I could—I could give the princess her medicine. I already take her the evening meal, after all. It would be no trouble to also give her wine too, before she sleeps." Priya paused. Then she added, "She trusts me. She won't fuss."

There was a moment of silence. Pramila shifted; the silk of her sari rustled around her.

"Despite what you may believe, and what is sensible, I love the princess," Pramila said haltingly, as if the words were being pried out of her. In a way, they were. Her voice wobbled. "I love her enough to want what is best for her, even if she doesn't."

"Then let me take this burden from you," Priya said. "Please."

"Fine," she said. "As long as you remember who you are loyal to."

"Of course, ma'am. Anything to be of use," Priya said earnestly.

Malini opened her eyes, just a little. In the thin crescent of her vision, she saw Priya—face wide-eyed and guileless, hand outstretched—and Pramila placing the vial of needle-flower in her palm.

Dusk fell. Pramila returned to lecture Malini about the mothers. Malini half listened as she watched the door, wondering what Priya was doing. Pouring a dose of needle-flower obediently into Malini's wine? Or perhaps tipping the whole bottle in, so that Malini would die swift and painless?

Unlikely. But she imagined it all the same.

Priya offered Pramila a bow and entered the room. As Pramila rose to leave, Priya spoke.

"Lady Pramila has given me the task of providing your medicine," Priya said to Malini. Then she gave Pramila a sidelong look, as if seeking approval. Pramila nodded, and Priya kneeled down, holding the carafe between her palms.

Malini stared at it. Then she looked at Priya.

"I know something of medicine made of needle-flowers," Priya said, voice quiet. Pramila, hovering by the door, was unlikely to have heard her.

There was a message, in those brown eyes, in the way she held out the wine as if it were a gift instead of poison; as if it were something precious cupped between her palms.

Trust me, her face said.

That was the problem with making allies. At some point, inevitably, there came a moment when a decision had to be made: Could this one be trusted? Had their loyalty been won? Was their generosity a façade for a hidden knife?

Malini made her choice. It was easier than it should have been.

"Do you?" Malini said, with equal softness. "Well. As it happens, so do I."

She met Priya's eyes. Without breaking their shared gaze, she took the carafe and drank deep.

19

RAO

After Rao heard about the executions and the women who were burned, he sat with Prem and worked through three bottles of wine grimly, methodically.

He was painfully relieved that Prem did not mock him for it; only poured out his glasses, and allowed Rao to lean on him, and told him rambling stories of their youth, to which Rao could only manage slurred responses.

"Remember," Prem said, "when you and Aditya tried to learn to dance for my aunt's wedding? Remember that?" Prem had long since stopped drinking, and was smoking his pipe, his face wreathed in a cloud of sweet-smelling smoke. "You were truly shit. Both of you. I couldn't believe it when Aditya gave you a black eye."

"It was a traditional Saketan dance," Rao managed to grumble out, even as the room kept on spinning dizzyingly around him. "We'd never danced with sticks before."

"Not much different from using sabers, is it? You should have been fine."

It hadn't been like using sabers at all. That had been the problem. They had both been clumsy, awkward, more used to scholarship and weapons than dance. And Aditya *had* tried to fling his twin dancing staves like sabers. That was how he'd thwacked Rao in the face.

Aditya had apologized profusely about the black eye. *I should have shown more sense*, he'd said, in that martyred, earnest way of his. *Sorry, Rao. I need to practice harder.* A pause. *On my own, probably.*

Rao told Prem as much, as he rested his head on Prem's shawl-cloaked arm, feeling the rise and fall of Prem's shoulder beneath him, moving in time with his breath. Prem hummed and laughed in all the right places, and Rao finally went quiet, closing his eyes. The room was still spinning. He was probably going to be sick later, he realized. He didn't care.

"How is he?" Lata's voice.

"Oh, fine, I suppose." Prem's voice was as light as ever. "He'll be asleep soon."

Lata sat down—he heard the rustle of her clothes, the thump of her body—and she and Prem began to speak in low voices, as Rao drifted in and out of consciousness.

"...the sacred wood," Prem was saying. His voice sounded muted. Rao heard the tap of his pipe, as Prem cleared it of ash. "Tell me if you believe it's true."

"The Ahiranyi believe that when the yaksa died, their sacrifice made those trees," Lata said, after a moment. "They believe its wood is imbued with the yaksa's power. As for what I believe— who can know for sure what it can do?"

He'd never taken Prem for a man interested in the faiths of others, Rao thought drowsily. Maybe one day, when this was all over, he would have to take Prem to the most ancient holy gardens in Alor—the ones where you could read old fates carved into the living trunks of trees. Maybe Prem would like that. Rao would have to ask him.

Then sleep took him, and he heard no more.

The next day he woke with a throbbing head and a woolly tongue, none of it unexpected. He allowed himself to feel sick for one morning, and one morning only.

Then he returned to the task of trying to see Malini freed.

Prem stared at him in silent judgment as he dressed like a Saketan lord, in clothes borrowed from Prem himself, all of it in pale greens and blues. As he tucked a shawl around his shoulders, Prem said, "At least take a blade whip with you. You can borrow one from one of my men, if you like." He gestured at the two guards standing at the door, neither of whom looked as though they welcomed the idea.

Rao shook his head.

"No Saketan highborn would go anywhere without his weapon," Prem said.

No Aloran prince went anywhere without his weapons either, as a rule. But Rao had put aside his chakrams and his daggers for the sake of subtlety. He didn't say so to Prem, who knew that perfectly well, and was just seeking to needle Rao.

"Anywhere?" Rao repeated, tying his sash. "The amount you drink, I'm surprise you still have all your limbs, then."

"We're trained to handle battle in any situation," Prem said, with mock affront. "Including inebriation."

"Well, I'd still rather not carry one. I'm more likely to cut my own hand off than defend myself with it, sober or not."

"I should teach you. Widen your repertoire."

"Maybe later," said Rao. Lata was waiting, and although she did not look impatient, there was a slight arch to her eyebrows that suggested she wasn't well pleased with the delay.

They rented palanquins to carry them from the pleasure house to the traditional Ahiranyi mansion where the lord they were meeting lived. Servants led them to a receiving room, where he was propped up by pillows on a low divan. There were vibrant red lilies carefully arranged in pots by the lattice windows. One pot sat by the side of the divan, a splash of color next to the old man's pale robes and the white blanket spread across his legs.

Lata had arranged this introduction, making subtle inquiries via the sages in the city who had received support and patronage from Ahiranyi highborn. There were always people who valued the conversation of a sage and sought to learn something of the scholarship each sage carried with them. This man was Lord Govind, the last male scion of an ancient Ahiranyi highborn family, who had expressed interest in Lata's teachings and wanted to meet her and her patron.

Today, Rao was that patron: Lord Rajan, Prem's cousin and a Saketan highborn with scholarly leanings. He reminded himself of this as he and Lata offered Lord Govind their greetings and respects.

Lata gave an elegant bow before kneeling down by the divan alongside Rao. She had carried gifts with her: books, written in her own hand, bound in silk. Rao could not imagine how long it would have taken her to complete such large manuscripts, the hours by lantern light, but she handed the books over willingly. She described their content as she did so—the tales she had gathered, the philosophies she had recorded and dissected—much to Lord Govind's obvious delight.

"These are a humble gift, my lord," she said. "But a gift nonetheless, from my patron Lord Rajan, who heard of your interest in my scholarship with great joy and interest."

"Ah, a gift from your patron! I see, I see. How generous of you, Lord Rajan," Govind said genially, taking the silk-bound books from Lata with hands that trembled. He placed the books upon his lap, pressing a frail finger reverently against the surface of silk. As he did so, Rao had a sense of how Govind would read those books when he was alone: slowly, savoring each page, cupping the spine to protect the fragile pages.

"It is a priceless thing, knowledge," Govind continued. "But the hours of work put into creating these are worth coin of significant measurable value, and that I appreciate even more. I thank you for your time, sage." Lata bowed her head in response, accepting his praise.

"What prompted such generosity, Lord Rajan?"

"Many things, Lord Govind," Rao said with a smile, allowing a little edge of a Saketan accent to inflect his words. Verisimilitude was important, after all. "But the joy of pleasing a fellow scholar cannot be underestimated."

Govind gave the mildest snort. "Parijatdvipan lords rarely visit Ahiranya for intellectual discourse."

"So I've been told," Rao said. He wondered if Lord Govind knew that Prem and his entourage were living in a brothel. He decided not to ask.

"They come here to do things that would be considered improper, beyond Ahiranya's borders," Lord Govind continued. "For example, I did not think Saketans considered it proper to travel with young women they are not married to. Did you bring no female elder as chaperone, Lord Rajan? For shame."

Ah. Rao had not even considered the impropriety, not as he should have. He had assumed there would be maidservants present in the room to attend on their master and his guests, but Lord Govind had waved any servants away upon Lata and Rao's arrival. And he and Prem had traveled with Lata enough that the strangeness of being alone with her had long since eased.

Despite himself, Rao felt his face go hot. It was tempting to keep his smile fixed, to wear it as a mask, but instead he allowed his face to grow solemn, and gathered up the sort of words and phrases he'd need to shave away the barbed edges of this conversation.

But Lata spoke first.

"My own teacher educated Lord Rajan's sister," Lata said. "That makes us family of a kind, my lord, in scholarship."

"Cousins in scholarship?" Govind asked, eyebrow raised.

"The bond of students who share a sage can be greater to us than a bond of blood," she said. "Or so many sages believe. In my eyes, it is entirely honorable to be in his company."

"And in the eyes of society?" Lord Govind murmured, something chiding in his quavering voice.

"Parijatdvipa is not an empire of unified values, my lord," said Lata, smiling.

"Indeed. Indeed it is not." There was a shrewd look in Govind's eyes. "Well, it's no business of my mine," he added mildly, as if he had not just *made* it his business. "You want something from me, I think, Lord Rajan. Perhaps you intend subtlety. But I am an old man. I have no patience for such games any longer."

Although Lord Govind was certainly old and frail, Rao did not think he lacked patience for politics. But Rao did not say so. He sat straight, clasping his hands before him with the neatness of the lord he was meant to be—a lord used to wielding pen and ink rather than sword, and leaned forward. Spoke.

"I seek a wise man's counsel, Lord Govind. You are my elder, a man who knows the…often tumultuous politics of Ahiranya intimately. I wish to understand Ahiranya's politics somewhat—better." These words were a risk. But when Lord Govind did not freeze in fear, did not react as if Rao was going to drag him before the regent as a traitor—only narrowed his eyes slightly in interest—Rao pressed on.

"We understand there are Ahiranyi highborn who fund poets. Singers. Scribes and sages. And…other rebels."

"Funding art should not be rebellion," Govind said, with what struck Rao as false mildness. "It should merely be a sign of culture."

"The rebels in Ahiranya do not simply write poems or sing songs," Rao pointed out. "We hear things in Saketa, also. We are aware of violent resistance. Of merchants and highborn of importance to the empire, murdered." He paused, thinking of the man he was meant to be, right now in this moment. "We are all three of us interested in scholarship, my lord, is it not so?"

Govind tipped his head in acknowledgment.

"Then let us speak as scholars," Rao said. "Theoretically, of concepts that have no bearing on what we may or may not truly do."

"We share an understanding," murmured Govind. "Continue, Lord Rajan."

"Theoretically, then—there is great anger here. I've seen hungry people, beggars, in Ahiranya, my lord. Far more than in Saketa."

Rao had never actually been to Saketa, but Prem had remarked on the number of sickly people in Ahiranya, the breadth of poverty. And certainly it was far more than Rao had witnessed in Alor or Parijat. "It makes rebel violence understandable. Sympathetic, to some."

"Anger," Govind repeated. He massaged his own throat as he coughed. "It is a shallow understanding of Ahiranya you must have, to call what fuels rebel violence *anger.*"

"Then what should it rightly be called?" Rao asked.

"You must understand, there is no one unified rebellion in Ahiranya," Govind replied. "The methods of each rebel group are different. But it is a vision that unites them all, not rage. A dream."

"What do they dream of, my lord?"

"For the sake of the scholarly interests we three share, I will hypothesize this: Every city-state of Parijatdvipa, every highborn and king and prince, is bound to Emperor Chandra by ancient vows. But Ahiranya is not bound by vow or choice. Ahiranya is a conquered nation. So of course, all rebels in our land dream of an Ahiranya that is free."

"But what freedom means, I imagine, is a more complicated question," Lata murmured.

Govind inclined his head. "And so, those Ahiranyi highborn who share the rebel dream—they fund it as they will. Some think freedom is won by killing. Some seek a path in art."

And what path do you take? Rao thought. *Do you have connections to rebels who seek blood? Can you ally with us, and see our princess set free?*

"Interesting," Rao said politely, instead. "That dream of a free country is—an admirable one." He waited a moment then added delicately, "The Ahiranyi are not the only ones with a dream of a different world."

He could have said it then: that there were many in Parijatdvipa who would see a different emperor on the throne; many who dreamt of an empire of joyful unity, instead of one crushed by an emperor who believed that Parijat stood supreme. But Govind scoffed, falling weakly back against his pillows, shushing Rao with a wave of his hand.

"Indeed, indeed. But what happens beyond our borders holds little interest to me. In truth, even what happens within our borders no longer concerns me as it once did. Dreams are dreams," he said. "I learned long ago the limits of a vision built upon faith and ideals. And the dangers."

"Lord Govind," Rao said, even as the man shook his head.

"You're a young man, Lord Rajan, and young people believe in things. Often they die for them. Kill for them. The regent burned women, Ahiranyi women, did you hear?"

Rao swallowed. Kept his expression calm. "I did, Lord Govind."

"Did the regent believe he acted correctly, in service of higher ideals? *Somebody* did, certainly," Govind said, and Rao had no doubt that by *somebody* he meant *Lord Santosh*. "But his act of faith will cost us all. He killed for faith, and now the rebels will do no less in return. If you will listen to an old man's counsel, then I advise you to leave the city while you still can. Leave Ahiranya entirely. Go swiftly. Forget our troubles. You will find no help here, Lord Rajan, from me or from any other. You would best be somewhere else, when the rebels seek blood in compensation. And it will not be long, I think."

"Think, or know?" Rao asked, doing away with subtlety. His heart was pounding.

Govind shook his head, which was no answer. Then he closed his eyes, clearly unutterably tired.

"It has been a long time," he murmured. "A long time since I have talked so much. I thank you for the books, Lord Rajan, young sage. These will bring me joy in the times to come. Whatever they may be. But I think now I must rest. You should be on your way."

20

JITESH

A warm night. Mosquitoes buzzing about, crickets humming, and the haveli lit so bright it was a small moon against the light-flecked black of the city. It was beautiful, but...

Spirits, he was tired.

He stifled a yawn—then yelped when he felt a hand on his shoulder.

"How's guard duty going?" Nikhil asked.

"Oh," said Jitesh. "Fine, you know."

"You definitely weren't falling asleep there." Nikhil's voice was amused. "At least try to look like a proper guard. This is a special night."

Lord Iskar had put on a lavish celebration to mark both the end of monsoon season and the birth of his first child. His second wife had given him a son, a fat and healthy baby with silver chains around his wrists and ankles to ward off ill luck, and an ash mark on his forehead for the mothers. Apparently mother and son were glowing and in good health, and Lord Iskar had arranged baskets of fruit and fine honey pastries to celebrate. From his position outside the celebration hall, Jitesh could just about see mother and child seated on a dais through the wooden window lattice, and the proud Lord Iskar standing at their side, greeting his guests.

All of Ahiranya's Parijati elite had come, dressed up in fine silks with gold pins in their turbans, expansive strings of pearls and rubies at their necks. Not a single highborn Ahiranyi—but that was no surprise. Jitesh had heard that Lord Iskar was becoming fast friends with some Lord Santosh from Parijat who was close to the emperor himself, and who apparently didn't think much of people who weren't from his homeland.

"Stand up straight," said Nikhil. "The commander's coming over."

His tone was derisive. None of the men liked their new commander, who was also Parijati, raised to his position because Lord Iskar wanted to please his new friend, instead of by any particular merit.

Both Jitesh and Nikhil were used to the way of things, of course. Lords did what they did for their own gain, and normal folk just had to accept it. But it was the man himself who irritated them the most. He insisted on talking to them. Trying to be their *friend*.

"He's going to talk about politics," muttered Jitesh.

"Spirits save us," Nikhil groaned.

Apparently, a forbidden verse from the Birch Bark Mantras had been daubed onto a temple to the mothers of flame the previous night. *Something about blood and righteousness*, the maid who'd seen it said, when Jitesh had asked her about it. *I don't know. You think I've got time for poetry, Jitesh?*

Jitesh didn't think it was a big problem. Words could be scrubbed away, after all. But the commander was furious about it and wanted everyone to know it. His men were, unfortunately, a captive audience.

"No one goes to war for poets and whores," the Parijati commander was saying to the soldier beside him, his Zaban rough and melodious by turns, as if he didn't know whether he wanted to speak like his compatriots or like his gem-dripping family. "Oh, people like to whine, that's true enough, but they should be glad those women were burned. They'll be worshipped now. Immortal." He sniffed, as if to say, *I wouldn't have been as kind.* "It was a generous death—better than having their skulls crushed."

"Yes, Commander," said the long-suffering soldier next to him.

"Are you listening to me?" the commander demanded. Jitesh didn't need to look at him to know his expression was sour, mouth twisted to one side. "You provincials, you don't know anything about how the world should be—"

The commander went silent abruptly. Jitesh nearly sighed with relief.

There was a gurgling sound. Jitesh looked over again, wondering what was amiss.

Then he saw the hilt of a blade protruding from the commander's throat.

The soldier who had been walking beside him gave a strangled cry of horror. Nikhil fumbled for his blade and Jitesh...stood there, frozen, catching sight of a figure on the roof.

He thought he would vomit, when the man leapt down before him.

The assassin wore an old-style Ahiranyi mask, dark mahogany with large eye sockets to allow for maximum peripheral vision.

"No one will go to war for poets and whores." He repeated the words slowly, levelly. "Isn't that what you said?"

Their highborn commander burbled out blood. Then he crumpled to the ground.

The masked man leaned down, twisted the knife, then drew it free. The commander was still.

"Come now, friends," the man said pleasantly. "You're going to have to move a little faster than you are. You may be traitors to Ahiranya, but you're still my people." He took another step forward. "I'd like to give you a fair battle. And a fair Ahiranyi death."

He drew a hand scythe from the back of his sash.

Nikhil finally lunged forward, sweeping his sword through the air.

The rebel slipped beneath the arc of his blade. In a motion as graceful as a dance, he moved behind Nikhil and cut his throat.

The other soldier cried out, helpless, as the rebel turned and stabbed the same sickle blade through his chest.

Jitesh was no idiot.

He turned and ran.

He ran into the haveli, ran down the corridor, straight into the arms of two other guards. He hit them with a thump so hard that one of them, winded, swore. Beyond them he could see the celebration—the guests, the gentle waft of music from a tanpura, the flicker of lantern light. He opened his mouth to yell.

It was already too late.

There was a scream as the first masked rebel emerged from nowhere—and truly they must have come from the air, because it looked as if they'd *peeled open* the thick lattice of wood, curling it away like mist, and surely that couldn't be possible—and slit a guest's throat. The screaming grew louder when three more emerged. Then another.

The guards holding Jitesh let go and reached for their swords. Jitesh stayed where he was, rooted by his horror.

By the dais, Lord Iskar drew his saber, face gray with fear. The regent was standing next to him. The regent was saying something, shouting, drawing his own saber, gesturing men forward. The rebels, Jitesh realized, were not indiscriminate. They killed one of the richest Parijati traders in the city. The wife of the most powerful tax collector. Then they strode toward Lord Iskar's wife, who screamed, clutching her child close. Her husband stepped in front of her.

Jitesh saw a knife fly through the air and bury itself point first in Lord Iskar's throat. Then the crowd of panicked fleeing guests crashed into him like a wave, and Jitesh was pushed back out of the room.

He ran through the haveli corridors, stumbling, blinded by panic. He ran even as he heard screaming begin from within the household's upper levels and saw the first hints of golden fire at the windows. He ran even as other guards spotted the blaze, shouted, "Water, water!"

He ran. And then there was someone standing before him, blocking his path.

"You did well," said a masked figure. It was not the masked rebel from before. The voice was younger, the eyes lighter. "A good run. I watched you. But now you're going to *stay still*."

He tried to run, but it was as if the ground tipped beneath him. He fell.

Frozen, he looked up at the figure above him.

"Thank you," the rebel said. They took a knife from their belt. "That will make things much easier."

21

PRIYA

It takes poison time to leave a body. And yet it seemed as if Malini improved almost immediately. She remained awake for once at night, instead of falling directly into a stupor.

"Light a lantern," she insisted. "I want to try walking about."

Would anyone notice that Priya had used more lamp oil than usual? It was something the senior maidservants in the mahal would have noticed. They would have remarked upon it. But Priya didn't think anyone cared here. Certainly not Pramila.

Malini clung to the wall for support and walked around the edge of the room on unsteady feet. Priya watched, seated upon the charpoy Malini had abandoned, as the princess pressed her hands to the stone, feeling the edges and curves of the obliterated carvings, a map destroyed. "It feels like the walls are always changing," Malini said with the faintest laugh, her eyes bright. "I feel like I'm swimming in this place, I'm so unsteady."

"Do you want to try letting go of the wall?" Priya asked.

"I'm not sure that's wise," said Malini. She looked at the blackened image of the yaksa on the wall. Then she exhaled and said, "Why not."

Priya stood up and walked through the spill of lantern light. "Here," she said, holding her hands out before herself, palms up. "Let me help."

"Thank you," said Malini. She took a tentative step forward

and placed her hands above Priya's. "I want to walk on my own, I think."

"Then let me just keep my hands below yours," said Priya. "You try to walk, my lady, and I'll be here to catch you if need be."

Their hands weren't touching but shared the same air, the same fall of shadow, as Malini took one tentative step after another, and Priya walked backward in front of her.

Malini's eyes met her own, face alight with a smile.

"You're doing well," Priya said, encouraging, and Malini's smile deepened.

"I feel less dizzy than I did a moment ago," she agreed. "I never thought I'd see the day when I would be complimented on not falling over. How my life has changed." Her voice turned wistful. "You've never seen me how I really am. I wish you could. I used to wear the most lovely silk saris in Parijat, and flowers twined in my hair like a crown. I was beautiful then."

Priya swallowed.

You still are.

"There is a way you have to move, when you're dressed like that," Malini went on, apparently oblivious. "A way you have to behave. You can't hold yourself hunched, as I am now. You can't lower your head. You can't show any weakness. You have to look strong."

"Strong," Priya repeated, turning a little to match the curve of the room. Malini turned too, as if they were dancing. "How so? You don't mean like a soldier, I think."

Malini laughed.

"No, not like a soldier. Strong like...Ah, perhaps it would be simpler to show you."

Malini straightened her spine. Lifted her head, her neck an elegant line, her eyes suddenly cool. She moved with grace, lifting her feet with a subtle kick that Priya could tell would make an overlong sari—the kind of impractical length Priya would never wear—flutter where it touched the earth. For a moment she was utterly transformed, untouchable and yes—strong. But it wasn't anything Priya had ever known as strength before.

Then Malini stumbled. Priya caught her hands immediately, taking Malini's weight. They were so close, Malini's face so near to hers, that their breath mingled. Their eyes met. Malini exhaled another faint laugh and drew back a little. Priya did the same. Her heart was pounding.

They were still holding hands.

"What was it like here, long ago?" Malini asked, voice strange. She was clearly trying to distract from whatever had just happened between them, and it was effective. Priya felt like she'd been doused in cold water. Malini had not said *before the temple burned*. But that was what she had meant.

If Priya closed her eyes she could envision it: carvings painted in rich shades of green and blue, with red eyes and red mouths. Blue floors, and gold lacquer on the great pillars that held up the walls. Lanterns of colored glass in sconces. Children laughing. The elders in their fine, soft silks.

But she looked around her, and nothing remained. Just motes of dust on the air, and the charred, empty walls. Just Malini watching her.

"What was it like in the imperial mahal?" Priya asked in return.

Malini offered Priya a sly smile that made clear she understood what Priya was doing but was willing to be led.

"It was beautiful. Sprawling. There were gardens everywhere, Priya. Such beautiful gardens. My ladies-in-waiting and I used to play in them, when we were small girls." She moved her fingers restlessly against Priya's own.

"I wish you would tell me about yourself," Malini added. Her voice was soft. "I want to know everything about you."

Priya's throat was suddenly dry.

"Me? I'm not very interesting."

"I'm sure you are. Let me prove it to you. A game." Her voice was almost teasing. "Tell me one thing you want right now, Priya."

"Want?"

"Yes. What do you want? Come, I'm testing if you're dull, after all."

It felt like a dangerous question. Priya shook her head, and Malini cocked hers.

"Come now," Malini cajoled. "Everyone wants something. Me, for example. I want the sweets my brother Aditya always brought me for my birthday when I was a girl. Ladoo, but like none you've ever eaten before, Priya. Soaked in rose syrup and sugared almonds, dusted in a filigree of gold. Oh, they were perfect. I haven't had them in years. So. What do you want?"

"Right now, I think I want those sweets," said Priya, half-serious. A ladoo soaked in rose syrup sounded decadent, and she suddenly wanted to be decadent. Craved something delicious.

"Don't cheat," Malini scolded. "You have to pick your own want. And no food. I've picked food."

"You can't pick *all* food!"

"I can and I have."

"Respectfully," Priya said, in a tone that was anything but respectful, "that isn't fair."

"I'm the one testing you. It's my right to decide the parameters of the testing. Now, go on: Tell me what you want most."

Priya didn't consider herself a complicated person. But she didn't often think of her wants. What did she want, anyway? To remember herself, her past. To see Rukh alive a few more years. For Ashok to be well and . . . different. Able to love her. And Bhumika. She wanted Bhumika to respect her.

Those were bigger wants than Priya wanted to admit . . . or than Malini surely wanted to hear, even if Priya were free to confess them.

"Maybe I want to learn to walk the way you do," said Priya, straightening her neck, tilting her chin just a little, in imitation of Malini's regal posture.

"Do you really? I could teach you."

"Spirits, no," Priya said, and watched Malini's lip twitch once more. "People would say I was pretending to be a princess. I'd be mocked, my lady. No."

"Then I need a different answer, Priya."

Priya considered for a moment. But it was hard to think, with Malini's hands in her own, with Malini's thumbs brushing the insides of her wrists, where her blood thrummed. There was a promise in this somewhere—in the touch and the smile and the joy written in Malini's face, the teasing edge to her voice. She didn't know what exactly to do with it, or with the way it made her own heart turn.

"There are coconuts that you can find growing in the forest," she blurted out. "Sometimes foragers or woodcutters collect them and sell them at the bazaar. Only the richest can afford to buy them."

"I said no food," Malini said in a chiding tone. But she was listening.

"They're not exactly edible. They're—the forest, my lady, is entirely Ahiranyi, and sometimes you find strange things inside it. Unexpected things. When you split those particular coconuts, you find flowers inside. Dark purple, violet, black. The color of shadows. The rich place those blossoms in their shrines. Or they used to." The wealthier pilgrims had brought those coconuts to the Hirana once, too. Priya had cracked one open herself, and nearly wept when the flowers had burst out, tumbling beautifully over her hands, a cascade of darkness. "I'd like one of those coconuts. I'd like to make that offering. It would be frivolous and stupid and...it wouldn't help anyone I've lost. Or summon any kind of luck. But it would be like a cry against the void. And that would be what some of the people I've lost would have wanted..." Priya trailed off. "I'm not usually frivolous. But that's why it's a want," Priya added. "Right now, in this place? That's what I want."

Malini was still staring at her, wordless. All playfulness had fallen from her features, leaving them blank and austere.

"Such a serious answer," she murmured.

"I'm sorry."

"You are," Malini said, "a genuinely interesting person. I thought it the moment I saw you, and I haven't yet been proved wrong."

Malini said it as if it were an accusation—as if Priya's words were somehow an affront, a blow, a thing that had harmed her. When Priya blinked at her, Malini released her abruptly, moving back to her charpoy and falling down upon it, head turned away.

"Are you well?" Priya asked, alarmed.

"Fine," Malini bit out. But she did not turn back to look at Priya again.

The sea change in her mood wasn't something Priya understood. But nothing about the curve of Malini's spine, the way her arms were wrapped around her body, suggested that she wanted to be asked further questions. As if reading her thoughts, Malini said quietly, "I would very much like to be alone."

"Of course," Priya said without thinking, and headed to the door. It was only when she touched the handle that she remembered she no longer possessed the key. The door was locked for the night.

Under her hand, the Hirana listened. The air shifted. The door swung slightly open.

Ah.

Priya glanced back. Malini was still curled up.

"I'll let you rest," Priya said. "I'm going for a little walk. I won't be long."

When Malini did not protest, Priya left the chamber.

The silence followed behind her. It was the kind that had thorns.

The triveni was empty. There was no rain. No cold wind. Perhaps the monsoon was passing. When she glanced up at the sky, she could see the wink of stars.

She took a few steps forward toward the plinth and—tripped.

With a quiet "oof" she regained her balance, straightening up. It was strange. She *knew* the triveni. She'd walked it so many, many times. The triveni had held her. But she'd missed, now—slipped against a groove. Her encounter with Malini had left her flustered, but not *that* flustered.

She looked down.

The lines upon the floor had definitely shifted. Instead of dancing like waves upon the shore, they'd merged together, jagged and strange.

They looked like flames. Like a *warning*.

There was a clattering noise. A shriek. She saw the shadow of one of the guards in the hall. Saw Pramila running toward her.

"The princess," Pramila cried urgently, breathless, "is she safe? Is anyone here?"

Priya shook her head, startled, her mind still trying to catch up. "Only—only the guards at the doors of the temple, I think, my lady. Is something wrong?"

Pramila strode over. There were high spots of color upon her cheeks. "There has been a terrible attack upon the city, on the home of one of the general's advisors—and no one has yet heard from the general himself—oh!"

Priya heard the whisper of Malini's footsteps behind her before she saw her, standing in the door of the northern chamber.

"I'm sorry," Priya said, cursing inwardly. She didn't want to break Pramila's fragile trust so soon. "I left the door open, I'm so—"

"Something is burning," said Malini. "Please. Tell me I'm not dreaming."

A deep slow breath brought an acrid scent to Priya's nose.

Priya went to the edge of the triveni, standing at its lip with nothing but the cracked surface of the Hirana below her to catch her, should she stumble. But she wouldn't stumble again. The Hirana was hers, and she belonged to it in turn. It was changing *for* her.

The temple ground held her as she looked out.

Below them, she saw yellow and orange flame.

Something was indeed burning.

The rebels had attacked.

PRIYA

Priya whirled without thinking, running toward the doors. Down the corridor. Beyond the lit lanterns. Then the guards caught her, shoving her back into the temple, slamming the gates behind them. One swore, fumbling with his blade—if he'd reflexively been trying to knife her, he'd done a piss-poor job of it—and the other held her by the upper arms and murmured urgent nonsense at her. It took a moment for the sound of his voice to become more than white noise.

"...no one can leave the Hirana. Our orders haven't changed. I know you're afraid, but you must be calm."

"I'm calm," Priya forced out, stilling her body. "I'm calm. I won't run again."

The guard released her and she edged back. Away. Walking until the guards and the gates weren't in sight any longer.

She couldn't escape via the doors.

Another hand grabbed her arm. Priya was already on a knife edge. She whirled, pinning the owner of that hand against the wall.

Malini gave a quick exhale. She met Priya's gaze without flinching.

"Let me go," she said. "We've no time."

"Where is Pramila?"

"I don't know. I ran after you. Come *on*. I want to talk to you alone."

In the end, Priya was the one to lead the way, dragging Malini down a rarely used side corridor, and from there into a cloister room. The room was small, intended only for meditation and prayer, but once the door was shut behind them, Priya tried to pace back and forth in the limited space afforded to her anyway. She thought of everyone in the mahal, panic gripping her lungs.

"I need to *go*," said Priya. "I can't remain here. I—"

"The guards stopped you," said Malini. "You think you can get beyond them?"

Priya shook her head, but it was no true answer. She could only think of Sima and Rukh and Bhumika, of the smell of fire, and her own blood seemed to sing a song in her veins: *run to them, run to them, run to them.*

"Priya," Malini said. Her voice was slow, deliberate velvet. "Listen to me. Calm yourself. Do you think you can get beyond them?"

It took a moment for Priya to realize that Malini was not trying to reason with her. She was genuinely asking if Priya could force her way past the guards. Priya's racing thoughts paused. Malini took her by the hands, threading their fingers together, grounding her to stillness.

"I don't want to ask this of you now," Malini said. "I truly don't. I thought perhaps in time...but there won't be a better opportunity, and we must seize it while we can. You could kill the guards, if you wanted to. You could remove Pramila. You could release us both. Couldn't you?"

"You overestimate my power," Priya said carefully. "I'm not— like that."

"You've done so much for me," said Malini. "I know you're attempting to save my life. Do you care for me enough to do more?"

Priya thought of pulling away. She tried to untangle her fingers from Malini's and felt Malini's grip tighten, drawing Priya in closer until there was no distance between them, and Priya was looking up into Malini's face—into the shadow gray of her pleading eyes.

"The guards likely won't obey their normal routine under these circumstances, but they all traveled with me from Parijat. I know them. The one with the thick mustache—he complains that his right knee pains him whenever it rains. And it rained a great deal on the journey here. The youngest of them is better with a long-range weapon than close physical combat. He prefers a chakram or bow if he has a choice. But if you attack his senior first, cut him at the knees, the younger one won't think to retreat, and once he's in close combat with you, you'll find it easier to manage him." Malini's fingers brushed back and forth over her own; a steady, almost hypnotic rhythm. "You can get us out, Priya. Right now, while they're distracted and there is chaos below us...You *can*. And I can help you."

Priya stared back at her. Numbly, she shook her head. She thought of the consequences for the mahal, for Bhumika, if the princess escaped the Hirana. "I...I can't. My lady."

"You don't need to kill them," Malini said quickly, still holding Priya close. "I don't ask that. I only ask you to consider what will happen to me if I stay here. My only hope is beyond the Hirana's walls. You could come with me, Priya." Her voice lowered. "Wherever I go, you could go."

Malini's expression was pleading, her voice was cajoling, wounded—but there was a hardness to her jaw, a desperation in her eyes that was at odds with her tone.

Her hands on Priya's were a light weight, fingers curled. Everything about her was a vulnerable entreaty. So perfectly vulnerable, that Priya could only think of festival plays, of actresses wearing theater masks painted saffron and vermilion, expressions fixed—stricken or joyful, sharp-toothed or soft-mouthed—to match their roles in the tale.

Priya felt as if her racing pulse, quick with panic, tripped over itself for a moment. Frozen, she felt her understanding of the princess—of *this*—shift upon its axis.

She thought of Bhumika's words from the sangam, suddenly. *I must use all the tools in my arsenal*, she'd said.

The princess was a daughter of the empire. The princess was trapped and desperate.

And Priya was...useful.

She'd been a fool.

"And what shall I get in return for helping you escape here?" Priya asked, rage and humiliation surging through her. "Were you hoping I'd risk my life for you just out of the goodness of my heart?" All those gentle touches, all those smiles—Malini's hands on her own, and shared breath that could have been a kiss. All of it, no more than a careful leash placed around Priya's neck, ready to be drawn at the right moment. "Maybe you thought I'd do it for a kiss? Do you really think so little of me?"

An expression flickered across Malini's face, too quick to decipher. "Priya, whatever you think, you're wrong."

"Pramila told me not to trust you. She told me that you make people love you. That you're manipulative."

Malini said nothing.

"You've wasted your energy on me," said Priya. "I'm not capable of what you want."

"You are," Malini said. "Please, Priya. If anyone can help me escape the Hirana, it's you. There's no one but you."

"Of course you think I can," said Priya bitterly. "You saw me after all, with Meena. You watched me kill her and you didn't even look afraid. Don't you know that you should be afraid of me? Don't you know how easily I could kill *you*?" She gripped Malini's hands harder in return, holding her fast. "I have so many reasons to hate you. You, with your imperial blood and your father and brothers who were happy to see Ahiranya's temple children piled onto a pyre and burned." Priya was surprised at the venom in her own voice, the way heat rushed to the surface of her skin, furious and prickling. "I have no reason to help the child of an imperial family that ordered my own family dead. I could break your neck, here and now, and you couldn't stop me. I could fling you from the Hirana. If you think I have the power to kill all the guards, then you know I could just as easily end your life and free myself."

"I'm not afraid of death at your hand," said Malini.

"And why is that?"

Some of the vulnerability faded from Malini's face. Leached away.

"The night you saw me, in my chamber, on the ground—I had convinced Pramila to leave the wine with me. I'd been nice to her. Sweet, biddable. For days. You know something about how that works. She left the wine. And I drank, and drank, and drank. I weighed up my choices. I thought: either I will grow sick enough that she will have to seek help, allowing me access to a physician who I can beg for aid to escape this prison, or I will simply die." Malini's voice trembled a little. "But then I grew afraid, and I flung the wine to the floor. I didn't know what was real any longer. And I did not want to die in a pool of my own vomit, after all."

And then, Priya knew, she had appeared. She remembered Malini's eyes in the dark. The rasp of her voice, her words—*Are you real?*—with a shudder.

"Does that disturb you?" Malini asked. Her voice hardened. "I like you, Priya. But I am afraid that I'm running out of time for the niceties of our relationship. If General Vikram is dead—who knows where my brother will send me next, or what will become of me?"

There was no distance between them and yet somehow Malini took a step forward, tugging her hands free from Priya's. She touched her fingertips to Priya's chin instead, so close to Priya's mouth, her fingers warm and steady, impossible to ignore.

"Kill me or save me," murmured Malini. "But do *something*, Priya. My brother wants me to waste away here, or beg him for the sanctity of an immolation—but I will not. I have been able to do nothing to change my circumstances apart from obtaining you, so please do me the kindness of ending my suffering, one way or another. Surely you're humane enough for that."

Priya wrenched back from Malini's hand.

"If you speak of what I am to anyone," Priya said angrily, "I'll force that needle-flower poison down your throat myself."

"I have never," said Malini, "threatened to tell anyone your secrets, Priya."

"You know nothing of my secrets."

"You know that I do."

"I am not ashamed of wanting you," Priya blurted out, even though she *was* ashamed of wanting Malini, because it made her a foolish love-addled thing unfit for the task her sister had set her. A failure. "But I don't appreciate you using my wants against me, and I won't let you do it anymore. Tell whoever you like that I want you. But if you speak of what you think I am—"

"I told you," Malini cut in. "I haven't threatened to reveal you. I could have long ago, and I have not. I won't."

That pulled a choked laugh from Priya's throat. "How generous of you! But you want to keep me on your side, don't you? Without me, you have no one here. *No one.*"

Malini said nothing to that. The vulnerability was gone from her face, and now her expression was nigh unreadable.

"Hide here from Pramila if you want," Priya added, as she turned. "I'm not going to help you."

"Would you really condemn me for doing what I need to in order to survive?" Malini asked. When Priya didn't answer, Malini said swiftly, "We could make a deal, you and I. There are other things I could offer you in return for your help."

Priya stopped. Turned back. "Like what? You have nothing."

"Tell me what you need and want. Bargain with me. So I am not as tenderhearted and naïve as you thought—so I want to live and I am willing to use you to do it—*so what*? Don't let that anger you, Priya. *Use* that. You will never have this kind of power over a royal of Parijatdvipa again. I am a princess. I know the heartbeat, the innards of the empire. Beyond this prison I have allies waiting for me. You have things you want, Priya. You told me. I know it. Use me."

Priya looked at Malini. At her pale brown, dark-eyed face surrounded by knotted curls, a face thin with sickness, and thought of how much of a fool she'd been to not see that Malini could read her like a book.

"You are useful," said Malini, when Priya continued to stare at her, heart pounding with fury and shame. "What you are—you have use. But so do I, to you."

"I make a good weapon, I suppose," Priya said faintly. She thought of Meena again—of rage, and Meena's body falling, and the smell of fire and cooked flesh that had haunted Priya for years.

Oh, spirits, thought Priya, with a kind of despair. *What am I choosing to turn myself into? What am I becoming? Is remembering myself worth this?*

As if summoned by her thoughts, a new memory came over her. A spill of water on the floor. The smell of ghee and resin in the air. One of her temple sisters turning to her, eyes wide, clutching her own throat. An elder, mouth curled downward, sorrowful, lighting a flame—

She didn't want to remember this.

"Priya." Malini exhaled. "Please."

Priya realized she was shaking.

"I can't," Priya said abruptly. "Not now."

"Priya—"

"Not now."

She left the room abruptly.

She didn't make it very far.

Away from the guttering lantern light, away from Malini, she knelt alone, crouched with her head on her knees. She was shaking.

She needed to know if Bhumika was safe. If the general's mahal—if Rukh and Sima and Gauri, if all those people who made up the mahal—if they were *all* safe.

If she could not go in person, she would take the only way out of the Hirana that she had available to her.

Ragged breaths. One after the other, and the other, winding deeper. Deeper.

She sank back into the sangam. The river water rose to meet her.

23

ASHOK

He always wore a spare vial of the waters around his throat. He touched it now, as they slipped through the forest, the smell of blood in their nostrils, caked in their clothes and their nails. Kritika turned back to look at him for a brief moment. There was a smear of darkness across her cheek.

"Keep moving," he said.

The vial was not hot, not burning with power the way sacred trees burned. But something felt—strange. Within the deathless waters in his blood. Within his skull.

Around him were his fellow rebels, winding through the forest with the familiarity of people born to it. A few wielded long-handled scythes and were clearing the way ahead of the rest of them. This was undisturbed land, untainted by the presence of empire, not even populated by Ahiranyi settlements. There were no shrines to the yaksa, hung in the branches or nailed to the vast trunks of the trees around them. It was no one's territory, and therefore ideal. They needed somewhere to hide. And rest.

They had hit the imperial regime with a strong blow. That was only right, only fair, after what the regent had taken from them. Parijatdvipa wanted to use fear, turning faith into a blade? Then so would Ahiranya.

There was a noise ahead. A thump. The others stopped, and

Ashok gritted his teeth and strode forward. Just like the rest of them, he knew the sound of a falling body when he heard it.

Sarita lay still where she'd collapsed, in a heap of bloodstained clothes and red-brown fingers, her scythe fallen at her side. Even standing above her, Ashok could see that her skin was wet.

When the vial waters were first consumed they brought on an intense rise in physical strength, along with some of the waters' magic. But as the influence of the waters faded, the body would begin to tremble, terribly weakened. After a short time, water and blood together would begin to leave the body, pouring out of the mouth, the ears, the eyes. That was the way a poisoned death began.

This one had taken Sarita fast.

She had drunk two vials, or three, in the time she'd served the rebellion, always struggling to hold at bay the death it brought. She had fought with ferocity in the old lord's haveli—broken a neck or four with nothing but the sheer force of her own strength holding those men still under her hands. And now she was dying. But a little more water would give her time. A little more—

A hand closed around his wrist. Kritika stood at his side.

"You have barely any left," she said in a low voice, so as not to be heard by the others around them. "Three or four vials at most, and who knows when you'll next be able to replenish your supplies? Please, Ashok. Don't do this."

He paused, his hand still on the vial in his pocket, ready to pull it free. Then he released it and kneeled down, placing that same palm gently against Sarita's forehead.

"Sarita," he said gently. "Brave woman. You've done so well."

Her eyes opened, just a little. All whites, the pupils a pinprick of dark, like two bloodied wounds welling up beneath the point of a needle.

"Sarita. Sarita." He repeated her name like a lullaby. His heart bled inside him at the sight of her. What a waste. "Does it hurt?"

Her mouth shaped a word, soundless. *Yes.*

"Kritika," he said. "Will you..."

"Yes," she told him, sadly. She gripped his shoulders, urging him up. "It will be done."

He stood and walked away.

He heard the scythe being lifted. A snap. Then nothing.

In the silence of the moment, with nothing to disturb him but the sounds of mortal breaths around him, the hum of insects and the call of birds among the trees, he finally understood what had disturbed him so. What called in his blood.

There was a voice in the sangam crying out his name.

He walked a little farther, until he found a tree old enough and large enough to lean against. It cradled him.

The follower closest to him saw him sit and nodded gravely. Ashok knew, without further confirmation, that no one would disturb him now, unless the general's soldiers found them. And that he considered unlikely.

He closed his eyes. Breathed. Breathed.

His sister had howled for him in the sangam, and he had come. She was a shadow kneeling in swift running water. She raised her head the moment he appeared.

"What did you do?" she asked him instantly.

"You saw the flames, then."

"Of course I did. Ashok. Why?"

"Justice," he said simply. "You think there shouldn't be consequences for burning women alive and crushing men's skulls? Come on now, Priya."

"Did you kill General Vikram?"

That question stopped him short.

"Do you really care?"

"I care because of what his death would mean," she bit out.

"I see. You care because of Bhumika." He drew closer to her. "No. I didn't kill him. I did consider it," he confessed, thinking of the regent's terrified face with no small pleasure. "But some things are not meant to be. I settled for Lord Iskar and his family instead."

"Ashok."

"The deaths of our people had to be repaid," he said calmly. She was still so naïve. She didn't understand the way the world worked, or the price power demanded. Not as he did. "And now they have been. Lord Iskar served the regent ably, didn't he? A great financial mind. Without him, Vikram will never be able to bring the other lords to heel. No one will know how to get anything done. Maybe when they're all bickering as their revenue streams crumble around them, they will remember that the Ahiranyi spirit isn't to be trifled with."

"You're escalating," said Priya. "You're going to make everything so much worse. The general is going to kill so many people to compensate for this, Ashok."

"*He* was the one who escalated," Ashok said. "All those men and women put to death for—what? An 'attack' in which no one died but Meena? Your regent is a fool, or his master is a fool. The emperor needs to understand that they can't take our language, ban our stories, let us starve, and then outright kill us, without consequences. I don't regret it, Priya. And neither should you."

"You'll see Ahiranya bathed in blood, between you." She sounded so much like Bhumika then—so disapproving and prim—that he could have laughed.

Instead, he kneeled down, mirroring her.

"Have you found the way to the deathless waters, Pri? If you really want things to be less bloody, that's what you need to do."

"If you're going to lie to me, at least do me the service of making it convincing," Priya scoffed. "If I give you the deathless waters you'll use them to build an army, to murder, to—"

"—live," he finished. "I need the deathless waters to live."

The blow struck, as he knew it would. He could hear it in the weight of her silence.

"It's like you're holding a knife to your own throat to make me obey," she said finally. "Everything you say feels like a threat."

"The truth isn't a threat," he said gently. "Pri, I never wanted this for you. I set Meena on this task for a purpose. But you're my only hope now. And I'm not lying. It will be less bloody, if my followers and I have the kind of strength we need to make a strike that snaps Parijatdvipa's control of Ahiranya at the joints."

In truth, they needed the waters if they wanted to be sure of success. He had plans. He knew exactly who needed to die to bring Parijatdvipa's imperial power to its knees. He'd spent a long time considering. Every murder he and his followers made was intended to weaken Parijatdvipa's control and pluck the weeds of imperial power out at their deepest roots. "You know what they say: in killing, a single blow of a scythe is cleaner than a dozen from the mace."

With the deathless waters they could be the scythe: stronger than their limited numbers and cobbled together, disparate funds would allow. They could kill accurately and swiftly, cleansing Ahiranya in one fell swoop.

Without the waters, there was little chance of success. They would have to be brutal. They would have to burn and gut Ahiranya, killing their own in order to destroy the empire. There would be no clean plucking of weeds: This would be the kind of war that set whole fields of crops alight, leaving nothing but ash and hunger in its wake. And even then—even after paying in Ahiranyi blood—there would be no guarantee of success. No promise that Ahiranya would be free.

Only Priya could find the waters. Only Priya could coax the way from the Hirana, and bring Ashok and his followers the strength they needed to succeed. Only her.

Priya reached for him, then paused. She drew her hand back reluctantly. Lowered it into the confluence of waters.

"I'm not sure I can give you what you need," she said finally. There was something vulnerable—almost a question—in her voice. "I'm not sure I can give you the waters. And I'm not sure I can give them to myself either."

"You agree with Bhumika now, then? You want to bow and scrape before the Parijati for what little they deign to give us? You no longer want us to have what is ours by right?"

"What will you do with that right, Ashok? What *are* you doing?" she demanded. "What are we meant to be?"

"We could do so much good, Priya," he told her sincerely. "The thrice-born could manipulate the rot, you know. It was so new then—as were we—but they could control it. You may not like my methods. You don't have to. But once we rule Ahiranya, we can make our country better. We can see our people put first, fed and cared for as a priority, for once. We can save our culture, our history. Perhaps even end the rot entirely."

"By becoming monsters?" Priya whispered. "By turning into weapons?"

Yes.

"You've killed too," he said. "There's no shame in being strong enough to take what is rightfully yours."

"Maybe there should be," she said. Another hesitation. Then the words unfurled out of her. "I remember more. The Hirana is beginning to respond to me. Sometimes I smell smoke and it's as if it's choking me. I hear screams. I..."

She looked at him, this shadow of her, who was only beginning to remember what he could never forget. "Ashok, can you promise me you won't...that you'll only do as much as you need to do, to see Ahiranya free? That you won't kill every Parijati on our land? I know your anger," she told him. "I feel it. And your grief. And your—hunger for something better. But can you promise me you won't drown Ahiranya in blood?"

"I promise to do what is best for Ahiranya."

"That isn't an answer," she said.

"I promise to make us what we once were."

"That still isn't an answer," Priya whispered. "Ashok. Brother. You cannot be trusted with the kind of power we once had."

Her words were like a slow knife, paring the skin from his ribs.

"I raised you," he managed to say around the pain of her condemnation.

"I know."

"When we were hungry, when we had nothing, I gave you

what little food we had. I stayed up with a dagger in my hand when you slept on the street so you wouldn't be harmed. In the Hirana I saved your life."

"I *know*," she choked out. "Ashok. I know."

But she said nothing more.

He thought of waking in the husk of the tree, knowing that Meena was dead. Knowing that his own weakness had left the rebellion without a spy, without a valuable weapon in its hands.

He had not cultivated Priya into a weapon. He had let her go to Bhumika. And this was how she thanked him?

"There is so much you don't remember of our childhood, Priya. But do you remember how we were trained when we were children?"

Silence. Then she said, "I remember pain."

"It was how we were taught to be strong. How we were all taught to be strong enough to survive, and to rule. Pain can be a loving teacher. Spirits know I've had my fill of it."

But you, he thought. *Have you?*

She was too weak, his sister. Too unaware of what she should have been.

"Do you know why we are nothing but shadows in the sangam?" he asked her then. "Have you ever questioned it?"

"No," she said.

"Some of us who were older—we spoke of it. All our gifts are a reflection of the powers the yaksa possessed. Even this. It was the yaksa who traveled the cosmic rivers, once, and came to our world. When we come here, I believe it's only the yaksa part of us that moves." He curled his hand to a fist, placing it against her collarbone, above her heart. "When you taste the deathless waters, they carve out a place for the gifts of the yaksa inside you. The power of the yaksa is a cuckoo in the nest of your body. But worse still, you convince yourself it *is* you. It's only when the power fades that you realize a part of you has been erased."

"You're not making any sense," she told him. But she was listening.

"The part of you that stands here is the part of you that isn't human," he told her. "The part of you that stands here is the part the deathless waters carved out, gutted and hollowed to make a space for power.

"You don't feel it day in and day out, but I do. Every time I drink the waters a new part of me is torn away." He steeled himself to do what was necessary. To teach her. "You want to know what we are, Priya? Here. Let me show you."

She realized a moment too late. Once, she would have known far more quickly—would have dodged or run or used her teeth. Life in the mahal had left her slow. But as it was, she could do nothing, before the shadow of his fist forced itself into her chest, the dark smoke of her unspooling.

He tightened his fist, close around where her heart should have been. And tightened, and *twisted*.

She screamed, the shadow of her a shimmer of agony.

"I know that it hurts," he said roughly. "I know. This is how I feel all the time. Scoured and twisted and—inhuman, Priya. This is our inheritance."

Like a hole through the heart, he thought. *Like your soul is a decayed structure, crumbling, the light pouring through you.*

There was something ugly and sweet about the feeling that ran through him in response to her pain. It was, he reasoned, the satisfaction of watching a lesson being learned.

"My will is stronger than yours, Pri. It always was. I saved your life time and time again, and now I tell you: Save mine. Your debt is due. Or you condemn me to die feeling like *this*.

"I want to make this ugliness in us worth something, Pri," he told her. "I want us to use it for something greater. For something good. For Ahiranya as it should be, free of the empire. For our *home*."

He wrenched his hand back. Darkness fell into the water from her shadowy form, bursting into black flowers before withering away. Her hands moved, fluttered, as if she wanted to touch her chest but didn't dare.

"You could have been kinder," she choked out. "You of all people, who suffered what I suffered—I thought I could trust you to be my brother."

He shook his head.

"Family don't have a duty to be kind to you. They have a duty to make you better. Stronger. I am being true to our family. Right now, Pri. And always."

His voice became more tender.

"Find the deathless waters. Remember who you are and be strong, Priya." And then, when she refused to look at him, when her head remained lowered, he said, "Priya. You had to know."

He reached for her but she stumbled back from him—rejected him, with a savage noise that was not words, only feeling. She flung herself back into the water, unspooling into nothing. Running from him, and from the truth.

Distantly, he felt the flicker of Bhumika. Of one of his rebels, the scant few left who'd drunk the waters to fight at his side. He closed his eyes and lowered his own face beneath the rivers.

24

PRIYA

Flung back into her body. A moment when she felt the waters of flesh and immortality and soul rising in her throat choking her and she grasped her own neck gasping, gasping. Her flesh burned—she did not know where the earth began or the sky ended, she did not know the way up, *out*. It was drowning, this feeling, or something so close to it that it did not matter if water surrounded her or if part of her lay ensnared in the sangam still, rended by Ashok's fury.

"Priya." A voice. "Are you injured? Speak to me. *Quietly*."

Priya's eyes cracked open. Malini knelt by her. She was not once-born or twice- or thrice-born: She was entirely mortal, gaze focused on Priya, her lips pressed tightly together. Priya was no longer in the sangam, then, and Ashok was not here. He could not harm her.

Ashok had tried to harm her.

Her hand went to her chest. He *had* harmed her. The place where he had hurt her was like a burning star within her center, and she could not breathe around it.

"Priya," Malini said again. Her voice was calm, utterly calm, but it was a serenity that Malini wore like armor. Her eyes held Priya's steadily. "You need to stop this."

Stop...?

It was only then that Priya realized they were surrounded by moss and flowers, vines twisting across the stone of the walls, unfurling through the cracks. In fact, the stone almost seemed to have moved, reshaping itself to let the greenery twine around it.

"Pramila," she gasped. "If she sees—"

"I don't know where she is," said Malini, "or when she will return, and that is why you must be *quiet*."

"I'm sorry," Priya gasped out, even though she had nothing to be sorry for, and Malini had *everything*. She tried to concentrate, to lift her head, but she could feel Ashok's fury as though his fist were still in her chest. She breathed—and faded into blackness.

Malini's face, cold and resolute, was the last thing she saw.

25

MALINI

The first time Malini learned how to hold a knife was also the day she learned how to weep.

She and Narina were playing in her mother's flower garden, profuse with both lilies and water lotuses in small ponds, zinnia and hibiscus. They were being Dwarali merchants, crossing the borders of Parijatdvipa into the dangerous wildernesses of nomadic Babure and Jagatay territory. For that, they'd needed thick cloaks—for some reason, Narina was insistent that merchants always wore thick cloaks—but they also needed weaponry.

"To protect our wares," Narina explained.

"I would expect we'd have guards to protect our wares," Malini had said.

"Not everyone has guards, Malini," Narina huffed.

"I see," said Malini. "We're not very good merchants, then. Or we'd be able to afford guards, wouldn't we?"

Alori gave a small sigh.

"Don't argue, please," she said. "Anyway, I know where we can get weapons."

Alori was the only daughter of the king of Alor, who had enough sons to constitute his own small army. Alori was quiet and small and had a gift for vanishing from view, fading into insignificance. But her quiet wasn't timidity, and she guided Narina and Malini confidently to the room where the youngest of her nameless brothers slept. On the way through the corridors, they could hear the sound of thudding wood and the clang of chains below. The sound was assurance enough that the imperial princes—Malini's brothers—and their attendant lords were busy sparring in the practice yard.

The girls went into the room and rooted through the trunk at the foot of Alori's brother's bed. He didn't keep his mace or his saber or any of his more impressive weapons in the room. But there were twin katara, sheathed in leather at the bottom of his trunk, and two daggers with carvings of beady-eyed fish at the hilts. It was only as they were leaving the room that Malini had the sudden thought to look beneath the mattress. That was where she stored her own treasures, and her instinct rewarded her when she grasped a simple knife. It wasn't a fine enough thing to be a dagger. There was no sinuous curve to the blade or decoration on the hilt. It was plain and brutal and sharp. Malini pocketed it.

They raced back to the garden, where they collapsed into fits of laughter.

It was Alori who offered to show Malini how to use the knife.

"My brothers taught me," she said. "Here, this is how to hold it."

There was a trick to holding a proper blade. Confidence, a shape to the grip. Malini extended the knife in front of her and felt a strange, blazing feeling unfold in her chest. She smiled.

"Let's protect our wares," she said.

She was pretending to be a Babure bandit, standing on the edge of a high rockery, waving the knife in front of her, when Narina and Alori—standing below her, yelling up at her valiantly—fell suddenly silent.

Malini was a sensible child. She lowered the knife to her side and straightened. Turned. Behind her, she saw a man's figure rising, limned to shadow by sunlight. But she knew the shape of those shoulders; that turban, with pearls around the edge and a single peacock feather stitched to the crown. The slippers of gold and richly dyed vermilion on his feet.

Chandra stood before her. He was young, only a few years older than her. But he already had a hardness around the eyes, a stony quality of someone furious with his lot in life. He looked down at her with disdain, and Malini was suddenly conscious of her uncovered hair, her bare and dirty feet. Her weapon.

"Malini," he said. "Where did you get the knife?"

Malini said nothing. Her palms were hot.

"I heard you in the corridor," he said, approaching her. "Oh, you thought you'd gone unseen, I know. But I wasn't in the practice yard with the others. I was praying at the family altar. Speaking with the high priest."

"About what?" Malini asked.

Perhaps if she pretended that nothing was amiss—that she couldn't see the curl of his lip, the narrowness of his eyes—his anger would melt away. Such wild hopes, she had.

Somehow his mouth thinned further.

"Give it to me," he said.

Alori had told her, with a laugh, how a jab beneath the hollow of the ribs could kill a man. How she could cut a tendon. How she could slice a throat.

She'd said it all mildly, easily. Those were all things Alori's brothers had revealed to her, as if a girl had equal right to weapons and knowledge, as if they expected her to spill blood by her own hands.

Chandra had taught her how fear felt. And shame. The way they could settle in your stomach, heavy as a stone. How they could alter your nature to something bidden and chained.

Malini thought of all the ways a knife could be used to kill or maim, her palm itching with bloodlust. Then she offered it blade first to her brother. Chandra took it.

"What did I tell you," he said, "the last time you behaved improperly?"

"I'm sorry," Malini said.

"Bow your head," he replied, as if he hadn't heard her.

He gripped her by her hair.

And then he began to cut.

"I told you," he said, sawing through her braid, his other hand roughly gripping her roots, "that women are a reflection of the mothers of flame. You were born to be holy, Malini. I told you if you refuse to behave properly, you'll have to *learn*."

Malini could see Narina right near them, her face red, her hands in fists. Alori had moved beneath the cover of the trees and was utterly still. Watching.

She'd never forget the look on her friends' faces.

She tried to shove him away—shoved hard, with both hands. He'd merely wrenched her head back and cut harder. She'd felt a piercing pain. He'd cut her flesh. There was a sting, and the heat of blood trailing down her skin.

She'd felt it then, as she'd feel it many times over, in the years that followed: the dizzying sense that when he hacked at her hair he wanted to hack her neck clean too. That hurting her made him love her more intensely and want to hurt her all the more intensely too; as if destroying her was the only way to keep her pure.

She began to weep, then. She wept because fighting had not helped, and she couldn't bring herself to beg. And his cutting gentled; as if her tears were a submission, a sign of defeat, and so he could afford to be kind to her. As if this was what he'd wanted all along.

She learned. Tears were a weapon of a kind, even if they made her fury smolder and rot and writhe inside her.

"Chandra," said a voice. And her brother's blade paused.

Malini's eldest brother, Aditya, stood on the veranda to the garden. He was still dressed for the practice yard, bare-chested in nothing but a dhoti, no turban to hide his sweat-slicked hair. He crossed the garden, his tread quick. Behind him, in the shadows, stood their mother. Her pallu was drawn over her face, her head lowered.

When Malini saw him she cried all the more furiously, great heaving sobs even as her heart stayed spiteful and furious inside her.

"Leave her," said Aditya. He sounded tired.

"She had a weapon. A woman should know better."

"She is a child. Let Mother deal with her discipline."

"Mother would ruin her if she could," Chandra muttered. "The priests say—"

"I don't care what the priests say," Aditya said. "Come with me, Malini."

She didn't have to be told twice. She ran to his side.

Aditya guided her to the veranda. After a moment, Narina and Alori followed.

"No one else thinks like he does, little dove," Aditya said gently. He lightly brushed the shorn ends of her hair. "This is a more enlightened time. But you've no need for a knife. You have guards enough to protect you, and two brothers who love you."

"And who will protect me from my brothers?" Malini asked.

"Chandra didn't really want to hurt you."

Malini knew Aditya was wrong. Chandra had wanted to. And he'd managed to.

But Aditya wouldn't understand, if she tried to explain it, so she didn't.

That night, when she and Narina and Alori had curled up like pups under one blanket, Alori tucked a sheathed blade between them. Another one of her brother's knives.

"He wants us to have it," Alori said. And: "He's sorry, Malini."

But no prince of Alor was responsible for Malini's pain.

She learned that day to turn to a carapace of meekness rather than showing the true mettle of her fury. She learned, when Chandra hacked her hair, that there was a way she was expected to be, and if she failed to be it, there would be a price to pay.

Only her mother knew what she was about. Once her mother sat beside her on the bench swing in the same garden where Malini had learned her lesson.

"I am going to tutor you and your girls," her mother said, after a long silence. "It's high time you learned. The philosophy of military strategy and leadership, the teachings of the first mothers—these are things a princess should know of."

Malini was silent. She had never been given the impression by anyone, not least her subdued mother, that such knowledge was for princesses.

"When I was a girl, my father arranged for a female sage to educate me," her mother continued. "I will try to provide the same to you, my garland child, but until that day, I can give you what I have. Such things will help you survive as a daughter of Parijat. A blossom with a thorn heart."

"I am not thorny," Malini said. "I *cried*."

"Weeping does not make you any less yourself," her mother replied. She touched her fingertips to Malini's shorn hair. "Be careful with your tears," her mother added, in a voice of cultivated restraint. "They're blood of the spirit. Weep too much, and it will wear you thin, until your soul is like a bruised flower."

Her mother had been wrong, though. Weep enough, and your nature becomes like stone, battered by water until it is smooth and impervious to hurt. Use tears as a tool for long enough, and you will forget what real grief feels like.

That was some small mercy, at least.

The walls were breathing. When she'd left the cloister room, slow in the guttering dark, she'd seen vines force their way through the walls, moss unfurl through the spiderweb cracks in the floor. Now those roots and leaves pulsed along with Priya's breath. Priya lay unconscious on the floor. Malini could see her eyelids flicker, restless, but never quite opening.

The catlike tilt of her eyes; the crooked nose and the sharpness of her bones. You couldn't dress this one and make a highborn woman out of her. She was unlovely and strong. She was exactly what Malini needed. Malini had known that, the first moment she'd laid eyes on her through the lattice in the dark.

She'd been sure of it when she'd heard screams from across the corridor, pressed her hand to her cell door, and felt the lock release as if it had been waiting for her touch. When she'd slipped free and watched Priya take the rebel's life.

Priya was a possibility, a hope. The only one Malini had.

"Priya. Wake up," Malini said firmly. She looked beyond the vines to the end of the corridor. All it would take was one guard seeking her here—or mothers forbid, Pramila turning the corner.

"Priya. *Wake.*"

With a groan, Priya opened her eyes once more.

Malini's own eyes were dry. She thought of feigning tears again, of being soft and softening Priya in turn.

But no. She'd failed to play the game adequately. The fire below had made her good sense lapse, and she'd revealed herself too quickly. All that carefully cultivated trust, the vulnerabilities she'd revealed—all of it, wasted.

Either she'd need to find a new ploy to win Priya, to snare her into service, or she would have to resort to honesty.

But first...

"Priya," she said. "Put an end to this. Your—magic."

"I'm *trying.*"

She watched the rise and fall of Priya's chest, the way her hands curled as she rose up onto her elbows.

"What happened to you?" Malini murmured.

"Stop talking," Priya said, "and let me think."

Priya's gaze was distant, fixed on a point far beyond Malini. She breathed slowly, deeply. Malini remained silent and kneeling. She did not touch the green around her—only watched as it receded, withering back into the floor and walls.

Priya looked down at her own hands with wonder and fear. "Soil and sky," she whispered. "It worked."

Then Priya raised her head, pushed herself up straight, and looked at Malini. Her expression was ugly—thin-lipped, jaw tight, narrow-eyed. Priya looked like she'd happily choke the life out of her.

"I have long known that I can't trust anyone," Priya said. "Known how the world is. But *you.* I was foolish about you. I thought I understood a little of what you were. I watched you sicken. And weep. And I was afraid I'd have to watch you die. But

everything you said and did...it was all a lie, wasn't it?" Priya
shook her head furiously and held a hand before her. "No, don't
answer. I know it was a lie."

I did not lie, Malini thought. She knew how to lie, of course.
She did so often. But the value of a truth, carefully carved to meet
the needs of her audience, was much greater, and far more difficult to disprove.

She liked Priya. Liked the steady grip of her arms; the way
muscle dipped and curved just so; the way she smiled, always
oddly guarded, no more than a flash of white teeth, a dimple
etched into one cheek.

Malini did not know how Priya's look of fury and betrayal
made her feel. There was a pain in her chest that reminded her of
the sensation of eating a fresh green chili whole when she was a
small girl, purely because her nursemaid had told her not to—a
pain throbbing and yet intensely sweet. She was not sure if she
hated it or hungered for more of it.

I do not want you to hate me, she thought. *I want you to like me.
It's absurd, but why else would I ask you to imagine me in my finest
saris? Why else would I ask you to imagine me beautiful?*

This truth could do her no favors. And she needed Priya.

"You should listen to what I have to offer," Malini said again,
instead. "Even if you will not help me escape—you should listen."

"With respect," Priya said, voice cutting, "I don't have to listen
to you. You have nothing."

Priya was right. Everything Malini had fostered in her time
at court—a garden of loyal highborn women and kings and
lords and princes, a network of whispers to feed her the nectar
of knowledge—was gone, withered or scoured by fire or simply
placed beyond her reach. Even her mind was not what it should
have been, thanks to the needle-flower poison. She had nothing
and no one. She could only offer Priya favors and debts she would
hopefully be able to pay one day.

She leaned forward, pressing a hand to the cool ground that
had been covered with moss. She did not play any game that Priya

would reject. Instead she met Priya's eyes and thought, *I am a highborn daughter of Parijat, I have outlived the sisters of my heart, I have won men to my cause. I still live, despite faith and flame.*

You will listen to me. I command it.

She poured the thought into every inch of her own limbs: into the tilt of her neck, the firmness of her hand on the ground, the proud jut of her shoulders.

It was enough to hold Priya fast for a moment. Just enough.

"You have little love for the Parijati, I know," Malini said. "But you do love Ahiranya. And you know that Emperor Chandra will soon remove your regent."

"What do I care if he does?"

"You want one of his cronies lording over your country? A zealous believer in the unity of Parijatdvipa under the one flame of faith? Whatever you may think of General Vikram, he's no idealist. Idealists are by far the most dangerous rulers."

What was she doing, trying to explain politics to a maidservant?

But Priya is no simple maid, a voice whispered in her head. It sounded like her own voice from—before. Before she had drunk poison day in and out and her thoughts had begun to fray within her mind. It was a sweet voice, speaking cultured court Dvipan with a cadence like a boat skimming deep, deep waters. *She is a temple child, isn't she? She has more power in one finger than you possess in your entire body. You do not know what she knows. You do not know what she can do.*

"What harm," Malini asked, "is there in listening to me?"

Priya hesitated. There was a sound somewhere in the Hirana. A name was being shouted. Priya's mouth firmed, and she took Malini by the elbow, hauling them both to their feet.

"Harm enough," said Priya. "But I'll do it anyway, I suppose."

The bitterness in Priya's voice...ah, if Malini were one to indulge in self-hate, she would have felt it then. There was something so blazingly soft about Priya's heart. She had never seen the like of it before. When Priya had spoken of making an offering of coconut and flowers to the Ahiranyi spirits, when she had spoken of grieving her dead, Malini had been sure she could *feel* that heart in her hands: a muscle as fragile as an egg with a world inside it, compassion flowing from it as terrible and nourishing as lifeblood.

But Malini was not one for regrets, so she felt nothing.

Pramila was not even angry. Priya glibly concocted a story of how Malini had raced away in fear and panic and Priya had sought her out, calmed her, and brought her back as soon as she could—a blatant untruth, but one Pramila was ready to believe. The older woman had been crying, and trembled still. Once she was assured that Malini was safe, she turned away and closed herself into her own room. To weep more, Malini assumed.

She and Priya were not the only ones with terrible memories of fire, after all.

Priya moved restlessly around the room as Malini sat still upon the charpoy, cross-legged, her spine straight. Without preamble Malini said, "My brother wanted me dead because I tried to arrange for our elder brother to take the throne from him."

Priya stopped pacing.

"Aditya left the faith," Malini added. She did not know what Priya knew, or did not know, about Parijati politics. Best to tell her everything. "He had a vision and became a priest of the nameless god. He could not do that and remain crown prince of Parijatdvipa. He could not be emperor. And so we were left with Chandra. But I knew in my soul Aditya should rule. I knew he would be so much better at it than Chandra, because he was so much better than Chandra in every way. And I knew his status as my father's firstborn—and his nature—would give him the backing of Parijatdvipa's nations. So I sought those kings and princes out, and cultivated them. I ensured their support. Then Chandra discovered my intent."

"You told me you were impure," Priya said. Flung the words out as if they were an accusation.

Impure. Yes, Malini had implied it—that her wants had been the thing that condemned her. It was not...untrue. But Malini had always hidden her desires well. If Chandra had known her true nature, her otherness, the fact that she preferred women to men, perhaps she would have ended up on the pyre sooner. But he had not known.

"I am," she said simply. Watched the way Priya looked at her—the flinch of her, the disbelief. "But it was what he called treason that brought me here."

"And was it not treason, to try to depose the emperor?"

"If I had succeeded, it would not have been," Malini said. "And I may still achieve my aim. The kingdoms of Parijatdvipa do not forget the Age of Flowers, or the sacrifice of the mothers. They made a vow to our bloodline, to unite around the rule of a son of Divyanshi's line. By their honor, they will not break it. But Chandra's vision places them not at his side but beneath his feet. I have offered them an alternative that provides them the status he wants to take from them. No more."

No more. As if building a coup against the emperor of Parijatdvipa, grand empire of city-states and forests and seas, were a small matter and nothing of consequence. It was a thing she had worked herself bloody for—risked *everything* for. And she had lost so much in the process. Her heart sisters, her Narina and Alori. Her standing at court. Her freedom. And her health and her mind, slipping from her, bit by bit. If Chandra had his way, her efforts to depose him would also cost her life.

"And you truly think this—this feckless brother who left your empire in the hands of someone everyone hates is fit to rule?"

Malini had to work to not flinch. She thought of Aditya—his morality, his goodness, the way he looked at her with fondness. Feckless, yes. She couldn't deny what he was. But he was a better man than Chandra. He had never held a knife to her. Never tried to burn her alive.

It was not, admittedly, a high standard to judge Aditya by. But ah, by the mothers, if the vow between the nations required a male scion of Divyanshi on the throne of Parijatdvipa, who else was there but him?

"Let me simply say, the men of my family have a problem with overindulgence in religion. But Aditya is still a good man. And Chandra is not."

"What makes him a bad man?" Priya asked.

Malini swallowed. "Is it not evidence enough, that he burns women? That he wants to burn me. He is—driven." She would not tell Priya about her childhood. All the years of creeping, terror, that no one had seemed to see or understand. She would not talk about all the Srugani and Dwarali, Saketans and Alorans he had angered, long before he even had the opportunity to sit upon the throne. "Chandra is a man with a vision of what the world should be. It's a horrible vision. And he will cut the world bloody to make it fit."

Something flickered in Priya's eyes.

Malini pressed on. "Chandra will destroy Ahiranya as you know it," she said. "But Aditya would not. And in return for you helping me...I can ask him for more than you have. More than this."

"Tell me."

"The same power all city-states of Parijatdvipa possess," she said. "Your own rulers. Places at court, to assist in the administration of the empire. A level of freedom, within the empire's hands."

"You can't promise me that," Priya said immediately. Her eyes were wide.

"Aditya has strong support," Malini countered. "And he has the element of surprise. Chandra does not know what forces have been amassed against him. He does not even know where Aditya is. He only knows that *I* betrayed him, stirring up ill feeling against his reign. I, and my ladies-in-waiting. And what could I, his whimpering child of a sister with her two simpering women, do to truly compromise his throne?"

"All that," said Priya. "For all that, what do you want? To no longer be poisoned? To be released from the Hirana? I won't free you. Not when it would put the regent's household in immediate danger. You need to ask for something else."

"I want to be free," Malini said. "You know that." She folded the want away. Let it sink, deep down. "But there are other things I need. I can't escape the Hirana, but—will your gifts allow you to?"

"Perhaps," Priya said. Guarded.

That was as good as a yes.

"A man loyal to me waits in Hiranaprastha," said Malini. Or so she hoped. "He waits for word from me. All I ask in return for Ahiranya's future is for you to take him a message and give me his response."

"What kind of message?"

"If you will not free me, then he will try to find a way," Malini said. "A quiet way that does not expose our plans. If there is one. And if not..." Her hands twisted, curling into fists. "Then I will be grateful to know how business proceeds, and to send word to Aditya."

Priya was very still. Malini looked at her, weighing up the tension of her body, the turn of her head, and wondered how close she was to breaking.

"You spoke of hating those with imperial blood," murmured Malini. "You spoke of your loved ones burning. Well, I have lost people I love to the pyre, too. At my brother's orders. Let us see him off the throne together, Priya."

There was an openness, a painful openness to Priya's face at that. Wide-eyed, mouth parting for words she couldn't speak. It faded, after a moment, leaving nothing but determination in its place.

"If I do this—if I help you—then we're not going to be mistress and servant," Priya said slowly. "Outside of here you may be the imperial princess and I may be nothing, but here I'm something useful. I have something you need. And I will not be your tool or your weapon. I will be your equal. Do we have an agreement?"

Priya hated being belittled. Priya hated not being seen. Hated being made small. Malini had seen it in her when Pramila had hit Priya—when a black, calculating look had flickered, just for a moment, through Priya's eyes.

It was lucky, then, that it was always so easy to meet Priya's gaze. To look into that face and give her what she wanted, simply by allowing herself to be honest. Not having to manipulate Priya felt like a small blessing.

"You are immensely powerful," Malini told her. "And if you choose to believe I am manipulating you, or not—please believe this: I am telling you the truth when I say I have needed a friend. And you have been—very kind." Ah, she would miss that kindness. "I must have your title, then. What would you be called? An elder?"

"Just Priya," she said curtly. "As you already call me."

"Then I must be just Malini to you, in return."

"Fine. We have a bargain," said Priya, and Malini's heart soared even as her stomach knotted. Bargains, and vows upon bargains. There would be no end to it.

"Now. *Malini.* Tell me about this man, and where I may find him."

26

BHUMIKA

She learned of the fire when the conches sounded. Someone had attacked Lord Iskar's haveli, a captain told her, when he came with extra soldiers to guard her manse. But he knew no more than that.

She waited in her rose palace to see if anything—anyone—would attack the mahal too. She had no idea if her husband was alive. She could only sit, and think, and force herself to remain calm.

The most vulnerable members of the mahal joined her: the youngest and oldest maidservants, a few children, and the handful of rot-riven who served quietly in her household. They stood at the very edge of the room, in shadow, as the children sniffled through tears and the maidservants stood in stoic silence.

Among the rot-riven, she saw the boy Priya had brought into the household. Khalida had *not* been happy when Bhumika had allowed the boy to have a position. But the boy had not caused any trouble since. No complaints had been brought to Khalida or, by extension, to Bhumika herself. Bhumika had, in fact, thought little of him since allowing his employment.

She thought of him now. It was easier to look at him—his hunched shoulders and his lowered chin, the way he held himself small and alert in the exact way Priya had, when Bhumika had first brought her home—than it was to contemplate what could be happening beyond her manse's walls.

"Come here, boy," she said, beckoning lightly to him.

He approached slowly, then stopped and sketched out an awk-ward bow. He was dressed in a serviceable tunic and dhoti, the kind of clothing given to any servant of the mahal, but the shawl he wore over it was dirty, frayed at the edges.

"Your shawl is filthy," she said. "Do you have nothing else?"

He shook his head. "No, my lady," he said, his voice a croak of nervousness.

"Did you ask?"

He shook his head once more.

She glanced over at Khalida, who communicated—by the arch of an eyebrow and a slight shake of her head—that the boy had not requested a new shawl or asked for help of any kind.

"If you could, Khalida," Bhumika said.

"My lady?"

"My spare brown shawl," she said. "Please."

Khalida brought the shawl over. It was plain, but well made from very fine and sturdy wool. It would keep him warm with-out showing stains easily. She placed it over his shoulders, telling him so.

She realized he was shaking.

"Rukh," she said, and he startled. "There is no need to fear," she told him gently. "We are at the heart of the mahal, and well protected. All will be well. You will be well."

The boy nodded slowly, not meeting her eyes. He wrapped the shawl tighter around himself, touching the cloth as if it were pre-cious, priceless. More worthy than his own skin.

A guard rapped on the doors and strode in.

"My lady," he said. "He's here."

Bhumika rose as swiftly as she could, which was not half as swiftly as she would have liked.

"Take me to him," she said.

Vikram was lying on the bed in his private chambers, his tunic removed. A physician was rebandaging a fresh wound in his side, a cut that was deep and bloody. He looked up at her and Bhumika exhaled, a wordless noise of relief and of horror. "Husband," she said, and moved to sit by his side. Vikram took her hand in his own. He smelled of smoke and blood.

"I am glad," he said brokenly, "so glad you were not there."

He told her everything. Lord Iskar had been celebrating the birth of his son. It had been a beautiful event. Then the rebels had attacked.

"And Lord Santosh?" she asked.

"Unharmed," he said. "He insisted on leading a force into the city to search for the rebels." His jaw tightened visibly with frustration and pain. "I tried to stop him, but my wound hindered me."

"Were the rebels found?" she asked. But that was not what she really wanted to know. What had Santosh done in the city, with no oversight from her husband? How many innocent bystanders had he injured? How many homes and businesses had he damaged? How much destruction had followed in his wake? Frustration and anger gripped her at the reality that her injured husband could not lead the charge; that Santosh was accordingly gaining power more swiftly than she had even expected he would.

"I don't know. I have sent men to follow him. I'll have news of the damage soon enough," Vikram said grimly. "But for now, I remain in ignorance. I could not leave. I could not follow him. I remained with Lord Iskar's body after—his wife..." He swallowed spasmodically. "There was so much blood." His voice was choked. "Forgive me. I shouldn't speak of this to you."

"Lord Iskar is dead?" Bhumika knew her horror had bled into her voice once more.

"Yes."

"And his wife?"

"Yes. Among others. Yes."

She made appropriately soothing sounds of comfort, brushing her thumb over his hand, even as her mind raced.

She thought of Ashok with fury.

"What happens now?" She kept her voice low. She tried to

sound as if she feared for Vikram specifically, and not for anyone or anything else.

"Lord Santosh is already using this tragedy as an opportunity to increase his influence," said Vikram. "And the emperor...the emperor will want what he always wants."

"I see," Bhumika said. "If that is the way of things...what must you do, husband?"

"I will remind Santosh that he is not the regent of Ahiranya. Until the emperor names him as such, that title is mine." His voice was hard. "I will maintain my rule. I will kill the rebels. Every masked one of them. And if the emperor demands that women be burned..." An exhale, pained. "I will do what I must. We will have peace."

This is not how you quell conflict, thought Bhumika. But she did not say so. She stayed silent.

"I am tired," he said, his knuckles against his forehead, his face a picture of exhaustion. "Tired of killing. Tired of trying to make something of this forsaken place. But it is the only throne I have, and I shall seek to keep it. I have done my best by Ahiranya and I will continue to do so."

"The rebels killed Lord Iskar, mothers ease him, because of the poet and his women who were put to death," Bhumika said gently. So gently, as if her voice were a footstep on the most fragile, spun-sugar ground. "Perhaps more death will only worsen this business."

"Be glad you were not there," said Vikram. "Or you wouldn't say such foolish things." He smoothed her hair. He believed he was comforting her. "There will be more death, one way or another. But I promise you, my path will be far less bloody than the one Santosh would carve."

Bhumika remained by her husband's side in the tense hours that followed, assisting the physician to administer a weak mixture of wine and needle-flower, and the maids to daub away the remaining blood and ash on her husband's body. After the physician had been dismissed, Bhumika helped her husband redress into a new tunic and dhoti of light silk that would not aggravate his injury. Although she was mindful of his wound, he was still grayer than ever with pain by the time the task was done.

A moment later, there was a clamor beyond the door. Commander Jeevan strode in without being announced, his white-and-gold armor scuffed with dirt and blood, his expression dark. His gaze flickered to Bhumika, then away, as he bowed.

"My lord," said Jeevan. "Are you well?"

"No pleasantries," Vikram said shortly. "Tell me everything."

Jeevan did.

As he described what Lord Santosh and his men had done in the city, Vikram's expression grew stormier. By the time Jeevan fell silent, Vikram's face was so tight with pain and anger that Bhumika reached automatically for the needle-flower concoction the physician had left. When she began to pour it, Vikram made a tight, angry gesture with his hand.

"No."

She lowered the cup and the pitcher back down, offering him nothing.

"Bring Lord Santosh to me as soon as he returns," Vikram said to the commander. "The second he arrives, I want him brought here. The *second*. Am I understood?"

"He's on his way back, my lord," Commander Jeevan said. "My men are watching his progress. I'll see to it."

"Go," said Vikram.

Commander Jeevan bowed once more, then turned on his heel and departed.

"Bhumika," Vikram said eventually. "You must leave now."

She shook her head and cupped one of his hands in her own, her eyes lowered. "I won't leave you until I'm sure you're well," she murmured, every inch the devoted wife. Before he could protest again, she squeezed his hand tight and released it, saying, "But I will wait on the balcony until Lord Santosh is gone. I promise."

She swept out onto the shaded balcony, giving him no time to order her away again. From here, she could see the grounds of the mahal. The sky. Standing at the far edge of the balcony, she was no longer visible to him from his bed. He would have to stand up if he wanted to seek her out, or shout if he wanted to send her away. She wasn't surprised when he remained silent.

It wasn't long before the door opened again, and Lord Santosh was announced.

The voices were muted, but Bhumika could hear the heavy thud of Santosh's boots. His greeting. Vikram did not greet him in return.

"I have heard what you've done, Lord Santosh," said Vikram.

There was a tone that Vikram used when he spoke to Santosh. It was a tone for diplomacy; for placating, for manipulating, for maintaining peace while navigating the thorniest of politics.

That tone was gone. This bloodied night had clearly shattered his patience. With a bite to his voice, he said, "Shall I tell you what my soldiers witnessed? Buildings ransacked. Men and women running for their lives, their homes destroyed. Beggars with their throats slit."

"Ahiranyi beggars," Santosh said dismissively.

"You also damaged the pink lantern district," Vikram said. "The source of income for Ahiranya's highborn. You're aware of the value of the pleasure houses to Ahiranya's economy, surely? To the *emperor's* coffers? You must be. So tell me, Lord Santosh. Why did you do it?"

There was a beat of silence.

"The Ahiranyi killed Lord Iskar," Santosh said slowly, incredulous. "They nearly killed you."

"Why did you do it?" Vikram repeated, voice clipped.

Bhumika winced. Her husband was not hiding his anger.

He should have consumed the needle-flower when she had offered it to him. Softened the edge of his pain, for the sake of controlling his usually well-restrained temper. Agony had unleashed it far too well.

"I did what was necessary to remind the Ahiranyi of their

place," Santosh said, after a pause. His voice was suddenly oily, cloying. Bhumika tightened her hand upon the balustrade and listened to the cadence of it—the warning his sudden obsequiousness carried with it. "You've long been absent from the heart of the empire, General Vikram. Perhaps you do not understand the kind of governance Emperor Chandra expects of you. When brutes like these Ahiranyi kill our own, they must be crushed with greater might. They must *all* face justice."

"You clearly do not understand Ahiranya, Lord Santosh," Vikram said, in a level voice that did nothing to hide his fury. "You do not understand its people. Not as I do. You do not know how to handle them. Your way will turn them into rabid dogs, biting the hands of their masters."

She heard a grunt, a noise of agony, as he adjusted himself on the bed. When she had left him, he'd been leaning back against the bolster cushions. Now, hearing the intentness of his voice, she could well imagine the way he was leaning forward, pulling his wound, his eyes upon Santosh. She wished she were in the room, where she could read their faces and their bodies. But she could stand and listen, measuring her husband's strained breaths and the weight of Santosh's heavy silence.

"Here is something I know about the Ahiranyi," Vikram said. "When a rebel is put to death—be he a scribe or a poet or a murderer—the Ahiranyi people say to themselves, 'The man broke the law. Perhaps he deserved to die.' When the women burned, the people said, 'She was a rebel, was she not? She must have done something that brought her fate upon her. What happened to her will not happen to me.' They look for reasons, for rules, and through those rules, they learn that as long as they are obedient, they will be safe. Their fear trains them. But tonight, Lord Santosh, you killed men and women who were *not* rebels, who knew nothing of what happened to Lord Iskar, who saw a lord of Parijat—*you*, Santosh— attack them without provocation. Those Ahiranyi will look at your work and they will be frightened. Angry. They will believe an injustice has been done to them. Highborn and commoner alike.

"When the temple children burned," he added quietly, "I learned exactly how far the Ahiranyi people can be pushed. How an apparently senseless act can make enemies of them. And you, Lord Santosh—you have pushed too far. You have united the Ahiranyi. The emperor will not thank you for that."

Santosh said nothing. But oh, Bhumika could well imagine the expression he wore.

You've said too much, husband, she thought.

Santosh was not a man who would take well to being chided. His pride was far too overblown, and Vikram had shattered it. She was afraid Santosh would gather the wreckage of it, all those splinters hewn off by Vikram's words, and make knives of them.

And her husband had not stopped speaking quite yet.

"I will have to be lenient, to make up for your lapse in judgment," Vikram went on. "I should shut the city, for the sake of safety. But the Ahiranyi will want to celebrate the festival of the dark of the moon."

"A heretical festival," Santosh said, in a thin, petulant voice.

"A festival of value to the Ahiranyi," Vikram said, still deliberate and level, "that I will allow them to celebrate despite the actions of the rebels, as a demonstration of the emperor's benevolence, and *my* benevolence. I will not make new rebels out of Ahiranya's citizens, Lord Santosh. I will let their gratitude soften their outrage."

Santosh made a noise. A laugh. Sharp, high. Oh, she wished she could see his face. The look upon it.

"I see," he said. "You'll make friends of them, will you? Of course you will. You, with your little Ahiranyi wife and your precious Ahiranyi highborn allies. You've practically become one of them." Disgust dripped from his voice.

She heard the thud of footsteps. For one moment, she wondered if he would storm out on the balcony, and readied herself, softening her shoulders, widening her eyes—she would make herself seem small, unthreatening, anything but the intent listener she was—and then heard him stop, and speak. His voice was more distant now, as if he had crossed the room.

"Ahiranya will not be yours forever," Lord Santosh said. "It is barely yours now. Try to win the favor of the Ahiranyi, if you like. Let them run their whorehouses and worship their monstrous gods. Let them! But winning their favor won't save your regency, *Vikram*. The emperor is the one who will decide who rules. The emperor sent me here. He will give me Ahiranya."

"Whatever the emperor asks of me, I will do," Vikram said. "Whatever he demands, I will give. But he has not named you as my replacement yet." A beat. "It has been a pleasure seeing you as always, Lord Santosh."

She heard a door slam. Santosh was gone.

When she was sure that he would not return, she stepped back into the room. Vikram was leaning back once more, eyes closed, his mouth slightly parted as he breathed through the pain. She moved beside him, already considering what consequences that unfortunate conversation would have for her husband's regency. For Ahiranya.

She carefully did not think of how her husband had spoken of her people. There were a great many things she was careful not to think about around her husband.

She poured the wine into the cup.

"Drink," she said, and placed the cup against his lips. She kept her voice tender, her expression compassionate, as if the conversation had meant nothing to her at all. "You need your rest. Let your wife take care of you, just this once."

Without opening his eyes, with utter trust, he drank.

27

PRIYA

It was one of the easiest things she had ever done. She prepared all the food, after all. She was the one who made the evening meal, the parathas, the pickles, the little pots of dhal or yoghurt if any happened to be available. She assembled a plate for Pramila and placed the smallest dose of needle-flower into Pramila's tea. The sweetness of the sugar she'd heaped into the cup would hopefully hide the taste.

With hands that shook far less than they should have, considering how nervous she was, Priya prepared the rest of the food. The maidservants had left bags of rice and wholemeal flour on their last visit, purses of ground spices, and bags of onions and ginger. As Priya heaved one bag of flour, she saw a piece of paper flutter to the floor. She leaned down and picked it up.

It was a letter written in indigo ink, smeared from long being folded between two sacks, though someone had gone to some trouble to dry it and had pressed a cloth between the two edges to blot the color. She recognized it as Sima's hand, crude Zaban. Sima was not a habitual writer, and her knowledge of written script was shaky.

Stay safe. Thinking of you.

Beneath it, Sima had drawn a little bird—a fat fledgling dove, marking in its dark eyes and fluffy down with painstaking care.

She thought of Sima sitting and carefully capturing words on the page for Priya's sake, and a lump rose to her throat.

She stuffed the note into her blouse, finished her cooking, and took the food to Pramila's chamber with a fixed smile on her face.

When she finally returned to Malini's room, she found Malini on the floor of her cell, her cheek pressed to the stone and her eyes wide. Priya ran over to her.

"What happened? Are you well?"

"Clearly I am not well," Malini gasped out. "I just—fainted."

"How ...?"

"My vision went black," Malini said. "And I felt sick. And now I'm on the floor. That's all I know. Please, help me up."

Priya did, taking Malini's weight as she rose to a seated position. She could feel the clamminess of the princess's skin.

"The dizziness will pass," Malini said firmly. She looked angry. "It's going to pass. This is a natural impact of giving up needle-flower, is it not?"

"I don't know," said Priya helplessly.

"You said you knew about the effects of the poison."

"I do. But I'm no healer."

"Well, then." Malini's jaw tightened. She raised her head higher, as if fighting some invisible force pinning her skull down. Carefully, she rose to her feet, then lowered herself to the charpoy.

Priya watched her.

"It's the lingering effect of the needle-flower," Malini added, eventually. As if to assure them both. "That's all. I'll be better in time. Are you ready, Priya? Is Pramila dealt with?"

"She's sleeping. I checked. If the guards come ..."

"They won't come to my room," said Malini. "They know better."

"But if they do?"

"I'll pretend to sleep," said Malini. "And if they wake me, I'll tell them I don't know where you are."

"Then I'm ready," said Priya.

"You remember—"

"I remember everything you told me," Priya said impatiently. "We have a deal, Malini. Don't worry about anything."

The palace of illusions, Malini had told her, was the place she needed to go. Priya knew of it. It was a pleasure house in a rather elegant—if not terribly reputable—part of the pink lantern district. Its name was both a joke and a mockery: It had been named for the palace in an old myth found all across the subcontinent, the palace of a beautiful queen who had many husbands.

She knew she was to meet the young lord who was staying there, a distant cousin of a low prince of Saketa—although that was not, according to Malini, his true lineage. She was to give him a message from Malini, ask Malini's questions, and then return. All before Pramila woke.

She would need luck on her side.

Priya threw a shawl around her shoulders.

"Priya." The expression in Malini's dark eyes was unreadable.

"Yes?"

Nothing. For a long moment.

"I hope you come back safely," Malini said finally. "I hope you're well. I'll be thinking of you."

Why did Malini keep insisting that she really cared? It made Priya feel raw. She wanted Malini to care for her—wanted to bask into that caring, *melt* into it. But the rest of her was wary. The rest of her wanted armor.

"Of course you will," Priya said. "I'm the only ally you have here. You'd be helpless without me."

Malini did not flinch, but there was something about her stillness that made Priya's own heart twist, just a little, with unwanted guilt.

"I'll be back soon," Priya muttered. "Just wait and see."

She left the room and walked out onto the triveni.

The darkness beyond was almost complete. The glow of the sickle moon was faint, the lights of the city mere scatterings of gold on black.

She closed her eyes. She felt the pull of magic, a river running beneath her skin. She thought of the way the Hirana had shifted beneath her; the way the carvings had become clearer, resurrecting from their old obliteration on the walls. She thought of the way her connection with the Hirana had grown too.

She sucked in a fortifying breath—and stepped down onto the Hirana's surface.

The stone was warm beneath her feet. She could feel new moss against her soles.

She took a step down. Another. Another.

28

RAO

"There's a woman here to meet your cousin, Lord Prem," said one of Prem's men. "A servant, looks like."

That was a surprise. Prem and Rao met each other's eyes. Prem's jaw firmed, mouth thinning.

In the three days since Lord Iskar's assassination, even the pleasure houses had been gripped by an atmosphere of unease. Prem's men had briefly investigated the damage to the local area, in the aftermath of the rebels' attack—and the reprisals from the regent's men that had followed. They had seen splintered stalls; ransacked houses; beggars dead, felled by horses, lying forgotten in street corners. The pleasure house they were in had survived, it seemed, by sheer luck.

They'd gleaned enough information to assume that Lord Santosh had been behind the damage to the city. "It's exactly the kind of stupid thing a man like him would do," Prem had said, distaste in his voice. Rao had nodded, and tried to make sense of General Vikram's decision to leave the city open in the aftermath. He wondered how the act of one lord tied into the act of another, how Santosh's brutality had triggered General Vikram's magnanimity, and what their choices said about the current balance of power in the regent's mahal. If he'd had more time—and more resources—Rao would have chased answers like a predator with the scent of blood in its nose.

"Who let her in?" Prem asked. "None of the guards stopped her?"

"Why would they stop a maidservant?" said Lata. She sat ensconced in a pile of pillows with a book in her hands. She didn't look up as she turned the page. "No one stops maidservants."

"After what happened to Lord Iskar—and at that Ahiranyi temple, let's not forget—they should," muttered Prem. "Besides, what if she's a spy from that jumped-up Lord Santosh? I don't think he was suspicious of me, but we should be a little careful. What is she—Parijati?"

"Ahiranyi, I think, my lord."

"Right, probably not one of his spies, then," said Prem, relaxing. He leaned forward, elbows on his crossed knees. On the ground between him and Rao lay a silk embroidered cross, the necessary board for a game of pachisa. He flung six cowrie shells to the floor with a little clatter. One shell fell aperture up and he swore mildly.

"I'm losing," he said, "so go if you want." He gathered up the shells. "Is this a pre-arranged meeting?"

"No," said Rao. To the guard he added, "Did she say why she needs me?"

"No, my lord."

Rao stood, wincing at the twinge of his still-healing wound. He listened to the quiet of the evening. The insects humming beyond the veranda. The sound of the fountain's running water. And he made his decision. "I'll come."

The maidservant stood waiting in the corridor. She was a simple Ahiranyi woman in a plain sari, perhaps in her early twenties, with loose black hair and dark skin, a crooked nose and penetrating eyes. She offered him a perfunctory bow of respect, then said, without preamble, "She told me to look for a man who calls himself Lord Rajan, a cousin of a low prince of Saketa. Is that you?"

Rao was taken aback by her directness. "Who asks?"

"My...mistress asks," she said haltingly, pausing before *mistress*, as if struggling to find the word she wished to use. "Are you Lord Rajan?"

"I am," he said. "Tell me the name of your mistress."

The Ahiranyi woman shook her head. "She told me to tell you that long ago she stole your knife. Not your dagger. Your knife." The maid repeated this as if she'd learned it by rote. "And she wanted me to tell you that she was glad when you returned it to your sister and to her. The weapon gave her hope." She met his eyes, the look ever so intent. "Perhaps you know my mistress now?"

"Come with me," he said quietly, and pushed open the first door that came to hand. She followed him into a bathing chamber and he shut the door firmly behind them.

"How do I know you're truly from her?" Rao asked roughly. Hope had cut his voice to shreds.

The maid shrugged, a single rise and fall of her shoulders. "I don't know. Does anyone else know the tale I told you?"

Rao swallowed. "No one else living," he managed. "But torture could have taken that story from her."

"Well, it didn't," the maid said tersely. "And I don't have long. I have to return to her, and I have questions for which she needs answers."

"Tell me."

"Can you save her?" the maid asked bluntly. "Can you get her out? Are you trying?"

"Trying, yes," said Rao. "But the need for secrecy has made success... challenging. I am not sure I can free her," he admitted with difficulty. "But I will continue to attempt to do so."

"Fine. Prince Aditya," she said. "He still lives? He's well?"

"As far as the reports I have tell me," said Rao. "He's alive and well."

"Does he have many supporters around him?"

"Maybe more than she hoped," Rao said. "I did my best to guide all those who were trustworthy to where they needed to be."

He did not mention his father's painstaking work to unite the kingdoms of Parijatdvipa against the emperor, in Malini's absence. Before the pyre, in the time when she'd first laid the groundwork for her machinations, she had written King Viraj a letter in fluent Aloran begging his help; had met with him in secret, with Alori's assistance and Rao's own, discussing her hopes and fears for rule under Aditya. His father had been nearly the first convert to her cause.

After Alori had burned, after Malini was imprisoned, his father had taken up the work. As had Rao, in his own small way.

But all of that was more than the maid needed to hear. He did not know if the woman was aware he was truly a prince of Alor—but frankly, he did not want her to be.

She was leaning forward, urgent now. "Who? Titles, at least, if not names."

"Lords from Parijat itself. Several low princes from Saketa, though the high prince has not been approached, or his closest favorites. Their men took the long way to Srugna, skirting the imperial borders. There's no sign they were spotted. You be sure to tell her that. She'll want to know."

"Who else? There must be more."

"Are you sure you'll remember this?"

"I'll remember," the maid said, an edge of impatience to her voice. "Go on, my lord."

"Dwarali's sultan has sent emissaries on his behalf, with their own horsemen." And hadn't they been conspicuous, on their pure white mounts with saddles of blood red. But the maid did not need to know about that either. "We have strong numbers. And Srugna's own king has thrown his lot in with us."

If the maid was impressed or alarmed by any of this, if she understood the implications of what he was telling her, she showed none of it on her face. He admired her impassivity. "Fine. I'll tell her so."

"And how is she? How does she fare?" Rao asked, and hoped he did not sound as he felt, in his heart.

The maid gave him a measured look. "She is not well. She's been sick for a long time."

"Has General Vikram arranged her a physician?"

The maid gave him a tight smile and shook her head. "The general has limited power over her care. On the emperor's orders, I'm told. Besides, it's her medicine that is killing her. She knows it's so."

"And who are you to her?"

"Her only attendant, my lord. And the one ensuring her poisoning does not continue."

"And how," he asked, "does that benefit you?"

"Ah, my lord," said the maid. "I do it for the love and loyalty in my heart alone."

There was a thread of truth in that quip, he thought. Something in the tilt of her chin, the shape of her mouth as she said the words, told him so. Malini had a way of winning people whether they liked it or not. And yet it wasn't the entire truth, of course.

"Have you anything I can use to free her?" Rao asked. Prem's efforts had failed. He had nothing but this—the hope that a maid carried a possibility and an answer. "Any knowledge, any information—any allies I can seek?"

Prem would have laughed at him for asking a maidservant for allies. But people who were invisible to others often knew far more than his highborn kind respected or understood.

"I don't know." The maid looked away from him as footsteps sounded in the corridor, then faded. "You shouldn't try to storm the temple, or anything equally foolish. There's no easy way up and down the Hirana. Its surface is dangerous. And there are guards, too. You'd have to make your way through the general's mahal, across the grounds, and climb without taking the safe path marked by the rope. You wouldn't be able to do all that. Not even with an army."

"But you can," Rao said.

A wry smile curled her mouth. "No one notices maids, my lord. And I'm Ahiranyi. I know the Hirana better than you ever could. But the princess cannot climb down the Hirana to her freedom, and I can't simply walk her out via the gates."

"She sent nothing for me?"

"Nothing but the information I've given you, of her health and her questions."

"She gives me no way to save her?"

"I believe she hoped you'll find one on your own. My lord."

That startled a laugh from him. Her Zaban was coarse, her expression hateful. He found himself liking her and was mildly appalled with himself.

"Would you offer me your name?" he asked.

"Priya," she said, after a reluctant pause.

Priya. A common name across all of Parijatdvipa. A sweet name for round-cheeked little girls and meek brides alike. This woman was neither.

"Priya," he repeated. "Thank you for coming to me. Please, give your mistress a message from me in return." A breath. "Tell her she must hold on to hope. Tell her that her work isn't yet done. Tell her—I will wait for word from her, and I will continue to try to save her. And tell her…" He blinked, not wishing to show his emotions before this woman. "I am her loyal servant. As I promised her. I have not forgotten, and never will forget, the vow we made over a knife."

She'd placed the cloth flat first, smoothing it down over the lacquered table with her fingers. The knife had followed. Compared to the table and the muslin, the knife was crude and ugly, unembellished, its edge a sharp and serviceable point.

But it was his knife.

He had not called for wine or tea or tall glasses of lassi or sherbet, dripping condensation on a hot afternoon. There would be no servants to disturb them. He had lived in the imperial mahal ever since he was a boy of eight, sent to foster ties between Alor and Parijat, and in all that time he had never been alone in a room with the imperial princess.

He was now.

They were quiet, for a long moment.

"My father is dead," said Princess Malini.

He almost jumped, when she spoke.

"I—I know. I'm sorry for your loss, princess."

"And my brother," she said. "My kind, honorable brother is gone, where no one can find him. Chandra is the only one left. To light my father's pyre. To sit upon his throne. I am sure when you took Aditya to the garden of the nameless, you never intended for this to happen."

"No, princess. I did not. But the ways of the nameless aren't in mortal control. One way or another, Aditya would have found the garden. And he would have heard our god. It is his fate, written in the stars of his birth."

"I don't believe that is the way things are," said the princess. "That we have no choices. And if fate must be star-burned into us, then I don't believe we can't bend to the needs of our times and turn from our prescribed path." She touched her fingertips to the dull side of the blade. There was still ash on her skin, from where she'd touched her father's remains, in a final ritual act of mourning. "I want to see Chandra removed from a throne he shouldn't have. And I want Aditya to rise to it. Can you help me?"

He met her gaze. No downturned, modest eyes from this one. The meek, quiet girl, easily given to tears, that Rao had expected her to be—had always known her to be—had fallen away. The princess who sat before him was stern and calm, her gaze pinning him as neatly as a dagger to the throat.

"That would put you and I, and everyone we value, in danger," said Rao.

"I have letters from Aditya," she said. "I know where he resides, and I will convince him to return. Fate or not, he knows his duty."

That made Rao's breath catch.

"You know where he is? Truly?"

"I have my own spies and my own women," she said. "And my brother did not have the heart, or the sense, to leave me without a word."

"How is he?" Rao asked. "Is he . . ."

Malini shook her head. She would not give him this. Not yet.

"You know what Chandra is," she said. "You know what he'll do. I can assure you, Prince Rao—your fears are not unfounded. My brother is the same creature he was as a boy and a young man. He thinks the tenets of his faith will purify his hands of blood. He thinks his atrocities are blessings."

"He's committed no atrocities."

"If fate is written in the stars, then I am sure his atrocities are already written too," said Malini. "Ask your priests. Or better yet, ask your own heart. You do not need to be a devotee of a god to know what he will do."

He thought of all he had seen of Chandra's nature. He'd grown up alongside him, after all. Shuddered.

Malini was still staring at him.

"We have a pact between us, Prince Rao," said Malini. "Do we not?"

He let out a breath and stood with her. He folded the muslin around the knife and took it.

"Yes," he said. "We do."

His sister Alori stood in the corner of the antechamber beyond, her arms crossed. Ostensibly she was on guard for visitors, but she wasn't visibly paying attention to anything. Her face was lifted up, catching a shaft of dappled sunlight come in from the high slat window. There were birds playing on its edge. Green parakeets with vivid orange beaks, the flit of their wings throwing shadows across Alori's upturned head.

She looked at him then, her eyes shaded by wings.

"Is it done, brother? Have you agreed?"

"Yes," he'd told her. "It is."

He returned to the apartment chamber. Prem still had the pachisa board in front of him, though a few of his men had now joined him at the game. He raised his head when Rao entered.

"Good talk in the bathing chamber, then?" There was a teasing note to his voice. "I have to admit, I never knew you liked them so dark."

"You're a fool, Prem," Rao said tiredly. He walked past him, and past Lata, still curled over her book, and stepped out onto the veranda.

He needed the cold air. He needed to forget.

29

PRIYA

She had no idea how long it would be before Pramila woke up, and reason told her it would be best to return to the Hirana as fast as possible. Certainly before dawn came.

But she'd been without her freedom for so long. She was used to being able to travel—to leave the mahal and go to the market, buying fresh fruit or morning dosas with sweet chutneys to cut through the fragile lattice of gram flour. She'd enjoyed hiding from Gauri with Sima, getting sick on palm wine in the orchard, laughing so hard her sides hurt. She missed lying on her own sleep mat.

She missed Rukh, a little. And when she thought of his face the last time they'd spoken, when she thought of Ashok and what a man like her brother could do with a starstruck child who was willing to die for him...

But she couldn't go to Rukh. She had no excuse to be in the mahal, or see Sima, or touch even the shadows of her old life.

But there was one thing she could do.

The house at the edge of the forest looked exactly as it had the last time she had visited; it struck her as odd, when so much else had changed.

She rapped lightly on the door. Waited.

It opened a crack, and Gautam's alert gaze met her own. He didn't look at all tired. There was something tight and terrified about his expression. Even in the dark, she could see that his hand was clenched on the handle of his scythe, holding it at the ready.

"Priya. What are you doing here?"

"I need to speak with you. I won't be long."

"It's the middle of the night, you stupid woman."

He looked as if he was going to shut the door in her face, so Priya leaned in, getting her body between the frame and the door itself. She stared him down, unblinking, keeping her expression calm.

"Gautam," Priya said. "My brother sent me. Let me in. And lower the scythe."

As she'd suspected, he hesitated. Then obeyed.

He led her beyond his workroom, beyond his own private chambers, into the central courtyard of the house. From there he led her to another room, dusty and quiet, and shut the door.

"How is business, Gautam? Still thriving?"

"Why did he send you?" Gautam demanded.

She shook her head minutely, never letting her gaze waver. He seemed to sweat more heavily under the steady pressure of her eyes. She'd learned that, at least, from Malini: how a gaze could pin and bind and compel, as powerful as any magic.

"He didn't," she said. "How long have you known my brother is alive?"

Gautam's gaze turned flinty. "Get out."

"You were friends once," she said.

"We were never friends."

"You owed him something. Or he knew enough to scare you into obedience. That's friendship enough. How long have you known?" When Gautam was silent, she said, "I've seen him again. Don't lie to me."

Gautam seemed to deflate. "I've known the entire time. I don't like him, you understand? But he's a hard man to refuse. He knows too many people. And he pays well. Not many people can, these days."

"With stolen money."

"Money is money," said Gautam. "I wouldn't expect a lecture on ethics from someone like you."

She ignored his pettiness. "And what does my brother buy from you, with his money?"

Gautam crossed his arms. "If your brother is back in your life, you should ask him directly. Don't involve me or mine in your family business again."

"You're afraid," she said. "You don't need to deny it, Gautam. I know what my brother's like. You're frightened of what he'll do if you tell me. But he doesn't know I'm here. And you have to know that when you take money from dangerous people, there are always consequences."

"Don't lecture me," he said tersely. "You're nothing but a floor sweeper, a rat. A whore probably too—"

"Stop talking," said Priya. The words came out of her with a vicious edge. In one motion she removed his scythe from his sweaty grip and broke the handle in her palm.

Gautam's throat clicked. His eyes widened.

"You forget," Priya said calmly, "that whatever my brother is, I am too. If you're afraid of him, then you should be afraid of me. Oh, I know I'm usually very nice, and I'd like to continue to be. You allowed me to sleep on your doorstep once, after all, and that was a service. I'm thankful for that. You may speak, if you like."

He gave a choked noise. Didn't.

"What," she said then, "does he buy from you?"

Gautam massaged his throat with his knuckles.

"I..." He cleared his throat. "He started coming a little more than a year ago. He said he needed supplies. His own were running low. The normal medicines, to heal wounds and hold back sickness. But also..."

"Go on," Priya prompted impatiently.

"My mother, when she still lived, was a regular pilgrim to the Hirana," said Gautam. "And she also paid other pilgrims for it. You have to understand. She knew it was dangerous, but kindling soaked in it almost passes for sacred wood. And for some of her clients, it was good enough. I've never sold it to *you*, though, Priya. I promise."

"Deathless water," Priya murmured. "I thought so. And where is it?"

He leaned down and lifted a covered slat in the floor. Below, a staircase descended into darkness.

Gautam pulled a lantern from the wall and lit it deftly; its dim glow guided them down, shimmering off a small, depleted collection of little bottles of fine colored glass that hung about the walls when they reached the bottom. The bottles were all carefully stoppered; all full of water that gleamed with its own muted strangeness in the flickering dark. Priya slowly touched her fingertips to one. It was cool, not fire warm like a sacred mask. But something in her heart—in the part of her that Ashok had twisted in the vise of his hand—recognized the call of it.

"You can't take them," Gautam said quietly, desperately, behind her. "You can't. I've thrown my lot in with him. I've promised them to him. Everything I have left is his."

"I won't take them," said Priya. She traced the edge of one vial. "But I should destroy them."

"Please," said Gautam. "No. Please."

She tapped the glass a little. Watched the vial waver on its hook.

"You called me a rat," she said. "And a few other things that you probably consider unkind."

He said nothing.

"I want you to remember that that's all I'll be—as long as you give me no reason to be more. And I want you to do this floor-sweeping whore a kindness and share a little of your knowledge with her." She turned to look at him squarely. "In return I'll leave these alone. My brother does not need to know anything."

Gautam's exhaled breath was shaky with relief. "What," he said, "do you want to know?"

"Tell me about needle-flower," she said. "Tell me exactly what long-term ingestion does to the body. And tell me what the consequences are when the doses are stopped."

30

MALINI

The dizzy spells grew worse after Priya left. Tremors shook her body, and there were times when she saw and heard nothing for long moments, then found herself in a new position. Leaning against the wall, or collapsed on the floor, her body not her own.

No one would come if she called. She and Priya had made sure of that, after all.

Priya was gone an hour. Two. Three. Malini forced herself to remain on her charpoy, curled up on her side like a small child, her hands bunched in the concave of her stomach, as if the heat of her own skin could ground her in place.

Perhaps Priya has died, Malini thought. Ridiculous. But time moved differently when you were captive and your body refused to obey you.

She heard the whisper of footsteps behind her. Raised her head and—

There was no one there.

She couldn't stay on the charpoy with strange noises brushing her ears. She felt vulnerable and scared, her heart howling in her chest. She climbed down—dizzy for a moment—and crossed the floor. Lowered herself down against the wall.

There was a memory of fire humming inside her. She closed her eyes and listened to the splintering pop of wood and flesh under flame. The hiss of it. The screams.

She was not well. Not well. Not.

She saw two shadows cross the floor. She watched them.

Not real. This is not real.

Not real.

"My la—" Priya stopped. "Malini. I'm back. Why are you sitting in the corner of the room?"

"It felt necessary," Malini said in a rasp. She didn't move as Priya approached her. She heard no footsteps this time, which was at least normal. Priya always walked with strange, silent grace. Her face was achingly alive—dark and real above Malini's own. "Did you find him?"

"I did," said Priya, kneeling down.

"Can he free me?"

Priya was silent for a moment.

"That's a no, then."

"He had messages for you."

"Tell me," said Malini.

Priya told her. There was comfort in knowing her work had not gone to waste. Aditya had all the tools she'd been able to provide for him—everything he required to crush Chandra to dust. But not enough to see her free from this: her prison, her poisoning, the black marks of fire upon the walls around her.

"Has Lord Rajan tried negotiating directly with General Vikram?" Malini asked. "Vikram has a great deal to lose from Chandra's rule—and more to gain from Aditya's. There could be a benefit."

"I don't know," said Priya. "I didn't know it was something I should suggest."

"No. You wouldn't have."

Priya frowned.

"Don't bristle, Priya," Malini murmured. "Such things are my business, not yours. I was raised to consider politics, always."

But she knew Rao. He knew the value of affability, of the subtler plays for power. It was why they had always gotten along so well, and why he and Aditya had been such fast friends. He would have approached Vikram in some form. That approach had clearly not borne fruit.

"You must go back soon," said Malini. "You must tell him . . ."

Ah. She could not remember what Priya needed to tell him. The words had slipped from her mind. Her hands shook a little.

This would pass.

"You need to take this," said Priya. She held a cup in her hands. When had she obtained it? Had she walked in with it? Malini did not know.

"What is it?"

"A very, very small dose of needle-flower," said Priya. Her expression was serious. "I spoke to a healer after all. Your body has grown used to the poison. Apparently reducing the intake too swiftly is just as likely to kill you as continuing to consume it. We need to give you a few more doses. Only a few. I'll measure them carefully and cut them by halves each time. Even that probably isn't safe, but it's . . . it's the fastest way we can see you free of it."

"Ah," murmured Malini. She looked at Priya's hand—at the cup, and her strong, fine-boned fingers curled around it. "That explains a great deal."

She reached out. Then drew her hand back. "Take it away," she said. "I won't drink it."

"Why not?"

"Because I don't want to," said Malini.

"Malini," said Priya.

"No. I won't touch it again. What it did to me . . ." The bile of poison on her tongue. Her mind in a terrible fog, a choking haze. Her grief, winding itself around her, a constant and whispering noose. "No. I won't take it."

"You'll die if you don't take it," Priya said bluntly. "You've trusted me with so much. Trust me on this."

Trusted by necessity. But yes. Yes, she had. She'd trusted Priya with the knowledge of Rao's existence, after all. Rao, who had kept his promise and awaited her word.

"Not yet, then," said Malini. "Not quite yet."

"Why not?"

Malini looked past her.

Beyond Priya's shoulders, in a room wavering as if through a mist of heat, stood two figures. They watched her. Smoke coiled from their hair. Their crowns of stars burning. Malini looked at them, reached out, as her vision wavered once more, as blackness came for her.

Narina had always been the prettiest of the three of them. A long, fine nose and arched eyebrows, which she plucked to an even finer arch. High cheekbones that she rouged. In the fashion of her father's people, she blackened her teeth, which made her lips look an even lusher red in comparison.

She stood and gazed at Malini with a singed smile. No teeth. Only char and ash.

"We've missed you, heart sister," she said.

"You needn't say anything," Alori said tenderly. "We know you've missed us too."

Time passed. Flickered. But Malini was still upon the floor, and Priya was shaking her, shaking her awake, as those two ghosts shifted about the room, mirages of colored smoke, red silk coiling and glistening, the stars in their hair glinting, fire-hot.

"Malini. *Malini.*"

Oh, her head ached.

"If this is a ploy to make me help you escape, it's a dangerous one," Priya said. Her voice was trembling. "Pramila is awake, and I've managed to distract her but—please. You need to drink. Please."

"How is my mother?" Narina asked. She cocked her head to the side, with a crackle like kindling wood. "No. I know. I don't even need to guess. She's twisted herself into knots of grief for me. She blames you for everything. Better than blaming the emperor. Better than blaming herself."

Alori said nothing. She looked at Malini with eyes like sad hollows, deep and dark.

"My mother will never forgive you," murmured Narina. "I hope you know that."

"Of course I do."

"What?" Priya looked confused. Alarmed. "I don't understand."

"Does she think I'm immortal now? A mother of flame? Do *you*?"

"I don't know what to believe anymore," Malini said honestly.

Kneeling before her, Priya lowered her head and let out a curse. Priya.

When had Priya spoken to Pramila? How long had Malini been on the floor, watching the slow coil of Narina's dead smile?

"Just drink," Priya said, her voice a fearful whisper. "Please."

Malini shook her head. And with a sickening lurch, Narina and Alori were beside her, before her.

"Do you remember how we both cut our hair, after your brother cut yours? We used silver shears and made ours even shorter. My mother was furious," Narina said. "She said, *What are you without your crowning glory?* But now I wear a crown of fire and I am gristle and dust, so I suppose it doesn't matter."

"You've lost so much," Alori said, infinitely gentle, infinitely sad, as her gossamer fingers brushed over Malini's forehead. And Malini felt . . . nothing.

Because they were not here.

"Your lovely silks. Your jewels. Your network of allies. Your friends. Your power. All gone. And who are you without them?"

"Cruel," murmured Malini. "You were never cruel, nameless princess."

"What is *your* name, beneath all the finery you've lost?" Alori whispered. "What did the nameless call you, on the day you were born?"

"That," Malini said, "is your faith, not mine."

"It doesn't make it any less true," Alori said. "Believe in it or not, fate will find you. As it found me. You were named long before you were born, princess. Your tale is written."

Was it written that Malini should live when Narina and Alori burned? Was it written that she should live and be reduced to this? She had tried so hard to build herself an impenetrable armor of power. She had learned classic texts of war and rule and politics, reading by moonlight when everyone else in the mahal slept. She had made fast friends with the wives of kings and the sisters of princes.

"And now you have nothing," said Narina, in a voice of wood sap and ash. "Not even us."

No sisters of her heart. No one to turn to.

"I have Priya," she forced out, and through the haze she heard the press of a voice on her ears. *Yes, yes, I'm here, please—*

A laugh.

"A maidservant with monstrous gifts, who doesn't even particularly like you?"

"Oh, she likes me."

"She liked a false you." Croon of a voice. "A you that you created for her. You crafted yourself into something warm and hurt, like a fat hare in a trap. I don't think she knew if she wanted to save you or consume you whole. But you're no hare, are you? You are a night flower if anything, precious only for a brief time before you decay."

That was not Alori's voice, or Narina's. They wavered and . . .

There was . . . herself. Princess Malini, daughter of Parijat, crowned in a profusion of flowers, pale jasmine radiating into marigold, to mimic the rising sun. Princess Malini, a sari of peacock-green silk, with a chain of knot-worked gold roses around her waist, a string of fat pearls around her throat.

She was everything Malini was not anymore. And she was smiling.

"You," said Malini raggedly, "are not real either."

It seemed easy—easy and correct—to push her old self away, to shove and then beat with her fists, as something ugly and furious rushed up into her lungs and her eyes and her mouth as she thought of Narina and Alori curled up with her in her bed, or her mother's funeral, or her father's, or Aditya leaving her behind with nothing but a letter and a kiss upon the forehead. The ugliness grew into a wail, and she was screaming and laughing, even as Priya hushed her and caught her fists, a furrow in her brow, and it was Priya she was fighting against after all—

"What is this?"

Pramila's voice.

"My lady, I don't know. She simply—turned on me." Priya's voice was frantic. She was gripping Malini's hands, forcing them still.

"She needs her medicine," Pramila said. "Do you have it? Give it to me, and—"

Malini laughed. And laughed. She could barely breathe through it, but she forced herself to, and bared her teeth into a smile, and thought of Narina.

"Your daughter," she said to Pramila, "your Narina, whom you mourn and mourn...the morning she died—did you know?— when she drank the opium wine and waited for the priests to come for us, she pressed her head to my arm, and told me, 'I want my mother.' Did you know she said that? I don't know if I ever told you. I think perhaps I wanted to spare you. I don't know why."

Pramila gave a full-body flinch, as if Malini had struck her. Had she struck her? Pramila's hand was on the wall. Was she weeping?

"I should get the guards," muttered Pramila. "I should—they can force her to drink, see if they don't—"

"My lady—"

"I don't deserve this," sobbed Pramila. "I..."

"I'll make her drink," Priya was saying. "I swear it. I'll deal with her. Please, Lady Pramila."

"I can't. I can't. I—"

"Please, Lady Pramila," Priya pleaded. "Please spare yourself."

Pramila gave another sob. She nodded, her face blotchy, unlovely. She turned. Left.

Priya exhaled, and Malini gripped her by the arms as her own body shuddered against her volition.

"You need to drink *now*," Priya said. "And as you've seen, I can make you, if I have to."

Malini turned her head.

"You're not yourself," said Priya gently.

"You're not the first to tell me so today."

"What?"

"I'm hallucinating," Malini said impatiently. "Do keep up, Priya."

She did not want to explain that when Narina and Alori had appeared before, she'd needed to speak to them. It did not matter if they were immortals or hallucinations. It only mattered that the loss of them burned, sore and powerful, and she had wanted to pick at the soreness, feel the fresh blood of them again.

"You need to tell Rao to go," Malini said, instead. "Tell him to go. Tell him Aditya needs him."

"Rao," Priya repeated. Her lips shaped the name with care. "Of course."

"It's not his name," Malini said. "None of them have names. Only words for the rest of us to use, to pin them like a cloth beneath a needle. You understand?"

"Not at all," said Priya.

"The royalty of Alor," said Malini. "They worship the name-less god. They keep their names a secret. A whisper. Because their names are their fates. I only...I only trust him, now. And I want something good to come of this. He cannot save me from this place. He knows it. You know it, too. His presence here is a waste. But if he goes to Aditya...If I can have even the barest taste of vengeance..."

Fire crept up her tongue.

The pyre burned, before her. Chandra stood before her. There were hands dragging her toward the pyre. None of her careful, cutting words had worked. They would watch her burn, all these princes and kings, so many of them allies she had cultivated with pretty words and pacts and—yes—coin. She reached for Chandra, fought furiously. *If I must burn, then I'll take you with me, throne and all.*

But there was no Chandra. Just Priya lying beneath her on the stone floor, pinned by Malini's hands, looking up at her with those clear eyes. Her eyes were surrounded by lashes more brown than black. Against her dark skin, they were like gold.

An absurd thought. But it brought Malini back to her own flesh again. It made her crumple down, as Priya took hold of her and held her steady.

"Hush," said Priya. "Or Pramila will hear you."

Was Malini making noise? She hadn't realized it. She ground her teeth together, lowering her head.

"You've let me hold you," said Malini, "when you could knock me down without even trying."

"I don't want to hurt you," Priya said, voice steady and sure. She had said it before, Malini remembered. A long time ago.

"And why not?" Malini demanded.

"Because we have a deal."

"Ah, no," said Malini. "No. That's not why."

She crumpled a little further, a spasm of pain running through her. Ghosts. Flame. The gossamer spirits of Narina and Alori dancing around her.

"Malini. Princess. Come on, please. Let me help you back to your bed."

Malini allowed herself to be moved. Priya gathered her up like a child, helping her onto the cot.

"You care," said Malini. "You care about me. You hate that I need you so much and that I tried to give you what you wanted from me—what I *thought* you wanted from me—to get what I needed from you. But you still care. Don't lie to me and tell me that you don't. I can see it in your face."

"You don't know what you're seeing," muttered Priya. There was a frown line creasing her brow.

"I know exactly what I'm seeing," said Malini. "But I don't

understand why. Oh, when you thought I was something gentle and wounded—that I could understand. But now, now you know I've lied to you and used you, now you know I am a traitor, impure, that I have a hard heart, that I am the empire and the empire is me—"

"I don't know," Priya said. Her voice was a lash. "I don't know why I care, is that enough? Perhaps I'm simply not monstrous enough to enjoy watching another human suffer, no matter how hard their heart may be."

"Sincere goodheartedness that has nothing to do with me," Malini said. Slow. The words came out of her slow and thick like honey. "I am not sure I can believe anyone like that exists. Everyone wants something. Everyone uses those wants. That's what survival is. That's what power is."

"Then your life has been terrible and sad," Priya replied bluntly.

"It has not. I have everything I need." Loyal friends. Loyal allies. "I used to have everything. I used to..."

She trailed off.

Silence. One beat of it, followed by another. Then Priya spoke.

"You're not proving your strength," Priya said, "by refusing the needle-flower."

"I can fight it," Malini said thinly.

Priya touched her hand to Malini's. Priya's fingers were rough at the palms. Her touch was utterly soft.

"I don't think you can," she said. "I don't think anyone can."

"All bodies suffer and die the same, like it or not," said Alori helpfully.

"You're not here," said Malini. "So shut up."

"Still rude, I see," Alori said, with an exasperated sigh.

"She can't help herself," said Narina.

"Even in my mind you're awful to me," said Malini. Her eyes ached. "If I tell you I miss you...well. You both would have known that, when you lived. And now, it matters to no one but me. So I won't."

"Malini." Priya's fingers threaded with her own. "Please. Focus on me. The needle-flower. Will you take it?"

Priya. Priya leaning over her. Priya squeezing her hand, trying to draw her back into the steady world.

Priya's hair was so very straight, so dark where it draped over the curve of her ear. Strange. She was not lovely, no, but parts of her were lovely. Parts of her.

"There are so many ways I could have convinced you to set me free." Dark thoughts, light thoughts, like a flicker of shadow on skin. "I wish I had the strength to use you as I need to, in order to escape here," Malini said. "And yet I'm rather glad I can't."

Priya just looked back at her, unflinching.

"Please," she said. "Drink."

And finally, Malini took the barest sip. Choked it down, acrid and sweet. And fell back into a dark slumber, her fingers still intertwined with Priya's own.

31

PRIYA

The first night, she didn't leave Malini's side. She measured out a careful dosage of needle-flower tincture and prayed that she hadn't made an error, that Gautam hadn't misled her, and that Malini would survive. Ever since her last dose, when she'd pinned Priya and raged, Malini had been utterly silent, eyes closed. If Priya hadn't held a hand to her mouth to feel the cadence of her breath, or touched the pulse in her wrist—and Priya had, over and over again—then she would perhaps have thought Malini was gone.

She sat beside Malini on the woven charpoy and urged Malini to drink the needle-flower, coaxing the other woman's mouth open. She propped Malini up in her lap and fed it to her, without even the medium of wine to make it easier.

"You're going to be okay," she told her, when Malini coughed and pressed her head against Priya's arm, eyes still squeezed tight shut. She ran a hand through Malini's hair, as if Malini were a child, easily comforted by kind touch. "It's going to be okay."

She hoped it wasn't a lie.

Priya slipped in and out of a doze, out of exhausted dreams. When she blinked her eyes open, shifting between sleep and wakefulness, the carvings seemed to dance on the walls before her eyes, surrounding her in an unblinking circle. The Hirana thrummed beneath her feet. And Malini slept on, breathing warm and steady against Priya's side.

The next day, Malini was still alive, but she continued to sleep, consuming no food, taking water and needle-flower only when she was coaxed. On the night that followed, Priya held her again, watching the rise and fall of her chest.

Let her live, Priya thought. *Don't let me wake and find her cold. Let her live.*

It was only human, only natural, to want Malini to live. No more than that.

She took Malini's hand in her own and held it firmly.

"You'll never get your revenge if you don't survive, Malini," Priya said to her. "If you can hear me, don't forget that."

It was the next day, in the middle of a rainstorm, when Malini finally woke. Drank a little water. She held out her hand—laced her fingers with Priya's once more.

"Tell Rao," she whispered, when Priya asked her how she felt; when Priya tried to convince her to eat, to rest more, to take her next careful dose. "Tell him to go."

Then she fell back asleep. Her fingers on Priya's were cool.

Priya drugged Pramila once more. Paced the triveni, waiting, anxious, then climbed down the Hirana in the dark of night.

The regent's men were patrolling in significant, intimidating numbers. But the night bazaars were alive with people regardless, all of them winding between the food stalls with stubborn cheer, their voices loud, their smiles defiant. Colored banners had been hung between the houses. There were lanterns set out on every veranda, not yet lit.

It took Priya, confused by the bustle of the crowd, a moment to remember that the following night would be the festival of the dark of the moon, when households donated lavish gifts to the poor, ate golden jalebis and milk sweets, and placed dozens of lanterns on their verandas to light up the dark. It took her significantly longer to gather—from the gossip of people around her—that the regent had given explicit permission for the festival to go ahead as normal. No one seemed to know *exactly* why he'd chosen to do so, but there were discontented murmurs here and there as she walked about things that had been done in the city by Parijat-dvipan soldiers. And sure enough, she saw a handful of buildings with their wooden frames clearly hacked apart, the damage still unmended.

She managed to enter the palace of illusions easily enough. All it took was approaching the servants' entrance confidently with a broom in hand—stolen from the veranda of an unfortunate household—and she was allowed in by the disinterested guards. After that, she was just another unnoticed maidservant slipping through corridors as distant sitars played and women warbled love songs.

Lord Rajan—or Rao, or the nameless prince, or whatever Malini wanted to call him—came to meet her. She'd asked one of the men for him—guards, she assumed, though they smoked and slumped outside his door far more calmly than any guards on duty she'd seen before—and he'd come, dragging on his jacket, as if he'd stumbled straight out of bed.

"What is it? What did she say?"

Priya told him. At the end, he gave her an incredulous look.

"I can't simply leave her."

"It's what she wants you to do. She said Aditya needs you."

Rao assessed her, his gaze taking her face in, as if he could read something in the look she wore, in the furrow of her brow and the twist of her mouth. "Yes," he said finally. "He does. But he needs her, too. Aditya is . . . not like her."

She didn't know what she'd expected of a man living in a brothel. But Rao was like a doe: gentle-eyed, but not without reflexive cunning.

"I told you she's sick," Priya said. "I . . . truthfully, I was afraid she'd die. And I am still not sure she won't. She can't help you. She doesn't have the strength to escape. And she has no one she can trust in her prison but me."

I could help her escape, Priya thought, as Rao's face crumpled a little and he brought a hand to his forehead. *I could bring her here to this man. It wouldn't be easy to get her down the Hirana, not as she is. But I could do it. Maybe—certainly—she'd be safer.*

But Priya's first loyalty wasn't to Malini. It was to herself, and to Bhumika, and to Ahiranya.

Rao's throat worked. "Are you sure?"

"As sure as someone can be."

"I cannot leave her to risk death alone," he said.

"She's not alone," said Priya. "She has me."

The prince bowed his head. "It's not enough."

"It's more than most people get," said Priya. "But...I promise, for what it's worth, that I'll do everything I can to keep her alive. I'll use what I have to help her survive until you or your prince can return for her."

It was more of a promise than she should have made—more feeling and more debt than she wanted to give Malini—but could Priya really leave her now, when she'd stayed up two nights watching her sleep, terrified the fool woman would die?

"I've done my duty by speaking to you," she said. "But now—I have to return to her. My lord." She bowed her head in acknowledgment.

He said nothing in return.

32

RAO

Prem was sitting alone, a great shawl wrapped around him despite the heat, an open carafe of wine in his hands. He was drinking directly from the bottle, a look of contemplation on his face.

"The horses are ready," announced Prem. "My men are arranging provisions. I tried to meet with General Vikram to give him my farewells, but praise the mothers, he's not receiving visitors at the moment. Share a drink with me?"

Rao leaned against the wall. "Princess Malini may be dying," he said. It was all he could manage.

Prem's eyes widened, then narrowed, in comprehension. "The maidservant was from her," he said. "I should have known the girl was one of *her* spiders. Gods, that woman has a way of collecting people, does she not?" Prem turned and thunked down his wine. He tugged the collar of his tunic. "What do you want to do?"

"I want to save her," said Rao. "But I know that isn't possible. And it isn't what she wants us to do anymore."

"Good. It isn't what I want us to do, either." When Rao gave him an incredulous look, Prem shook his head. "Don't stare at me like that. You know there's no easy way to save her. And brave as she was at court, as excellent as she was for putting together Emperor Aditya's cause, she's not . . . vital."

"Is she not?" Rao murmured.

"Aditya will come back for her, Rao. When the war's won."

"He can't if she dies."

"Then she'll be remembered for her sacrifices, and Emperor Aditya will honor her," said Prem firmly. "The promise of death awaits us all, Rao. Some of us get a good death and some don't. At least she won't die burning."

"As my sister did."

Prem didn't flinch at that. Only nodded and drank. "As your sister did, yes." He drank again, then sighed. "Ah, I'm sorry, Rao. I'm not good company."

"It's fine," Rao said.

It was not, in fact, fine.

"I am sorry for your loss. I am. But…" He shook his head. "We've lost so much already, and this coup isn't yet really begun. But that's how it goes, isn't it? Removing a despot from power comes at a cost. I just didn't particularly want to pay it."

A maudlin comment, from the usually lighthearted low prince. Rao waited, frozen for a moment, as Prem looked at him in return.

"You can't pine after her forever, Rao," Prem said finally. "She was never for you anyway."

Rao had to bite back a laugh. Prem didn't understand anything at all. Didn't understand what Malini was to him; what had been whispered to him long ago, a secret, a thing that was his and his alone, in the dark.

"I'm sorry," he said, straightening. "I've been a fool. I—" He turned. "I'll be back in a moment."

"Rao—"

"In a moment!" he shouted, and pelted out of the door.

He should not have been able to find the maid. In the dark of a crowded night, on a street that never slept, it should have been impossible. But when he ran out of the pleasure house, he saw the shadow of her, the shape of her shoulders and the paleness of her sari, as she moved between lantern-lit market stalls. He caught up with her. Gasped out, "Wait."

She turned, one swift arc, and he saw her hand clench into a fist. There was a knife in her grip, an ugly kitchen blade. She had the sense not to brandish it. It was held tight at her side, her arm at an angle, as if she were ready to gut him if need be. Her expression was tight, and only thawed minutely when she realized who he was.

"What do you want?"

"To give you a message."

"You've given me a message. I've given you hers. What more is there?"

"Just this. You tell her, I'll be beneath the entrance to the seeker's path," he said. "We'll wait for her at the grave site."

"The bower of bones," corrected the maidservant. "That's what we call it."

"The bower of bones," he agreed. "Tell her I'll wait until the festival of the dark of the moon is done. If she can escape, we will take her with us. If she sends word, we'll try to come for her. *I'll* try to come for her."

"She wouldn't want that," the maid said tightly.

"I know," said Rao. "But...she may weigh the risks and change her mind. I want her to have the choice." And then, with embarrassing sentimentality, he said, "If she is dying, she may want to be cared for her by her own people."

"More than she wants her cause to win?" The maid laughed. "You don't know her as well as you think you do, my lord."

"I know as much as I need to," he said.

He could not tell her that he knew deep in his bones that Malini would live. Such things were not for outsiders. He could not tell her the secrets of the nameless—the whispered answer that lived in his blood, that told him more about Malini than even Malini knew.

"Tell her that," he said. "That's all I ask."

After the maid had vanished, he made his way back to the pleasure house much more slowly. His side ached. Prem was gone. To organize his men, no doubt, or sleep off the drink.

Lata found him seated on the steps to the veranda of their ridiculous room. "You've delayed long enough," she said into the silence. "It's time to go to Aditya. He's been waiting for you."

"After the poet, when I was injured—you asked me what I wanted to do."

"You can't do what you want," Lata said. "Can you?"

"No." He shook his head.

She gazed back at him, entirely calm. She'd nominally been a servant in the imperial mahal, before Malini's fall from grace. But in truth, she'd been an apprentice to the sage who had educated Malini and Alori and Narina as children. She was as familiar as anyone could be with the strange weight of the nameless faith—its joys, its demands. Its price.

"Lata," he said. "Why do you never call me Rao?"

She gave him a considering look. Then she crossed the floor and sat beside him.

"I may be no priest of the nameless, but I am a sage," she said finally. "I understand the value your people place on names. And I know Rao isn't your true name. I know you keep to the oldest ways and pay the price those ways demand. I don't need to call you by a pet name. I honor the name that was whispered at your birth."

"Do you know what it is?"

She shook her head. "How would I?"

"My sister knew it," he said. "She told me her own, before she died. And I . . . I told her mine."

"I had no opportunity to speak with the princess before her immolation," Lata said quietly. "And she would not have told me anyway. I understand the telling is . . . significant. Special."

Rao nodded. "When your name is a prophecy, it is wise to keep it secret. Or so I was always taught. We only speak of it when the time is right. When the prophecy nears its fulfillment. When our voice has a purpose."

He knew the tale of his own naming. How his mother and father had carried him to the temple garden of Alor, a gentle, swelling valley full of trees that dripped with jewels upon threads. How the priest, in his pale blue, had taken Rao into the monastery and sought out his name from the fathomless dark of god. Rao had returned to the garden, at age five, and been given the gift of his name. He'd carried it ever since—the weight of its sharp consonants and its soft vowels. The weight of its promise.

"Alori…" He swallowed. "My sister. Her true name was—old Aloran is hard to translate but—but she was named She Who Will Burn upon the Pyre. And so she did."

"A death name is a terrible burden," Lata said, with such learned compassion that he did not dare look at her.

"She was strong. She managed it—well." Better than Rao would have. "My name doesn't prophesize my death. My name…"

"You can tell me if you wish," Lata said gently. "Or not."

He looked up at nothing. He thought of his sister, with her silences and her cleverness, and the way she'd touched her forehead to his arm and told him, *Don't weep, please don't weep. I'm okay. I've known all my life that one day I'd burn.*

"No," he said. "It isn't the right time. I know that."

He stood, wincing a little as the wound in his side pulled.

"But it is the right time for me to begin my journey to Srugna. I've done all I can here. Princess Malini's fate is out of my hands."

33

PRIYA

She climbed the Hirana with her eyes closed, the wind biting her cheeks, her hair catching in the breeze. At one point she stopped, pressed her head to stone, hooked a foot into a crook of broken rock and moss, and used her free hands to loosely plait her hair.

There. Much better.

What would Bhumika say if she saw me now? Priya thought, with no small sense of amusement. *Balanced on a deathtrap with nothing but my thick head?* Perhaps Bhumika would enjoy the excuse to yell at her.

When she entered the Hirana—slipping through quiet halls, under the shadows thrown by the guttering lanterns—she checked on Malini.

She was asleep. There was color in her cheeks; something easier about her form. And the minuscule dose of needle-flower Priya had left for her had been taken.

Perhaps she'd survive after all.

Priya lowered her head to the weave of the charpoy at Malini's side. Listened to her breathing—the steady, comforting rhythm of it.

And entered the sangam.

She'd avoided this for longer than she should have. The thought of seeing Ashok again had made her chest burn with an echo of pain, the memory of betrayal. But what scared her most was the falsely kind way he'd looked at her and spoken to her, in the moments before she'd flung herself beneath cosmic waters and returned to her flesh.

He'd hurt her for love. That was the way of strength, in their family.

She opened her mouth. Called for Bhumika in the fathomless winding of waters. She had howled for Ashok; this was something quieter. A beckoning.

And Bhumika came. She rose, a shadow spooling out of the water.

"Tell me," Bhumika said simply.

She told Bhumika everything as succinctly as she could. She spoke of her pact with Malini; of her meeting with one of Malini's allies, and of Malini's efforts to see Emperor Chandra replaced on the throne by his brother, Aditya.

"So war comes for us no matter what," Bhumika said. "Parijatdvipa turns upon itself. We're in an even greater mess than I thought." She sounded tired.

"What will you do?" Priya asked, thinking of the general, the children housed in the mahal. The future.

"I don't know. I don't have the power to fix everything, no matter how capable I may seem."

"That isn't what I meant."

Bhumika clicked her tongue, as if to say, *It doesn't matter*. "I should be asking you how you fare. Ashok harmed you."

Priya resisted the urge to touch a fist to her chest, to the place where Ashok had shoved his hand into her soul and twisted.

"I know Ashok is strong. That he can be dangerous when he needs to be. I just thought..." Priya stopped.

"You thought he was still a good man, beneath it all."

"He is a good man," snapped Priya. Then she forced herself to stop again, and looked away from Bhumika, at the winding cosmos around them, liquid and strange. If he was not good, how could Priya be good? How could any of them?

"You remember the boy he was," said Bhumika. "You don't—see—the man he is now."

"I remember that he saved my life. That he cared for me. Sometimes I feel like I can almost remember *that* night and I cannot hate him because..." Her voice cracked. "I don't like to talk about my feelings. I don't like any of this, Bhumika, and I swear if I could rip this anger out of me, if I could not feel what I feel, if I could erase that night entirely—"

"I know," Bhumika said. "I know. Do you remember how I would bring you up to my rooms and speak with you alone, from time to time, when you first came to the mahal?"

"You always had sweets," Priya said immediately. It was her strongest memory of that time. After years of starvation, she'd had a strange preoccupation with hunger. "Once you even had rasmalai. Covered in rose petals."

"I convinced Vikram I was brooding for a child," Bhumika said. "He liked that idea. So I had sweets for you, yes. And time for you, Priya. For a little while." A hesitation. "Pri. I did try to be family to you. I really did."

There was something aching in Priya's chest.

"I know," she said, with difficulty. "I do know that. You shouldn't listen to me when I'm angry. Or at all. I'm never particularly fair to you, Bhumika."

"Is that an apology?"

"No," said Priya. "This is an apology: I'm sorry. Savor it, because I'm not going to do it again."

The apology dropped between them heavily, awkward as a stone.

"Please don't," Bhumika said finally. There was something softer in her voice, as she shifted in the water, as it rippled soundlessly around the shadow of her. "You—and you won't remember this, I expect, Priya—you were so quiet when you first came to the mahal. Not...shy. But unwilling to speak. I would try to talk to you about our childhood. About the Hirana. About how you and Ashok had escaped. You refused to tell me anything.

"I thought at the time that it was trauma. You were a child. You were frightened and hurt and abandoned. But now, I think not. You made a choice, Priya. There was something you wanted to discard."

"You can't know that."

"I know how stubborn you are. You've never obeyed me," Bhumika said. "Not really. There is something in you that is...elemental. As there is in Ashok."

"Are you saying I'm like him?"

"I'm saying that you've sought the deathless waters. Allied and broke with Ashok. Made a pact with a princess of Parijatdvipa—all without me, of your own volition. You follow a path I can't walk, Priya, and you never look back at what you leave behind." She spoke gently. It only made the words cut more deeply. "You're driven by a moral code I can't fathom. In your own way, Priya, you're as dangerous as Ashok. Yes. I should have recognized that about you long ago."

Bhumika's sense of who Priya was—the fact that she saw Priya as some kind of staggering, strange, fierce, and elemental creature—made Priya want to laugh incredulously.

"I have never done anything—anything," said Priya. "I've been...nothing but a maidservant. Parts of me are broken and I stand in the middle of all those pieces and don't go anywhere. I'm stuck, Bhumika. In all this time, I've just been quiet. I've just survived."

"A biding quiet, I think. And now you're exactly where you were intended to be all along: on the Hirana, with the deathless waters almost in reach." Bhumika's voice was knowing. "I can tell that you're growing stronger."

"I never planned this."

"Did you not?" A pause. "I won't try to control you anymore, Pri. But I do ask you to think: Are any of the people you've trusted truly worthy of it?"

"I trust you," Priya managed to say.

Bhumika shook her head, slow and sure. "No," she said. "I don't think you really do. Go back, Priya. And please, keep the princess imprisoned and safe just a little longer. For my sake."

"What will you do?" Priya asked, not for the first time.

Bhumika was silent for a moment. Then she said, "I don't know, yet. But I'll begin by speaking with Vikram. I'll counsel him to carve a path through war that sees us all survive. And if he will not listen..." A shadow passed through her voice, black-winged. "Well. You and Ashok are not the only temple children."

"I wish you luck," said Priya. "For all our sakes, I suppose."

"Yes," said Bhumika. "For all our sakes."

She returned to her skin. Glanced at Malini's sleeping form, then slipped from the room to walk the triveni. It had been raining again. The ground was slick, almost a pool, a great mirror.

If Bhumika was right... If she had chosen not to speak. If she had chosen to forget...

She tilted her head back. Rain was falling again. One last shower for a fading monsoon. She rose to the plinth of the triveni, the stone cool and damp beneath her bare feet, her face raised to the sky. Soil. Sky.

Just show me the way.

"Why," she whispered. "Why did I have to show you the way, Ashok? What did I know that you didn't?"

The answer lay inside her. It always had. But she had folded herself small. She'd held that night of fire and death in a closed fist. She'd been too frightened that it would be stolen from her to let it go, to do anything but conceal it. Through grief and hunger and loss, through her arrival in the mahal, to drinking and laughing with Sima under the cover of trees—she'd carried it with her. She'd held it so it couldn't be touched or altered.

It was time to unfurl her fingers. It was time to see what she held.

For the first time in a decade, Priya thought of the night the temple children burned.

34

PRIYA

Priya tugged at the heavy bucket of water, swearing as it tilted precariously, a wave spilling out over the hem of her ghagra choli. "Nandi! Help me!"

"I can't help," Nandi said, sounding affronted. He was sitting in the center of the room with his hands clapped pointedly over his eyes. He had been sitting that way, wailing, for a good ten minutes. He'd had a run-in earlier with the handiwork of some of the elder temple children, who'd been growing deep bursts of spores on the walls. Nandi had touched where he shouldn't have, and a burst of yellow pollen had hit him square in the face.

Usually, Priya would have dragged him directly to one of the elders for a scolding and to have his eyes washed clean and a tincture applied to stop infection, but the elders had expressly forbidden Priya's group of children—the youngest and smallest—from leaving their rooms this evening. One of the twice-born had lost control of a seething knot of vines, which had cracked stone and burrowed their way under the surface of the temple, causing a fair amount of destruction. They'd already shattered the steps up the Hirana, stopping any pilgrims from making the journey.

The Hirana was always dangerous and changeable. Sometimes the path the pilgrims took vanished overnight. Sometimes strange wildflowers grew even upon the triveni, in violet and black and vibrant pink, and had to be plucked away with murmured prayers and reverence by the elders. But the Hirana was not vicious in its shifting moods, in the way mortals could be. Or so Elder Bojal said. Elder Bojal complained vociferously, to any other elder who would listen, that the "cursed" children had ruined the Hirana, totally and utterly. He'd only shut up when Elder Sendhil had cornered him and asked, in a low voice, if he wanted to confront the children directly himself.

Elder Bojal hadn't been able to answer that.

Elder Chandni hadn't commented on the changes to the Hirana. Not even the new cracks that opened to darkness, which had caught some of the general's own men in their maws. No one had died—the elders had intervened—but one man had broken his leg at an awful angle, and that had made thrice-born Sanjana and Riti—who were elders now, although none of the other elders called them such—laugh and laugh, as if blood and bones were a terribly funny business. But when Priya had asked Elder Chandni about it, she'd only shaken her head and told Priya to be careful.

"You're not quite like they are," she said. "Be glad of that."

Priya had thought that was an odd statement. Priya was exactly like the rest of them, even if she was only once-born. She had passed through the deathless waters during the festival of the dark of the moon, along with all the others: the youngest children trying to become once-born; the once-born ready to be twice-born; the twice-born seeking to rise to elderhood. She'd risen from the waters, gasping, when three of her age-mates had not. She'd sat in the sickroom, waiting to see if the waters would take her belatedly, with fever and wasting, as they sometimes did.

And like all the children who'd survived *that* journey, that unnatural and ill-starred journey, she'd grown...strange. The twice-born had suddenly been able to coax small blooms, burst pollen through buds. The thrice-born had sheared stone with leaf and thorn alone. And Priya and Nandi had stumbled through dreams of waters meeting, walking the sangam of ancient tales.

No elder has walked there in centuries, Elder Kana had

whispered. And of the rest, as the keeper of old lore she'd said: *No elder has had such power since the Age of Flowers.*

Mythically gifted they might be, but Priya and Nandi were still children, and Nandi was still a crybaby. Priya thumped the water down, struggling not to snap at him again.

"Lean back your head and open your eyes," she said.

"Don't yell at me!"

"I'm not!" Priya. "And if you don't want me to shout, stop being so, so..."

Nandi sniffled.

Relenting, Priya went over to him and tugged him gently forward. When he was near the bucket, she pried his hands away from his eyes and washed the pollen away as he blinked rapidly.

"Does it feel better?" she asked.

"I—I think so."

"Good."

"Are you two getting ready?"

Priya and Nandi turned as one to see thrice-born Sanjana leaning against the door. She wore a deep yellow sari, her hair loose over her shoulders, the maang tikka on her forehead ruby red, like a heavy drop of blood. A trail of moss had grown beneath her bare feet, but withered as she took a step forward.

"You're taking absolutely ages, and I'm bored," said Sanjana. "Riti's grumpy today, and Ashok's got some awful stomach ailment, he's refusing to eat a single thing, and there's so much lovely food laid out. Why are you dawdling?"

"Nandi got pollen in his eyes," said Priya.

"Ah," said Sanjana. "And—is that why your clothes are wet, Priya?"

Priya scowled in response, and Sanjana chuckled.

"Why did you hurt those men?" Priya asked suddenly, thinking of the man whose leg was broken. Maybe she shouldn't have asked. Maybe Sanjana would box her around the ears for asking. But Sanjana's expression was easy, her brow soft, and Priya didn't think so.

"Who?"

"The Parijati soldiers."

"Did it scare you, little dove?"

"I'm not easily scared," Priya said. They both knew that wasn't exactly a no.

Sanjana's answering smile was crooked. "Because the Parijati should be afraid of us," she said. "But you don't need to be afraid of me. We're family."

Sanjana had hit Priya more than once, and stolen her dinner, and laughed uproariously when Priya fell during training or fell asleep at meditation. But Priya also knew she meant what she'd said. Cruelty was part of their training, callousing the heart the way a knife calloused the hands. Weakness had to be burned away. Sanjana had always tried to make Priya strong, so that Priya would survive two more journeys through the waters. So that Priya would live.

"They're going to name Riti and me elders tonight," said Sanjana. "So I want you to look nice."

"I do look nice."

Sanjana kneeled down. She touched her fingers to Priya's hem. "Here," she said. "Let's make you a little prettier. Only a little, mind. I'm not a yaksa proper, I can't do such great magic."

"Ha-ha," Priya said flatly. But then she fell silent as Sanjana lightly brushed her fingers back and forth across her skirt, and the distant sound of rustling grass filled the air.

A faint tracery of real leaves, their veins fine as spun gold, lined the damp hem of Priya's dress.

"There," said Sanjana. "Doesn't that look lovely?"

She let the hem drop. It made a crinkling whisper as it brushed against Priya's ankles, as if the leaves still lived. "You look very smart too, Nandi," Sanjana added.

"Thank you." Nandi's voice was small. He was still hunched next to the bucket.

Sanjana laughed—not quite cruel and not quite kind—and swept out of the room.

To make his tears up to Priya, Nandi combed her hair, applying a little oil to it so that it would be shiny and supple and smell sweet. She dabbed a little on his head in return, and checked his eyes once more. They no longer looked swollen, and Nandi wasn't sniveling, so Priya dragged him from the room toward the feast. She could smell something roasting and wondered if the servants had made her favorite festive platter, of rice dyed green and yellow and studded with almonds, pistachios, and fat raisins, heaped with dumplings, and a broth both sweet and intensely spiced.

"Wait, Priya. We should put the bucket back," Nandi said to her urgently. "If Elder Chandni sees it, she'll know we didn't do as we were told. Stay in the room and go straight to the feast, she said, and she'll know we didn't."

"She'll only shout at us," Priya said with a shrug.

"Or she'll make us leave the feast early. Or tell us we can't have any of it."

It *was* the kind of punishment an elder would choose. Thinking longingly of that colored rice, Priya sighed. "Fine, let's go put it back. But quickly, or we'll be really late."

It was easier work, carrying the bucket between the two of them, though Nandi whined at Priya for bringing such an overfull bucket, and Priya snapped back in return that she'd just filled it and brought it without thinking, and it was Nandi's fault for hurting his eyes in the first place...

They heard voices. Stopped.

"The elders," hissed Nandi, and without bothering to respond, Priya hauled the bucket into a side cloister room and dragged Nandi in after her.

Footsteps drew in closer.

"We should wait until Bhumika returns." That was Elder Bojal's voice.

"You think she'll come back? Truly? The minute she passed through the waters the girl ran straight back to her family's bosom like a coward," Elder Saroj replied.

"Her family keep the faith. They'll bring her back."

A snort. "Keep the faith? Barely. The Sonalis know the direction of the wind. They'll never return her, you mark my words, they'll throw her into a suitable alliance and forget she ever served."

"Still..."

"They've grown so much stronger." The new voice was an urgent whisper. Elder Sendhil. "Every minute. Every hour. You can't waver in this now. Soon we will not be enough to manage. The emperor will send armies. Ahiranya will bear the consequences."

Nandi opened his mouth. Priya clapped a hand over it before he could let out a noise. "Make a sound," she whispered, "and I'll pinch your nose shut too."

He went silent.

"They're strong in the way we've taught them to be strong. Perhaps this is needful."

"What Emperor Sikander demands is unconscionable. *Inhuman.*"

"That is why we go with them," Elder Saroj said calmly. "They are our family. We go together."

"But surely we must discuss—"

"No." Elder Chandni's voice. It was sad but unwavering. "No, I think not. And we've discussed this enough. We agreed."

A silence. Then, Saroj spoke, her voice heavy: "It will be the end of us."

"A necessary end, I think," Chandni said softly. Priya bit down on her lip at that. "In this, the general isn't wrong."

There was a murmur that Priya could not catch, and then footsteps once more.

Elder Bojal. Elder Sendhil. Elder Saroj. Elder Chandni. All of them, conferring over strength and strangeness. Over the temple children.

Priya had never been commended for her intelligence, but she knew enough to feel a bristle of fear. She met Nandi's eyes. Uncovered his mouth.

"What do you think they meant?" Nandi whispered.

Priya swallowed. "I don't know."

The feast was in full swing in the northern chamber, cushions arrayed in a circle, platters set on the ground including—as Priya had hoped—the dyed rice and dumplings. Once they arrived, Elder Chandni shut the doors behind them. They were the last children in attendance.

There were cloths draped across the walls, in a vibrant array of colors. Priya brushed near one. It smelled sweet, resinous, like ghee or sugarcane, and was faintly...wet.

Elder Chandni touched a hand to Priya's forehead. Then she leaned down and kissed her cheek.

"The left door," Chandni murmured.

The elder's fingers felt cold and trembled a little.

She said nothing else to Priya, and that—ah.

"Stay here," Priya hissed at Nandi, and he sat down without complaint.

Sanjana and Ashok were seated next to one another, and when Priya sidled up next to them, Sanjana said, "Finally. What are you going to have? Not wine, I hope, though it would be funny to watch you be sick, I suppose."

"I need to tell you something," Priya said in a quiet voice. She must have sounded upset, because they both looked at her— Ashok clutching a tepid glass of water and looking faintly ill— and listened intently. As Priya continued, Sanjana's face went pinched with fear or fury, Priya couldn't tell. Sanjana took her by the wrist and said, "We'll talk to them. Now."

She stood up and...stumbled. Raised a hand to her head, fingertips to her temple, and swallowed.

Fell.

Priya would never be able to remember what followed with any clarity. She remembered only shouting, and her siblings trying to use their water-given gifts. They managed, somewhat. The ground splintered. The stone churned, moved by vine and root, by their magic-flecked fury. But there was something wrong with all of them, and little by little they all slumped, sickened.

"The food," Ashok murmured suddenly, his face twisting as he looked around them. He stood rapidly and took Priya's arm. "We're going."

He dragged her forward, between fallen bodies.

She heard a noise—a puncturing noise, and a cry—and Ashok dragged her forward farther, farther, aiming for the left door as she'd told him to. She turned her head back. Nandi, she needed to get Nandi—

"Come on, Priya," Ashok said sharply. "Come on. *Ah*."

There were soldiers, Parijati soldiers, blocking the doors. It made Priya's stomach jolt to see them here, these outsiders in a place reserved for Ahiranyi pilgrims and servants and her own temple family.

Ashok shoved Priya behind him.

He had always been a good fighter. They all were. But the other temple children were drugged and barely conscious, unable to fight as they normally would have. Ashok wasn't similarly stricken. He raised a hand before him, and vines shot through the walls and floor. One soldier made a noise of horror—there was a clang of falling steel.

Ashok took the soldier's weapon and made a slash, his arm jerking.

Priya felt something wet and hot against her face and forced herself not to squeeze her eyes shut. Instead she grabbed a little carving knife from the table, from beside where one of her siblings had fallen unconscious, their forehead pressed to an upturned plate of food, and clutched it in a sweat-slippery hand.

She and Ashok rushed forward, and there was no grace to it: just an ugly press of bodies and blood, and Ashok dragging her, and Ashok slamming the door with his hands, and Priya turning back, meeting Nandi's eyes across the room, his head at an awful angle, nothing living in the wrongness of it.

The last thing she saw before Ashok grabbed her in his arms

was Elder Saroj touching a lantern flame to one of the hanging cloths. The room began to burn. Saroj dragged the cloth from the wall, and Priya saw it fall on one of her siblings.

"Don't look." Ashok dragged her out.

He attacked the soldiers brutally, economically, slicing through one artery, breaking another neck, losing his knife in an eye socket. He lowered Priya so he could fight, but when a dagger hit the ground at her feet, he swept her up into his arms and ran.

"Priya," he bit out, against her hair, his voice breaking through the pounding clamor of her own blood. "Priya, where is the way to the deathless waters?"

"I don't know!"

"You do. You do. Don't fail us now."

Like all other parts of the Hirana, the entrance to the deathless waters moved. Sometimes the Elders made a ritual of seeking it out. But Priya had never struggled to find it. She was not the best fighter—not the cleverest or strongest—but even with her eyes closed she could find the way unerringly.

It had astonished Elder Chandni when she'd realized. The elders had all tested her. Blindfolded her. Spun her about until she was dizzy with it. Asked her at night, at dawn, in the heart of the day. She always knew the path.

No one could explain her gift. She'd heard the elders discuss it once, in Chandni's room, when she'd been curled up asleep on the floor beside Chandni's pallet.

"It's a strange affinity," Saroj had murmured. "Oh, the longer we're here, the more we feel connected to the Hirana, to be sure. But the girl is...different."

Chandni's fingers had carded gently through her hair.

"Not many children are born on the Hirana," she'd said. "It's no surprise that she shares a special bond with the temple."

"Children shouldn't be born here," Sendhil had said, and there had been something in his tone that had made Elder Chandni still.

"As you say," Chandni had murmured, drawing the covers over Priya.

She hadn't mentioned it again. And it didn't matter anymore. Priya squeezed her eyes tight shut. Raised a trembling hand from Ashok's shoulder, and pointed the way. He swore an oath—of fear or thanks, she didn't know—and followed her guidance.

The entrance was set into the floor of an unlit corridor. Ashok skidded to a stop. Still holding her, he jumped into the darkness, stumbling a little down the first step, then the second. Priya opened her eyes then, and watched as he used his twice-born gifts and touched his fingers to the aperture above them.

The way closed, and they were in darkness.

They made their way down. Down to the heart of the Hirana, the yolk in the egg.

They reached ground. Even through the closed lids of her eyes, she could see and feel the press of the luminous water. The tug of it, more stars than river.

"Don't look, Priya," he whispered. So she didn't. She pressed her head against his shoulder, hard enough that she could feel the firm pressure of cloth against her eyes, sticky with her own tears and his sweat. She could smell smoke, still. "Don't look. Just show me the way."

"The way where?"

"Out of here," he said. His voice trembled, faintly. He smelled of copper. "You know the Hirana better than anyone. And it knows you."

The distant drip of water. Luminous blue light, all around them, seeping under her eyelids. He wasn't wrong. Sometimes the Hirana felt like another limb to her. He carried her near the water's edge, seeking a way through. She pointed the way. Tunnels. There were tunnels after.

"I can't touch the water," she gasped, "I can't, I can't. What if I die?"

"Hush," he whispered. "Hush. I won't drop you."

He tucked her face beneath his chin. He was holding her up, even though his arms trembled, even though he was sweating and she could hear him crying.

"We're going to be fine," he said, muffled and shaky. "Just fine."

They opened the way together, in the end. Reshaped the stone and emerged free and alone, on the green surrounding the Hirana.

Above them the pyre still burned.

"Don't look," Ashok repeated. And though he should have been too weak to pick her up again, she heard him inhale and do it anyway. She wrapped her legs around his waist, her arms around his neck, and didn't try to be strong. And for once he did not ask her to be.

It took two days for the leaves on Priya's skirt to die.

Years. Years she and Ashok had spent on the streets, hungry and mosquito-bitten, stealing food and begging for it when there was none to steal. He'd beaten other men a few times, taking their coin. He'd made allies out of bad men, and men like Gautam, who could be bound by fear and favors and debts unpaid. But as he'd grown sicker, his gifts had seemed to fade too. And Priya's gifts had always been small. They'd grown smaller, beyond the Hirana, along with her grasp on her own memories.

Chandni had seen something in her. But that had been in another life.

Now, Priya stood on the plinth, the rain in her eyes, and heaved such deep, sobbing breaths that her lungs ached with them.

She'd found the way through. That night. She was the one who'd saved Ashok, and he had saved her.

He saved me. I saved him.

She realized she was crying. She dashed her eyes with the backs of her hands, furious with herself for weeping like a little girl. No matter how old she grew, family it seemed still had the power to hurt her.

They had saved each other. He'd left her for Bhumika to raise, because he'd loved her. He'd hurt her because he loved her.

Love. As if love excused anything. As if the knowledge that

he was cruel and vicious and willing to harm her made her heart ache any less.

She stepped down from the plinth. The cloth of her sari blouse clung to her skin. Her hair was dripping. Her footprints, as she crossed the triveni and walked out into a corridor leading to the kitchens, were damp, the stone beneath them shimmering with movement, as if it walked with her.

There was no void in her any longer. Whatever she was— weapon, monster, cursed or gifted—she was whole. Beneath her the Hirana was warm. An extension of her.

She'd known the way all along.

The Hirana led her to a cloister room—a small, unassuming cloister room—that had once been tended to carefully. Even in those days long gone, it had been plain, bare but for the pattern of waves etched into the walls and floor.

The lines flowed around Priya's feet as she walked.

The way to the deathless waters was not fixed. It appeared where it chose to. As a little girl, Priya had sprawled more than once over the opening, her head tipped over the edge in room after room, listening to the howl of the cavern beneath, the hollowness inside its stone shell. It had sounded mournful. Like sea. Like song.

The floor had no opening now. But Priya kneeled down. She set her hands to the stone.

She should not have been able to open the way alone, only once-born, with none of the stronger gifts of her fellow children. But the deathless waters wanted to be found. The Hirana had been shaped by temple hands, temple child flesh—living and dead—and it moved and clung and changed around her with the ebb and flow of her own heart. It wanted this for her.

The ground rippled beneath her, great waves of stone drawing back. The earth opened.

Priya stared down into the darkness. Pressed her teeth to her tongue, a light and grounding pain, and sat on the edge. She lowered her feet. Nothing met them, for a moment, and then the earth moved once more, vegetation forming a step beneath the soles.

She straightened. Took another step. Another.

It was a long way down into the dark. At least her memory hadn't lied about that. By the time she reached the bottom—felt cool loam beneath her feet, and the chill of deep darkness around her—she was parched, all the magic in her run dry.

But she didn't need it any longer. The deathless waters lay before her, a long coil like the great sinuous curve of a snake. In the dark beneath the world, it glowed a faint blue. She heard it in the silence: a drumbeat, a whisper, a music in her soul.

Priya looked at the waters. She thought of Bhumika begging her not to follow this path, the look in her eyes saying she'd had no real hope of controlling Priya and never had. She thought of Ashok, twisting his hand in her chest, driven by fury, and how he had held her when she was small and they were alone. She thought of Rukh, whom she'd tried, in her own small way, to hold and protect in turn, living her childhood all over again.

Priya was not here for them, or despite them. Their voices remained with her, but underneath it all was one simple truth: Priya had wanted to find the deathless waters not for Ashok or her dead temple siblings, but for herself. She had always hungered for it. And now she was here.

She didn't allow herself to think anymore. She took a step forward, and another, and immersed herself.

A rush of water. The grip of pressure around her skull, a band like clutching bones around her lungs, luminous blue meeting the snap of her opening eyes and—

Silence.

35

ASHOK

"So how do we proceed then?"

"Proceed?" Kritika's voice was deferent, as it always was. Ah, ever-watchful Kritika.

"What," said the man, an edge of impatience in his voice, "will you give us for the weapons?"

The men before him were Ahiranyi and Srugani, and they'd taken this village, abandoned when the rot overran it, as their own. Someone had done a poor job burning the rot away, and it still hung about them: vivid flowers hanging from the walls, slick and venom-bright. Great curling roots, pulsing with a fleshy sentience, poured through the cracks in the floors. Most of the men had some hint of rot about them: a dust of strangeness to the veins of their hands, or pollen in their hair, or a quality of bark to their faces.

They wore sacred wood, for what little good it would do them. It was the only reason they weren't all yet dead.

Ashok and the brothers and sisters who'd joined him in drinking the deathless waters were safe from the rot, or so it seemed. The rest of his followers had taken suitable precautions, and wore cloth bound about their mouths and noses, their hands swathed in gloves, beads of sacred wood bound on long threads around their throats.

These thugs—this militia—had nothing to live for and no one else willing to barter with them. Although rot couldn't be spread between people, the rot-riven were still shunned. There were precious few other gangs that would consider causing them harm, but none would trade with them either, and from the pinched look of the man's face, the starkness of his cheekbones, food was running scarce. It made them both willing to sell their fine weapons for any ridiculously low barter they could manage, and also made them entirely volatile. Either Ashok's people would leave with everything they wanted, or the thugs would try to ensure they left with nothing at all.

Ashok was half tempted to throw a bag of rice on the floor, just to see what they would do. But instead he chose to be sensible. "I'm not unreasonable. I—"

It hit him, then. Like a wave. Starry power rushing through him. The feel of her, through the bed of the undergrowth, the sap veins of the forest, the drumming heart of it all. He felt it through the root that had wormed its way inside him, when he'd entered the waters once, then twice, hollowing himself so the river was forever winding inside him, binding him to the source.

Kritika whirled to look at him.

"What's wrong with him?" the man asked.

One of Ashok's own boys took him by the arm. Acting as a crutch, the boy led Ashok out of the hut, the two of them lumbering into the light.

"Don't worry," he heard Kritika say. "We're not actually here for your weapons, after all..."

Two more of his people waited outside the doors. They ushered him away, into the shadow beneath the trees, away from the suspicious eyes of the rot-riven men.

Without guidance from him, his followers fell into line, guarding him in a loose circle, their scythes ready and their feet grimly planted.

"What happened?" asked one.

"I need silence," he said. "Please."

They nodded in acknowledgment. The barrier closed in tighter.

Priya. She'd found the way.

His equilibrium steadied, his pulse settling into a less frenetic rhythm. He needed to be calm. He breathed and breathed. He needed to enter the sangam.

He entered like a creature stumbling, ungainly. Fell to his knees in the water.

"Priya!"

He had trained her. He had made her. He'd kept her safe, when everyone else had died and they'd had nothing but each other.

"Priya!"

He'd begged coin and food from strangers. Or threatened them for it. When he'd begun to grow sick—blood in his cough, his lungs bands of agony—he'd knifed a man for the parcel of food tucked under his arm. He'd watched her eat it and been glad he had strength enough to kill for her, terrified that he would soon not even have that.

He'd given her up. Abandoned her to Bhumika, their sister who had looked like a stranger, with her finely woven saris and her cold eyes, her husband whose hands were stained in their siblings' blood. He'd cut out his heart. When he'd been a dying boy and nothing but that, Priya had been his heart.

He yelled for her in the sangam and she did not come.

The water moved around him. He felt Bhumika, the alarm of her, across the water. But she knew as well as he did what had happened; felt it through whatever bonded them, temple-raised and gifted, together.

He realized then that Priya was not coming.

The girl he'd saved. The girl he'd abandoned.

Fine. So be it.

She had the deathless waters. She'd opened the way. And the way was all he needed.

He returned to his flesh. His family of followers had surrounded him in a circle, all thirty of them looking down at him.

Some held metal weapons. Others, stakes and staves carved from sacred wood, burning with heat and the promise of violence.

Kritika crossed through them. She was wiping her scythe clean of blood.

"We've dealt with those men," said Kritika. "And we have what we need."

They were always underestimated, until they drew on their masks.

They still had safe houses untouched and unknown by the regent. But they needed food and weapons and sources of coin. The nobility who had funded them were more wary, after the attack on Lord Iskar, unsure of what would happen under Lord Santosh's regency. And his regency was coming, sure as the sunrise.

But these rot-riven outcasts had also possessed something Ashok needed far more than food.

"You have it?"

Kritika nodded and held it forward.

The villagers had once had a proper traditional village council. Most of their wealth had been stripped away by the carrion birds that were the militia and any other bandits or desperate folk who had passed through the region, but no one had taken the most precious item the council had once possessed.

It looked like a sack of odds and ends: bottles of glass or wood or dried leather, bound bead-tight. Nothing of worth, to ignorant eyes.

He reached in. Felt that pull, that poisonous yearning. Pulled out the vials of deathless water, one by one.

They buried the bodies. He took three of the strongest of his followers with him to do it. Then, as they made their camp a safe distance away, he told his followers everything.

Kritika was silent for a long moment. Behind her, around her, the others listened and waited, watchful. Then she said, "What shall we do, Ashok?"

He thought of Priya. Trying to make her strong.

The absence of her.

"We find her," he said, "and we take the way from her. Being strong means doing what is necessary, no matter the cost."

Kritika nodded. "Then you will allow us all to drink the water with you," she said. "And join you in saving our country."

Thirty drinking. A high number. They would need more water to sustain them, and Ashok—who had spent years sourcing vials of deathless water—knew it wouldn't be possible. If they drank today, this would be a final gambit. If they did not find the deathless waters soon, it would be the literal death of them.

"You have sacrificed enough. I cannot ask this of all of you."

"I am older than you, Ashok, but not as old as you seem to think," Kritika said, with her usual gravity. "I still have the desire in me to seek freedom. To burn Parijatdvipa's soldiers and lords and see the regent strung from his neck. Allow me that. Allow us all that."

"We may all die," said Ashok, finally. "We may not obtain my sister. We may be killed by Parijatdvipa's men. This may be our end."

Kritika said nothing. She knew the shape of Ashok's thoughts, his words, his silence. She knew he was not done.

"Knowing this may be our death," he said slowly, "knowing this may be the last time we are so strong, we should destroy as many of our targets as possible. The nobles and the wealthiest, the merchants and physicians that Parijatdvipa needs to keep its claws in our land—we need to kill them all. Whether we obtain my sister or not, we must have some sort of victory." He looked at Kritika. "Are you ready?" he asked. "Are you ready to risk everything we have?"

"You have prepared for it," said Kritika. "We all have."

Yes. They'd accumulated weapons. They had loyal men and women, and the people they'd bought loyalty from too, with fear or hope or coin or some alchemical combination of all three.

"A little poison," said Ganam, "is something I am willing to take."

"We all are," said another boy. "For this, we all are."

His mind was moving, bird-swift. They could leave the ones who could not fight in the forest. The youngest and oldest. The rest...

The rest were already standing before him. The men and women who had allied to see Ahiranya free. Who rejected the shackles of outside rule. Who sought better than the rot that had stolen their homes and killed their loved ones; the hunger that followed when the regent did not care to ensure that they were fed.

And Kritika, the woman who had saved him when he had thought he would die, her lined face already set and implacable. She knew what was coming. They all did.

"We can't be cautious any longer," he said. "You're right. Care has not won us anything. This is our last stand. Our last howl of rage. Let us show them that we are heirs to the forest, brothers and sisters. Heirs to the deathless waters. Let us show them tooth and claw and put an end to Parijati rule."

Kritika apportioned out the vials. Only a taste. It only required a taste.

She placed a vial in his hand, too. His fingers trembled. He did not have long.

"We're taking the Hirana. We're taking its magic," he said. "We're taking Ahiranya."

"A last stand," said Kritika.

The circle around him lifted the vials and drank.

36

BHUMIKA

She returned to her body with a ragged groan.

Ashok. Damn him. She felt as if the poison of his rage were swimming in her own skull. She rose up from the ground, her maids fussing about her, and said, "I need to see my husband."

"Shall I fetch the physician?" a maid asked.

"The physician? No. Fetch my husband. Him alone."

She settled on a floor cushion. Accepted a glass of something sweet and cool, drinking it swiftly to settle the shiver of her limbs. Vikram entered, walking slowly still as a result of his wound, followed by his closest guards. He'd been at some kind of meeting, she guessed, from the tired look of his eyes. She'd seen that expression before.

"Is the child unwell?" Vikram asked abruptly, looking her over with concern. She rose to her feet, shaking her head.

"I'm well," she said. "And so are they, I expect."

"Then why am I here, Bhumika?"

"I asked to see you alone," she said, glancing briefly at the commander, who was staring straight ahead, his eyes fixed on nothing in the distance.

"Leave us, Jeevan," Vikram said shortly, and the commander bowed his head once in acknowledgment and departed.

"Well?" Vikram's voice was edged in impatience, his attention already wandering, now that he knew there was no immediate danger to her health.

"I have news," said Bhumika. "A terrible warning. I cannot keep it from you any longer."

His face was like stone. "Speak," he said.

Here, she hesitated, then said, "My family are old and venerable, Vikram. And I am…approachable. Sometimes people feel more—comfortable—speaking to me, than they would perhaps feel speaking to you. And I have heard whispers about the rebels. I believe we're in great danger. The city is in danger. The mahal must be protected, and the people must be drawn into its walls."

"Tell me who has spoken to you," he said. "Ahiranyi highborn, is it? Gossiping maids? A guard or a merchant?"

"I would rather not say."

"Bhumika. I need names. Now."

"If someone approaches a woman of position with a warning, and asks not to be named," Bhumika said carefully, "then revealing their name would ensure that that woman would never be warned again."

"No one should have approached you at all," he said, the stony look on his face now lending his voice a leaden quality. "You are my wife. I am the regent. They should have approached me."

"I have told you nothing untrue," said Bhumika quietly. "I am sorry I am the source of this. But I am your wife. I would not lie to you about this."

"Anyone with knowledge worth having could have spoken to any of my advisors," he said, with a belittling gentleness. "Or my guards. My men. Not you. You have been given baseless, poisonous gossip, Bhumika, nothing more. They should not have approached you in your fragile condition."

It hovered on her tongue, the full truth.

There were so many times she had wanted to be honest with him. There were so many times she'd almost told him what she was.

There was an illusion that had fallen over her when she'd wed him. It did not always hold her. But sometimes the veil of it covered her eyes. Sometimes she believed she loved him. Sometimes she was grateful to him, for the fine mahal, for the opportunity to keep a handful of people safe.

Oh, she was careful to sweep it away, to remember the bare bones of the business at hand. She'd married the regent of Ahiranya. She'd married the man who'd instigated the murder of her siblings and would have seen her burn too, if she'd not had a blood family who loved her too well to truly let her go, and the political clout to erase her past and save her. But live with a person long enough, lie in their bed, no matter the politics of it, and you will feel something. Such things were inevitable.

But now it was not love that tugged the truth to her tongue. It was furious spite that made her want to speak.

He thought so little of her. So little.

You know so little, husband. My temple brother has been biding his time, building his strength, waiting until he could take the powers of the deathless waters before murdering you and every Parijati in this country. And now my fool sister has found the way to the waters, and has taken their power herself, instead of giving it to him. So if you want your rule to survive, Vikram—if you want to save Ahiranya from the promise of blood—you will listen to me. You will listen.

No. She couldn't tell him that. But there was venom in her, regardless, when she said, "When the rebels claw this city apart— when our home and those dependent upon us burn—will you remember my warnings? You will regret not listening to me, Vikram, simply because I am merely your wife. If you cannot trust me, why did you marry me?"

She'd said too much. She knew it, looking into his face.

"You speak out of turn," he said. "It is not your place to direct me. It is not even your place to counsel me." His face tightened; she saw him wrestling with his own spite, resisting. Then, giving in, and saying, "If I had wanted a wise and clever wife, I would have married a woman of Parijat."

"You gained the loyalty of the Ahiranyi highborn because you married me, a Sonali woman," she said, not without pride and certainly not without anger. "That is worth something, I know.

After you killed the temple children they would sooner have spat on your shadow. And what highborn Parijati woman would have had you, a man only regent by merit instead of the shallow business of blood?"

He was before her then. His hands on her upper arms. It took a moment for the pain to register—for her to feel the bite of his fingers, the casual, unknowing strength of them, grinding the meat of her arms, her bones.

"*Enough.*" He shook her—just a little, as if she were an animal to be bidden quiet, and her teeth rattled, and her insides curdled from it. "Names, Bhumika, or nothing at all."

She did not bare her teeth at him. She did not set her own hands neatly around his throat. She lowered her eyes. Names or silence? Well, then she would have to give him silence.

Her sudden demureness must have given him pause. She felt his grip loosen a little. Raising her gaze, she saw him glance at the curve of her belly.

"I will call for the physician," he said, and in that she heard a wealth of things: his fear that he had, perhaps, hurt her and by extension hurt the child within her. The belief that all she'd said was a product of her flesh—her pregnancy, her so-called womanly weakness of heart and body—and not evidence of her intelligence, her political acumen, and all that she was.

"No more of this." He placed his hand upon her stomach; a warm, proprietary hand. "This is all that matters, Bhumika. Focus upon it."

A child should not be a chain, used to yoke a woman like cattle to a role, a purpose, a life she would not have chosen for herself. And yet she felt then, with an aching resentment, how Vikram would use their child to reduce and erase her. She hated him for that, for stealing the quiet and strange intimacy of her and her own flesh and blood and making it a weapon.

"I will," she said placidly. "I'm sorry."

Her arms ached. She could not rely on Vikram. Could not even use him. She would have to fight Ashok herself. So be it.

37

PRIYA

She was under the water for minutes, or hours, or centuries. She did not know.

The water coursed through her. It swept through her lungs. Through her blood. It wasn't cold or sweet. It was like fire, eating through her flesh and her marrow, relentless. *I'm dying*, she thought, at first wildly, and then calmly, as her fear was carried away along with everything else inside her. She felt as if she had been scoured clean. As if she were one of the coconuts she'd longed to place on a shrine, once. Split, her insides, bruised and flowering, scraped away.

Images slipped from her mind's eye as swiftly as they arrived: great carved faces of wood turning toward her, eaten by flame that poured from their own mouths. Bodies splitting, three rivers of waters pouring from their insides, which were empty, open to the void. Voices clamored in her ears, but she couldn't understand them. She kicked her feet and moved her arms, rising up, or diving deeper. She couldn't orient herself. She needed to breathe. She needed to get *out*.

There was a drumbeat of silence.

In the places inside her soul and her bones that had been hollowed—magic poured in.

She saw the sangam beneath her. Saw the whole world. She felt the forest of Ahiranya—every tree, every crop, every creeping vine, the insects that burrowed through the soil. She felt her kin. Bhumika, there in her rose palace. Ashok, deep in the forest, walking on earth rich with bones. And she felt other souls. Other kin. In the forest, others who were like her moved and breathed and lived.

She wasn't as alone as she'd believed for so long.

She gasped out—surprised, or laughing, or spasmodically seeking air, she didn't know—and the water rushed in deeper and vaster, swallowing her as she swallowed it in turn.

There was nothing, after that. Not for a long time.

Later. Later.

Her head broke the surface of the water and she was breathing cold air, gasping, her lungs aching.

She'd survived. She was twice-born.

She couldn't feel anything beneath her feet, as she kicked to keep herself afloat. There was just water, fathomless underneath her body. Around her the water flickered, as if dappled by sunlight through leaves. But there were no trees and no roots this deep beneath the ground. Above her was only the dark cavern of the Hirana.

She swam to the edge of the water and dragged herself up onto the cold earth. Her clothes were soaking, heavy. Her hair was a weight of water. She wrung it out a little. Her insides still sang and burned but she was cold.

She couldn't remember exactly what had passed when she'd stepped beneath the waters. Already the memories were beginning to slip away from her like sand. But she knew what she felt now: power, dripping from every inch of her. Power bursting like flowers beneath the closed lids of her eyes, when she squeezed them shut and let out a ragged, joyful laugh. When she opened her eyes once more, she saw that small buds had unfurled from the surface of the soil beneath her knees. She curled her fingers around one. It was warm.

She released a slow breath, feeling magic pour through her with shocking, glorious ease. The ground trembled, a little. Then its surface burst, and there were buds all around her, roots and leaves rising from the maw of chill soil.

Priya started to laugh again. She couldn't help it. She was twice-born, she'd found the waters, she was strong. She felt invincible. She felt as if she could turn around right now and dive back beneath the water, take on all the power of the thrice-born.

But no. That had never been done. For a reason, surely? She didn't know. She knew nothing. But it didn't matter what she knew or didn't. She had this. A gift, living inside her.

She remembered that some of the children who rose from the water had died...later. But if that was to be her fate, it wasn't something to think of now. Through the invincible glow of power she could feel Ashok rattling in her skull, calling for her, furious.

He wanted what she now had. And she knew—with the bone-deep assurance of a woman who'd felt his fist around her heart—that she could not give it to him.

She made her way up, up, up. And when she rose to the Hirana's surface, she turned back and looked at the entrance to the deathless waters. She leaned forward. Touched her fingers to the stone. With the same bleeding, lacerating power, she drew the rock together. Sealed the way shut.

Ashok would not be able to find it without her now.

She crossed the Hirana: the empty corridors, the triveni. The air was cold and soft, the ground strangely warm—as if the Hirana came alive, sang, at her presence, at a twice-born crossing its surface.

The corridor to Malini's room was quiet. She pushed open the door softly, expecting to find Malini as she'd left her, sleeping on the charpoy. Instead Malini was sitting up, clutching her cheek. Even between her fingers, Priya could see the dark shadow of a bruise.

She felt a movement behind her, from the corner by the door. There was suddenly something sharp beneath her chin. She felt something hot. The wetness, not of water, but of blood, as Pramila's hand trembled around the blade.

MALINI

You poisoned me first.

Malini did not say it, of course. But she thought it. She sat very still, her hands in fists in her lap, her eyes wide, and thought it with all the fury in her. She had not had to feign softness or weakness when Pramila had first confronted her and slapped her, accusing her of poisoning Pramila in secret, of being an impure and evil creature down to her core. Malini's tongue was thick with the taste of metal, the clinging memory of needle-flower, gently administered by Priya the last time Malini had briefly awoken.

The second—and third—time Pramila had hit her she'd refuted everything Pramila had said. No, she had not poisoned Pramila. No, there was no plot against her. Malini had been consuming her wine obediently, taking her medicine as was expected. No, Priya had not betrayed Pramila. Priya was loyal.

And yet. For all her lies, spoken with all the earnestness she could muster, here they were: Pramila, red-eyed and furious, her hand trembling around a knife. Priya, with her head slightly raised, a thin rivulet of blood winding its way down her throat.

"Why are you holding a knife to my maid's throat?" Malini asked, letting a quiver shake the last words. It was not difficult. It was amazing, really, how close a tremor of fury sounded to a tremor of fear. How dare Pramila. How *dare* she. "Pramila, I don't understand. Why are you doing this? What have I done to offend you?"

"Oh, don't try that with me, you sly bitch," Pramila said. Her voice was savage, and her hand twitched a little with the force of her feeling. "It may have taken me time, Malini, but I know now. You used this maid to poison me, didn't you? You want me dead. Well, I can't kill you. I ..." A shuddering breath. "But this one is a traitor."

Priya was soaked. Her hair was plastered to her shoulders. Water was dripping from the hem of her sari, and the blood at her neck had turned from red to a washed-out pink. Where in the world had she been? Malini had been trapped in a haze of sickness for mothers knew how long, and clearly much had passed in the time she was in a void. Curse it.

Priya looked strangely calm. She met Malini's eyes. What did she want to tell Malini? What did that calmness mean?

Malini could not understand it. She was tired, hollowed out by grief dreams and poison.

"Priya has been a loyal maidservant," Malini managed to say in a wavering voice.

"Loyal to *you*."

"She's a good girl," said Malini, even though she knew it was useless to continue the lie. Still. The *knife*. "A simple girl."

"I don't even know if you'd be sad to lose her," Pramila said thickly. "You probably didn't even weep over my Narina, did you? And she was meant to be like a sister to you. Oh, but you let her die happily enough. What will a simple, stupid maid matter to a monster like you?"

This time it was not an accidental flinch that brought blood to Priya's skin. It was a deliberate movement of Pramila's hand. Priya's mouth parted, just slightly.

And Malini felt something inside her tighten.

Being locked here had made Malini a shadow of herself. She'd been haunted by her own past—by a flower-wreathed princess of Parijat with a shrewd smile and a voice full of secrets, who had the hunger and the wherewithal to tear Chandra from his throne—and by how beyond her grasp even the possibility of being that woman lay.

But suddenly it no longer mattered. Suddenly her spine was iron. Her tongue tasted of blood, as if Priya's hurt lay inside her. She did not need flowers or court or the graces due a princess, to be what she was.

"Pramila," she said. Her old voice came out of her—water-deep. "Lower the knife. You've never killed before. Will you start with this one?"

Pramila went quite still. After Malini's trembling, her sudden strength was a weapon all its own.

"I can do what is needful," Pramila gritted out.

"Is killing a mere maid needful?" Malini asked, letting her voice spool from her lips like a silk noose. "Come now, Pramila. You've never been cruel." A lie. But it was a lie Pramila believed, and it would strike her like truth. "The only needful murder you must commit is mine. And you balk even at that, don't you? You feed me needle-flower, but not enough to kill me quickly. You entreat me to choose the pyre, but you will not light one beneath me yourself.

"In that, you are very like my brother." Malini let pity seep into her tone. "He cannot stand to have blood on his hands either. He chose to place mine on yours, after all. Tell me, is he displeased I still live? Is my continued survival a failure?"

"I have dreamt so many times of killing you myself," Pramila spat. "Believe me, I have. I don't fear blood on my hands. But unlike you, princess, I try to do what is right. I've tried so hard to ensure that your death would purify you. But now, now I've woken time and again from a sleep riddled with nightmares, now I've dreamt drugged dreams where my daughter screams..." Pramila swallowed. She raised the knife an increment further.

A thicker rivulet of blood snaked down Priya's throat.

"Don't hurt her," Malini said, and was horrified to hear her voice falter all of its own accord. By the mothers, it was one thing to tremble when she had chosen to do it. It was quite another to do it now, when an air of command had momentarily held Pramila still, and perhaps could again. "Don't—Pramila, she is nothing."

"Nothing," Pramila repeated. "Nothing and yet—look at you. Are you going to weep? I think you might. If you're debased enough that you'd cry over a maid, then—good. Good!" Pramila's laugh was more a sob, a haunting ribbon of grief. "You took *everything* from me!"

Malini had felt helpless in the past. She did not feel helpless now, although she should have. Her cheek was throbbing. Her head was spinning with stars.

"If you kill her," she said, in a voice that seemed to come from somewhere far beyond her, from somewhere old and beyond mortal lifetimes, "you do not know what you will make of me. I will see you ruined, Pramila. I will see your living daughters ruined. I will blot all that brings you joy out of this world. I will murder more than your flesh. I will murder your heart and spirit and the very memory of your name and your lineage. I vow it."

"Will you? Will you truly?" Pramila's hand was steady now on the blade, holding it so close to Priya's throat that surely Priya could not breathe around it. "You are not in Parijat anymore, Princess Malini. You have no ready spies, no slavering fool boys following at your heels. You're a filth-ridden, impure traitor and you will die in a foreign land like the shame you are."

"I am still what I have always been," Malini said, although Pramila would not understand. Pramila had never understood even her own child, her clever and prickly Narina, who had died believing in something, who haunted Malini still. "I've set many things in motion, Pramila. I can set a few more, before death comes for me."

Pramila laughed. "Such empty threats, Malini! I never thought I'd see you stomp and shout like a small girl, but here we are. You—"

Pramila stopped abruptly, choking. There was something

around her throat: a great, knotted skein of green and earth and root.

Malini had been so focused on the knife against Priya's neck that she had not seen what was happening on the ground. But she saw now that thin tendrils of thorny vines had crept their way across the floor, winding through the lattice hidden behind its curtain and the crack beneath the heavy door. They'd crept up the side of Priya's body, up her wrist and her shoulder, up behind her neck until the whole tangle of them had met, squarely around Pramila's throat.

The vines tightened further. Looking—if anything—slightly irritated, Priya reached for Pramila's wrist and clenched it tight. Pramila's fingers spasmed, as she struggled for air and against Priya's hold. Seconds later, the knife clattered to the ground.

"Sorry," said Priya, leaning down and picking up the knife. The thorn tendrils slipped away from her, her clothes and skin unmarked. "I didn't know if I would be able to do that."

"Have you done anything like it before?" Malini asked, feeling a strange hunger at the base of her skull as she watched Priya turn the knife over in her grip. *Tell me what you are*, the hunger was saying. *Tell me what you are, every layer of you, tell me how I can use you—*

"No." Priya tucked the knife away. "No, I found something that belonged to my people once. And now I have—new gifts. And new weapons."

It was Malini's childhood teacher—the sage that her mother told her must be called her nursemaid, should anyone ask—who had taught Malini and Narina and Alori about the Ahiranyi and their old council leadership. Although Malini had learned something of what the Ahiranyi had once been able to do, gleaned through a mix of old history scrolls on the Age of Flowers and common tales alike, it was her sage who had detailed all the gifts they'd supposedly once possessed. Inhuman strength. Power over nature, so strong they could rend the earth and turn it to their will. A fragment of the yaksa's terrible magic, all of it born from a trial performed within sacred, deathless waters.

Waters that were lost when the temple elders and their children died.

Priya looked at Pramila, who was still gasping for air. The knife was still in Priya's hand.

"Will you kill her?" Malini asked, leaning forward upon her charpoy, the pain in her cheek and jaw only making her thirst for blood stronger.

But perhaps she sounded too eager, because Priya shot her a look, a frown creasing her brow. "No," Priya said, as Pramila crumpled to the ground behind them. The woman's eyes had fluttered closed. "She's unconscious now. She can't hurt us. We're not going to be here much longer, after all."

"I wish," said Malini, "that you would kill her."

Priya was silent for a moment. Then she held the knife, hilt first, out to Malini. Priya's catlike eyes were hooded, her mouth a thin line. She looked like a carving of one of the mothers, all austere fury.

"If you want her dead, then do what you will," she said.

For a moment Malini considered it. Truly considered it. The knife was before her. Pramila was still upon the ground. It would be easy.

But she could not forget Narina's face. Her whisper, before they had walked to the pyre.

I want my mother.

Priya waited a heartbeat longer. Drew her hand—and the knife—back. "I thought not," she said.

The thorns slithered across the floor, following her as she moved. She looked exactly as she always did: crooked-nosed, dark-skinned, her hair perhaps a bit damper and wilder than usual. And yet there was power like an aura around her, in the stone and green, in the way Pramila lay unmoving behind her.

In the way she'd held the knife, no deference in her at all.

Priya had called them equals before. But she looked at Malini now as if Malini were the servant and supplicant, and Priya the heir to an ancient throne.

"A final deal," Priya said, voice a hoarse rustle of leaves. She reached up a hand, absently brushing the blood from her throat. "Malini. Make one final deal with me."

"What would you have of me?" Malini asked, throat dry.

"There isn't much time. Someone is coming for me." Priya said the words carefully. Her eyes were unblinking. "Someone wants the waters that gave me this gift. Someone wants new power, greater power, so that they can destroy Parijatdvipa's hold on Ahiranya."

"How does a rebel know you've found these magical waters?"

"They felt it," Priya said simply.

"Are so many people gifted with magic in this place?"

"Ahiranya isn't like Parijat."

"You know nothing about Parijat."

"I'm part of Parijatdvipa, aren't I?" Priya said. "I know a lot about what it means to *belong* to your country. I probably know more than you do."

Malini look at Priya's face. Thought, *I do not know this woman at all*.

And yet that did not frighten her as it should have. She knew how many faces people possessed, one hidden beneath the other, good and monstrous, brave and cowardly, all of them true. She had learned young that a fine-bred brother could turn into a brute over nothing. Nothing. She had sat with lords and princes and kings, binding them to the vision of Emperor Aditya upon the throne. She had known the size and clout of their personal armies, the names of their wives, their greed and whispered sins—she had met them and learned them as one learns any stranger. She had learned them in person; pried them open and controlled them, and had still been aware that beneath all their carefully cataloged hungers and weaknesses likely lay a multitude of selves she would never see.

The face Priya wore now was a familiar one. She'd worn it when she killed the rebel maidservant on the triveni; when Malini had first looked at her and thought, *I could use this one*. It was the face of a temple daughter, formidable and strange. Priya was not just a maid or a weapon. She was something more, and Malini had no words for her.

"Malini," Priya said, with sudden alarm. "Can you understand me?"

"I can."

"You need a dose of the needle-flower." Priya touched a hand back to her throat—not to the wound, but to the stoppered bottle, still safe upon its thread.

Malini shook her head, after a moment. "I don't need it," she said. It was not sickness that had distracted her. Her fingertips tingled as if there were fire inside them. "Continue."

"Malini—"

"Tell me your deal," Malini said sharply. "You said there wasn't much time."

Priya's hand paused.

"Fine," she said. "I want Ahiranya's freedom. Entirely. No kindness or benevolence from your Emperor Aditya—no graciousness bestowed from on high. Ahiranya doesn't need to be another nation bound to the empire. I want our independence. I'll set you free, Malini. I will make sure you reach your nameless prince and his men. And in return, you will vow to me that you will give Ahiranya to me."

"To you," Malini said slowly. "And what would you do with it? Become its queen?"

Priya's mouth quirked into a smile.

"Not me," she said. "But belonging to Parijatdvipa has done this country no favors. No matter how kindly you say your brother Aditya will treat us, we'll always be dogs at the table. We'll always be angry if we remain chained to your empire."

Malini said nothing for a moment. There were consequences to such a vow. She could not unilaterally alter the shape of Parijatdvipa. She did not know what Aditya or his men would say, in the face of a woman's foolish promise.

Oh, vows could be broken. Of course they could. And yet

Priya was...not entirely a safe person to lie to. And worse still, Malini did not *want* to break a promise to her.

There was a sound, somewhere below them. Priya's jaw hardened.

"Promise me this, or one way or another, you die here."

"You'll kill me after all, Priya?"

"No, you fool woman," Priya said, eyes blazing. "No. Never me."

Malini was not sure she understood what she felt in that moment—the furious storm of feeling in her—but she knew the choice that lay before her.

"I vow it," she said. "If you save my life—if I am reunited with Rao—then Ahiranya is yours."

"Well, then." Priya exhaled, long and slow. The thorns around her receded. The vine at Pramila's throat crumpled. "We need to go. Now."

39

BHUMIKA

When the conch sounded, Bhumika was prepared. She sat in her room in the rose palace with the window lattices thrown open. She listened to the bellow of sound, echoing over the Hirana, over the city that flickered already with burning light.

It was difficult to trace the path of fire, but Bhumika tried nonetheless. The strongest light lay close to the mahal itself, in the district that housed the wealthiest of Ahiranya. All her husband's advisors. Highborn Parijatdvipans. Merchants. The oldest highborn families of Ahiranya.

Her uncle.

She turned and met Khalida's eyes.

"Summon the servants to my rooms," she said. "Quietly."

Now was the perfect time. The guards would be busy ensuring that the mahal was secured. They wouldn't question a handful of women and children running for safety, especially not when Khalida was so clearly escorting them on her kindhearted mistress's orders.

She waited. Listened to the distant screaming. In her mind, the sangam flickered, full of Ashok's fury and pain, wet with blood.

The servants and children were ushered in. They looked at her nervously. Some of the younger ones were weeping.

"The city is burning," said Bhumika without preamble. "The rebels have attacked those they consider a threat to Ahiranya, and its potential freedom." And everything and everyone else—the wooden houses of Hiranaprastha, their residents, even the innocent servants of the mahal—were acceptable collateral to her brother. "They will attack the mahal. They will, perhaps, break the perimeter. And they will come for us." She looked at each one of them. "I promised you when I gave you a place in this household that you would be safe. I will not allow this night to break my vow."

A breathless silence surrounded her. Even the children had quieted.

"You will have weapons," she said. "I have bows, for those of you who used to hunt before you came here. Axes for the strongest of you. Daggers for the smallest. Khalida will guide you on preparing boiling water and oil that can be thrown over the walls, if need be. But I hope it will not come to such measures."

"It will," a voice said. "Lady Bhumika, I am sorry, but it will. We have a traitor."

One maid—Gauri—dragged Rukh forward by the arm. Dropped him to the ground. His shawl was gone. His bare, rot-riven arms were encircled with leaves, spines of sap prickling from his shoulders.

"Tell her," said the maid. "Tell her what you told me."

"It's my fault that they'll breach the mahal," the boy choked out. "The rebels asked me to spy for them. To watch..." He faltered, mouth failing to work. "To watch...someone. And find a way in."

To watch someone. Of course.

Oh, Priya.

"And did you find a way in, as they asked?" Bhumika said, keeping her voice calm.

"Sometimes the guards don't watch the doors properly," he said. "Sometimes when supplies are brought in...I eat in the kitchens sometimes, and I see...sometimes a person could slip in. I told the rebels that."

"These rebels will not be slipping in like thieves," said Bhumika, thinking of the fire, the smoke. The blunt force of Ashok's rage, rending the city. "Nonetheless, you have betrayed the household that has cared for you, Rukh."

He flinched. "I'll accept any punishment you think is right, my lady," he whispered.

"And what punishment should be given for assisting in the killing of innocent servants in this mahal? For the deaths of my husband's men and perhaps the regent himself?"

The boy swallowed again. He did not want to say it. But she waited.

"Death," he said. "My death."

"Your death is coming for you swiftly, whether I arrange it or not," observed Bhumika. "That sacred bead around your wrist cannot hold at bay the rot I see in you."

He bowed his head.

Another maidservant pushed forward. "He's with us now, my lady," she said hurriedly, her hand coming to rest on Rukh's shoulder. "Surely that's all that matters. He's—he's only misguided. He's just a child."

Priya had saved this boy. Bhumika knew that. This dying boy, who was young and silly. And the maidservant who was Priya's friend was standing and watching Bhumika warily, her posture radiating defensiveness.

Rukh's expression, when Bhumika looked at him, was somehow just as brave. His small hands curled up into fists. "I didn't have to tell you the truth, my lady. I didn't. No one would have known. But I didn't want anyone here to suffer. I've always... always wanted to do something good, something important." There was a hunger in his voice too big for his years. "I helped the rebels because I wanted to fight for something. I wanted my life to matter. But here..."

Again, he paused. Sima's hand tightened on his shoulder.

"No one has ever protected me," he blurted out. "Or been kind to me. And here—she—you—some people are."

He had not said Priya's name. But her name was written in his face and his words regardless.

"Whatever the punishment, I'll take it," he said, in his wavering voice. "I'll—I'll even die, my lady. But I'd rather do whatever I can to protect the mahal. That's what I'd like to do."

"Then this is my punishment to you, boy," Bhumika said. "If you wish to make a difference, you will do so in my service. You will serve me loyally until death. There will be no more betrayals. You will be my creature until your last breath. Will you swear it, upon your soul and your life?"

Beyond him, in the shadows, figures moved in through the door. She saw a gleam of silver. Thin as a sickle scar.

"I will," he said.

"Vow it."

"I vow it, Lady Bhumika."

"Good. If you betray me or mine again, you will die."

"Yes, my lady," he said in a small voice. Sima's hand finally loosened on his arm, her own shoulders relaxing.

With that resolved, Bhumika looked at the people still surrounding her. They had very little time.

"You'll be shown your weapons," she said. "And you'll be shown what to do. The soldiers will direct you," she added, inclining her head at the man standing at the door, his arm cuff of command glinting, his white-and-gold armor pristine. He nodded, gestured, and his men fanned out.

Khalida helped Bhumika settle comfortably upon the floor cushions, beneath an open window that allowed in the smoke-tinged breeze.

She was surrounded by roses, growing in profusion in their clay and lacquered jars. Flowers, sweet and delicate, peeking from their thorny vines, twining from the gardens up to her windows. Soft, feather-leafed plants, dripping from the flat roof. Every single one had been grown by her own careful tending. By her hands—and most importantly of all, by her magic. Every time she breathed they moved with her, as if her own rib cage were their soil, the home for their roots.

There is power that is showy and fierce. And there is power grown slowly, and stronger for the time spent braiding its ancient strength. An old lesson from Elder Saroj. Bhumika held it in her mind's eye as she waited.

"Ashok," she whispered. "Come for me. And we'll see who is stronger."

MITHUNAN

The regent had been shouting for some time, demanding Commander Jeevan be brought to him. But there was no sign of the commander, or of any of the regent's personal guard. Lord Santosh's men were gone too, and no one could say exactly where they had gone, though one of the gatekeepers claimed they had left via the stables hours ago, fully armed.

Everything was chaos. Somehow Mithunan—no more than a lowly guard who kept watch on the walls, trained to shoot the occasional arrow and ring the bell for the changing hours, and not much more—had been given a sword and sent to fight.

And somehow, he'd found his neck in the hands of a rebel.

The rebel slammed him to the ground by the throat. Once. Twice. Released him. Above Mithunan, the rebel's masked face wavered. Behind him, another mask appeared. Two of them.

The sound of a booted foot, striking a body to the ground. Three.

There were a lot more, beyond the mahal's walls.

"Show us the way to the lady of the house," said the kneeling rebel. "Or we kill you right now."

He didn't want to. It would be wrong. He knew that. But he could hear yelling, and the whistles of arrows falling. The thud and hiss of steel. He could hear the gasp of other guards, wounded and dying, around him.

He did not want to die.

To his left, one of his fellow guards was rising up on his elbows, gasping for breath. "We won't do it," the guard choked out. "Won't—"

His words stopped. A wooden sword had been shoved into his chest. Around the hilt, his skin burned, blistering with heat.

Mithunan shuddered.

"So," said the kneeling rebel, still watching him. "What will you do?"

"I'll show you," Mithunan said. Swallowed. "Please. Don't."

The rebel dragged him to his feet.

The wife of the regent had her own palace in miniature, in the central courtyard of the mahal. As Mithunan stumbled toward it, a strange burning knife at his back, he could only wonder at how the smoke and the fighting had transformed even the normally prosaic miniature fort of flowers. The trellises of roses, the white and yellow blooms upon the windows, all looked somehow thicker and darker. The green of the vines was deeper, almost oily with color. The window shutters were absurdly open. In place of lattice were leaves, entwined with shadows.

"It doesn't look like much," the smaller rebel muttered. A woman, by the sound of their voice.

The male rebel grunted in response.

Shoved his knife forward.

Mithunan felt nothing for a long moment. He looked down and saw the shaft of the blade protruding from his stomach, surrounded by blood, as if through a dream. Then he began to shake. Fell, as the knife was drawn free.

You should not have trusted rebels to spare you, he thought, and the voice in his mind sounded like his commander's—a low, derisive rumble of judgment. *They were always going to kill you. Fool lad.*

"It will take you a while to die from that," said the woman. She stepped over him.

But as the two rebels approached the rose palace, a rain of arrows was upon them suddenly—from the roof, the windows. They cursed and leapt, with terrifying swiftness, between the arrow-fall. It was like a dance.

And then the ground...shifted.

Flowers, jagged as glass. Thorns burrowing out of the earth, sharp as knives. As teeth.

He heard them as if through water. Saw them wavering, shifting as his vision failed.

The earth was swallowing the woman's feet. She screamed, fighting it, but the gentle expanse of flowers the Lady Bhumika had planted with her own hands, long ago, had somehow consumed her up to the ankles. The ground was bloody around her.

Something green speared through the male rebel's chest.

It will take you a while to die from that too, Mithunan wanted to crow. But he had no words left in him. Everything had seeped out of him.

The darkness enfolded him like a cloak.

41

MALINI

They made their way to the triveni. Here, Malini could smell smoke. Hear far-off sounds—like voices, wailing.

"I can guide you down," said Priya.

Malini looked down at the Hirana, over the edge of the triveni. The surface was uneven, all slick edges, sharp crags. The last time she'd climbed the Hirana, she'd had a guiding rope and guards to keep her alive. But the parts of the Hirana below her had no rope. Even with Priya beside her, she felt a nauseous swoop in her stomach.

"I suppose there's no other way," she murmured.

"No," said Priya. "Not anymore."

Malini steeled herself. She had to do this, if she wanted to be free. And to die by a fall rather than by poison or fire would be—novel. At least there was that.

She let Priya take her hand. Her first step was on ground that was treacherous and fragile. She felt as if she stood on a broken shell with nothing but a void beneath it. Then the surface steadied beneath her feet. Moss seeped up between her toes. She swallowed, and fixed her eyes on Priya's face.

"Tell me where to place my feet."

"Just follow me," Priya said. "That's it. Just like that."

The breeze swirled around them. On it she smelled burning once more.

She kept her eyes on Priya and followed.

"That's it," Priya said, in a voice like the wind through leaves. Perhaps she intended it to be soothing. It was—not. Not exactly. "Quicker, if you can."

"I can't," Malini ground out.

She wanted to explain to Priya how little strength she had. But there was a sudden whistling noise in her ears, and a thud, and Priya swore, her grip slipping. An arrow had landed in the ground by their feet. Malini flinched, fighting the instinct to curl into a ball or worse, throw herself backward. She teetered for a moment, supporting her own weight, balanced on nothing but one small outcrop of rock.

Another arrow hissed through the air and Malini jumped to escape it.

The ground gave with a snap and ah—she was stumbling, teetering for a second with nothing to steady her, meeting Priya's horrified eyes. Fear jolted through her. She was going to *fall*. She dropped with a noiseless scream—

And was caught. Moss, like a netting at her back. Her heart was pounding, and she clasped one sweat-slippery hand on rock. Any rock. She could feel the moss hissing and forming behind her, knitting together with unnatural speed, cradling her body up.

"Priya."

Priya was staring at her, openmouthed.

"I didn't know I could do that," she said faintly. And then, as if startling herself out of a stupor, she strode forward and heaved Malini back to her feet. She did not do it by physical strength alone, although Malini could feel the iron grip of her hands and see the way her jaw clenched as she strained to drag Malini back up; Malini could feel the green push too, as if it were an extension of Priya, responding to her movements.

She gripped Priya's wrists.

"Don't let go of me again," she gasped.

"I won't."

"Even if we risk being skewered. Don't let go."

"I won't." Priya's fingertips were gentle on Malini's skin—on the race of her pulse. She tightened her grip, eyes on Malini's. Her face was very gray. "I won't," she repeated.

They made their way down the Hirana. Slow, slow. Another arrow landed, and Priya swore violently and dragged Malini down to hunch against the rock. She bared her teeth—the only rage she'd shown since they began their descent—then drew Malini back to standing and continued to guide her.

"They're not trying to hurt us," Priya said to her in a low voice. "They're trying to scare us into staying still so they can collect me. So we'll survive this, Malini. I promise."

Malini could have wept, when she felt steady soil beneath her feet once more. But she was not that sort of woman, so she merely gave Priya a nod and straightened her spine, looking toward the general's mahal.

The mahal itself was well protected, with high, impassable walls. Like any busy mahal, it would usually be porous, with servants and visitors pouring in and out—but Malini could see that the work of shutting the way had begun swiftly. The lattice windows were black. On the roof stood archers, their arrow tips lit by flame.

Beyond the mahal the city of Hiranaprastha was burning. Smoke coiled in the air, a halo of it.

"One of them is here," Priya said tightly. "No. More than that." She was still holding Malini's hands, and she gripped them even tighter for a moment before finally letting go. Then she turned, facing the open expanse of land, marked only by outcroppings of trees.

A shadow moved beneath the trunks of those trees. Just for a moment.

Malini stood very still, the wind whipping her hair.

Then, suddenly—there they were.

Two people wearing wooden masks, great fearsome carved faces, raced toward them. Priya shoved Malini gracelessly down against the ground, and Malini flattened without complaint. She did not want to die like this, not when freedom was so close, not when she had a chance of reaching Rao and Aditya and the vengeance she craved. And combat had never been her strength.

But it certainly was Priya's. She moved with a snake's venomous swiftness. She was not a tall woman, but there was strength in her shoulders, in the corded muscle of those arms. She caught the first rebel with a shoulder to the stomach, tackling them to the ground. The rebel was winded, but they recovered quickly, throwing a fist at Priya's face.

She dodged, but the movement dislodged her hold, and the rebel was up, turning on her again. This punch didn't miss. Priya was caught on her side and hit the ground hard. The masked rebel was on her, fists flying. And Malini was on her feet after all, propelled by some wild instinct, as if her meager strength would be enough to see either of these rebels away.

But Priya—Priya was laughing. The rebel paused, as their companion slowed to a stop behind them, no longer running to join the fray.

"If you kill me, the way will go with me," Priya hissed. "If you kill me you all die, desperately sipping your vials."

The rebel above Priya froze.

"I closed it," she pushed on. "Hid it again. The way to the deathless waters is gone."

The rebel hesitated a second longer.

The ground shook beneath their feet, huge thorns bursting from the sod. The standing rebel yelped, falling backward. A line of blood bloomed on their arm. The wood of the mask was scored with a white line of damage, dangerously close to the eye socket.

The smaller rebel—possibly a woman—had their hand open before them. As if that motion could hold the thorns back. And perhaps it could.

Upon the ground, those thorns were twisting, curling upon themselves.

"You're not the only one with gifts." Through the mask, their voice was hollow, distorted by wood. "I'm water-blessed too."

"Vial-blessed," Priya gritted out. "A dead thing walking. You won't live long."

If the rebel had any thoughts on that statement, their feelings were well hidden by the mask. "You could save us all, if you only showed us the way. We should be on the same side."

"Tell your leader that," said Priya. "You tell him he was the one who brought us to this point. Not me. I want what I've always wanted." Priya did not move a hand, and the thorns slowly began to uncurl again, bristling. The movement was slow. Too slow.

"Your will isn't stronger than mine," said the rebel. "You are not a creature of conviction. You serve nothing."

"I'm stronger than you think," said Priya. And then the ground began to break beneath the rebels. The thorns bent in closer, menacing. "Your leader doesn't want my corpse," Priya said, as they struggled to maintain their balance. "We both know that. But me? I wouldn't mind killing you at all. So my advice to you is simple: *Run*."

They didn't want to. That much was clear. But the sod was churning beneath them, new thorns creeping free like spindly fingers, clawed and curving. So they turned and made their scrambling retreat.

Priya did not even watch them go. She was panting, her arm already livid with bruising, staring at something beyond them. Malini followed the tilt of her head. Saw what Priya saw.

There was a man near the mahal. He was not moving toward them. Malini was not even sure he was watching. The eyes of his mask were black pits. He stood with a bow propped against his leg, making no move to use it. His head tilted back. Like an acknowledgment, or a challenge.

"Come," muttered Priya, taking a step back. Another. Malini sucked in a breath and followed her.

It seemed it was now their turn to run.

They didn't stand out in the city as Malini had feared they would, because the violence of the rebels and the equally violent response of the general's soldiers had sown chaos. The wooden houses of Hiranaprastha had been no match for it. Soon they were darting through a burning maze of buildings. Even if Malini had not spent months trapped in a single room, she would have been overwhelmed by the scope and size of the madness.

As it was, all she could do was grit her teeth and force herself to keep moving, no matter how her body threatened to betray her. The crowd jostled her, the pressure crushing, and Priya gripped her tighter. "Don't let go of me," urged Priya. "Hold on to me like we're still climbing down the Hirana. Just like that."

"I can smell the fire," Malini said, voice throttled by the taste of it and the memories it dredged up in her.

"I know," said Priya. "I know." She was blinking hard, her eyes streaming, the whites red from smoke. For the briefest moment, she was not looking at Malini but through her: caught up in the darkness of her own past. "Don't think of it." She tightened her grip. "We can't think of it. We need to keep moving."

Priya led them on, a woman on a mission. Through narrow alleys and wide streets full of people and shouting and chaos. She gestured at Malini to cover her face with her pallu, to keep out the acrid scent, as Malini's eyes streamed from the smell and the feel of the smoke. *Keep moving,* Malini told herself. *Keep moving, you're so close. We're so close.*

She could see the forest in the distance when Priya suddenly veered to the right, dragging Malini beneath the cover of a stone alcove. The crowds still surged by them.

Priya's expression was resolute.

"You go," said Priya. "Go to your loyal follower, whatever his name is. He's waiting for you, under the bower of bones. I'll tell you the way; it's not far from here. Go and he'll take you to your brother."

"You think I can survive here alone?" Malini asked incredulously. "I have a high opinion of myself, I promise you, but I'm hardly capable of making my way through a burning city without dying."

"We all learn this way," said Priya.

"By hoping we won't die, when the odds are thoroughly stacked against us?"

Malini did not mean it seriously, but Priya's mouth was firm, her eyes solemn as she nodded.

"Yes," said Priya.

"You asked me to make a promise," Malini tried. "You asked me to make a vow to you, for the sake of your Ahiranya. Won't you try to ensure that I live to see it fulfilled?"

Priya said, in a choked voice, "My friends are in the mahal."

Her friends. Those other maidservants. Malini swallowed and said, calmly, "Then they're behind strong walls, and as safe as they can possibly be."

But Priya was not listening to her. "I have this power. This gift in me. And it's stronger now than it will ever be again. I need to help them. If anything happens to them, I..."

"Are you stronger than every rebel attacking the mahal and burning this city combined?" Malini asked. "Are you more cunning, are you cleverer, better equipped, and better placed to conquer them?"

"You only want to convince me to do what you need of me."

"Yes," Malini acknowledged. "But that doesn't make me wrong. Save me, and you may save your Ahiranya. Save me and your country has an option beyond the rebels and whatever fate the emperor has in store for you. Please."

Priya was not sure what to do, Malini knew that. She saw it in Priya's eyes; in her downturned lips, tight as a bowstring drawn taut. And Malini could do no more to convince her.

"You're right," Priya said. "I made you a promise. And you made me one in return."

And then she whirled, heading toward the cover of the forest, and Malini had no choice but to follow her.

They were deep into the dark and winding maze of trees when Priya suddenly stopped.

"Priya," Malini said. She spoke quietly. Had she heard something? Seen something? "What is it?"

Priya was swaying faintly on her feet. She turned to face Malini slowly, blinking. She reached an arm up, wiping her eyes.

The hand she drew back was streaked with blood.

"Something," Priya said. "Something is—wrong."

Malini had no time to do or say anything before Priya crumpled to the ground.

42

ASHOK

He could barely feel Priya any longer.

He stood before the squat little fort—the rose palace, Bhumika's ugly creation, of that he had no doubt—that lay at the heart of the mahal. Surrounded by gardens, its walls were a knot-work of thorns. Thorns as wide as a man's arm. Thorns as sharp as a blade. They were gristly with blood.

She was within those walls. But Priya was not.

"I could reach you, Bhumika," he murmured, eyes closed. "If I tried, I could do it."

"They have archers on the roof," one of his girls said quietly. She was standing in the cover of shadow, her mask raised.

"Not very good ones," Ashok said calmly. "Those they lost on the outer walls."

The boiling liquid they kept flinging down concerned him more. Cheap tricks, but they were effective, in light of her limited resources.

The mahal, after all, was shattered.

Ashok had only lost a few men and women. It wasn't clear if the thorns or the arrows had killed them, in the end, but he thought it unlikely that anyone but Bhumika had put their lives to an end. His soft-spoken sister, too highborn to dirty her hands, had always been a monstrous opponent when she allowed herself the indulgence of proper battle. That apparently hadn't changed.

No matter. Let her molder in this place. He didn't need her anyway.

When he returned—when he was thrice-born, with all the strength of the waters in him—then they would talk about Ahiranya's future. And his will would overpower her own.

"With me," he said, and turned. He walked from the rose palace; walked from the broken mahal to the Hirana. It loomed above them. Together, they climbed, using the rope for purchase.

The last time he'd been upon the Hirana, his temple siblings had burned. He'd had nightmares for years after their deaths. An old rage rose in him as he climbed and looked at the carvings, both familiar and made strange by the passage of time. This had been his home once. This had been *his*.

On the Hirana, he put his rage to good use. The few guards they found, they killed efficiently. They explored the rooms. Found nothing. There was one woman only, unconscious on the ground in the northern chamber. Not, he thought, the imperial princess. A pity.

Ashok beckoned over one of his men. "Wake her," he said. "Interrogate her. Find out if she knows anything useful about my sister."

His man nodded and removed his scythe from his sash.

Ashok left him and returned to the triveni.

You are mine, he thought, speaking to the Hirana in the quiet of his own skull. He placed his hand upon the plinth. *And I am yours. I did not die in you for a reason. So show me the way.*

Beneath his hand, the stone was cold and unresponsive. He couldn't feel the warmth of it, as he had as a boy. It was still and cold, a corpse of stone. He'd hoped, perhaps, that he could find the way without Priya. Now that the regent's power had been broken—now that Hiranaprastha burned, and the Hirana was as good as his—he had hoped the temple would yield to him. It had been a small hope, against all reason.

No matter.

One of his women entered the room, wiping her hands clean

of blood. Behind her were three more rebels, watching him, waiting for orders.

"We keep searching," he said. They did so. He walked the length of the Hirana—entering each cloister room, every space where his siblings had once run and fought and played and prayed. He entered the sangam, hoping the Hirana would feel it and yield to him. But the entrance to the deathless waters did not appear. He could not find it.

Perhaps if he meditated—if he spent days upon days here, as she had—he would find the way.

But there was no time. The deathless waters swam in the blood of his followers, quickly turning to poison. Leaching away their strength. Their lives. He needed to act before they ran out of time.

Damn you, Priya.

"We're leaving," he told his followers eventually, defeated by a pile of stone. "We're going to seek out my sister once more."

"I'm sorry," another of his men said. Through the mask, Ashok couldn't see his expression, but he sounded ashamed. "I shouldn't have let her escape."

"There's nothing to be sorry for," he said. "We still have our new strength. We'll find the way."

43

PRIYA

The first step, after entering the deathless waters, was to emerge at all. If you could fall beneath that cosmic blue and come back out again, your body still in working order—well. You'd already managed a minor miracle.

The next step was surviving the hours that followed. Priya had not forgotten the sickroom: not forgotten the twice- and once-born who'd died there, lost and feverish in their beds. But she had not thought it would come for her now, when the Hirana had called her to the waters, when she'd felt nothing but a kind of bliss as she'd lowered herself into them and the sangam had unfurled for her.

But here she was. Burning. Spitting bile into the bushes.

It was her own fool fault for thinking she was somehow special. She wasn't. And now she was dying.

Weeds withered and resurrected in a frenzied cycle beneath her hands as she dry heaved. She swore, dizzy on her hands and knees.

"Can you get up?" Malini asked. Her voice was near. She was kneeling by Priya, her own eyes fixed on the path behind them. Looking, perhaps, for other people running for refuge, or soldiers.

"I can. Just give me a moment."

With great effort, Priya stumbled to her feet.

Fell.

"Well," said Malini. "Apparently not."

"I'm going to have to," Priya gritted out. "We can't stay here. Not with the city in the state it is."

Malini was silent for a moment. Then she said, "You understand that my strength is—limited."

"Of course I do."

"Then you'll forgive me if this ends badly. Come. Put your arms around me."

Priya did. Somehow, Malini managed to leverage them both to their feet, with Priya's face against the crook of her shoulder and Priya's hands clutched tight against the cloth of Malini's blouse.

"What on earth has happened to you?" Malini whispered, voice feather-light on Priya's hair. And Priya shivered, not from the fever alone, and said, "I can't explain it."

"Can't?"

"Won't, then. My magic is—my business."

"Leave your magic and your gifts a mystery, then, if you must," Malini said. "Just tell me where we need to go, to reach this bower of bones."

Priya told her. And Malini began to walk—slow, careful steps, mindful of the stumbling weight of Priya in her arms. Priya forced herself to move one foot in front of the other, again and again, even as her blood felt like a tide turned backward inside her body.

"Priya," Malini whispered. "Priya, Priya. Listen to my voice."

"Why are you saying my name?"

"Because you're not answering me."

Priya's breath gusted out of her. "I'm sorry I'm scaring you."

"I'm not scared," Malini said, sounding furious. She was still holding Priya—still using her strength to drag Priya through the fronds of great dark leaves.

"Of course you're scared," said Priya. She meant her words to sound gentle, understanding, but they came out of her slurred with pain, and Malini ignored them.

They walked. Walked.

"I can't drag you any farther," said Malini, after an age. "We're going to need to wait here."

Wait for what? Priya thought. But she didn't ask. Malini was trembling and sweating, gray-faced as she sank against the knotted trunk of a tree, the light of the sun streaming over her. Her cheek, where Pramila had struck her, was livid.

"The needle-flower," Priya said faintly.

"I wish you would shut up about the needle-flower," Malini said. But after a moment, she swore and reached over Priya. Priya turned her head so that Malini could remove the chain from her throat.

Malini took a dab of the tincture on her lips. Grimaced. "There," she said. "Now we don't need to discuss it further."

"Put it—round your neck."

Malini gave her an unreadable look and slipped the chain over her own head, the small cask settling at the hollow of her throat.

"Why do you want to know about my magic?" Priya asked. "Why does it matter to you?"

"I told you that you interest me," said Malini. "I told you that I want to know everything about you."

"You said that to make me think—you liked me," Priya said haltingly.

Malini's dark gray eyes fixed on her own. "I do like you," said Malini.

"Please don't say that."

"You have helped me. You tried to save me from poison. You comforted me. When reality felt far away, and I didn't know what was real, you—"

"Please," Priya said, and knew she sounded like she was begging this time. "Don't."

She didn't want to be convinced into foolishness again, to let herself like Malini too much. She didn't want to trust her, or want to be friends. She didn't want to *want* her. And it would have been so easy, after all they'd been through together—after she'd seen Malini nearly die and watched the way Malini's eyes had gone wide and cold with fury when Pramila had held the knife to Priya's throat. She was teetering on the edge. She did not want to fall.

A silence settled between them.

Then, in an unreadable voice, Malini said, "If you say so. Perhaps this will be more palatable to you: I want to understand the world I live in, strange though it may be. I need to understand, in order to survive it. I learned young the importance of understanding the nature of those around me, but also the need to understand greater things: religion. Military strategy. Politics, and all its many games. Your magic is no different from any of that."

That was better. Easier to handle. It made Priya's heart feel less open, less bruised.

"There is a river beneath the Hirana," said Priya, into the velvet quiet of humming insects, of Malini's uneven breath. "Your nursemaid was right about that. But it isn't accessible to just anyone. I think if General Vikram or any imperial soldier tried to hack their way through the stone to it they would have found nothing. It's... magic. And living, and it let me find it because of what I am.

"All rituals are in three parts in Ahiranya," continued Priya. "I don't know if it's the same in Parijat or any other place, but we always knew as children that we'd have to pass through those waters three times, if we wanted the gifts of the yaksa. Since the founding of Parijatdvipa, the ritual has only given our elders the smallest gifts. Power to control the Hirana. No more. But we traveled through the waters, me and my siblings, at the festival of the dark of the moon, and... suddenly, we were as the elders had once been, in the Age of Flowers.

"The ones like me, who were passing through for the first time, we were changed. But the ones who were passing through the second time, or the third..." Priya shook her head. "It was as if a seed had been planted the first time, and it had been growing inside them until that moment. Something that had been growing in the waters, perhaps for years, bloomed in us. Our elders, they...

they should have been pleased. But they were not. Because they thought..." Priya swallowed. Should she admit this? The terrible suspicion they'd had, of her siblings, of her? "The rot arrived when our powers did," she said eventually. "It was smaller then, weaker, but they were afraid. They thought we were the cause. And that we were monstrous. We were too strong. So they killed us. Died with us."

Priya propped herself up on her elbows. The green beneath her was soft. Soothing.

"I've been seeking the waters again," said Priya. "Seeking the way. And I found it. But the finding—it has a price. And I'm paying it."

Malini made a choked noise. But Priya did not look at her. "I don't want pity," she said, still staring at the green.

"What were you hoping to accomplish?" Malini said after several heartbeats, her voice low.

"I was trying to find...myself. After the others died, I...I think my mind tried to protect me. I forgot so much. I couldn't use even the gifts I already had any longer."

"And have you found yourself, Priya?"

Priya shook her head. "I don't know what it means to be a temple child anymore. Maybe it means being useful to people who seek power," she said, finally looking at Malini. "Maybe it means being monstrous. Sometimes it feels like it. But maybe...maybe it means something else. The children and I, we could control the Hirana. Control nature. Someone once told me that the strongest of us could even control the rot. Maybe what it means to be me is to...to be a cure."

It was a hope she'd only started to consider now that she could feel the power fading out of her, ebbing and flowing. Now that she'd felt the heady sweetness of it. Could her magic really be monstrous, if it felt this sweet?

"You think you may have the power to end the rot?" Malini asked.

"Maybe," said Priya. "It's all—everything is *maybe*. I don't know. It doesn't matter now, does it? I'm not going to survive to test my strength."

The tree roots on the surface of the forest floor gave a little flutter, shivering, creaking their way across the soil as they reached for Priya.

"Should I beat them away?" Malini asked in a strange, dry voice. "Or are you calling them?"

Priya sighed, suddenly weary. "Leave me. Go to that Lord Rajan of yours. Go to your brother. Do—exactly what you'd hoped to. I know you want to. Don't pretend you care what happens to me."

"You saved my life," Malini said. "You saved it more than once."

"And you still don't care," said Priya. "I know that. So go."

She could feel Malini considering it. Malini had the needle-flower now. Priya had told her to take it exactly for that reason. She could leave Priya here and walk to the bower of bones and begin her journey to Srugna. If she was swift, perhaps she would even catch up with Rao and all the other men.

"I'm dying anyway," Priya added. "What does it matter?" *I've served my purpose.*

"What indeed," Malini said, in a voice that was too sharp by far. Suddenly she wasn't sitting back against the tree trunk. She was leaning over Priya, gaze intent, something fierce in the curl of her mouth. *That* held Priya's attention, even through the stupor of fever. Malini was often vulnerable, or cunning, or as blank as glass. But fierce? No. She was rarely that.

"You don't have to believe that I care for you, Priya. You only have to believe that I need you. And I do need you."

"You have the needle-flower. You know the way."

"I need you," Malini repeated. And there was so much in those words—in the set of her lips. "So, what can I do to ensure that you live? Do you know a healer?"

Priya thought of Gautam and how they'd parted. "No," she said.

"Then how can I help you?"

A shiver racked her. Cold. She was beginning to feel cold. That was a bad sign with fever.

"There is someone out there who will save me." The strength in her was fading, but she knew what she'd sensed in the waters: the sangam, the forest, intertwined. She'd sensed other kin. Perhaps even thrice-born, because their presence had felt nothing like her twice-born siblings—somehow sharper in the sangam, distant and brighter all at once.

"Where?"

Priya tried to speak. Swallowed. She lifted a hand, pointing the way, and marks carved themselves into the trees in response. Her heart raced.

"Through there. Follow—marks on the trees. Like fingers."

"How helpful," Malini said. But even in her daze, Priya could hear the fear beneath her wry tone. "Here," she went on. "Lean on me again."

It took a long time to lift Priya to standing once more, and Malini was panting when it was done, wan with exhaustion. But she held Priya with a grip like iron.

"It wasn't my nursemaid who told me tales of Ahiranya's yaksa and magic waters," she said. "No self-respecting maid would risk her position like that."

"No?" Priya thought she knew something of what it meant to be a self-respecting maid.

But Malini only smiled at that, a thin, tight smile, even as she stumbled forward on unsteady feet, and said, "No. No normal maid who has to worry about losing her position. It was my teacher, my sage who told me. She educated me. As the women of my mother's family were educated. As princes are. And she taught me this too: no wars are won without allies."

"Your allies are at the arch."

"But I'm here, in this forsaken forest. And so are you."

"Are we fighting a war right now, Malini?"

"Yes," Malini said. "We always are."

44

RAO

They waited at the bower of bones for a long, long time in the dark of the moon. They waited as Hiranaprastha began to glow with festival lights, which grew bright enough for the glow to be visible even through the dense forest. They waited as dawn approached, rosy-fingered, for Malini to come.

Rao had promised to wait through the night for Malini, and he did so, along with Lata and Prem and all of Prem's men. Day came. The city continued to flicker, alight with both sun and flame. Surely the festival was over? But Rao knew nothing of Ahiranyi traditions. He couldn't be sure.

He kept on waiting.

The men were restless. One of the messengers in Prem's service—a man used to traveling across swathes of the empire—entertained the others by telling them about the strange nature of the seeker's path.

"Srugna lies beyond the woods, on every map. It's a long journey, usually. Weeks. But Ahiranyi's forest doesn't always obey normal rules, and on the seeker's path time moves differently," the messenger told them.

"Differently?" another man asked, clearly skeptical.

The messenger shrugged. "All I can tell you is that if you travel this path, you'll make it to Srugna in days, not weeks. The locals say the yaksa built it. For all I know, they did."

"Does it demand a price?"

Rao and the others turned. Lata was standing back, in shadow beneath the trees. He couldn't quite make out her expression.

"I don't know what you mean," said the messenger.

"No tale would claim yaksa are inherently benevolent beings," said Lata. "Not even to their own people. If they have made a path, if that path still exists long after their demise—I have no doubt that the magic of it is a double-edged sword."

"Well, it's not a *safe* path," the messenger said thoughtfully. "Sometimes people go missing along it. Or turn up dead. But that's no different from traveling the woods the normal way. You could just as easily be shot by a poacher or eaten by some wild animal."

"Did you last travel it alone?"

The messenger shook his head.

"And how many of you made it to the other end?"

"That isn't important." Prem interrupted firmly. "We're going the swift way, like it or not." His voice held nothing of its usual languorous gentleness. It was a voice that brooked no argument. "We've stayed in Ahiranya far too long."

There was a noise from behind Lata. One of the men who'd been on watch appeared, his expression grim.

"The city's on fire," he said.

"What do you mean, on fire?" Prem barked.

"I don't know," the guard said helplessly. "I went near to the edge of the forest and, my lord, the smoke isn't from the festival lights. It's something far bigger."

Alarmed, Prem and Rao went to look for themselves. The smoke from the city was beginning to billow into the forest. From here, it was difficult to tell the cause. But Rao could smell burning wood and the distinct, cooked char of flesh on the air. He covered his nose, staggered that he had not smelled it sooner, or felt the sheer heat of the blaze.

Ahiranya's forest did not obey normal rules. Somehow, the forest's strangeness had muted the worst of it until they had stepped nearer to its borders.

"Someone needs to be sent back to find out what's happening," Rao told Prem.

Prem crossed his arms. "I think we should head directly to Srugna," he said. "As fast as possible."

"There are Parijatdvipans down there, and we need to know what's become of them," said Rao grimly. "We need to know what kind of dangers we're leaving at our back."

The guard who had been on watch volunteered to go.

"If there's any trouble at all, you come straight back," Prem told him. "You understand?"

"Yes, my lord," the man said. He bowed his head, then straightened, adjusting the whip at his waist. "I won't be long."

"No more than an hour, or we'll have to leave you behind."

"My lord," agreed the man, and then he bowed once more and strode off.

Rao slumped against a tree, rubbing his forehead. Prem joined him, sitting on the ground by his side with a wince.

"Are you hurt?" Rao asked.

"Me? No. Besides, Rao, I'm more interested in talking about you."

Rao looked at him. Prem offered him a lopsided smile.

"So much yearning," Prem murmured. "I don't think I've ever felt like you do."

"I'm not in love with Princess Malini," said Rao. "That isn't why I've waited here."

Prem snorted in disbelief. "Whatever you say."

"Prem. She was my sister's closest friend."

"Are you telling me you've left your family behind, hid here under an assumed identity, consorted with Ahiranyi, and refused to leave with me, because you think of her as a *sister*?"

"No! No." Rao took a deep breath. "I'm here because I know Aditya." He lowered his voice to a whisper. "He needs her."

Prem was silent for a moment. His smile turned into something more thoughtful. "He's managed to gain plenty of followers without her."

"Has he? I was there when he chose to leave," said Rao. "When he decided to become a priest—to abandon the role of crown prince and choose another way."

"And now he's seen the error of his ways."

"I was there," Rao pressed on, voice as low as he could make it, "when Malini wrote him letter after letter, convincing him to take up his birthright again. I was there when she convinced lord after lord, warrior and prince and king, to join her brother's cause. I was there when...when she stood before the court and called Chandra a false emperor on a stolen throne and proclaimed that she spoke for the mothers of flame. When she promised he would fall."

"You put too much weight on her dramatics," said Prem, eventually. "Those lords and kings have good reason not to want Chandra on the imperial throne. They would have turned to Aditya without her."

"I'm not so sure. Aditya removed himself from politics. Perhaps some would have sought him out. But the power that's amassed around him...She saw a weakness, a need, and she took advantage of it. She gave him this. And without her—"

"He'll be fine."

You still think I love her, thought Rao. "Without her," he continued, quietly, "he won't know what to do. I was raised alongside him, Prem. I was his companion, one of his closest lords from boyhood. I *know*."

Prem glanced at him. But all he said was, "Someone's coming."

Rao heard it then: the clatter of hooves. The swish of metal against metal, sabers drawn from sheaths. Prem gave a low whistle, and a moment later his own men appeared in the trees behind him.

There was a distant, frightened whinny of horses. The noise of men dismounting. Beasts of burden were too frightened of the forest to enter it. The Ahiranyi knew that. Even *Rao* knew that. But the men approaching were dragging their wild-eyed mounts with them, apparently on the orders of a man shouting from behind them.

"We should go," Rao murmured.

"I thought you were the one who wanted to know the dangers at our back," Prem whispered in return. His gaze was fixed forward, mouth barely moving. "Well. Now we'll know."

After a moment, ten figures appeared in their line of sight. A contingent of soldiers, dressed in Parijati white and gold. Prem's man, who'd gone into the city, was at the forefront. There was a saber to his throat.

Immediately, Rao reached for a chakram at his wrist. Around him, Prem's men touched hands to their whips. The ones at the back, nearly in the shadow of the seeker's path, reached for their bows. Behind them, Lata sank back deeper into the gloom, seeking cover.

"Ah. There's no need for that. Lower your weapons," a voice said. The figure stepped forward, and Prem swore, unraveling his whip from his belt in a slithering hiss of steel.

"Santosh."

"We went to collect you from your whoring, Prince Prem," said Lord Santosh, eyes glittering. "And you, Prince Rao," he added, bowing his head in a mockery of respect. "Although I expected to find a Lord Rajan. What a pleasant surprise, to find you instead! The brothel burned down, unfortunately. And you weren't there."

"Let my guard go, Santosh," Prem demanded. "Or you'll be committing a crime against the royal blood of Saketa."

"I act in the emperor's name," Santosh snapped in return. "I protect his interests. And it has occurred to me that it's curious for a low prince to spend so long in Ahiranya just when the emperor's sister happens to be here, imprisoned. Very curious."

"I told you," Prem said, baring his teeth into something that vaguely approximated a smile. "I came to Ahiranya for pleasure."

"And you, Prince Rao? For pleasure alone?"

"What do you want?" Rao asked bluntly. The Saketan man was blinking hard, obviously terrified, struggling to breathe around the press of the blade, and Rao suddenly found he had no patience for games. "For the boy's life."

"I want to know why you're here," Santosh said. "I want to know where you're going. I want to know who you're working with against our emperor."

"I'm afraid you don't have the authority for such invasive questioning, Lord Santosh," Prem said. "Let me explain it to you, since you strike me as particularly slow: You're nothing but an inbred Parijati lord who loves licking the sweat off Chandra's feet. We, on the other hand, are royal-blooded sons of the city-states of Parijatdvipa. You are not our equal. Unless Chandra has already handed you Ahiranya's regency?"

"I am an advisor to the emperor," Santosh said through gritted teeth.

"All our ancestors, since the Age of Flowers, have been advisors to emperors," Prem countered, gesturing to himself and Rao. "Our kin are the emperor's counselors and have always, always placed their blood and their hearts in the service of the whole. You're nothing but a lackey."

"You don't deserve to serve him," Santosh said, a hectic light in his eyes as he drew his own saber. "You've been given too much freedom. It was Parijat that saved your people and Parijati blood that should stand first. Your betrayal only proves it. He is far superior to you."

"He isn't your friend," Prem goaded. "You know that, don't you?" He tsked. "Poor dove. I can see that you don't."

"I'll peel your skin off your bones, low prince."

"Grand talk. Come closer, if you mean it."

Together, Rao and Prem took a step back, and another, moving deeper into the seeker's path. The air rippled strangely around them. They saw the hesitation in the eyes of the Parijati soldiers, who clearly feared the odd stillness of the forest and remembered the horrifying tales they'd been told about Ahiranya as children.

"Go back the way you came," Prem called out. "Go squat on the regent's throne. It's clearly where you want to be anyway. Or does Chandra need you to prove yourself first?"

"Speak," Santosh commanded angrily. "Lower your weapons and tell me how you've betrayed the emperor, or your man dies."

The Saketan boy was watching them.

"My men know their loyalties," said Prem.

The boy closed his eyes. Jerked forward, yelling, as he tried to make a bid for freedom. The Parijati soldier holding him wrenched his saber back.

There was a burst of blood, and Prem's man was dead.

In almost the same moment, a volley of arrows broke from behind them, responding to Prem's command.

"Quick," Rao said, as Prem's hand lowered and the Parijati ducked, raising shields or arms—one receiving an arrow through the wrist for his trouble. "Into the forest. We can try to outrun them."

"And lead them right to Aditya?" Prem said, incredulous. "Come on, Rao, if we stay and fight—"

"We die," said Rao.

"I'm not afraid of death," Prem said.

"Maybe not," Rao replied. "But you'd like to win, wouldn't you?"

Prem hesitated.

"Trust me, Prem. They don't know the terrain. We have a guide. They won't know what to expect in there. I have a plan—"

"Whatever you're thinking," Lata yelled, with more volume than Rao had ever heard from her before, "*hurry up!*"

"I'm trusting you," Prem said roughly. And with another gesture, a sharp whistle, his men were turning down the seeker's path.

The Parijati, overcoming their hesitation, took hold of their horses and followed them.

45

BHUMIKA

There was a burning, charred metal smell upon the air. Bhumika sat very still, surrounded by her people, and felt the drip of blood from thorns—smelled the wafts of smoke rising from the city and seeping in through the wefts of vine barring the windows.

Jeevan entered. Stood before her. Shook his head.

"Bad news, my lady."

"Tell me."

"Your husband lives."

Any normal wife would have been thrilled to hear that her husband had survived. But Bhumika bit down upon her tongue until she tasted blood.

Her brother hadn't even done her the kindness of taking this choice from her hands.

"What shall I do with him?" Jeevan asked.

"Bring him into the rose palace," she said. "Find a room where he can be locked away. And then I'll see to him."

Jeevan placed Vikram in Khalida's own room, which adjoined Bhumika's sleep chamber. Vikram lay half-conscious upon Khalida's sleep mat. There was a great wound gouged in his side, mirroring the one he'd received in Lord Iskar's haveli, hastily bandaged with cloth torn from a soldier's tunic. She wondered which poor soul had saved him, perhaps at the cost of their own life.

Bhumika sat upon the ground beside him.

"The rebels," Vikram said. His voice was a hoarse question, bloody with fear.

"A wall of vines grew around the rose palace," said Bhumika. "No one can enter."

He didn't question her words. Perhaps his injuries had temporarily addled him.

"They've overwhelmed the city," he said. "The mahal—they should not have been able to break the mahal's walls. They were not an organized military force. Nothing like Parijatdvipa can muster. How did they break the walls?"

Bhumika was silent. She watched his face twist with torment.

"So many of my men are dead," he said.

She had not known what she would do once she saw him. But the look on his face softened her treacherous heart.

"Even my uncle's home has burned," she said quietly, thinking of that beautiful old haveli with a heartache. The flowers she'd grown for her uncle—deep red lilies, fed by her own heart and her own magic—had turned to ash at his bedside. She'd felt it. But there was no room for her grief, in this task or in the role she now found herself in. She could only fold it away, shelter it, until a time came when she could indulge in feeling her sorrow. If such a day ever came, of course. "There are highborn who have fled the city, and perhaps my uncle joined them. I do not believe he had the strength to do so, may soil and sky protect him. But I will imagine that he died in his bed, at peace. That is a kindness I offer myself."

Vikram looked through her. He barely seemed to hear her voice. "I don't understand," he said. "I can't. It's almost as if..."

He fell silent. She knew then that he was thinking of the temple children.

"I'll seek the aid of the emperor," Vikram said eventually.

"He'll have you removed from your post," said Bhumika. "Or killed. And then you will have nothing."

"I have connections," said Vikram. "There is nowhere in

Parijatdvipa that would give me a throne, certainly, and I have no heart for military campaigns any longer, but there is always work for a man who knows how to tend to power." A pause. "Saketa, perhaps. It is a green place. Beautiful. It would make a good home for children."

"I don't wish to leave Ahiranya. This is my home."

"You know nothing but Ahiranya," he said dismissively. He tried to sit up. Gasped in pain. "You'll learn. Where is the damnable physician?"

"I won't leave Ahiranya," said Bhumika. "I intend to remain here. My apologies, husband. You cannot make me leave."

He was gray-faced with pain, his lips pinched a mottled purple.

"You're my wife," he said harshly. "And you carry my child."

"Yes." Simple words. "But I do not belong to you. And the child is still mine, my flesh and blood, and body and milk. One day that will change. All children outgrow their mothers. But for now, they remain with me, as they must."

"No more of this, Bhumika. Call me a physician. I have work to do, if we hope to survive."

She shook her head.

"What do you mean, *no?*"

Vikram had not been prepared for what those touched by the deathless waters could do. And those rebels of Ashok's had not been prepared for her. But then, Ashok had always underestimated her. Just as Vikram had. Just as Priya had.

Fortunately, Bhumika never underestimated herself.

You should have listened to me, she thought of saying. *You should have avoided escalation with the rebels. You should have known better than to throw your lot in with the emperor who burns women, who dashes down his allies, the emperor who dreams of a world purified by faith and flame.*

You should have trusted the woman you married.

"I never wanted this," she said instead. That, at least, was true. "I wanted peace. I was willing to pay the price that peace demanded, however broken that peace was. But now it's gone, husband, and now that the rebels and your men have torn Hiranaprastha between them like dogs, I will do what is needful. I will take up the role that was once mine."

Finally, he looked at her and saw her. The flush of her face, suffused with power. And behind her...

The thorns, coiling through the window with unnatural, winding sentience.

She saw the realization dawn in his eyes. It was a cold, pure horror, a horror that told her he had never suspected her, never feared her. Never known that his Ahiranyi highborn wife, married for politics and for her beauty, for the possibility of the child she now carried, was the kind of monster he had once sought to burn.

"You will not return to your emperor," she said. "I am sorry for it, Vikram. But there are lives I value more than yours. And truly..." She swallowed. "Truly, I tried."

She rose to her feet. He grasped at the hem of her sari. She stepped away before he could touch her.

"A physician," he called after her. "Bhumika. At least that."

He was trying to rise to his feet. She heard him groan once more in pain.

She shut and bolted the door behind her, without looking back.

Everything she had built had shattered.

Her safe identity. Her marriage. Her nation of fragile peace. She could no longer use the strength of Parijatdvipa to protect her own. It was Ahiranya's strength she needed now. The strength of the deathless waters and their magic of root and vine.

She needed Priya.

Many of the survivors in the rose palace were very old, or very young. But some were Jeevan's men, or guards who'd run to safety. Some were strong-armed gardeners, or cooks from the kitchens with burn-scarred and callused hands. And some were maidservants, used to the hard work of hauling water and firewood, of climbing the Hirana. And these were the people she spoke to.

She told them that not all the temple children had died.

She told them of Priya's gifts, so like her own. She told them that the way to the waters had been found. She told them there was a chance the power that had once existed in Ahiranya could be restored. She gave them more honesty than she had ever afforded Vikram.

"And if you come with me, or guard the rose palace for my return," she said. "If you act as my retinue and my loyalists, if you help me find my fellow temple child, you will ensure that Ahiranya has hope. That it may survive, still, even if the empire turns upon us. So." She looked between them. "Will you come?"

"We all know the tales of the temple council," one cook said gruffly. "Some of us who were city born and raised met them in person. We know what was done to them. The children." He looked down at his hands. Raw now, not just from cooking scars, but from handling a bow. "I'll come."

"I want to come too," said the maidservant Sima. A few other voices joined in, offering their presence on the journey or their arrows on the palace's walls.

"This won't be an easy journey for any of us," she said, once all the volunteers had spoken and roles had been delegated. "And to those of you who remain—I will pray every night for the strength of my thorns to hold."

There was no rest after that. Only planning, and more planning, and then when she finally found a moment alone, to close her eyes, she heard footsteps. Looked, and saw the child with the rot upon him standing before her, a hopeful look in his eyes.

"Rukh," she said. "What do you want?"

"I'm coming with you," he said. "Aren't I? You made me promise to serve you. So I must come. I need to help you find her."

The journey ahead of them was not suitable for a child. She should have refused him. But leaving him behind would crush some of the hope in him. And she found she could not do that.

"Yes," she said. "Go and pack your things."

This journey was no place for her either. She could not even imagine her own child yet. When she tried to, she saw—nothing. Only felt the alienness of her own body, the tug and pain that pooled at the base of her spine. And yet she loved them, because they were her own, and breathed and dreamt with her.

"You deserve better than this," she murmured, moving her hand back and forth over the curve of her stomach. Back and forth. "But here we are. The work must be done."

46

PRIYA

A bed. A green bed. A bed of water. She was beneath a swirling river, and it was overgrown with lotus flowers, their roots snarled around her wrists and her throat.

She twisted and turned within them, disturbed by the fact that the liquid around her wasn't cold but hot. She had a distant memory that it had been painful once, a scalding heat, but now it moved around her with the same warmth and sluggish consistency as blood.

She reached for her own throat, untangling the roots, rising to the water's surface. She was in the sangam, or something that looked very like the sangam, with winding rivers, and stars racing in skeins and knots upon the water. But the water was deep, deep, and overfull of flowering blooms—lilies and other strange, curling flowers she had no names for.

She shouldn't have been here. She had been somewhere else, only moments before. Hadn't she? Malini holding her up. She remembered that. Malini holding her, and her voice, commanding Priya to remain with her, to stay, please—

Sapling. Look.

She looked again at the water she'd risen from. Through the dark, she saw a body.

Her own face lay beneath the sediment. Her own hair, a loose cloud of black fronds. Those were her own eyes, closed as if in sleep. From her chest bloomed a great lotus, bursting through exposed ribs. From her eyes streamed marigold petals, flecked gold and carnelian, seeping from beneath the closed lids.

Not a reflection. She knew it wasn't that. And if she hadn't been sure, she saw beneath it, in the slow shifting gray of the water's bed, a dozen more tangled figures, held by lotus roots, their hair coiling in water, their bodies half root and half flesh, beautiful and strange.

The body that was so like her own, that lay above the rest, was moving. The mouth opened and within it was a flower that unfurled in thorns, virulent blue and black, its heart a cosmos.

She gave a gasp and shifted back in the water, trying to swim, to turn—but the ropes of those great lotus roots held her.

The body was rising from the water. Its eyes opened. Gold-petaled. Crimson as blood.

It waded toward her. Touched fingers to her jaw. Its fingers were warm as sacred wood. Its smile was red. It wasn't her. Couldn't be her.

It stroked her cheek.

"Look at you," it said, in a voice that wasn't her own. "You're so new. And yet so hollow."

"What are you?" Priya whispered.

"Don't you recognize what you worship?" her reflection asked. It smiled.

Priya flinched—a full-body flinch of surprise—and the yaksa laughed. The water was blood hot, the yaksa's form carved wood and flesh, its eyes a bloody bloom.

"You've cut out your heart to meet me," it said. "Won't you ask me a boon?"

Priya said nothing. She couldn't. She was silenced by awe and wonder. And the yaksa only shook its head, black petals falling from its shoulders, and kept on smiling.

"I want to go back," Priya said finally. "Please."

The yaksa nodded. Its fingers drew back—but not before one fingernail sharpened, fine as a needle, and drew a line of blood from her cheek. It held a hand that was like her own to its face. Touched her blood to its lips.

"Oh, sapling," whispered the creature. "We'll meet again, you and I. One way or another."

And the creature reached for Priya and kissed her, square on the mouth.

For a moment, she saw the whole world.

She saw the ocean roiling at the edges of Parijatdvipa's great subcontinent. She saw the mountains capped with snow at the border of Dwarali. She saw Dwarali's Lal Qila, a fort that stood on the edge of the known world. She saw Parijat, and the imperial mahal in Harsinghar, surrounded by flowers.

She saw the rot. She saw it everywhere, everywhere. And she saw it grow, and change; saw it was not rot at all, but a flowering, a blooming; saw a dozen creatures with river water seeping from their fingers and carnations for eyes lift themselves from the world's soil, and *breathe*—

She woke, not with a gasp or a start, but slowly. As if she'd only been dreaming. As if she had not been in the sangam at all. She lay on a sleep mat on the floor of a house that was squat and cool, smelling sweetly of damp. Malini sat next to her, on her knees.

She flung herself over Priya, embracing her.

What...?

"What is this place you've led us to?" Malini asked, voice dangerously low. "The woman won't let me leave this room. And the man—"

Malini went abruptly silent. Priya felt her pull back, her face calm again, her eyes demurely lowered.

And there, behind her, was Elder Chandni.

Priya's heart gave a sharp thud.

She'd felt the presence of a sibling, or so she'd thought. Someone like family, a sharp needle-thorn in the tangle of the forest. She had not expected this.

Childhood. Chandni at her writing desk. Chandni's hand in her hair.

The feast. The blood. The fire.

Chandni stepped farther into the hut, into its semidarkness. But Priya could see her. Her face, with its angular cheekbones, and hair that had gone fully gray, bound back in a bun low at her neck. She had new wrinkles, and a way of walking that spoke of pain.

"Your companion brought you here," said Chandni. Her voice was soft. It took a moment for Priya to realize she was speaking in classical Ahiranyi, excluding an uncomprehending Malini from the conversation. "She said you asked to be brought to this place."

Priya swallowed. Her throat was dry. She felt a little like she was still trapped in some terrible fever dream.

"I did."

"And yet I don't think you knew you would see me. Did you?" Chandni's eyes tracked every movement of Priya's face—every tic and twitch of muscle in her body.

Priya wished she had Malini's ability to leach all feeling out of her own expression, but she didn't. Still, she wouldn't flinch. Not here. She stared at Chandni unblinking until her eyes burned as fiercely as the thing knotted in her chest that she had no name for.

"I sensed someone like me was here," said Priya. "But no. I didn't expect—you."

"Did you think me dead?"

I hoped you were, thought Priya. But in the next beat, she knew it wasn't true. However, neither answer was going to help her or leave Malini unscathed.

"All the temple council are dead, elders and children alike. Or should be," Priya said.

You killed us. You should have had the decency to die with us.

"Some of us chose to die with the children," said Chandni. "And some of us chose this."

This. Priya looked around. Mold upon the wooden walls. The scuttle and worm of insects through boards decayed and speckled with damp. The drip of a broken roof.

Malini was watching her with hooded eyes, apparently indifferent. But Priya knew better.

"It isn't much of an exile," Priya managed to say. "You're still in Ahiranya."

"Not exile," Chandni said. Still soft. So soft. She took a step closer, and Priya realized it was not gentleness as she'd first supposed, but the lulling voice one uses with a feral animal. To calm it, before the leash or the slaughter. "We still had work to do. Or thought we did."

"Who else is here?"

"Just Sendhil, now. The rest are gone. But he won't harm you."

Chandni leaned down, with difficulty. She placed a hand on Priya's forehead. Priya did not move. Only stared back at her.

"How did you save me? I thought the waters had me."

"I didn't," said Chandni. "You survived on your own, Priya, just as the children taken to the sickroom at the temple did. Or did not."

They looked at one another, distrustful, distorted reflections in the half light.

"Your fever is gone." Chandni lowered her hand. "That's good. You'll live, then."

"If I'd known it was you, I would never have come," Priya said. "I would have expected you to kill me the moment you laid eyes on me."

"I should not have let you live, Priya," said Chandni. "Not—then. And not now. I should have killed you when your companion brought you here. That's true enough."

"So why didn't you?" Priya asked, suddenly angry—so angry that she could feel now that she was shaking and hadn't even realized it. "I could hardly have stopped you."

"When you're better, we'll talk."

Chandni began to rise and Priya gripped her by the shoulder. She did not hold tight. She didn't need to. Chandni's bones were sharp points beneath her hand, fragile as shell.

"I'm well now," Priya said in Zaban—the common tongue flowing so much more easily from her lips. "I'm well now. And now, we'll talk."

I am the stronger one, Priya thought, holding Chandni's gaze fixedly. *I am not a child anymore. And you will give me answers.*

"Well, then," said Chandni, now in careful Zaban. "If you're healthy, get up. Follow me outside, and we'll talk. Alone."

Chandni didn't do her the kindness of looking away as she struggled to her feet. Malini stood with her, hands clasped neatly before her. She didn't follow as Priya and Chandni made their way out of the room, though Priya could feel the weight of her gaze.

Priya ached. Every part of her. The great strength she'd possessed right after rising from the deathless waters was gone, leaving her completely drained. But at least she was no longer feverish or dying. She felt mostly like herself. And her self was furious and tired, flayed bare. She didn't know if it wanted to strangle Chandni or weep over her.

"This way," Chandni said. Using the wall for support, she guided Priya toward the back of the hut. Sendhil sat by the edge of the hut, a hood drawn low over his head. He looked to be sleeping, but Priya was sure he was not. You didn't sleep when a child you'd tried to murder returned to your home full grown.

"How have you lived, since the temple council fell?" Chandni asked.

"*Fell*," repeated Priya. "That doesn't really capture what happened."

Chandni was silent for a moment. Then she said, "Never mind."

Some of the softness seemed to leave her then. In its place were slightly bowed shoulders, a sudden lowering of her head. She looked defeated.

"What is worship called, in the oldest Ahiranyi texts?" Chandni asked eventually.

"I don't know," said Priya.

"I taught you, once."

"I don't remember."

Chandni turned to look at her. In the daylight, her face was pinched and creased, almost brittle.

"The hollowing," Chandni told her. "It is called the hollowing."

She looked away from Priya then, making her laborious, slow way around the building's perimeter. "We believed we understood it. Hollowing, to scrape you clean of weakness. Hollowing, to make you a vessel for truth and knowledge. Hollowing for purity." A pause. "Then your siblings entered the deathless waters and returned with strangers living behind their eyes. And we understood that we were wrong. Whatever returned wore their skins. But it was not them. And then the rot began. Whatever lies in you—whatever returned within them—was the mother of the rot. A blight. We had to end it before it ended the world. The emperor feared you and wanted you dead. We wanted the rot to end. We thought it was right."

Priya thought of her siblings. Little Nandi. Sanjana. Her voice shook when she spoke. "We were just children."

"The thrice-born were young elders, ready to join our circle. Not children anymore. And the rest . . ." An exhalation. Priya was not sure if it was a sigh or a pained breath as Chandni stopped and steadied herself. "Children who can change the shape of mountains and compel root and leaf—they are not children anymore. They are something that only looks like a child. We had a duty, Priya."

"Then why did you save my life?" Priya asked. "If we were monsters that needed destroying, for the sake of your duty, *why did you try to spare me?*"

"Sometimes we do foolish things," Chandni said, sorrow in her voice. "It doesn't matter any longer. That time is long gone. You need only understand this, even if you do not forgive it: We sought to stop the rot from growing and spreading. We were afraid of what would become of the world. And we came here to seek a way to protect our Ahiranya. To destroy the rot that remained. And to—mourn." Her voice cracked a little. "Now. For your own sake—step carefully. Follow my lead."

Behind the hut where Sendhil and Chandni lived lay an empty glade. Perhaps it had once been used to grow vegetables or keep animals, but now its ground was untouched by human hands, covered in a whirling knot of grasses with the slithering thickness of hair. At the center of the glade was one single tree. In the ground around it were stakes, pieces of wood, hammered deep into the soil.

"You may look at the tree," said Chandni. "Inspect it as is needful, but don't cross the perimeter of sacred wood."

It was a great mangrove-like thing, that tree, with a wizened trunk and drooping branches laden with small leaves, as pale as pearls. Priya walked toward it, the heat of sacred wood a pulsing heartbeat before her.

"What is this?" Priya said. "What...?"

She'd been wrong to think the trunk was simply wizened. Here, close now, she could see the rot of it: the pink of wounded flesh between the striations of wood, the breathy pulse of the roots, loose-limbed against the soil.

The faces.

Saroj. Bojal. Not all the elders. But enough of them.

Priya felt the bile rise in her throat.

"It began soon after we arrived here. The first began to sicken and die. As he died, the tree changed. Stole his soul, I think. Then the second. The third. Now only Sendhil and I remain. Waiting." Her voice was terribly calm. "Whatever curse lay in you and your fellow children...well, it lay in us too, it seems. Although it manifests as you see."

"Their bodies?"

"Burned. But it doesn't matter. The rot has us. A curse beyond death, I think." Priya heard Chandni step closer and thought for the first time that there was an almost wooden creak to her movements; that her skin had not simply looked pinched but fissured like bark, in the light.

Priya stared not at Chandni but at the tree before her. The rot of it. The justice of it.

"You're wrong, to think we were a symptom of the rot. We're the cure. I'm sure of it." She tilted her head until she was staring at canopy-slashed sky, blinking back unwanted tears. "I've been told the thrice-born could control it. Maybe banish it."

"Who told you?"

"Was it true? Could they control it?"

"They could," Chandni said, after a pause. "Yes."

"You were fools," Priya said, choking on her grief, her anger. All of the children had deserved better than the death they'd had. She thought of Sanjana's smile, Nandi's gentle eyes, and was crushed with the weight of how hollow they *hadn't* been—how hollow the world was without them. "We were the answer all along, and you discarded us. Destroyed us."

"Perhaps," Chandni said heavily.

"There's no 'perhaps,'" Priya said thickly. "Was it worth it, then, murdering my brothers and sisters? For a belief?"

Priya turned. Chandni was looking at the tree. Perhaps she was thinking of the other lost elders, who had been like kin to her. Perhaps she thought of the children they had murdered.

"It was the choice we made," Chandni said finally. "We believed you were monsters. You believe you are not. We did what we thought was right, and you may now condemn us for it. But it changes nothing."

"Why am *I* still alive?"

"You were born on the Hirana," Chandni said, resigned. "Not simply temple raised but temple born. You know that."

"I do. But born or reared, we were all taken from our birth families and given a new family, old bonds severed," Priya said. "That was the price of rising to the status of a temple elder, wasn't it? Give up blood family. Choose a family of brothers and sisters in service. And my family burned upon the Hirana." She thought of Chandni's hand upon her hair as she slept. She thought of what it meant to be temple born when all the other children were adopted into service. She knew what it meant, what was unsaid between them. And it didn't matter. "If I had blood family, that's what I would tell them."

"Ah," said Chandni. "Then I suppose I saved you for sentimentality. For a dream I should have put aside. I told you it was foolish."

"It was."

Chandni's smile was sad.

"Exactly right," she said. As if she'd known it would come to this in the end: Priya standing before a tree that was not entirely tree alone, its roots swelled with the blood and flesh of the dead.

"Some things are inevitable," Chandni said. "The tides. The sunrise. Perhaps despite our best efforts, the rot is inevitable too. And you are inevitable." She looked, once more, at the tree. "I am too old and tired to do more. So this is my answer, Priya: I allow you to live now because I cannot stop the tide." Chandni shook her head. "Now, if you're well, you should go."

47

VIKRAM

The pain and the betrayal had left him in a fog he could not rise from.

All his hard work. His years of sacrifice for the empire. The wars he had fought, the pacts and alliances he had made, the regency he had been granted. The wife he'd wed. The children he'd burned. All of it, gone.

The door clicked open. For a moment, the men who entered were in shadow. He heard their booted footsteps. With difficulty, he raised his head and watched them approach. The first man was a young guard, a stripling with cold eyes, who did not even bow his head. The second...

"Jeevan." Vikram exhaled heavily, more relieved than he could say. "Thank the mothers you're here."

Jeevan closed the door quietly behind him. He was not wearing Parijatdvipa's colors—no pure white, no gold. His tunic was plain and dark. But the cuff marking his status as head of the regent's personal guard was still upon his upper arm, and he wore a shawl bound from shoulder to waist, knotted at the hip, embroidered with the jasmine flowers of the empire in white thread.

"My lord," said Jeevan. He kneeled down. "This is a low day indeed."

"Can we escape unhindered?" Vikram asked. "Jeevan, my wound is grave. I will need a physician before we begin our journey to Parijat." He grunted, drawing himself up on his elbows. "Help me up," he said. "Quickly now. Are there any rebels in the corridor? Have you more men?"

Jeevan helped him sit up straight. The commander's hand was firm against Vikram's back. The other guard kneeled down next to him as, one-handed, Jeevan unknotted his shawl.

"What are you doing, man?" Vikram demanded. And then, when the shawl was loose, he finally understood.

"Ah, ah," said the young guard, pressing a hand to Vikram's chest. "Stay still, my lord."

"You work for her," he whispered. The commander of his personal guard. The man who had kept him alive all these years—protected him at his most vulnerable. How could it be? "You work for my monster of a wife—my—"

"Do not say it, my lord," Jeevan said calmly, gripping him hard to hold him steady. "Ill words are beneath you."

Vikram laughed, a helpless laugh, because he could not believe what had become of him and his life, even the ruins of it turning to ash around him. What could be beneath him now?

"Lady Bhumika's health does not allow her to do what is necessary," said the soldier who'd served him so long, gruffly. "And besides. That's what I'm here for. This is my purpose."

"Can I truly trust no one?" Vikram gasped out. "After all I've done? How hard I have striven to make something of this place? Will you condemn me with no mercy, no trial, no justice?"

"I'm sorry, my lord," Jeevan said, although he did not sound particularly sorry. "There'd be a trial in another life and place, I expect. But not here and now."

The cloth was looped around his neck. He struggled but the young guard pinned him down efficiently, driving an elbow brutally into his stomach to leave him momentarily winded, stunned to stillness. That moment was enough. It was too late.

Vikram felt the noose draw tight.

48

RAO

Santosh's men had tried to drag their horses with them onto the seeker's path, which bought Prem's people time, just as Rao had suspected it would. It was just enough time to arrange an ambush.

"I grew up in the imperial court," Rao said to the assembled men, as they stopped to catch their breath. "I learned the traditional methods, the grand strategies that date back to the Age of Flowers. If Santosh is as much of a purist as I remember, he'll adhere to the rules of fair warfare. Without horses or chariots, he'll struggle. He'll use sabers. No archers or chakram throwers— certainly no whips," Rao said, gesturing at the steel whip coiled at Prem's waist. "He won't sully his men with the weapons of other nations. He'll be badly equipped to face an ambush."

Prem wiped the sweat from his forehead. He was still in his heavy shawl, knotted tight to keep it out of the way.

"He's a purist, true enough," Prem said. "Fine. Let's try it."

"I can use a bow," Lata offered.

"You're going to keep well away from the battle," Prem told her firmly. Lata inclined her head in agreement, but Rao made sure she had a throwing knife regardless.

The Saketans stood in the shadows, steel whips readied. The archers climbed into the trees. Rao joined them, one chakram drawn from his wrist held steady between his fingertips.

When Santosh's men appeared, all but one of their horses were gone. Run off, most likely, utterly spooked by the forest. Poor beasts.

Prem held his men until Rao threw the first chakram. When he threw the second, they rained down their arrows. As soon the last arrow was loosed—the Parijati either huddling together in the center of the path to avoid the blows, or bleeding and prone on the soil—Prem and his men reared forward, their whips cutting through the air.

Rao leapt down from his branch, skirting around the melee to avoid catching the edge of the whip swords himself. That was when he saw Santosh, crawling away from the battle.

He drew a dagger from his belt. He leapt at the man and—missed, as Santosh rolled away from the blade and jumped to his feet with more agility than Rao had expected of him.

Rao swore, flipped the blade in his hand, and slid it back into place on his belt as Santosh drew his saber.

The saber was little good against a blade whip, but it was very effective in close range against traditional Aloran weapons, which were all intended for throwing or for prosaic close-range stabbing. Rao had four chakrams left on his arm—a handful of throwing daggers at his waist. He jumped back, flinging a blade at Santosh. It missed.

It would have been nice—pleasant even—if Santosh had been a bad fighter. But he'd grown up noble if not royal, and he knew how to handle a Parijati saber. His movements were perfect—sharp slices and stabs at precise angles, which Rao had to dart to avoid, wishing he had a blade whip of his own.

The Saketans suddenly moved as one, shifting, and Prem leapt out, flinging his whip in a rippling slice that caught Santosh on his saber-wielding arm. Slashed through to the skin. The man cursed in pain—but did not drop his blade.

"Two against one? Where is your honor," Santosh roared.

"Be sure to tell Chandra what dishonorable dogs we are, if you win," Prem said cheerfully, his steel whip slicing a sharp arc through the air that Santosh stumbled to escape.

Behind the flash of the whip, Rao saw a figure move in close behind Prem, saber drawn, breaking through the defense provided by Prem's men. There was no time to think. On instinct, Rao drew a chakram from his wrist and flung the sharp-edged discus at the Parijati soldier.

It went through the man's skull. But not before the man's blade caught Prem at the arm.

Prem's whip dropped. His shawl, torn ragged by the blade, fell from his shoulder.

And Rao—froze.

On Prem's exposed throat, his bleeding arm, were—marks. Bruises.

No. Not bruises. Whorls of bark, large as Rao's palm. Veins, spidering from them, limned in green. The blood that poured from his wound was not quite red. Not quite human.

Santosh took advantage of Rao's shock, of Prem's stagger as he tried, despite his wound, to draw his shawl back into place. He lunged for the low prince.

Prem's eyes widened. He fumbled for his whip. Rao, horrified, scrambled for one of his chakrams, his knives, anything—

Prem's whip flashed through the air, cutting through Santosh's armor, bloodying his arms and blowing open his lip. But Santosh had already thrust forward. His saber had slid, cleanly, straight through Prem's stomach.

Rao's mind went white for a moment. He saw an arrow fly past him. Heard shouts, muted, as if his ears were beneath water and the water were the thud of his own bloody rage pouring through his skull. The next thing he knew, he had Santosh pinned beneath him. Santosh was yelling for his men, for Chandra, for help, for anyone to help.

In a haze, Rao drove one of his steel chakrams by hand into Santosh's palm. He drove it hard and vicious, feeling the bones snap under it like the necks of small furred creatures.

"He is a royal of Saketa," Rao said raggedly. "You had no right, no right. All your talk of honor—you had *no right*."

"The emperor," Santosh gasped out. His teeth were washed red. "For the emperor, for Parijat, my men, protect me!"

But one of Prem's men was now at Rao's back. Another was leaning over Prem, talking to him urgently. And there was Lata, trying to staunch the flow of blood, tears streaming down her face. The battle had to be over, and Rao knew, knew distantly that he should take Santosh hostage, that Aditya could use him as leverage.

"Chandra is not our emperor," Rao said, voice rough.

Santosh's mouth was open, still yelling, so Rao lifted his bloodied hand and took one of his daggers from his belt. Without pausing, he drove it to the back of Santosh's throat.

They set up camp. Prem's men didn't leave. It was a miracle that they remained, but Rao accepted it. He had thought the rot on Prem's skin would send them running. But they merely shook their heads. "We knew what he had, my lord," one said. "He was our lord. He told us. He explained. It doesn't spread. Not between people."

Together, he and the men set up a tent for Prem to be settled in. He kneeled on the ground, once it was arranged, and watched Lata work, preparing her tinctures. Preparing the bandages, her eyes red. She'd known. All this time. Only Rao, it seemed, had been in the dark.

He couldn't ask Prem now why he hadn't told him. He could only feel the blood drying on his clothes, and watch the saber-wounded mess of Prem's stomach rise and fall. He could not see how Prem could survive this.

"It can't infect you," said Lata. Her voice was careful, calm. "He wasn't lying about that. Where is his pipe?"

"His pipe?"

"An analgesic," she said. "It dulls the pain. He's found it help-ful these past months."

"Won't do any good," said Prem. He sounded hoarse. "It hasn't worked for a while. And now…" He touched a hand to his upper abdomen. Swore.

"Don't touch it," snapped Lata.

"What difference will it make now?"

She said nothing. Prem closed his eyes, his skin pale and drawn.

"You should never have come to Ahiranya," Rao said, a knot of helpless sickness in his stomach. He wanted to scream at his friend, to shake him. "You should have remained in Saketa, drinking wine."

"That was never my way," said Prem, with difficulty. Already, the bandages Lata had applied to his stomach were wet with blood. "Don't get me wrong, Rao. I like a good wine. But seeing the right man on the throne..."

"Ahiranya has done this to you. Trying to see Aditya crowned has done this to you."

"Ahiranya didn't do this to me," Prem said hoarsely. "I was sick before I came here."

Rao shook his head. "What do you mean? How can that be?"

"This rot," Prem said. "I don't know how it's spread, but it exists in Saketa too. Hundreds have died of it. The high prince has managed to keep the whole business quiet for now, but..." Prem coughed. A wet sound, bubbling with blood. Lata moved quickly, daubing the blood from his lips. "The last two years. It's dug its roots in. It's becoming hard to ignore. It must be everywhere."

"It hasn't reached Alor," Rao said.

But did he know that for certain? He had been to Alor only rarely, after his fostering to Parijat. His elder brothers supported his father ably, but there were aspects of governing the city-state of their birth that they had never involved him in. If a strange blight had attacked Alor's fields and farms, its herds of cattle, would any of them have told him?

"Rao. Chandra. He. He's made the mothers angry. Using their names for political ends. Great, good women of old, they didn't die for the likes of him. Now they're punishing us all."

"You can't believe that's why you're—like this."

"Why else would the rot get so much worse?" Prem asked. "I

know the will of the mothers. I feel it." He grimaced again. With a shuddering breath, he said, "What does your nameless god say? Does he disagree?"

"No theological arguments," Rao said. "Not now."

"I don't know," said Prem. "Now feels likes the perfect time." He tried to reach out, but groaned in pain. So Rao reached for him, taking his hand.

"We need him gone, Rao," Prem murmured. "And mothers help me, I respect your faith, strange as it is. But Prince Aditya needs to put the priesthood aside and become the emperor Parijatdvipa needs."

Rao swallowed. Nodded. Beneath his grip, he could feel the bark on Prem's skin, fibrous and rough.

"I didn't stay because I hoped to save *her*," Prem said. "I stayed because I knew he wouldn't listen to any of us but you. You share his faith. You're his dearest friend. If you tell him to return, to take his crown, to make a sacrifice of his calling..." Another cough. Then: "I had to bring you to him. I'm sorry I won't—finish it."

"No," Rao said. "No."

In the dark of a tent, on a path through a forest, so far from home that Saketa and Alor both felt like distant dreams—this was not how Prem should die.

"Tell me one thing," said Prem. Voice wet. "Consider it a boon."

"Anything."

"Who are you really?" Prem asked. "What prophecy were you named with by your nameless god? What do you know of what's coming?"

"Some prophecies are small," Rao said.

"But yours isn't," said Prem.

A name should not be said until the time is right. A name should only be spoken when the fulfillment of a prophecy is at hand. And yet.

It was not like telling his name at all. A secret told to the dead is a secret still untold. And from the look in Prem's eyes—from the profile of Lata's turned-away face, the hunch of her shoulders—Prem did not have long.

Rao leaned forward. He whispered against Prem's ear. Syllable after syllable.

For a moment, Prem was silent. Then he let out a choked laugh.

"No wonder you stayed for her," said Prem. "No wonder."

Lata was waiting outside the tent. It was light. "I can perform his last rites," she said. Her voice was thick.

Rao swallowed. He felt as if his throat were full of glass.

"In Saketa, they don't allow women to perform funeral rites."

"There's no one else." Her voice was gentle, her expression remote.

"They don't allow it in Srugna. Or Dwarali. Or Parijat. They don't..."

"There's no one else," she repeated.

He nodded. He felt impossibly tired.

"Thank you," he said. "For taking care of him."

"What is the point of knowledge that isn't used?"

The men had all waited. They listened, as Rao told them Prem was dead.

"He wouldn't want us to return to Saketa," one of Prem's favorite pachisa players murmured. "We're going to Emperor Aditya. It's what he would have wanted."

They buried him. There was no choice, here in the woods.

They had to keep walking. They had no choice about that either. Malini had not come, and Prem was dead.

"Tell me what it's like in the lacquer gardens," Rao managed to say to Lata as they trudged along.

Take me away from here, he wanted to say. *Spin me a tale that allows me to leave the pain and the loss and the rot of this place for a time. Please give me that comfort.*

Lata's feet crunched down the long grass. She ran a stick along the ground ahead of them, warning any sleeping snakes that humans were passing, and it would be best to slither away and leave them be.

"I know less of the gardens than you do," she said.

"Anything you've read. I know you have. Please."

"It was a place built for the sake of a vision," she said finally. "And like all things vision born, it is an irrational artifice."

"You sound like you're quoting."

"Very perceptive. I am. The texts of my own teacher."

"What does it mean—irrational artifice?"

She raised her head, squinting against the sun.

"You'll see for yourself, soon enough," she said. "Look."

Ahead of them stood a gorge, and across it lay a bridge of root, carved between walls of mountain rock. Through the path, he could see a temple garden. A great monastery.

They had reached Srugna. They'd found the lacquer gardens, where Aditya awaited. There were men, watching for them at the top of the path. Not soldiers of Parijatdvipa, in imperial white and gold. Dwarali horsemen. Saketan liegemen. Even Aloran warriors. His father's men, sent to ensure that Aditya would take the throne.

Rao looked at them all and thought of the words he would have to say.

The low prince of Saketa is dead. Prince Prem is dead. But I am here, Aditya. I'm here.

CHANDNI

Sendhil entered the hut, removing the hood from his head. Without it, the patches on his skull where moss had formed were entirely visible. He kneeled down, holding his gnarled hands loose before him.

"You should have killed her."

"Mm."

"Should have let me do it, if you couldn't."

"There would have been no point," Chandni replied. "Nothing we've done can put a stop to it now. Besides, she isn't the only one who survived."

Sendhil gave a grunt in response. He'd been so eloquent once. So incisive. She remembered still walking beside him and all her fellow elders, a mixture of children who had grown up alongside her and the people who had raised them, dressed in their fine silks with the wind that wound through the Hirana on their skin.

All of them, gone now.

She looked down at her own hands. Her fingertips were whorled like the heart of a tree. In her veins was an ichor, a poisonous sap, and soon enough it would kill her. Soon enough her face would stop being her own.

She thought of Priya's face, twisted into a rictus of hate.

You can have a child, and hold that child against your own skin, and raise it.

You can betray yourself and your values for that child. You can let the child escape, even though you know it should die—know, no matter how strong and firm its hand is in yours, that it is a blight and must be hollowed from the world to give the world chance enough to survive.

And that child can look at you, with fury and contempt, and leave you to die.

She and Sendhil sat, wordless for a long time. Then Sendhil exhaled, low and slow, and said, "I can hear people coming."

Chandni thought of the agony it would cause if she stood, forcing all her bark-whorled joints to creak into motion. So she did not rise. When men and women entered the hut, she was still crouched on the floor. She could hear more of them surrounding the outside. Counted the footsteps. At least twenty.

She looked up and met Ashok's eyes.

"She's long gone," she said to him. "But you know that."

He kneeled down. "So. You live."

Chandni inclined her head. She wondered if he would strike her then, or simply gouge her neck through with the fine scythe in his right hand. Behind him, his people were exploring the hut, some walking out and toward the treacherous garden and the tree of flesh. None of them were children she'd taught or raised.

That, at least, she was glad of.

"What did you do to her?" Ashok asked.

"I nursed her to health, after the waters sickened her," Chandni said levelly. "And when she was well, she left. I know no more."

"We should have cut her throat," said Sendhil. "But the fool woman did not."

Ashok gave him a sharp look. Then he turned his attention once more to Chandni.

"Where did she go?"

"I don't know."

"You must have seen the direction she walked, when she left."

Chandni shook her head slowly. "I think, perhaps, you mean

her ill." She sighed. "You always had strong passions, Ashok. I'd hoped they would leave you in time."

"Strange, when your intention was to ensure I had no time. But no matter—I still live, and you're dying. So tell me where my sister is, elder," he said, in a voice that trembled, venomous and childish in its grief, a wobbling, teetering fury born from broken love. "Tell me, or I will be forced to take the answer from you."

Suddenly, he seemed to remember his people around him, and his expression went firm again. In a far more even voice, he repeated his command. "Tell me where to find Priya."

She said nothing.

"Ashok." A woman spoke, reentering the hut. "There's something you need to see."

He rose to his feet and left the hut. When he returned there was a solemn turn to his mouth. He kneeled once more by her, looking at the rot upon her skin, the sharp mottle of her changing bones, against her bark-like flesh.

"If I'd known you were alive, I would have killed you long ago," said Ashok. "Now I see that life has shown you justice. But I can still hurt you, elder. And I can kill you—swift or slow. I don't wish to give you pain, but I will for the sake of finding her. She is more important than you now. I value her above any justice you deserve to face."

"And yet, I have no answer for you," said Chandni. "Hurt me if you wish. Hurt Sendhil. Kill us both. We cannot give her to you."

Ashok nodded.

"Tell me," he said. "She was upon the Hirana long before any of us. She was there as an infant. Is she yours?"

"It doesn't matter," said Chandni. "Whether my flesh made her—whether she was left a foundling at the base of the Hirana, with birth blood still on her—what difference does it make? I thought of her as my own. That was my error."

Ashok nodded again. Rose to his feet.

"Tie her to the tree," he said. "Tie them both. We'll see what becomes of them."

50

PRIYA

Priya told Malini curtly that they would head directly to the seeker's path. When Malini suggested the bower of bones, Priya shook her head. "Your prince will be long gone," she said. "Better if we try to catch up with him."

She strode ahead, leading the way. For a time, they walked. And walked. The trees were thick around them, with heavy leaves that drooped over their winding path between the trunks and branches.

"So," Malini said after a time. "Your elders live after all." Priya could hear Malini's careful footsteps behind her. "It was very strange in their home. They barely spoke to me."

Priya actually bit down on her tongue. She was so—so *angry*.

"Priya, will you stop for a while? Or slow down." Malini's voice sounded strained. "You must be exhausted. I certainly am."

Priya didn't want to stop or slow down. Stopping meant thinking, and she didn't want to think. Not of the tree with its faces of flesh and bark, or Chandni's resigned, rot-riven face, or how all of it had made her feel. Scared and grief-stricken, but more than anything, angry.

"Priya." Malini's hand closed on her shoulder. Her voice was gentle when she said, once more, "Stop."

Malini's palm felt overwarm on her shoulder. Priya could have shaken off her hand. But she didn't. She stood still and closed her eyes, calming her breath, and listened to the rustle of the trees. The faint rush of water.

"I don't want to talk about it," Priya said tightly. She swallowed. "I can hear a stream. I'm thirsty. Come on."

The thick maze of trees soon parted, opening to a slope of gray rocks that ringed a pool. The pool was fed by a silvery, snaking waterfall, pouring over the low, green-dusted rocks. The water rippled faintly as the waterfall rushed to meet it. It was clear, unmarked by anything resembling rot. Priya clambered down to it. She heard Malini huff out something that might have been a swear, and follow her.

Priya kneeled down on the edge and cupped the water, cold and clear, and lifted it to her lips. She drank. Then she splashed her face, blinking water from her eyes. Ah, spirits, she felt unclean, as if her own mind had stained her skin. The sight of Elder Chandni, Elder Sendhil, the tree—

"My elders," she choked out. "I don't want to talk about my elders."

"I know," murmured Malini.

"They—Chandni—said they thought…they thought we weren't even human. That I'm not even human. She thinks I'm monstrous. My own—my own family. That's what they think of me. Do you think I'm monstrous, Malini?"

Priya heard Malini's footsteps drawing closer. But she didn't really want to hear Malini's reaction. She was afraid suddenly that Malini would say yes. So she spoke again instead, the words tumbling out of her. "Because I think *you* are. Or I'm afraid you are. Oh, you're so lovely to me, you're very good at being lovely, but you're also the woman who organized a coup against the emperor. You're deep waters, Malini. You're so much more than you're willing to show me, and that scares me. I think I'm always waiting for you to turn on me."

"I've been myself with you, always," Malini said. Her voice was careful. Steady. "But we all have more than one face. We have to have many faces in order to survive, don't we? That's natural.

Normal." Malini was at her shoulder now, kneeling also. "This face you know didn't abandon you in the forest when you collapsed. I carried you when I was weak, to people who frankly frightened me, and I stayed with you. That was all me."

Priya knew that was true. But how could she trust Malini? How, when she couldn't trust herself?

"But the rest of you," Priya said unsteadily. "Your other faces—"

"Some parts of me are monstrous," Malini said, and when Priya turned to look at her she saw that Malini was clutching the needle-flower cask at her throat. "You know why? A woman of my status and breeding, Chandra told me, should serve her family. Everyone told me I should be obedient to my father and my brothers and one day, my husband. But Aditya and Chandra made their choices, and I didn't simply accept those choices. I didn't *obey*. Because my brothers were wrong. But more than anything, Priya—more than that—I'm monstrous because I have desires. Desires I have known all my life that I should not. I've always wanted things that would place me in danger."

Her voice shook, a little, as if she trembled on the same edge as Priya. "I've avoided marriage. I'll never willingly beget children with a man. And what is more monstrous than that? To be inherently, by your nature, unable to serve your purpose? To want, simply because you want, to love simply for the sake of love?"

Their eyes were fixed on each other. Priya couldn't look away.

The gap between them was so small.

For so long the void inside Priya had been between her past and her present. But this...Priya could cross this distance. It would be simple. The thought made her breath catch and her skin feel too small, hot and prickling.

Instead she turned away and lowered her legs into the pool, sliding into the cold water. When she stood, the water reached her knees.

"I'm going to wash," she said. "I...I'm going to." She swallowed. "Who knows when we'll get the chance to again."

There was sweat, blood, and dirt all over her, so the water was actually very welcome. She waded deeper, until she was in the wake of the waterfall, submerged to her waist. She dunked her face under the water. Raised it, tugging her fingers through the damp snarl of her braid.

"Here," said Malini. Abruptly, her voice was in Priya's ear. She was right there, standing in the water alongside her, the folds of her sari billowing around her. "Let me help."

Malini touched her fingers to the end of the braid, tentative. There was a question in her eyes. And Priya...nodded. Turned her back.

Malini took up the sodden weight of Priya's braid and began to unravel it, working her fingers through it with care.

"My hair is easier to manage than yours," Priya managed to say. "No curls."

Malini worked slowly, sliding her fingers gently through the tangles. "I know you're trying to avoid talking about us."

Us.

"Will you let me?" Priya asked.

"Do you really want me to?"

She could feel the tug of Malini's hands—the tingle of it in her scalp. She shook her head, and knew Malini could see it, feel it.

"I was never lying about wanting you," Malini said in a low voice. "Never with my eyes or my words. Never when I touched you. All of that was true." Another tug. Priya felt the last of her braid uncoil, the pressure on her scalp releasing. "You're already helping me. You've saved my life, Priya. I'm free. There's no benefit—nothing I gain for the empire, for my goals—by telling you this. Do you understand?"

Malini placed her hand flat against Priya's back. The water was cold and the heat of her skin—of her outstretched fingers—burned. She'd placed her hand against Priya's blouse, under the drape of her sari, between her shoulder blade and her spine, where her heart thumped inside the cage of her ribs. It was like she was trying to hold the frantic rhythm of Priya's heart in her palm.

"Why?" Priya asked. "Why would you...?" She trailed off. She didn't know how to ask, *Why would you want me? Why would you follow me into the water, and hold my heart and speak to me in a voice like that, like you're yearning for me?*

As if Malini had heard her, she said, "I thought you might die." A small, hitched breath. "I thought that it might be the end, when you collapsed in the forest. And I..."

Priya turned. The water moved around them.

"Priya," said Malini, and her voice was dark and hungry and drew Priya in like gravity.

"Malini," she said in return. She pressed a hand to Malini's jaw.

And then Malini's hands were clenched in the seams of Priya's blouse and dragging Priya forward. There was a moment, a single moment, when Priya was looking into Malini's eyes, and Malini was looking into hers, and finally, finally Priya stopped thinking and simply moved. She leaned in.

Malini's mouth was on Priya's then, punishingly sweet, a bruising warmth that made everything vicious and hungry rise up in Priya with a swiftness that devastated her. Somehow, Priya's hands were in Malini's hair—that ridiculous, tangled hair that would never be unknotted—and they were stumbling back, back, until Priya could feel cold stone against her spine, the falling water around them, and Malini's hands now upon her shoulders, her throat, her jaw. And Malini was tilting her face up, kissing her with a fury that melted into sweetness, with a tenderness that was strong as lifeblood, and burned. Burned.

RAO

The lacquer gardens of Srugna were an interlocking maze of monasteries. Rao walked through them, barely seeing anything around him. Priests had gathered. There were lords of Dwarali in high-necked robes, bows at their backs; Srugani, lances in hand; Saketans with their steel whips wound at their waists; his own Alorans, blue-turbaned with bands of daggers wound at the hip and steel chakrams at their wrists, and even Parijati, clothed in light weaves with sabers and prayer stones to mark their status. There were enough disparate lords and nobles to fill the monastery steps nearly entirely.

A man walked down the steps on the path left between them. He wore a dhoti and a shawl of pale blue, his chest bare and his hair bound back in a long braid. Even before he raised his head, even before his mouth shaped a smile, Rao recognized him.

"Emperor Aditya." Rao kneeled. Behind him he heard Prem's men—*his* men—kneel down too, a chorus of creaking leather and armor. "We've come."

"Rao." Aditya's voice was gentle. "I'm not emperor."

"Not yet," said the Dwarali lord, from the edge of the steps. "But you will be. We've come to see to that."

Aditya crossed the ground. Beneath his bare feet the green leaves crumpled noiselessly. The birds sang. He held his hand out to Rao, who took it. When Rao stood, he found himself drawn into a fierce hug, Aditya's cheek pressed to his own.

"Rao," said Aditya, drawing back, eyes bright. "Ah, I've missed you. Why have you taken so long to come?"

"Malini," Rao managed to say.

"You have her with you?" Aditya asked. There was such hope in his eyes.

Rao shook his head, and the hope dimmed.

"Come then," said Aditya. "And we'll speak of what has passed."

They settled into what could only be Aditya's own room. It was neat and plain, entirely a priest's chamber, with a charpoy for sleeping, and a box of books, carefully sealed to keep out heat and damp. There were no candles. The only light, at night, would come in through the vast window, which opened to a garden of lacquer and of green. Golden songbirds flitted from branch to branch, trilling brightly.

"I am glad you tried to save her," Aditya said, once Rao had stumbled through the business of explaining what had passed. "And—I am sorry for your loss."

Rao swallowed. If he spoke too soon, he was afraid he would begin to weep. His grief lay on him like heavy hands. But he couldn't allow it to hold him.

"Yes," Rao managed. "Prem. He was." His lazy grin. The ever-present wreath of smoke from his pipe. Those shrewd eyes, and the sheer kindness of him, always folded around the shape of a joke, a laugh, a drink. What was Rao meant to do without him? He shut his eyes. One heartbeat, that was all he took, to breathe through the sorrow that rolled over him. "He was your friend once, too, Aditya."

Aditya nodded. "One of his cousins is here—Lord Narayan. He will need to be told."

"It will be done." He studied his friend, worry pushing aside grief for the moment. "Are you—well? You seem unlike yourself."

"I'm sorry," said Aditya then. And there was real sorrow in his voice, at least. Now that they were alone, no longer before the

Saketans and Dwarali, the Srugani and lords of Parijat, his shoulders had bowed. The calm of his face had faded. "I'm not the friend you once knew, I'm afraid. And not the would-be emperor these men require. I told them...ah." He touched his fingertips to his forehead, as if trying to smooth away an invisible pain. "I told them I awaited a sign from my god. Releasing me to the task of war."

"And they've stayed?"

Aditya's smile was tight. "No man of faith, whatever he may worship, willingly perverts the will of a god."

Rao thought of Prem, rotting, blooming, blaming Chandra's perversion of the faith of the mothers of flame for the sickness that had fallen over him and his people.

"And will you wait for our god to speak, Aditya? Because these men will not remain forever, and Chandra must be removed."

"If they want Chandra deposed, they will wait."

He was right. Parijatdvipa was born because of the sacrifice of the mothers of flame, and flourished under the unifying rule of their descendants. The Age of Flowers was such a strong cultural memory in all of them—a faith that went beyond gods or spirits—that replacing the imperial bloodline that held them together, like a thread through frayed cloth, felt anathema.

If they wanted Chandra gone, they needed Aditya. There was no one else.

"Must he truly be deposed?" Aditya said, suddenly, as if reading Rao's thoughts.

"Yes," said Rao, just as swift. "My father has joined this cause. My sister died for it. Your own sister is imprisoned or dead also, for the sake of removing him from the throne. And Prem..." Rao stopped. "Yes. Chandra must be removed. You know it, no matter how priestly you may be now."

All the imperial siblings had the same eyes, Rao thought, as Aditya looked at him—deep and dark, with a gaze that could pin a body and hold it, by sheer force of charisma alone.

"Will you tell me your name, Rao? Your true name?"

"As a priest of the nameless, you should know better than to ask me that."

"I don't ask you as a priest," Aditya's said quietly. "I ask you as your friend."

"No," said Rao. "You ask me as the prince named emperor. You ask me because you gained a revelation when you entered the garden of the nameless all those years ago with—with me. I expect you've had many other revelations since, as a priest. But still, the picture is incomplete, isn't it? The future is a shadow thrown by a great beast, or light seen through shifting water. You just need a little more. A clue, a word, and you'll be sure that what you think is to come is true." Rao swallowed, and looked away, out at the gardens. He saw blue birds. Gold. "The whole of fate isn't for mortals like us. So no, I won't tell you my name. It isn't for you."

"One would think you were the priest, not I," Aditya said mildly.

"I've been a faithful of the nameless far longer than you've been a devotee, Aditya."

Aditya had never been quick to anger, and that hadn't changed. He inclined his head wordlessly. The only sign that he was at all perturbed or wounded was a slight thinness to his mouth.

"Come," he said. "I have a vision to show you. Something the nameless god revealed to me."

Aditya led the way to a quiet segment of the garden, surrounded by a protective wall of spindly lacquered trees laden with heavy red leaves. At its center stood a pool of water upon a plinth.

"We feed it with water drawn from the reservoir that lies beneath the gardens." He gestured at the channels on the ground. Walked over to the plinth. "Do you remember," Aditya continued, "the night you took me to the gardens in Parijat?"

Of course Rao did. "We were drunk," he said. "If we'd been sober I never would have taken you."

But they had been drinking, and Aditya had been asking about his name again, in that way he always did: insistently, steadily, but charming, a grin on his mouth.

"You don't tell a prophecy just like that," Rao had said with a grin of his own. "No matter what it is. You know, my great-aunt's name was a prophecy three pages long? And all about how fields would be irrigated in fifteen years, in eastern Alor."

"Truly?"

Rao had nodded. "Well, at least she made the farmers very happy. Increased our crop yield."

"And what will your name change, Rao?"

Rao had shaken his head, a queasy feeling in his stomach that wasn't from the drink alone.

"If you're so interested in the faith of the nameless," Rao had replied, not knowing what his words would result in, "then get up—leave your wine—and I'll show you the future."

They had entered the gardens of the nameless, laughing and stumbling, and found themselves at a plinth just like the one before them now.

Now, Aditya took the role that Rao had taken so long ago. He placed his hands on the edges of the basin in quiet reverence. He traced the edges. Back. Forth. Began to murmur a prayer in archaic Aloran.

Rao steeled himself—approached the plinth—and mirrored Aditya's stance. Lowered his head to stare at the water.

Around them the leaves of lacquer clicked and rustled, and then fell eerily silent.

When you commune with the nameless—when a priest or a drunken Aloran prince lays hands on a seeing basin and sings the ancient prayer—you seek the voice of the universe.

There was a door in the water. A door in his mind. Rao looked once at Aditya, then walked through it.

There is a void that holds the world.

Some countries, some peoples, some faiths think it resembles water or rivers. But Rao knew better. As a boy, before he'd been fostered to Parijat, he'd been taught by the family priest, in the garden of the nameless that bordered the Aloran royal mahal.

Before there was life, there was the void. And in the void—in its lightless unknowability—lay the truth of the nameless god.

He gazed into it now. Hung in its black nothing and waited as the voice of the nameless unfurled around him, opening like stars.

He saw the voice of the nameless and heard it ring in his ears. A mask—a mask of wood. A mask that was a face of flesh and jasmine and needle-flower, bright marigolds and heady sweet roses. A face on a body crawling free from waters deep and strange. He heard the nameless's voice.

A coming. An inevitable coming.

He saw flowers wither in fire. Saw a pyre. The screams of women. His sister's voice.

A coming, a coming. They come in water, they come in fire. They come.

This sliver—this fragment of Aditya's own visions—speared through him.

They returned to the garden. Returned to themselves.

Their shared breathing was hoarse and unsteady, but Aditya found his equilibrium first.

Aditya's expression was otherworldly, his eyes entirely black. He blinked, and blinked once again, and they returned to their normal dark gray. But the gift of the nameless was still in his voice when he spoke: the sure knowledge of what was preordained.

"There is a sickness coming to Parijatdvipa. There is a sickness coming to every land, imperial or not, a sentience rising that will destroy everything that matters to us. That is what I saw when you took me to the prayer gardens and the nameless spoke to me. If I had been named by prophecy at birth it would have been like this: 'You will see them come, and in the nameless god's eye, you will see the way to make them go.'" Aditya's expression was tortured. "Now you have seen them, you know why I put aside the throne. Why I seek the way to understand what the nameless promised me."

Rao did. The vision was so overwhelming that he reeled from it. The earth turned monstrous. The body turned monstrous. He thought of Prem, dead, with marigold petals seeping from his eyes.

"What are they?" Rao asked, choked.

"That I don't know," Aditya said somberly.

The way of priests was isolation and meditation—a surrender to fate. The opposite of kingship, where a man inevitably held the fate of swathes of people in his grasp.

"Then why agree with Malini? Why allow this rebellion at all?"

"The nameless gives me no answers," said Aditya. "And in the silence of the nameless, my sister speaks. We're told to trust fate, Rao. I wonder—I wonder if allowing the force of my sister's will and belief to carry me is what the nameless wants from me. Or if…if her dream leads me astray from the truth. So I let men surround me, and name me emperor, and hope the answer will come.

"And of course, I miss myself," Aditya added, in a voice so quiet it sounded like the confession it was. "I miss my old fate and my purpose. And for all that Parijatdvipa—the throne, the crown, the empire, all of it—is insignificant in comparison to the dangers that threaten this world, I miss my old life still." Aditya released the basin. Moved away from it, to stand by Rao instead.

"The throne of Parijatdvipa—rule over my father and his land, and all the lands of the empire—is not a small thing," Rao replied.

"I know you believe so. Part of me continues to also, despite the truth. You must see now," Aditya murmured, "why I seek your name? Perhaps no mortal man deserves a complete image of fate. Perhaps no man can comprehend such a thing. But I have two great purposes tearing me in two. I need guidance. And when you've come so far to serve in this war, come with a name that is a prophecy—I have to ask. And hope you're my answer."

"I can't speak it," Rao said sadly. "Not yet."

"And yet it concerns me, doesn't it?" When Rao said nothing in response, Aditya exhaled and nodded. "I only wish you would tell me, so that I would know what to do."

"That isn't how it works," Rao said. "You know it isn't. And... Aditya. I." He stopped. "I'm not a man who gets angry easily," said Rao. "But what Chandra did to your sister, and mine, and Lady Narina, the way he mocked faith to burn them..." Rao grappled for calm, gazing fixedly at the neat lines of Aditya's priestly shawl. "He was always cruel, Aditya. Cruel and vindictive. But I don't need to be a priest of the nameless to see that this is only the start of what he can do, and will do, now that he has a measure of power. And if you cannot see that—if you cannot see that you must put him aside—then you are indeed not the friend I once knew. Whatever vision the nameless granted you when I took you to the gardens—the answer to what you need to do is plain."

Aditya flinched as if he'd been struck. Rao ran a hand over his own face. "I—need to rest," he said raggedly. "Aditya. About your sister..."

"I have men, watching the seeker's path," said Aditya. "Watching for lights, or strangers. If Malini comes, we'll know of it. I promise you."

"She was trapped in Hiranaprastha. On the Hirana," said Rao roughly. "Dead, perhaps."

"Ah, Rao." Aditya sounded pitying. "We both know she isn't dead. Now rest. You've had a terrible journey."

We do not know, thought Rao, his thoughts sharpened by a hysterical edge of fury and despair. We *do not*.

But I do.

52

MALINI

They lay side by side on the bank of the rockpool, letting their saris dry out in the heat. There had been no rain, which was a relief. Just the day's sunshine, and a faint breeze that mingled with the coolness of the water below them.

After all that Malini had been through—the burning of her heart sisters, her poisoning and imprisonment, her escape with Priya through a city aflame, and Priya's near death—being here felt like a blessing. Kissing Priya in clear water, holding her arms, her warm skin—lying beside her here in the quiet warmth of sunlight—made Malini feel closer to happiness than she had been in a long time.

Maybe the foolishness of her decision to enter the water with Priya, to act on her want, would strike her later. But right now she felt no shame or regret. She wanted simple things: to savor this moment—stone digging into her hip and all—as long as she could. To have the time to memorize the shape and feel of Priya's mouth, to learn her skin by blind touch. To laugh with her and talk with her and learn her, no pacts or painful debts between them.

"You know this doesn't make you a monster," Priya murmured. She lay facing Malini, sun on her deep brown skin, her hair a loose sheet of darkness around her. "Wanting me. You know that, don't you?"

Malini wanted to explain that being monstrous wasn't inherent, as Priya seemed to believe it to be. It was something placed upon you: a chain or a poison, bled into you by unkind hands.

But that wasn't what Priya needed to hear.

"I know," Malini said simply. "This part of me isn't anything I'm ashamed of."

She felt much greater shame at her own rage: the cold iron weight of it, ever present and ever steady in her heart. It shamed her, all the things she dreamt of doing to Chandra, but only because of how much pleasure the thought of his suffering brought her. He deserved to suffer. But to enjoy the thought of his pain made her more like him than she wanted to be.

"I think you may be a good person after all," Priya said slowly.

"Oh?" Malini smiled. "You change your mind so swiftly?"

"Parts of you, then," said Priya. "Parts of you want the world to be better. You want justice for yourself and the people you love, because your rights have been denied. You think the world owes you for that."

"You need to work on your love talk, Priya," Malini said dryly, and Priya laughed, a warm sound. "And I hope you realize you could be speaking about yourself, temple child."

Priya shook her head. The laughter faded from the shape of her mouth, her eyes, as her expression turned contemplative.

"I've never wanted justice. Maybe I should have, but the thing I truly wanted was myself back. And now I just want to know— to prove—that the temple elders were wrong. Parijatdvipa was wrong. My brothers and sisters and I, we were never monsters. We didn't deserve what was done to us. I want to believe that. I want to *know* that. I want that to be true, and if it isn't, I want to make it true. But you, Malini," she said. "You want to remake the world."

"I just want to change who sits on the imperial throne," Malini replied. But that didn't feel entirely like the truth, even to her own ears.

Priya reached out, tracing Malini's jaw with her fingertips. Priya was gazing at her with clear eyes and a furrow between her brows, reading her bones as if they were a map.

"This face. This face right in front of me. The face you've shown me, the fact that you kissed me. I know it. I know you," said Priya. "I know exactly who you are. There are other versions of you that I don't know. But this one..." Her fingers were against Malini's lips. "This one is mine."

For a moment, Malini felt as if maybe this was all that she was. There was nothing more to her, no princess of Parijat, no politician, no royal. She was just this, just herself, under Priya's sure hand. Someone content.

She rolled over, placing distance between them. Priya drew her hand back, and perhaps she understood the gesture, because she rolled over onto her stomach, propping herself up on her elbows, no longer touching Malini. Instead, she lowered her gaze to Malini's throat, where the cask of needle-flower hung on its chain.

"Do you have enough?"

Malini clasped her hand around the bottle. Its weight in her palm was heavy, the chain a cold shock of metal.

"I don't need it anymore," said Malini.

"Are you sure?"

"I have no physician to advise me, so no. Of course not. But I feel well enough now." *Well enough* would have to do. She wouldn't swallow needle-flower again unless she had no other choice.

"If you don't need it any longer, why wear it?"

"You want me to discard it?"

"No," said Priya. "But—I thought you would want to."

"And you know me so well," Malini said, without bite. She lowered her hand. "It's a reminder."

"Of what?"

She could have been flippant again. She could have denied Priya a true answer. But instead she said, "Of the price I've paid to see Chandra removed from his throne."

"May I?" Priya asked.

Malini did not know what Priya planned to do. But she nodded regardless and said, "You may."

Priya touched her fingertips to the bottle. A firm touch that pressed it against the cloth of Malini's blouse. "A reminder," Priya said softly.

The plants in the soil around them and the silt of the rockpool shivered. The air went still. There was a sound. A splintering.

The remnants of needle-flower essence had furled into new life, splitting through the bottle until it was in shards, falling to the ground. The flower was ugly, all points, and a deep black like a river on a moonless night.

Malini thought of the tale Priya had told her, of worship, of a hollowed coconut shell filled with a profusion of flowers as an offering of devotion to the yaksa and the dead. A thing frivolous. A thing of heart.

"It won't die," said Priya. "Not until I do, I think. It's a memento but not . . . not only of loss."

She lowered her hand, and Malini immediately raised her own, touching those needlelike black edges. They were strangely silken beneath her fingers. The flower was alive, despite the chain threaded through it, metal through bud—and she drew the chain so that the poison flower was hidden beneath her blouse, a strange weight on her skin.

"You're terrifying," Malini said. There was no fear in her, though. She almost wished the flower were sharp-edged so that she could feel the pain of it against her breast.

Priya snorted. "Hardly," she said. And then, with endearing self-consciousness, she tucked her hair behind her ear and looked away. "We should keep moving."

Priya knew more of Malini than she thought she did. And Malini was struck, absurdly, by how much she liked the woman Priya had made her be, however fleetingly.

I know you.

Priya stopped. Turned her head just slightly. She was close enough that Malini could see the tension in her shoulders. The flare of her nostrils, like an animal scenting the air. Priya rose abruptly to her feet.

"We need to go," said Priya. "Quickly. As quickly as we can."

"What is it?"

"The people we met at the mahal. The ones I fought. They're here. I can feel them. Come *on*, Malini."

Malini asked no more questions. She let Priya drag her to her feet. She followed Priya through the undergrowth, between the tall spears of the trees. And when Priya began to run, she did the same.

Sharp wood beneath her heels. The stinging snap of leaves and branches against her face, her arms, as sunlight blinked in and out of sight above them. Malini could hear nothing but the thud of her own heart, the ugly wheeze of her own breath in her ears. She wasn't built for the business of running for her life.

"Don't look!" Priya yelled. "Don't look, just keep running—"

And Malini intended to follow Priya's orders, she truly did. But something grasped at her ankle—a root she hadn't seen perhaps, but it felt like something new, pushing through the soil, shoving her off-balance. She fell, and let out a gasp, and Priya caught her, and then they were both stumbling to a stop, surrounded by tall trees and ten figures in masks who slipped out from the shadows.

They were surrounded.

Priya turned, taking Malini by the arms, as if she wanted to push Malini behind her. But there was nowhere for Malini to hide, and no way for Priya to defend her from the circle of rebels, in their masks of dark wood. Priya's hands tightened on Malini for a moment. Then she released her.

"Stay still," said Priya. She raised one hand in the air.

The earth splintered, grass bending upon itself as thorns like spears shoved through the sod. Malini held herself perfectly still as they drove up through the ground around her feet—as the trees creaked, as if they were being drawn by some terrible gravity to bend toward the place where the rebels stood.

The rebels raised their own hands. Pushed Priya's work down.

"That won't work, Pri." A man's voice. Low, even. One of the rebels stepped forward. "We've all drunk from the vials today." Eyes black, shadowed by the mask. "Put your hand down and come along obediently, hm? You're wasting your energy. You have to see that."

His words were echoed by the other rebels, with a susurration like wind through leaves. *Obey. Obey.*

Priya's hand trembled. She opened it to the sky, the trees groaning dangerously. In response, the masked rebel tilted his head and a root forced its way from the ground, lashing tight around her wrist.

"I don't want to hurt you," he said. "But I will if I need to."

"Ashok," she said. "Let me go."

"*Kneel,*" he said, and there was that whispered echo again. That chorus.

One of the thorns in the ground snapped. Ricocheted. With her free hand, Priya shoved Malini farther behind her. Priya made a noise that sounded as if she'd been punched, and then in the silence that followed, Malini saw a rivulet of blood snake down Priya's hair, staining her neck and the back of her blouse.

Priya looked back wildly at Malini.

Malini was struck, in that moment, by their shared helplessness.

Then Priya turned away. Slowly, she kneeled.

The rebel took a step forward. For all his size, his footsteps were almost soundless upon the ground. He removed his mask, revealing a face that was all angles, brushed dark at the jaw by stubble. He did not look at Malini, or the other rebels. He seemed to see nothing but Priya.

"I don't want to fight you," he said.

"But you have," she said. Her voice was strained, as if she were pushing against a great weight.

"I will die, Priya. All of us will die." He kneeled down too. "Do you want that?"

"You know I don't."

"Then tell me the way," he cajoled. "Show me. We can go together." He held his hand out, palm open. "I've bested you. I've proved myself stronger. It's only right."

A sharp shake of Priya's head.

"Will you really deny me my rights as your temple brother?

You would deny me the chance to give Ahiranya the freedom it needs to survive?"

Of course. Of course he was a fellow temple child, Malini should have *known*. Should have pieced together the nature of this. But she didn't move. She listened, and hoped there was an outcome from this better than all the dire ones that seemed to lie before them.

"Would I deny you the right to make us into exactly what the elders feared we'd become?" Malini could not see Priya's face, but she could imagine what expression Priya wore: the bared teeth, the challenging set to her jaw. "I would."

"You're acting like a child," he said. "You know what needs to be done. You know Ahiranya's only chance is freedom from the emperor's control and his ideology. Our only chance to be more than rot, degraded by Parijatdvipa's idea of us, made smaller day by day, year by year—is *this*. The deathless waters. Their blood on our righteous hands. And yet you still refuse."

"I'm not refusing," snapped Priya. "But I won't give it to you like this. Ashok, not like this. Not the way you want it."

The man—the rebel, the temple son—named Ashok stood, drawing himself to his full height.

"Then how?" he asked, voice dangerously calm. "You want me to grovel, Priya? Maybe there will be time to make a world and a rule more like you want in the aftermath. But right now, you have a weapon you have no idea how to properly use. And it's mine by right."

"I want you to talk to me. I want you to use your reason. But you've backed yourself into a corner, haven't you, Ashok? You're killing everything you love. Yourself. Your followers. And you can't see any way out but this." Priya's head was still bleeding freely, dripping onto the soil. "Maybe I should thank you after all for abandoning me. If I'd stayed with you, you'd be killing me too. At least now you're only hurting me."

"I told you. I have no desire to harm you."

"Whatever you say," Priya said, and Malini could hear the sneer in her voice, goading him.

Ashok's face darkened.

Priya had moved a little in the time she'd spoken, carefully trying to angle her body in front of Malini's. But finally—unfortunately—Ashok looked at her. He tilted his head, examining her.

"A lady of Parijat," he said softly. "What should I make of this, Priya? Is she a hostage?" He took a step toward her. Looked her up and down, measuring her.

"Ashok," Priya said. "No."

"There are so many ways to hurt someone," he said pleasantly. "Do you remember when Sanjana hit Nandi once, to make you give her something she wanted? What was it—a hairpin?"

"A bracelet," Priya said thinly.

"She did it because she knew you wouldn't give in if she hit you. But you cared too much about Nandi to watch him suffer. I'm sure the principle still applies." A pause. "This is your last chance, Priya."

Malini met his eyes. The glint of them. She knew a man who took pleasure in pain when she saw one, and this one did, whether he admitted his darkness to himself or not.

Priya turned her head, looking between Malini and Ashok not with fear, not with helplessness, but with a kind of mulish fury.

"I really hate you sometimes, Ashok," Priya said in a low voice. "I swear it."

A noise, like a splintering. The thorns unbowed their heads. Priya rose to her feet and flung herself onto her brother's back, clawing his face like a cat. He swore and drove an elbow into her stomach. She made no noise—he must have winded her—and fell back hard against the ground.

The other rebels moved forward, but the ground rumbled, and split, kicking her back up into the air. She leapt onto her feet. Grabbed Malini's arm, holding her, keeping her close, a manic light in her eyes.

"They need me," Priya said, ragged. "Don't worry. Stay near."

There were hands, suddenly, against Malini's throat, her shoulders—she twisted, furious, flinging a fist up without any sense of where it would land, and felt a burst of pain in her knuckles. Wood. The mask. She should have been more careful, but she was no warrior and did not know what to do.

Vines clambered up her arms, vicious spines digging into her attacker. And just to help things along, Priya threw a punch that knocked the mask askew. The rebel swore and let her go, and then Malini was upon the ground, and Priya was circling her, desperately outnumbered. Trying to keep her safe.

They were carrying weapons of wood, and this close Malini could feel the heat pouring off those weapons—a strange, immutable magic.

Think, she told herself. *Think, think.*

The heat was closer than it should have been. She looked down.

There was a dagger on the ground. It was made of wood, polished and honed to a sharp edge, and when she reached for it, it burned her fingers. She bit down on a curse and dropped it. Then she wrapped her pallu around her palm and grabbed it.

She thought of the lessons Alori had taught her. Of how to use a knife. Of how to gut or kill. The hollow concave of a heart. She thought of the fragility of her own flesh and bone, and how much she still had to accomplish.

Malini held the wood tight, adjusting to the burning warmth of it in her grip. She straightened. In her mind, she put aside the Malini she'd been beside the waterfall; put aside the woman she'd been for weeks on end, saved and seen by Priya's eyes and hands and heart. She thought of pain, and how it could be leveraged, and the lessons your enemies can teach you, however unwitting.

She thought of her own ghost haunting her: a princess of Parijat, eyes cold.

She thought of Priya's utter trust under her touch.

Malini rose up and darted against Priya's back, clutching at her side. She could feel the stickiness of Priya's blood—her own panicked heartbeat. She forced herself not to shake. Nothing good could come from an unsteady hand.

And then, without trembling, without hesitation, she placed the point of the knife beneath Priya's ribs.

53

PRIYA

Priya didn't know what she was feeling at first. Hands on her waist. Arms. She almost flung them off, but she heard a murmur against her ear. Malini's voice.

"Priya. Please."

Still, she considered throwing Malini back. Malini's grip was limiting her movement, and they were entirely surrounded. Priya needed to move—needed to protect her.

Priya could feel the pull and tug of her magic moving the soil, trees, the plants to her will. She could feel the unnatural strength of her own hands. But none of it was enough. She was surrounded by rebels who had drunk vials of deathless water. And Ashok was watching, pity and amusement in his eyes.

Eyes that widened, in the half second before she felt the press of a knife against her skin.

"I'll kill her before I let you take her," said Malini.

She'd positioned the knife in the concave area beneath Priya's ribs. It was a good place to angle a weapon. Better than the neck. Here, at the angle she held the blade, she could slide it up into Priya's heart.

The rebels stood, shocked into stillness. And Priya...

Priya did nothing. She could feel blood still trickling down her scalp and shoulders from the wound in her hair.

"Priya could kill you where you stand," said Ashok.

Malini laughed—a glorious laugh like the sound of a blade unsheathed.

"She could. But she won't."

Priya's breaths were shallow. She didn't know if she was afraid or not. Sweat stood out on her skin. The wooden knife burned. She was not sure she even felt betrayed.

"I know Priya. Every inch of her heart." The way Malini said *heart*, so savagely—it was as if she were truly talking of the muscle pulsing in Priya's chest, and it made the breath seize in Priya's throat. "She won't touch me. She could snap my hand clean, but she won't do it."

This was a game of wills. Ashok, staring at Malini, staring at her straight in the eyes. And Malini staring back. Priya knew he was thinking: *This is a ruse.*

But it wasn't. Priya could feel the steadiness of Malini's hand and Priya did...nothing. Still nothing. Stood and breathed and breathed as if the knife beneath her ribs were a welcome friend. Maybe it was the shock of it. She didn't know. She felt the warmth of Malini at her back. The beat of Malini's heart, fast with terror.

"Step away from her, Priya," said Ashok. Low.

"She won't," Malini repeated. "She'd rather I hurt her, rather I kill her, than give you what you want. It's in your best interests, *Ashok*, to let us both go. Because I assure you, I can't lead you to your deathless waters. If Priya dies, the knowledge dies with her. And I will be glad to die too, knowing I have kept my empire safe from you and your ilk."

Something flickered in Ashok's eyes. She saw the way he took Malini in, weighing up her skin, light enough to reveal she wasn't accustomed to outdoor labor; the thinness of her, the lack of muscle in her limbs; the sari she wore, more expensive than anything he or Priya had ever owned. He shifted, just a little.

And the knife moved, just a little. Just nicking skin.

"You may be quick," Malini said more loudly. "But I can be quicker. So. What will you do?"

Ashok took a step forward. Another. Malini held steady.

"What is this, Priya?" His gaze flickered over. "Will you let this Parijati whore murder you, to spite me?"

"You shouldn't be so rude to women holding knives," Malini said, holding Priya tight, tight. "It isn't wise."

He looked at Malini once more. Something ugly twisted his mouth. "Kill her, then," he said. "Go on."

"I would rather leave."

"Well, you can't. So kill her, or lower your weapon. I'll wait."

"You need her," hissed Malini.

"And you," Ashok said, eyes narrowed, "won't kill her. Not a soft thing like you. I know your people. You're more likely to cut your own throat than hers. I will not let you go. What will you do now?"

Ah, Ashok, Priya thought, despairing. *You don't know her at all.*

Priya felt Malini's wrist move, the muscles holding her knife steady tensing.

The moment stretched and stretched. Was she loosening her grip or driving the dagger up? In that moment, Priya wasn't sure, couldn't be sure. She could only stand there and feel the green magic of life in the forest around her, in the soil beneath her.

The magic shifted. *Lurched.*

A rain of rocks was being thrown, slung by the hands of people hidden behind the trees. The ground shuddered, seismic, as figures appeared in the shadows between those trees. The rebels who surrounded them were now surrounded in turn by maidservants and cooks and gardeners that Priya had known almost her whole life.

And there, leading them, was Bhumika.

She had real soldiers with her, too. Soldiers, including some of the regent's most loyal men. Priya recognized Jeevan, no longer in the colors of Parijatdvipa, though he still wore his commander's armlet of curved and polished silver. Khalida, wielding a scythe like an extension of her arm. A glut of maidservants in armor, the head chef holding a huge mace.

Ashok spun wildly.

"Did you not hear me coming, brother?" Bhumika's voice rang

out, sweet and pure. She stepped out of the crowd, face flushed from the heat but smiling.

"Don't come any closer, Bhumika," Ashok said. "Or I'll be forced to deal with you, and I have no wish to."

"Will you fight me, as I am?" Bhumika asked, placing one hand on the curve of her belly. She quirked an eyebrow in challenge.

"I'll fight you if it comes to it," Ashok said roughly. "But I don't want to."

"It's odd how you never want to fight, and yet you always do." Bhumika continued walking forward with a pointedly calm air. Some of the rebels edged away from her, as if they did not know quite what to do. She soon stood inches from Ashok, staring him in the face. "And when we were children...well. You remember. I always won."

"We're not children anymore," he said.

"No, indeed," agreed Bhumika. Her hand at her side, visible to Priya, who was still held frozen at the point of a knife, twitched a little. It was a small motion, but one Priya had learned early on as a maidservant, back when there'd still been hope she'd develop the fine manners and demureness to serve at feasts and functions, at the beck and call of highborn women. The gesture meant, *Watch me. You may soon be needed.*

"You won't defeat me," said Bhumika. "You have your vial-poisoned followers, the taint of the water in your veins. But I am not the only twice-born in opposition to you today."

Priya placed her own hand over Malini's. She felt Malini flinch like a hound used to the lash. Malini's hand was trembling now, where it gripped the knife, hot from the sacred wood and damp with sweat.

"Let me go," Priya whispered.

"I can't allow him to take you," Malini said roughly.

She could have broken Malini's grip. She could have broken Malini's fingers. She could have bound her with vine and thorn and stepped easily to freedom.

"Let me go," she repeated.

She had never needed strength to break away. Only this. The gentlest shadow of a touch, the barest press of her fingertips, on Malini's arm. Only her own voice. She leaned back into Malini, letting Malini take a little of her weight.

"Please, Malini," she said. "Trust me."

Malini released a shuddering breath. Released her.

Bhumika's hand moved in an arc. And Priya moved a hand too—moved it as if through water, and drew on the power that lived inside her, just as Bhumika did the same.

The air was a shower of glittering, deadly thorn shards.

She had never seen anything like it before. She had never *done* anything like it before. She felt the roots beneath the soil—every deep root and every shallow curl of green—and drew them out. The ground crumbled unevenly, sinking and lashing tight around the feet of the rebels, throwing them to the ground and swallowing their weapons whole.

Priya grappled clumsily with her new strength, pouring it into the task. She wouldn't have been able to do any of it without Bhumika. It was Bhumika's skill that broke those thorn shards into razor-edged fragments; Bhumika who coiled the earth around limbs.

Priya understood for the first time the sheer power Bhumika had concealed all these long years. She saw the rebels try to draw on their cursed abilities and falter, under the strength of the thing she and Bhumika wielded. Their gifts seemed to feed on one another, a rush of water all the stronger for its weight, all the stronger for their shared power.

Ashok stumbled back. He reached for his own gifts, but it was like moving against the tide. She felt him in the sangam. The flicker of him.

"We are stronger than you, brother," Bhumika said, and her sweet voice was a vicious kiss.

The ground roiled beneath him, knocking his feet from under him. He fell to the ground.

Imagine what the thrice-born could have done, Priya thought wildly, *if they'd known what their powers could do together. It's like a song, a howling song—*

Ashok drew his mask down over his face to protect himself. The other rebels did the same. She saw his shoulders rise and fall. His chest heave.

He slammed his hands down, the grass rippling under him in a wave. Where Priya had used the momentum of her fall to fling herself back to her feet, he used it to launch forward, all brute strength. When Bhumika flung a heavy vine at him—thicker than his torso—he caught it, winding it around his arm. Drawing it like a lash, he whipped it back at Bhumika.

Bhumika broke it into halves in the air. The two pieces crashed to the ground.

Slowly, Bhumika walked between the cleaved halves toward him.

"Will you hurt me, then?" Bhumika asked, voice mild. "Your own temple sister?"

Priya saw his hand curl into a fist. Saw him raise it. Priya moved forward, her own hands upraised.

He doubled over, clutching his chest.

His mouth parted, and a rush of blood and water poured from it. Two of his rebels who had fought free from the earth's prison ran to him, gripping him by the shoulders as he forced his head up, touching his fist to his mouth.

"Perhaps not," he said, voice thick.

Bhumika took advantage of his lapse in control. Her eyes narrowed, and she broke the earth beneath him again. He fell forward, and the two rebels grabbed him.

"*Retreat!*" one yelled, and as the soil churned up around them, the trees collapsing, they stumbled back and began to run, Ashok held unsteadily between them.

"Let them go," said Bhumika, and the people behind her, who had begun striding forward, came to an abrupt stop. She touched her own knuckles to her mouth as Ashok had done, a calculating and almost sorrowful look in her eyes.

"We have what we need," she said. "Priya. Are you well?"

54

PRIYA

"I'm fine," said Priya, dazed. "I'm fine."

She was suddenly kneeling. Had she planned to kneel? She wasn't sure. Malini was beside her, knee touching her own.

"Priya," Malini said, teeth chattering, as if cold or shock had overcome her. "Priya. Are you hurt?"

"No," Priya said. "No, I'm not hurt."

"I didn't mean," Malini began. Then halted. "I would never. I. I don't think I would have."

All her words were fragments. And Priya did not know how to feel, looking at her. She was perhaps a little shocked herself.

Priya pressed her forehead to Malini's.

"Breathe with me," she whispered, as the world steadied around them, and Bhumika's power and her own wove the forest back into place. The soil smoothed, the trees settled. The leaves rustled in the wind.

When Malini pulled back, she had a brilliant streak of blood on her forehead. Priya touched a hand to her own scalp and winced.

"Here," said Bhumika. She was looming over them, a cloth in hand, which Priya took and pressed hard to the wound. She didn't think it was deep. Head wounds always bled far too much, shallow or not.

Finally, Priya looked around in wonder. Then she began to laugh.

"You're—all of you. Is that really Commander Jeevan? *Billu?* You—Bhumika!"

"You seem to have lost your words, Priya," Bhumika said serenely.

Priya felt tears threatening at her eyes, through the laughter. She forced them back.

"I was afraid for you." Priya's voice was rough.

"And I for you, although I don't know why I bother, when you're always throwing yourself into trouble." Bhumika glanced at Malini, who was now standing behind Priya, watching them with the attention of a hawk. "Why," Bhumika said, "are you in the forest with the emperor's sister?"

"She would have died if I'd left her on the Hirana," said Priya.

"That doesn't answer my question."

"Lady Bhumika," said Malini, bowing her head, just slightly, in the gesture of a noblewoman greeting a respected equal. After a moment, Bhumika returned it.

"We should speak privately," said Bhumika.

The three of them walked some distance away from the traveling household—though Priya turned as they walked, looking for familiar faces in the crowd. With difficulty, Bhumika sat on the severed trunk of a tree, using Priya's arm for support as she lowered herself. Priya kneeled down, Malini mimicking her. A small distance away, Khalida hovered, eyes narrowed and arms crossed.

Now that she was not using her twice-born gifts, Bhumika looked pained and tired. Her child was due so soon, Priya knew, and she felt a pang of worry run through her as Bhumika carefully straightened in her seat with a quiet sigh.

"Speak," said Bhumika.

Priya was the one to explain the new agreement between them. The possibility of self-rule for Ahiranya—freedom entirely from the control of Parijatdvipa. As she spoke, she watched the way Malini looked between them, weighing up all she'd seen— Bhumika and Priya's shared gifts, the informal way they spoke to one another—drawing her own conclusions about the bond between them.

At the end, Bhumika nodded. Said, "I see." Then she leaned forward a little, expression thoughtful. "To me," she went on, "the difference between a place in the empire and a place beyond it, as an ally nation, is—negligible. You may have noticed that our crops and our farmers have suffered greatly. We cannot easily feed ourselves. Our position is weak. To survive as an independent nation would require us to be like any city-state of Parijatdvipa in all but name. And we would *still* have no power at the imperial court."

"I cannot promise you power at court *and* freedom," Malini said. "But as for independence... Lady Bhumika, surely the symbolism is important, is it not? No one forgets what the Ahiranyi were in the Age of Flowers. Parijatdvipa does not forget the way your temple ancestors and the yaksa nearly took everything. Ruled everything. And my own people think, on balance, you would not have been kind masters.

"Your subjugation, as a vassal nation, has been a symbol to Parijatdvipa," Malini continued. "A symbol of great power, demonstrating that no one may stand against Parijatdvipa's nations without consequence. Your freedom, however yoked to the empire by commerce or need, will be a symbol to your own people, that you are no longer under the empire's feet. Perhaps it would even be enough to make Ahiranya's rebels obey you."

Bhumika looked no less pained or tired, but there was a new light in her eyes.

"Should your brother Prince Aditya win, we can perhaps agree that symbolic freedom would be—helpful," Bhumika said, with care. "But until he wins, Ahiranya will be vulnerable to Emperor Chandra, and to the other nations of Parijatdvipa. We do not have the strength to fend them off."

"I believe you have a source of power that can protect you," Malini said. "The rebels sought it. And Priya has the key."

Finally, the two of them looked at Priya.

"Princess Malini. I think you and I should, perhaps, talk further alone," said Bhumika.

Priya thought about protesting. She was, after all, not exactly uninvolved in any of this. But then Bhumika said, "Priya, I think there's someone in my retinue you may want to go and meet." She smiled, only slightly, but it was a true smile.

Malini did not touch her. Did not try to stop her. Her fingers twitched faintly where they rested on her knees, and in an even voice she said, "Thank you, Priya. You can go. Lady Bhumika and I will both be fine."

Priya began to walk away. She glanced back only once. Malini's back was to her. Her face was turned away, invisible, unknowable.

Priya didn't touch the wound at her ribs. She took the blood-soaked cloth away from her head, crumpled it up, and kept on walking.

There's someone in my retinue you may want to go and meet.

Sima. There was Sima, standing among the other maids, talking to a warrior who held his mace at his side. Sima, looking up, then running across the forest.

"Priya!"

Sima, hugging her fiercely.

"You've kept so many secrets from me," Sima gasped.

"I had to," Priya said, then coughed as Sima squeezed tighter. The burn beneath her ribs *hurt*—a pain she didn't want to contemplate, a pain deeper than skin and her capacity to understand her own wayward heart. "You're hugging me too hard."

"You're a big girl, you can take it."

"Your hair is in my mouth."

Sima laughed wetly and pulled back. She gave Priya a huge grin, even as her eyes streamed.

"I'm sorry," she said. "I'm just so glad you're not dead."

"I'm so glad you're not dead too," Priya said. "What are you doing here? And is that—are you carrying a scythe?"

"Isn't it obvious? I'm here to bring you home safe. And

because—because the city is in ruins, and Lady Bhumika is leading us now. So. There's that." Sima's smile wavered, then faded. "I can't exactly rely on my wages, now that the regent is dead."

Priya looked at the people around her—at Commander Jeevan, watching her with flinty eyes. Of course the regent was dead.

"Rukh," said Sima. "You'll want to see him."

Her heart was suddenly in her mouth. "See him? He's here?"

Sima nodded.

"What is he doing in this place?" Priya asked. Who had brought a boy—a child—to the deep forest, to blood and to war?

"Lady Bhumika ordered him to come," Sima said. She hesitated, then added, "Lady Bhumika... she knows Rukh did something he shouldn't have. Spoke to people he shouldn't have."

So Bhumika had found out, then.

Maybe Rukh's presence was a punishment. A punishment for Rukh—or a punishment for Priya, for bringing him into the mahal. But such viciousness didn't seem like something Bhumika would willingly choose, so Priya was not sure she could believe it.

"I do want to see him," Priya said. "Please."

Sima nodded. Then she said, "Just. Prepare yourself, Priya. He's not like he once was."

And indeed he'd grown so much worse. All of his hair had the texture of leaves now, dark as ink. His veins stood out, a strange green against his skin. There were rings like the secret heart of bark, inked along his arms. Even the shadows beneath his eyes were more wood than flesh. He'd been sitting a little apart from the rest of Bhumika's retinue, wrapped in a blanket beneath the cover of a tree. When she approached, he stood and let the blanket puddle at his feet.

He looked at her. She looked at him.

"Rukh," she said. "Won't you greet me?"

"Are you sure you want me to?" he asked.

She could have told him the rot had never scared her. She could have assured him in a dozen different ways.

Instead she walked over to him, bent down, and hugged him carefully. It was the first time she'd done it, and she wanted him to know he could push her away. But he didn't. He stayed very still.

"I'm so glad to see you again," she said.

She felt the tension in him. The way he held himself, wound tight with his fists clenched, ready for anything that could be thrown at him. She felt it break.

"I'm sorry," he gasped out. "I'm sorry."

She held him tighter then, fiercely, as if she had the power in nothing but her arms to keep him safe.

"I'm sorry I joined the rebels," he said. "I'm sorry I wasn't loyal. But I am now. I'm staying here, with you and Sima and Lady Bhumika, I made a promise, and I'm *sorry*."

"It doesn't matter," she told him. "None of it matters. You're okay."

"I told Lady Bhumika what I was. I told Gauri. I . . ." He trailed off, as if he couldn't explain himself to her. As if he didn't have the words for why his heart had changed. Why he wanted to remain with her, with Bhumika.

"It's different," she said. "Having a home. Isn't it?"

He pursed his mouth to stop his lip from trembling. Nodded.

"You're okay," she said gently. "We're both okay. You have nothing to apologize for, Rukh, nothing at all." She hugged him again, pressing her head to the leaves and curls on his head. "I'm sorry I'm hugging you while covered in blood."

"That's fine," Rukh said, muffled, sounding calmer now. He sniffled a little. "I don't care. It doesn't smell great, though."

"I bet it doesn't."

She let him go then, before either of them could begin to feel awkward. Rukh smoothed down his clothes. Rubbed his eyes dry.

"There's a lot that's happened in Hiranaprastha since I left," said Priya. "Will you both tell me everything you can?"

Some of that awful guilt finally dimmed from Rukh's face. Sima drew in closer, and the two of them began to weave the tale as Priya thought of the deathless waters. The promise of them. The hope.

She thought of her dead siblings. The thrice-born, like Sanjana, who could manipulate the rot. She thought of what she might be able to do to save Rukh, if she had the same kind of power.

She could make something of what she was—of what she and Ashok and Bhumika were—that wasn't only monstrous or cursed. She could make something good. She could save him.

Cure. Not curse.

Perhaps.

55

ASHOK

They began to die. One, then two. Then a third.

"Thrice-dead," he murmured, as he closed eyes. Felt silent wrists. If only there were a magic in this, as there was in surviving the waters. But death was a failure, and the deathless waters granted nothing in return for their due.

He listened to labored, water-laden lungs heaving for breath around him, and felt the tightness in his own. He felt the tremor of his own strength beginning to seep out of him.

They kept on walking. He could feel Priya and Bhumika. He could follow the pulse of their presence in the sangam and the green of the soil until he found them once more, and then he would take Priya's knowledge, by trickery or violence or if it came to it, by pleading at her feet.

Then Ashok began to grow more ill: blood rising in his sweat, in his eyes.

He and his followers stopped to rest, under the shade of a bower. There were no bodies buried here, but Ashok could only think of what a peaceful place this was, and how good a resting place it would be for his own bones.

He did not want to burn when he died. He'd had enough of fire.

"Ashok." Kritika's voice. She kneeled down beside him. She opened her satchel, removing a crown mask with careful hands, making sure to only hold it by the cloth that bound it. She lowered it to the ground. Then she lifted out a small thing. A thing of glass that glowed faintly blue.

There was only one vial left.

Kritika held it upon her palm.

"You must drink," she said. When she blinked, he saw blood upon her lashes, and wondered what dread thing the water was doing to her from within.

"You must drink," she said. "You must survive."

"Kritika."

"You must become thrice-born, and become the high elder, and wear this mask." She nudged it forward. "You must save Ahiranya. So drink."

He wanted to. He thirsted. He was parched and empty, a husk on the verge of inward collapse.

But he could not drink.

"You have been with me longer than any of the others. I will tell you the truth," Ashok murmured. Kritika leaned in closer, to listen to him. "I don't have the strength to do what needs to be done. I will not survive to find my sister and fight for her *and* return home to the Hirana. So I will not drink."

Kritika said nothing and nothing, but her lip began to subtly tremble. The sight of her distress almost weakened his resolve.

"You are our only hope, Ashok," she said. "You always have been. Do not give in to despair now, I beg you. There is a future for Ahiranya still, and for us."

A trickle of blood escaped her nose.

He could not bear to see her dead. He could not.

He thought for a dark moment of ending it for them both. It would be simple. Perhaps honorable even. Like something for a dramatic tale, enacted by players in masks on a village stage. He had a knife, a fine sharp blade, in his belt.

"I am grateful beyond words, that you saved me, all those years ago," he said instead. "If you had not given me the waters, I would have died of the sickness eating my lungs. Died in shame, and alone. If this rebellion has accomplished anything, it is because of you."

"I was a pilgrim to the Hirana for the same reason as all the rest, Ashok," Kritika said, moving the vial back and forth gently between her palms. "I wanted better for myself. My family. Ahiranya. And when all was dark, and I thought nothing could be saved—ah, finding you saved me."

"I never had a mother," he said. "And—you are not my mother." A choked laugh. "A mother doesn't follow her son to war." He took her hand, curling her fingers around the vial. Pressed it back to her.

"You will drink it," he said. "Or no one will. Do you understand? My vision must survive me. Ahiranya must be saved. Must be free." His voice was suddenly ragged. "This country needs protectors. If my siblings will not allow me to do it, then they must. Or you must."

"You want me to pass through the waters three times." She sounded disbelieving. "I am not a temple child, Ashok."

"We were trained for it," he said. "Trained to be strong enough to survive it. It would be a miracle if you did, and yet that's what I ask of you, Kritika. Seek a miracle. You and the other rebels. If even one or two of you can find the deathless waters—if you can survive the process—your strength would be enough. It would be enough."

"I would do anything for Ahiranya," said Kritika, voice trembling. "I drank from the vial, even knowing it would mean my death. We all did. But there are limits to what any of us can do, no matter what we may wish to."

"Then convince my sisters to be more than they are," he said tiredly. "Only drink, so that you have the time to do it."

Kritika bowed her head, elegant in obedience.

She touched her fingertip to the top of the vial. Pressed her finger to her tongue.

"Drink it," he said hoarsely. "Don't simply dab it. Soil and sky, you will not survive like that. It's not enough."

She stood. She reached down, picking up the mask and the vial once more. He saw then what she hadn't removed from the satchel: a square of fermented rice, a rolled-up roti. Fruit, carefully swaddled in cloth to keep it free of ants. She had provisions. And a tight, serious look upon her bloodied face.

She placed the vial in his belt, carefully, then straightened.

"Rest, Ashok," she said gently. "I'll return."

56

MALINI

I almost killed her.

That would be a new nightmare, to fold in with the rest. Already, she dreamt of fire, the smell of burning flesh, Narina's blackened smile.

Now she would dream of Priya's heart in her hands. Pulsing. A hairsbreadth from her blade.

She did not allow herself to reveal how she felt. She walked with Lady Bhumika's strange retinue of people—soldiers, maid-servants, cooks—and ignored the looks they gave her.

Bhumika had agreed to ensure that Malini would be returned to her brother Aditya's side, so that Malini could carry out her part of their bargain. Then, in turn, Bhumika would return to Hiranaprastha, where she would protect Ahiranya with all her and Priya's full might and wait for Aditya to succeed or fail. For now, Bhumika directed her retinue to continue along the seeker's path, and insisted on keeping Malini close, often leaning on her arm for support. As Bhumika did so, she made a point of asking Malini small, prying questions about her life at court. About imperial politics. About Chandra and Aditya.

Malini should not have underestimated Bhumika, when she first met her. That had been a grave error on her part.

Malini answered as best as she could. They did, after all, have an alliance. And she was glad to have made an ally of the Ahi-ranyi woman rather than an enemy.

Malini asked after the fate of the regent only once.

"I think you know the answer," replied Bhumika. She said it without any visible emotion, but Malini knew how little that meant. She did not pry further. What lay in the privacy of Bhumika's mind was Bhumika's business.

"My condolences," Malini said simply.

"It was necessary," Bhumika said tonelessly, which was... revealing.

Malini nodded, walking sedately at Bhumika's side, to match her pace. To her distant left, she saw Priya, walking with a child and another maidservant. As if sensing her gaze, Priya turned to look at her. There was a question in the shape of her mouth, the tilt of her head. They hadn't yet had a chance to talk alone.

Malini looked away and found Bhumika watching her with an unfathomable expression.

"Are you happy with our pact, Lady Bhumika?"

Bhumika considered this, turning her head forward once more.

"Yes," Bhumika said finally. "Symbolism is important. And freedom... You will not understand this, Princess Malini. But there is a subtle pain the conquered feel. Our old language is nearly lost. Our old ways. Even when we try to explain a vision of ourselves to one another—in our poetry, our song, our theater masks—we do so in opposition to you, or by looking to the past. As if we have no future. Parijatdvipa has reshaped us. It is not a conversation, but a rewriting. The pleasure of security and comfort can only ease the pain for so long." She clasped her hands before herself. "And yet I never wanted this—this collapse of the regency. This end. I understand that to ease the pain of being a vassal nation comes at the cost of mortal lives. Now bloodshed is inevitable... I gladly enter a pact that allows the death to be minimized, and even a shade of our freedom, our *selves*, to be saved.

"Besides," Bhumika murmured, "who am I to undo the vows made between my sister and yourself?"

Malini glanced at her. Bhumika looked weary, but there was a smile on her lips, small and knowing.

*   *   *

Later, when everyone stopped to rest, Malini slipped away and found a place to sit alone—the trunk of a fallen tree, beneath the cover of an old banyan that had sucked the moisture and life from the earth around it, leaving a private glade. She waited.

It wasn't long before Priya arrived.

"Finally," Priya said, approaching. The ground whispered beneath her feet, small plants turning around her heels. Malini wondered if Priya even realized it was happening. "I've wanted to talk to you."

"It's been difficult," Malini agreed. "There are—so many people. I'm not used to it any longer. It was so much quieter on the Hirana."

"Malini," Priya said. "I just..."

Malini watched Priya draw in closer, until Priya was standing over her, one arm wrapped across her stomach.

Malini braced herself. Waited.

"I understand," said Priya, "why you threatened what you did. It was the only weapon you had."

Malini tilted her head back, looking into Priya's eyes. "But do you understand that I almost killed you?"

Priya was silent. She didn't look away from Malini. Didn't move.

"Do you understand what I'm saying?" Malini asked, looking up, up. "If you had lost—and you were losing, Priya—he would have killed me or hurt me, or used me as a hostage in order to use you. Better to have killed you than that. Better to have killed you than let an enemy of Parijatdvipa have that kind of power. That...that is what I told myself before Lady Bhumika came. I told myself to drive the knife into your heart. I would have done it. I would have..." She squeezed her eyes shut. Images of Narina and Alori and the blood in Priya's hair seared themselves behind her lids. She opened them again. "I couldn't," she admitted. "I couldn't do it."

Priya exhaled. The light was behind her. Malini could only see her eyes—the fall of her hair, black haloed in gold.

"Then you're not the person you think you are," Priya said.

"But I'm going to have to be, Priya. I need to be—the part of me I need to be—can't be good. Or soft. Not to do what's needful."

Priya said nothing. She simply tilted her head, listening.

"I am going to have to carve out a new face. A face that can pay the price I need to pay. I am going to become monstrous," Malini said, tasting the weight of the words upon her lips, her tongue. "For so long I have only wanted to escape and survive. But now I am free, and for the sake of my purpose...for the sake of power," she admitted, "I am going to become something other than human. Other than simply *not good*. I must."

Priya hesitated. Said, finally, "I'm not sure that's what being powerful means. Losing yourself."

"As if you haven't paid a price," Malini said. "As if your Bhumika hasn't. Or your brother."

"Fine. So power—costs. But what you do when you have power, when you've gained it—that's the key, isn't it?" Priya took a step forward. "I know what my brother would do. And...it's not exactly that he's wrong. But he's not clever enough to make something that lasts out of the carnage he'll bring. I should know. Neither am I. But what will you do, once you have your justice?"

"Once Chandra is dealt with? I don't know," Malini said. "I can't imagine it. To even hope—it's been beyond me for so long."

"You could do something good," said Priya. "No—you've already promised something good. Ahiranya's freedom."

"And that's kind of me, is it? Freeing Ahiranya so rebels like your brother can seize it and ill-use it in Parijatdvipa's place?"

Priya sighed. "I don't know what it means to be a just ruler, all right? I don't know what you want to hear. But I think you can figure it out. You're going to be influential when your brother Aditya claims his throne. I know it."

"Priya. I almost slid a knife into your heart. How can you be here? How can you speak to me?"

"Well, if you had, I'd be dead, and we wouldn't be talking about anything." She shrugged.

"Priya." And oh—the voice that came out of her was pleading. "Please." What was she pleading with Priya for—honesty? Forgiveness? Whatever she wanted, she knew only Priya could provide it.

Priya gazed back at her, keen-eyed, unsmiling.

"When I was small, when I began as a temple child, I learned how important it is to be strong. We were trained to fight—to fight enemies and fight each other. To cut away the parts of us that were weak. That was what surviving—and ruling—meant. Not being weak." Priya paused. "And still, most of us died. Because we trusted the people who'd raised us. I suppose that was weakness, too."

"What are you trying to say?"

"That...that the people you care about can be used against you. And strength—strength is a knife turned on the parts of yourself that care." Priya's fingertips touched at the hollow of her own ribs.

Malini swallowed. She thought of the night when the needle-flower leaving her body had nearly killed her, and she had pinned Priya beneath her. She thought of the blazing softness of Priya's beating heart.

"I know what it means to have power," Priya continued. "I know the price. I don't know if I can blame you for wanting to pay it."

"You should," Malini rasped. Her throat felt raw.

"Maybe," Priya admitted. "Maybe if I'd been raised gently by people who taught me to be kind and good, I'd know how to do it. But I was taught goodness and kindness, or what passes for it, by other damaged children, so I can't." She came forward. Sank to the ground by the tree stump where Malini sat. "My own brother ripped my heart out in a vision. That part doesn't matter," Priya said hastily, when Malini's mouth began to shape an alarmed question. "What matters is that my own brother hurt me, horribly, and I don't think I can hate him, even now."

Malini pushed the obvious questions aside. "When my brother hurt me, I made it my life's purpose to destroy him."

Priya laughed softly. "Maybe that's the better way."

"I'm not so sure." She couldn't smile. Her heart felt like a howl. "You need to forgive less easily, Priya. You need to guard yourself."

Priya looked up at her through those eyelashes like strange gold, those clear eyes pinning her soul.

"You couldn't use the knife on me," Priya said. "Do you think one day you'll turn yourself into someone who'll be able to? Who'll carve out my heart with no regrets?"

Malini thought of Alori and Narina and burning. "Priya," she said finally. Her voice was choked. And in it were all the splinters of her, all the things frayed by loss and fire and prison, isolation and fury, by the tenderness of Priya's mouth on her own. She did not know. She did not know.

Priya's expression softened. There was something knowing about that look—knowing and fond.

"Malini," she said. "If you do, if you change—I won't let you do it. I may not be canny or clever or—or anything you are, but I do have power." The leaves around them, as if in response to her words, rustled and drew closer. The trees were a wall around them. "I'll stop you. I'll turn any blade to grass, or to flowers. I'll bind your hands with vines."

"Will you hurt me?" Malini demanded. "You should, to save yourself."

Priya shook her head. "No."

"Priya."

"No. I'm sorry, but no. Because I'm strong enough not to need to."

"Don't be sorry," said Malini. "Don't—"

Her own words left her. Her own words broke. This was what she had needed. Not forgiveness, not a balm for this strange writhing fury inside her, but the promise of someone to care for—to love—that she could not harm. Even if she had to. Even if she *tried*.

She leaned forward, and Priya took Malini's face in her hands, as if she'd been waiting to trace Malini's cheeks with her thumbs, to look up at her with that utter, terrifying softness.

"I'll never understand your magic," said Malini, as Priya gently stroked her brow. "And I'm glad. So furious, and yet so glad."

Priya made a noise—a noise that meant nothing and everything, and raised her head, and kissed Malini once more. This time there was no fury in it. Only the warmth of Priya's skin. Only her soft breath, and the pin-straight fall of her hair, brushing Malini's cheek like the flat of a wing. Only a feeling like a deep dark well, a feeling like falling without the desire to rise.

Bhumika went into labor the next day.

Malini was standing near the lady's palanquin when a gasp came from within it. She turned and was suddenly surrounded by a throng of people as the palanquin was hurriedly lowered.

"We'll need to stop," said Bhumika tightly. "For a time. Just for a time."

"Someone set up a tent," barked her maidservant.

Malini stepped back, back. She watched Priya crouch at her sister's side. After a moment, she slipped away. She wasn't needed here.

As she walked, she glanced around. She'd expected the soldiers to come running the minute the lady cried out, but they were disturbingly absent.

Malini walked farther up the path, still alone. She hadn't been alone in a long time.

I should be afraid, she thought. She'd seen enough of the strange tree behind the hut where Priya had recovered to give her a healthy terror of this forest—of its waters and its soil, and most certainly, its trees—but she was not.

She finally saw Bhumika's Ahiranyi soldiers in a clearing ahead. As she approached them, their commander whirled. He turned the sword on her. Aimed it, with instinctual swiftness, at her sternum.

She didn't flinch. To flinch was to invite the first cut. Chandra had taught her that. She simply met his eyes and waited. She could see the moment when he realized who she was—and saw, too, the moment that followed, when he considered skewering her through anyway.

He lowered his sword.

"Princess," he said.

"Commander Jeevan," she said. She'd heard his name often enough already on this journey to remember it. "What has frightened you?"

His jaw tightened. He didn't sheathe the blade.

"I am not frightened." His voice was a whisper. "And keep your voice low. There are men farther along the path. Setting up camp. We can't skirt them without being seen."

And they couldn't move anyway. Not easily. Not now.

"I'll get Priya," she said.

"No. Lady Bhumika needs her."

Ah. So someone had told him what was happening. "She has plenty of women to rely on," Malini said. "But you will need Priya's strength."

She turned to go. He grabbed her arm.

She met the soldier's eyes. "They are Parijati, aren't they?"

He said nothing.

"Don't fear," she murmured. "If they're Chandra's men, I have no qualms about you killing them."

"And if they are your priest brother's?"

It seemed too much to hope, that they would be Aditya's soldiers. But nonetheless she said, "Then, knowing the pact I made with Lady Bhumika, you should allow me to join them."

"I'll get Priya," one of the other soldiers muttered. Jeevan gave a curt nod and did not let go of Malini.

"You accompanied me to the Hirana," Malini said. "I remember."

"I did," Jeevan said.

She tilted her head a little, considering him. "You feel no pity for me," she murmured. "But you took no joy in my suffering either. Curious."

"Not so curious," he said, gaze still fixed on her, though a muscle in his jaw twitched a little. "I care about only a few things. You are not one of them."

After a long moment, someone approached.

"What is it?" Priya's voice was low. She drew near them, her footsteps silent on the ground.

"Men ahead," said Jeevan. "Camped. They don't yet know we're here. They will soon."

"Are they dangerous to us?"

"They're Parijati."

Priya met Malini's eyes.

"Protect us however you see fit," said Malini.

Priya huffed out a breath. "Jeevan, why are you holding her hand?"

"Someone is approaching," one of Jeevan's men said, quiet, sword at the ready.

Jeevan swore, finally releasing Malini, who had just long enough to wish she had a weapon herself before a man appeared ahead of them. There was no way for them to hide from view. Jeevan and his men stepped forward with their swords, and Priya straightened, drawing on the strange magic within her.

The Parijati man turned on his heel and ran.

For a moment, they simply stared at his retreating form.

"Does no one have a bow and arrow?" Malini murmured.

Priya gave her a look. Twitched her fingers, and a branch flung itself through the air and hit the man on the back of the head. He crumpled to the ground.

He yelled as he fell. Priya winced, swearing.

"Be ready," Jeevan said. The men fanned out as racing footsteps converged, and more Parijati appeared.

"There's more of them!" One of the Parijati men shouted the words, then something incomprehensible that drew more footsteps, men running along the seeker's path. Men of Parijat and men of Alor, in the sharp blue turbans of their people.

Wait—Aloran.

Jeevan and the others met them with a clash of steel, swords a dancing arc against the air. Priya spared Malini a glance—mouthed at her to run—then turned and strode into the fray. No weapons were in her hands—nothing but the thing that lay in her blood.

Malini should have fled. Common sense demanded it. But there was something more than sense, common or otherwise, at play. Aloran men. Men of Parijat, but—for all they wore Parijati clothing, in pale weaves, with prayer necklaces wound about their throats—they did not wear the white and gold of the imperial army. This was an opportunity, a possibility.

More fool her. Of course one Aloran man broke through Jeevan's ranks. Of course he ran, and swung his sword at her.

"Rao," she gasped out. "I know Prince Rao, do *not* harm me!"

The Aloran's eyes widened.

Unfortunately, words did little good against a moving blade. Malini could only watch as it descended toward her—and then Jeevan was there. His sword met the Aloran man's at an angle, knocking it aside and out of the Aloran man's hands. He struck, and the Aloran ducked, rolling to the ground.

Malini stumbled backward, away from the fight, and felt the earth shift beneath her, carrying her farther as if on a green wave. Priya had not turned back, but of course Malini knew it was her hand in that moment of strangeness.

Run. Even the earth was saying it, speaking in Priya's voice.

But Rao.

It was not her finest moment. It was not an act of subtle politics or cunning. It was only this: her hands clenching into fists as she sucked in a deep, deep breath and yelled with all her might.

"Rao!" She nearly winced at the sound of her own voice, so shrill and sharp. "Rao, I am here! *Rao!*"

"Stop." A voice. *Rao's* voice—a whipcrack of command, achingly familiar. "Peace, brothers. Peace!"

It should have done nothing. But Priya swore, and then the earth moved, the soil sinking, holding all their feet fast.

Everyone froze.

As the chaos settled, Malini took in the sight before her. Men with swords. And there—Rao.

Rao, with Jeevan's sword tip beneath his chin. The two of them were caught by the earth, fused into the moment before the cut of the blade.

Here was the moment when she would know if she was a hostage after all.

"Let him go, Commander," Malini said. "Lower your blade. These men are my brother Aditya's."

A pause. "Are you sure," Jeevan said flatly.

"Yes," said Malini. "In honor of the vow I have made. Yes."

"Jeevan," said Priya. "Come on. Lower it."

Clearly conflicted, Jeevan finally let the tip of his sword fall. And Malini looked at Rao—that pleasant face, that dark unbound hair—and nearly shook from the familiarity of it. Of him.

"Hello, Prince Rao," she said.

"Malini," Rao said, by way of greeting. He blinked at her. "I—Priya?"

"Lord Rajan," Priya said. "How nice to see you again."

"Priya is my ally, Rao," said Malini. "I think there has been a…misunderstanding. These Ahiranyi have allied with me. With Aditya."

"Of course they have," he said, the strangest smile gracing his face, for only a moment. "Stand down. All of you."

His men lowered their own weapons, with a reluctance mirrored by Jeevan's own soldiers. After a moment, the ground rippled, releasing them all, and Jeevan stumbled back with a curse. Carefully, Rao took a step forward. Another.

And then he was before her. He did not touch her. He merely bowed his head and touched his fingertips to his forehead, in a gesture of love and respect. Malini held her hands out before her, glad they did not shake.

"Prince Rao," she said. "I know you waited for me. Sought to save me."

"I did. I'm sorry I did not accomplish my goal."

"No matter," she said softly. "But tell me. Why are you here, upon this path?"

"Our scouts brought news of people here. Women, men, and children. And I hoped, but I didn't know, couldn't be sure...ah. Malini." His voice lowered. "I am glad you're here at last."

He took her hands in his own. Looked at her, as if her face were a blazing light, as if she shone brighter than a statue of a mother.

"I'm here," he said, "to take you to your brother. Your brother is here, Malini. He's here."

57

PRIYA

"Go back to Lady Bhumika," Jeevan said quietly.

"And if they turn on you?"

He gave her a sidelong look. "Go back to her," he said.

Priya understood. She gave him a nod of assent and turned back to the camp.

She could feel the Parijati men watching her as she walked. Her back prickled. She wondered if they saw an enemy when they looked at her. She did, when she looked at them.

Malini...Malini hadn't looked uneasy when she'd entered the Parijatdvipan camp. Instead she'd stood taller, her chin rising. There was a sudden, new grace to the way she'd crossed the ground. For a moment, Priya saw the Malini who had glided across her prison, her hands hovering over Priya's own, as she'd tasted her first moments of freedom from the needle-flower. Looking at her now, though, Priya realized that she had never truly seen Malini in her element, a royal surrounded by those who venerated her for her blood. What Priya had witnessed in the intimacy of the Hirana, in the lantern light, had only been a shadow of this woman.

Priya pushed her sudden yearning to know *this* Malini—as she'd known the one who had kissed her beneath a waterfall—away.

She returned to the main camp, where people were milling around Bhumika's tent. The tent itself was silent. As she approached, Khalida emerged, grim-faced. She looked a little ill.

"Where have you been?" Khalida barked.

"There's a group of Parijati ahead up the path," Priya said in a low voice, drawing closer so she wouldn't have to speak up. "They're allies of Prince Aditya. The princess is with them, and Jeevan and the men are there. I'm going to remain here to keep Lady Bhumika safe."

"Prince Aditya's allies," Khalida repeated. "You're afraid the Parijati will turn on us?"

"Jeevan is with them," Priya repeated. "And if they attempt anything, I'll use everything I have—we all will—to keep them at bay."

"You have a deal with the princess," Khalida said, in a voice that needled. Her eyes glittered. "Are you telling me you don't trust her word?"

"I'm telling you that when there's a large group of men with weapons who aren't my friends, even *I'm* not stupid enough to trust them," Priya said evenly. "I want to see Bhumika."

"And how will you guard her from in there?" Khalida gestured at the tent.

Priya's power was depleted, but she let it touch her voice, just a brush of it, when she said, "I'm strong enough to make you move."

"You can't scare me," Khalida retorted.

"I'm not trying to," said Priya. "We're allies, Khalida. Don't be dense. Just move aside, or I'll make you. And you won't like that at all."

"You," Khalida hissed, "bring her nothing but grief. You know that, don't you?"

Priya stared at her. Stared, and said nothing.

Without another word, Khalida drew the tent flap aside.

Bhumika was kneeling on the ground. She was nearly silent, but there were low, animal noises of pain coming from her. Her face was damp with sweat.

It was a dark, intimate terror that consumed Priya when she kneeled by Bhumika's side.

"Priya?" Bhumika gritted out.

"I'm here."

"Come closer."

Bhumika reached a hand out and Priya took it.

"I don't know anything about birthing," Priya confessed, holding Bhumika's hand tight.

"Oh, good," said Bhumika. "Well. Neither do I. A shame that we're going to need to learn like this."

"I thought you'd know what to do," Priya said, appalled.

"Well, I thought I'd have trained midwives with me," Bhumika said through clenched teeth.

"You have me," Khalida said, sounding hunted from the entry.

Priya gripped Bhumika's hand tighter in comfort—a difficult task when Bhumika's own grasp was iron.

"Khalida," said Priya. "Get Sima."

"Why?"

"Her mother used to deliver the babies in their village," said Priya. "She'll certainly know more than either of us."

Khalida left at once. A few moments later, Sima's quiet voice cut through the dimness. "I can help."

The tent flap opened again, another woman entering with water. "And I'll need some of the other maidservants as well. I'm sorry," Sima added.

"This tent is becoming overcrowded," Bhumika gritted out.

"I'll go and keep watch." There was an edge of relief in Khalida's voice.

Women came back and forth, bringing water from the fire, boiled clean, and cloth, as Sima whispered to Bhumika, guiding her to breathe, coaxing her into one uncomfortable position after another. Helplessly, Priya sat and held Bhumika's hand and talked nonsense at her.

She was watching Sima rub Bhumika's back through the next set of pains when she felt one of the maidservants kneel at her side, passing her a wet cloth for Bhumika's forehead.

"I have the boy," a voice said quietly. "Come and speak to me, and I'll return him to you alive."

Priya looked up.

She did not know the woman's face. But she knew those eyes. She'd seen them through a mask of wood.

Before she could do anything, the woman was gone, and Priya was clutching the cloth in her hands, the water dripping against her palms.

"Priya. Priya? Give that to me." Sima pried it away. Then she turned back to Bhumika, and Priya could only rise to her feet. Turn to the entrance of the tent.

"Priya—where are you going?" Bhumika asked, alarmed.

"I'll be back."

"Priya—"

"I'll be back."

58

MALINI

The encampment was larger than their first sight of it suggested, long rather than broad, winding to match the narrowness of the space the seeker's path allowed between the arch of trees. There were fine tents, and men sharpening their swords. No horses, and no fires—just a silent watchfulness that swelled into something new when Malini entered the camp with Rao at her side and Commander Jeevan and his small force of soldiers at her back.

Priya had vanished. Malini bit down on her tongue, a light and assuring pain, and did not look for her again.

She looked at the men in the camp instead. Dwarali. Srugani. Saketan. Aloran. These were men of Parijatdvipa, of her family's great empire. She straightened, wishing she had some of her finery about her—her crown of flowers, the armor weight of her jewels—but she would make do with what she had, even if all she had was her mind and her pride. She had accomplished plenty with less, in these past harrowing months.

"Here," Rao said, ushering her forward. He guided her to a tent, opening the way for her.

She turned back for a moment. Met Commander Jeevan's eyes, steady and unwavering, even with enemies at his back.

She faced forward. "Rao," she whispered. "Make sure the Ahiranyi men aren't harmed."

"I will," he told her.

Good, she thought grimly. *Or Bhumika and Priya will see us buried.*

With a nod, she entered the tent.

It was no fine Parijati royal tent. There was no carpet rolled out across the floor. No cushions, no braziers burning, beneath a canopy of gold and white cloth. The tent was well made but plain, a Srugani domed construction. There was only a low writing table upon the floor. And a man standing before it.

Aditya.

His face was familiar and strange to her, all at once. There was that same firm jaw, those same arched brows. Those wide, dark eyes, exactly like her own. Her memory of him had always been so clear to her, so unchanged. But she had forgotten, somehow, the length of his nose. The mole under his left eye. The way his ears stuck out, just a little. The way his face warmed, always, infinitesimally at the sight of her. Her brother. Here was her brother.

"Malini," he said, and he smiled his old smile. He held his arms open, fingers curled toward her, openhearted and beseeching. "You're here. At last."

Malini had never been the kind to fling herself into embraces with the ease of a small child, even when she *had* been a child. She gripped his hands instead. Then his arms. She simply held on to him, just to assure herself that he was real.

She had worked so hard to be here. It had seemed impossible, at times. But here they both were. At last.

"I've dreamt of being here," Malini said. Tears threatened, despite herself. "For so long, I thought perhaps I'd not . . . not live to see you again."

"You're here now," he said, his voice low and warm. "You're safe."

Safe.

That shook some of the fog of emotion away. Left her cold and still and once again, herself.

"Malini," he said. "Sister. You're so thin."

She shook her head, wordless. He could draw his own

assumptions on why that was the case. As if he understood that she was not disagreeing, that she was simply shaking his words off, like cold water, he smiled again. Said, "We'll get you as much food as you want. Anything."

"When we're home in Parijat and all is well, and you have the throne safe in your grasp, I will do nothing but eat my fill," she told him. "But where is your army?"

"We don't need to discuss that now," he said. "Not when we've only reunited."

She shook her head at this, too.

"I sent you men from across the empire, and I see many faces, but no horses. No elephants. You lack the numbers to see yourself on the throne."

"They can't fit upon this path," he said with grating patience. "The forest disturbs them. And the monastery has no place for war elephants."

"Monastery," she repeated. "You still remain at the monastery?"

He inclined his head.

"The bulk of forces await orders upon the path to Dwarali."

"Then why," she said, "are you not on the path to Dwarali, leading them?"

"I was waiting for you." But she knew at once that was not the entire truth.

"Aditya. Don't lie to me," she said.

He hesitated, drawing back from her, his hands clasped behind him. "I have a task here, among the priesthood. A purpose. And I am not sure how yet to proceed." A pause. "If you call Rao back, he can, perhaps, explain."

"What is there to explain?" Malini asked. "What is there to do but wrest the throne from Chandra's hands?"

Aditya studied the writing desk, as if the answers he sought were etched there. Then, finally, he looked at her. "I am not sure that is what I am meant to do, Malini. I am not sure if ruling Parijatdvipa is the right path."

Fury, pure and ugly and hot, rushed through her. It cut

through her elation like a knife, leaving her raw. She had not been braced for it.

"You're not sure you want to rule Parijatdvipa," she said slowly, trying to keep the coldness from her voice. "Do you think that surprises me? I know you, Aditya. But I thought you'd put aside your reluctance, after I wrote to you what Chandra had done—the advisors he replaced, because they were not Parijati. The ones he *executed*. The frothing priests he raised above our father's wisest holy confidants—and you still think your *desire* to rule matters? The throne is yours. If not by desire, then by necessity and by right."

"You're always so very sure," he said.

"Not always. But of this, yes, I am sure."

He shook his head. "I have seen something, in the visions granted to me by the nameless. I have seen..." He trailed off. "Let's not talk about this now, sister," he said. "I am just so glad you're here."

Fine. If he didn't want to argue, then she wouldn't argue. There would be time enough for that. What her letters to him had not accomplished could perhaps be done in person.

She forced her body to relax. Forced down her fury and said, "I have brought allies with me. Ahiranyi who have rebelled against Chandra."

"And they want to join me, these Ahiranyi?"

"They want their freedom," said Malini. "Their independence as a nation. And I have offered it on your behalf, as thanks for saving my life and seeing me into your care."

Aditya blinked at her, startled. "You would carve a piece from the empire, in my name?"

"If my life is not worth such a price—and surely, brother, to you it is—then consider only the liability that Ahiranya represents. It suffers a crop blight that can infect flesh. Its people rebel against our rule. Soon it will be a nation without resources with a people that hate us. What use is that? We don't need this country," Malini said, with utter conviction.

He shook his head.

"Perhaps this is fated," she added. "Once, we quelled Ahiranya for trying to conquer us all. It was a righteous punishment. Surely now that the Ahiranyi have helped me, we can consider their debt paid."

"Malini. I can't give anything to your Ahiranyi now," said Aditya.

"But you will be able to, when you are emperor."

He gave her a considering look. "It matters to you so much, does it?"

"Yes," Malini said simply. He did not have to know the well of feelings that lay behind those words. "The fate of the Ahiranyi matters to me a great deal. Promise me this, Aditya. Vow it to me."

"Whatever you want," he said.

She was not satisfied with that answer. He should have had questions for her. He should have been weighing up the consequences of such an act, measuring whether the promise was worth fulfilling. These were the calculations that leadership required. But he was not, and his casual agreement, his tired disinterest, filled her with unrest.

Aditya looked at her, something pained in his dark eyes. "We'll return to the monastery," he said eventually. "And from there—we'll see, Malini."

"When?"

"After a night's rest," said Aditya. "Or whatever passes for night in this place."

So. Soon she would be in the monastery. And from there, at Aditya's side, she would see Chandra's removal truly begun. She would do so as a free woman, the threat of fire no longer hanging over her head. She would begin reshaping herself into the kind of person she needed to be in order to destroy Chandra—to claw him from his throne and see his name disgraced and erased from Parijatdvipan history.

Why did she not feel entirely exultant? Why had her initial joy become a spear point of pain beneath her ribs?

She thought of Lady Bhumika laboring upon the path, and Commander Jeevan looking at her and considering whether to run her through.

She thought of Priya.

"Tomorrow," said Malini. "I look forward to it."

59

PRIYA

There was no sign of the woman who had whispered to her in the tent.

But Priya strode into the dark of the trees surrounding the seeker's path, where time tugged and pulled strangely, the uneasy blur of light beyond the maze of trunks breaking into even deeper fractures. She felt movement around her, like water. Then she left the path and felt the strangeness melt away.

There was the woman. Waiting.

And there was Rukh, bound to a tree by its own roots. There was a gag in his mouth, and when he saw Priya he made a guttural noise that would have been a shout if it were not muffled.

"I expected him to come quietly," the woman said. "But the boy was—reluctant." Her mouth pursed. "How quickly the loyalties of children change."

"I should fashion a spear of wood and set it through your skull," Priya said, clenching her hands tight. "Or perhaps I should sink you into the ground and let the worms have you."

"I have roots around his throat," the woman said calmly. "I can strangle him before you can save him or murder me."

"You can't."

"Strangulation takes time," the woman agreed. "Instead I'll just snap his neck."

"He was one of your own," said Priya. "Loyal to you and your cause. You'd really kill him?"

"If still he had any loyalty, he'd die willingly for the sake of seeing Ahiranya free."

"He's a child," Priya snapped. "You'd truly murder a child you know, with your own power?"

There was a noise—a hiss, as the roots coiled tighter, and Rukh kicked his feet furiously against the ground.

Well, that was certainly an answer.

A line of watery blood oozed from the woman's nose. Trickled down her lip. She brushed it away with the back of her hand.

"We're spitting distance from Parijatdvipans who'd be happy to see rebels strung up," said Priya. "And the people traveling with me have no reason to like you very much either."

"Well, they didn't stop me," said the woman, who wore no mask and carried none. There were strands of silver in her hair, lines around her mouth. "Without my mask, you and I are alike enough. Maidservant and maidservant. Common woman and common woman. Invisible."

"We're nothing alike."

"No," agreed the woman. "You are a temple child. You have a duty to Ahiranya. When I was your age, I was no more than a worshipper, a pilgrim at your temple. And now I am your brother's follower, here to seek your help and ensure that you fulfill your duty. All you need to do is tell me the way."

"And where is Ashok? Why are you here, and not him?"

The woman cocked her head slightly. "You won't give me the way? Even now?"

"If Ashok wanted to hurt or manipulate me, he'd do it himself," said Priya. "He doesn't even know you're here, does he? But you're loyal to him. Obedient. Why would you come here without his blessing?"

The woman said nothing.

"He's dying, then," Priya murmured. She hated the way her heart twisted at the thought, a dull ache in her breast and throat.

The woman said nothing again, but Rukh made a choked noise, low and terrible, as if the roots had tightened further still.

"I can't simply tell you the way," Priya said quickly. "The way must be shown. And if Ashok is dying, there's a high possibility he won't have the strength to reach the Hirana before the end."

The woman shook her head. "The way alone isn't all I desire from you. Ashok has a vision that must be fulfilled whether he... whether he lives or not." The woman swallowed, grief flickering over her face. "You have condemned him. But I know the vision is greater even than him, so I will put any thoughts of justice aside if you will come with me, and hear him speak."

She could not leave Bhumika and Sima and the rest of them vulnerable. But she couldn't leave Rukh either.

"Come with me and listen to your brother," said the woman. "Or the boy dies."

"Let him go now, and I'll come."

The woman snorted. "No," she said. "He comes with us."

Priya looked at Rukh. His hair was stuck to his sweat-damp forehead, his face flushed, terrified and angry.

"Fine," said Priya. "Let's go."

The woman's name was Kritika. She'd been a pilgrim once, one of the men and women who climbed the Hirana and collected deathless waters, to place at the feet of the yaksa upon their altars, or wear as a talisman of power and fortune. But when the temple council had burned, she'd kept all the water safe, knowing it would one day be needed.

She told Priya all of this, as she dragged Rukh forward on a leash of vine. His hands were bound. He looked at Priya, now and again, and she looked back. *It's going to be okay*, she tried to say with her eyes. But Rukh still looked afraid, and there was an angry twist to his mouth, as if he didn't know if he wanted to yell or cry.

Priya saw other figures in the shadows as they slowed down. The figures wore scythes, their narrowed eyes fixed on her as she passed them. Some were still masked, their identities hidden behind rictuses of wood, but others were bare-faced, their expressions tense.

Kritika stopped before a small bower shrouded in flowers of pale umber, with drooping leaves like veils. Kritika entered the bower with Rukh still bound to her. Time passed. Ashok's presence was a quiet drum beneath the earth—a song reminding Priya of the ways, large and small, that the waters bound them.

Kritika returned with Rukh.

"He's waiting for you," she said.

"Was he angry at you?"

The rebel gave Priya a level look. "Speak to him," she said. "I'll wait with the boy."

"I'll be back soon," Priya said, meeting Rukh's eye. Then she entered the shroud of the leaves.

The world lay in muted shadow. Ashok was lying on his back on the ground, wrapped in a long shawl. He watched Priya approach with eyes that glittered with something akin to fever. His face was gaunt.

He looked like the brother who'd abandoned her on Gautam's veranda, so many years ago. The brother who had been dying.

"I came here to die in peace," whispered Ashok. "But I am glad that Kritika did not obey my wishes." His fingers twitched against the edge of the shawl. "Come closer."

Priya drew closer. Kneeled down beside him.

"Are you sad, Priya?" he asked. "You knew this would be the consequence of refusing me the deathless waters, after all. My death and theirs." He gestured weakly at the entrance to the bower, and the watchful figures who lay beyond it.

"Don't place your death on my shoulders," she said roughly. "You chose this. You knew the risks."

"So what happens now, little sister? When I am dead, will you let the empire rip us all apart in its teeth? Will you lock away the deathless waters until you find someone you consider worthy of that power?"

She shook her head, heart aching. "You're getting what you want after all, Ashok," she said quietly. "A free Ahiranya. And it'll be Bhumika's doing, and my own. Not yours. We made a deal."

He tried to sit up, his eyes focusing intently on her.

"What kind of deal?"

"Politics aren't my strength," said Priya. It was only partially a lie. "You'll need to ask Bhumika about that. But however it was done, Ahiranya's independence has been promised, and we're going to use the strength of the deathless waters to hold on to it. Just as you think we should."

Ashok gave a choked laugh.

"My two sisters listening to me. I never thought I'd see the day."

"Your Kritika brought me here against my will. But—it would be useful to have strong fighters working with us in defense of Ahiranya. To have a network of loyal hands and eyes. To have a new temple council that already knows the taste of the waters, and the risks."

There was a heartbeat of silence as Ashok looked at her. Perhaps it was the sickness that had left him so open and raw, but she could see the hope in his face—in the shape of his mouth. He wanted his followers to live.

"And what will my dear little sister, who claims to know nothing of politics, ask in return?"

"You accept Bhumika as our leader," said Priya. "You must vow never to try to overthrow her. You must promise, on the yaksa and the waters in your blood, that you will never fight her for control of Ahiranya. Let her be the best of us, Ashok. She's the only sensible one of the three of us, after all."

"I cannot promise not to fight or test her," he said immediately. "She doesn't understand what Ahiranya should be. She doesn't care."

"You're in no position to bargain, Ashok," she said.

A rattling cough escaped him. He wiped water and blood from his lips, then said, "My followers—they'll have a future? As leaders?"

"Yes," Priya said, and hoped desperately that she was not making an error.

"Alongside you and Bhumika?"

Priya was not sure she wanted her own name mentioned alongside leadership, but said, "Yes."

"Then I accept," said Ashok. "Get me to the waters, save me and mine, and I'll serve Bhumika. For Ahiranya's sake, we all will."

Priya nodded, relief pouring through her. "Can I trust you? Truly?"

"We're still family, Priya," he said. "There's no one in the world exactly like us. Who knows what we know, or has suffered as we have."

"That isn't a yes, Ashok." She squeezed her eyes shut. Opened them again. "But it will do. I need one more thing from you."

"Tell me."

"Your Kritika has a boy as her hostage," she said. "Rukh. I want him back. Or there is no deal between us. This is our business, Ashok. Our family. We don't need to involve anyone else. I'll speak to Bhumika, and once she agrees to our deal, I'll return with her."

"Fine," he said.

She thought of standing and leaving him there. Their deal was done, after all. There was nothing more to be said.

Instead, she leaned forward and touched her forehead to his, smelling the sweat and sickness and home of him. She was still so vulnerable to him and to love and to the strange, broken family that had shaped them into . . . whatever it was they were.

"I'll be waiting," he murmured.

You don't have any other choice, she thought.

She bit her lip and nodded, then pulled back.

"Kritika," he called.

The pilgrim entered at once.

"Let the boy go," he said. "My sister and I have come to an agreement. She'll return to us soon enough."

*   *   *

The camp was no longer quiet when Rukh and Priya returned. There was a great deal of noise from the other women, and Khalida emerged from the tent, white-faced and furious over Priya's absence. She was still berating Priya when the tent flap was pushed back, and Sima peered out. She caught Priya's eye. Beckoned.

"Lady Bhumika wants you," she said, as Priya extricated herself from Khalida's wrath and walked over. "Come. See for yourself."

Someone had burned sweet incense to improve the smell of the tent. Bhumika was half sitting up, face sweaty and flushed. And there was a squirming bundle, squeaking like a newborn kitten, in her arms.

"It's..."

"A baby," Bhumika said. "A girl, apparently. I suppose that's good. Will you hold her?"

The baby was small and did not smell pleasant, and when she was placed in Priya's arms, Priya felt something overpowering—a kind of terror and wonder at the revolting beauty of life, that made her want to hand away this small human as quickly as possible, and also hold on to her forever.

"She smells," said Priya, staring down into the baby's tiny face.

"The first words the poor thing gets to hear, and that's what you offer her," Bhumika said. "Give her back to me."

Priya did. "If we were still in the temple, you'd consult star charts to choose the right letters and syllables for a name, as we did for the babies of pilgrims."

"We're not temple children anymore, thankfully," Bhumika said. "Her name is Padma. That's the name I've chosen for her. It will do. Now tell me what Ashok offered to you."

Priya raised her head. "You knew?"

"I felt him too," Bhumika said. "How could I not?"

There was no end to it. Even now, in this moment, there was no end to their duties. Their war, and their work.

Priya took a deep breath and began.

*   *   *

After Commander Jeevan had returned to guard Bhumika and the others—after he'd learned everything that had passed—Priya slipped away.

She moved silently, carefully, making her way through the woods to the Parijatdvipan camp.

Malini had a tent of her own—Jeevan had seen it erected, and sketched out its location to Priya with his words before she departed.

Priya waited until no one was looking, then slipped inside.

Malini watched her enter. She didn't appear surprised.

"Priya," she murmured. She crossed the tent and took Priya's face in her hands. But she didn't kiss her. Merely looked at her.

And Priya...

"What, by soil and sky, is this tent?" Priya said, looking around. "Is that gold on the ceiling? And why do you have a writing desk?"

"It's actually modest by the standards of my youth," said Malini, a smile curling her mouth. But her eyes were guarded when she said, "You shouldn't have come here."

"Those soldiers couldn't have harmed me."

"Nonetheless," said Malini. "Why have you come?"

Priya looked at her and looked at her, struggling for the words.

"Malini," she said, shaping the name carefully on her tongue, as if this way, she could keep it. "You're where you need to be. My part of our bargain is done. And I'm... I'm here to say good-bye."

She watched the smile on Malini's face fade and die.

"I... In truth, I don't think I should be here telling you this at all. This is—an act of trust," Priya admitted.

"Leaving," Malini said. "You're leaving."

"You knew I would have to eventually," said Priya. "Bhumika and I—all of us—have to protect Ahiranya until your brother Aditya takes the throne. Until you're able to see your vow to me fulfilled."

"I know," Malini said numbly. "I know. It's just so—so swift."

Her forehead creased, just slightly. She touched her fingertips to her throat.

There was a tightness to Malini's face as she very gracefully walked away and sat down at her writing desk, her back to Priya.

"Thank you," Malini said, "for coming to speak to me. Knowing how I feel—it was kind of you." She bowed her head a little, the nape of her neck bare as she drew her braid over her shoulder. "And thank you, too, for . . . everything. For the time we've had together. I won't forget my promise to you."

Priya swallowed. Her throat felt tight. Her eyes stung.

"We're not done with one another, Malini," she said. "This isn't the end."

"Of course it is, Priya. You said it yourself. We're on different paths now. Isn't that what an end is?"

To be nothing but a part of Malini's history, and for her to be part of Priya's in turn . . . no. That felt wrong, viscerally wrong. It couldn't be that easy to erase what they felt for each other—the wonder and hope of it.

"Malini," Priya said. "Malini. I . . ." She swallowed. "You'll see me again. I know it. No matter where you go or what you do, I'll find you eventually, because you're taking a piece of my heart with you. You carved it out, after all."

Malini jerked to her feet. She strode over to Priya. Touched their foreheads together, setting Priya's pulse thrumming. She smelled of clean skin and jasmine and she was too close, too close for Priya to see her clearly. All Priya could see was a shadow of dark hair. The flicker of the oil lamp, casting shadows on Malini's cheek. Malini's clenched jaw. Her lashes, damp.

"At least kiss me good-bye," whispered Priya. "At least do that."

Malini cupped her face in her hands and kissed her. Malini took her lip between her teeth, soothed the sting of it with the gentleness of her tongue, and kissed her deeper. Priya, her blood singing, cupped the back of Malini's neck in her palm, the warm, silky skin, brushed her thumb over the feathery, faint tendrils of her hair at her nape and the faint silver of an old scar and drew

Malini closer again, and again. It was a lush kiss, a biting one. It was a good-bye, and it made Priya's heart hurt.

"I could make you stay," Malini whispered, drawing back, her breath unsteady and a wild look in her eyes. "I could convince you. I've convinced so many people to do what I want in the past. If I can cajole someone into treason, surely I can convince you to stay by my side." She leaned into Priya's handhold. "You want to, after all. You don't want to leave me. You wouldn't be here, if you really wanted to leave me."

There was want in her words, but fear too. Priya knew. It was the same fear Malini had admitted when she'd spoken of how she had almost placed a knife in Priya's heart. It was fear of herself.

"You couldn't convince me," Priya told her. "Couldn't trick me. I'm absolutely sure of that. I have a purpose and a goal and even you can't make me give it up. I promise, Malini." She kissed her again—the lightest brush of her lips against Malini's cheek. "I promise."

Malini exhaled.

"Good," she said. "That's good." And then she turned her head, meeting Priya's mouth with her own, brushing their lips together once again before she drew back. Drew back and turned away.

"You should go now, if you want to leave before it's light. Go now, Priya."

Priya looked at Malini. At her back, a forbidding line.

"I promise you I'll come," Priya said to her. "I know you don't think much of prophecies. Or portents, or fate, or anything of that sort. But one day I am going to come and find you. By then, I expect you will have long forgotten me. Maybe I'll only be able to walk the edges of whatever mahal you live in, but as... as long as you want me to, I'll come. If you want me to find you, I'll come."

There were so many things Priya didn't know how to say.

The moment I saw you, I felt a tug. You are the feeling of fall-ing, the tidal waters, the way a living thing will always turn, seeking light. It isn't that I think you are good or kind, or even that I love you. It is only that, the moment I saw you, I knew I would seek you out. Just as I sought the deathless waters. Just as I sought my brother. Just as I seek all things—without thought, with nothing but want.

Priya said again, "If you want."

"You'll always be welcome," Malini said abruptly, as if the words had been wrenched out of her. "When you come and find me—you'll be welcome. Now, Priya. Please."

Priya swallowed. "Good-bye, Malini," she said.

60

MALINI

Malini waited until she was sure that Priya would be long gone. She waited hours, in the strange light of the seeker's path, sat at the writing table, no pen in hand. Then she rose to her feet and left the tent to ask for the whereabouts of Commander Jeevan.

As she'd expected, she was soon informed that Commander Jeevan and his men had returned to Bhumika's retinue some time ago. When one of Rao's party had gone to seek them out, approaching cautiously with a lantern held above his head to mark his presence, he'd found no signs of the camp.

"The Ahiranyi vanished," said Rao. "Left, as far as anyone can tell, of their own accord."

Rao had brought her food. Clean, simple fare, carried from the monastery: pickled vegetables; fermented beans; roti, cooked to char over the shared fire. She ate it without really tasting it. She'd thought—hoped—Aditya would come question her. But his reluctance to engage with his fate apparently extended even to this. It was Rao instead who stood in her tent, his hands clasped behind him, watching her with careful eyes.

"I told them to go," Malini said.

Not true. It didn't matter, of course. Truth and lies were both tools, to be used when most necessary. And she had made a vow to Priya that she intended to keep.

"They could have been useful," Rao observed.

"Most were not," said Malini, bluntly.

Rao's eyes narrowed, a little. Canny. "The one who saved you..."

Malini shook her head. "I am in their debt," she said. "They saved me from prison, and saved my life. If they've chosen to return to defend their nation—I cannot begrudge them. I can only be thankful."

"Aditya told me you made them a promise."

"I did," said Malini. "And I'll see it fulfilled."

Rao looked at her for a long moment. "Malini," he said. Hesitated.

"Yes?"

He lowered his gaze. "Nothing. The camp is packing up. Shall the men arrange you a palanquin?"

She shook her head.

"No need," she said. "I'll walk."

As they neared the end of the seeker's path, sunlight bled through the trees, untainted by the strange rain-like wash of night.

"No candles," one of the men was barking at the others. "No pipe smoking, men. Don't forget that."

At first glance, the lacquer gardens of Srugna were a grand valley monastery, an ideal worship ground for the nameless. The valley walls were covered in a delicate, rich profusion of leaves of deep green and burnished yellow. The ground was rolling grass and meadow flowers: purple, pink, blue, as small as beads. Between them were trees, delicate and long-limbed, heavy with the weight of fruit and young leaves, berry dark.

But none of it was real. The weather in Srugna was not suitable for the meadow flowers of Dwarali, the sweet grasses found in parts of Alor.

Malini looked at the high tree-ringed slopes that surrounded the gardens, encircled by a vast reservoir of water; the narrow entry across a bridge of woven root and vine. The monastery was both well protected from invasion and terribly vulnerable.

She felt that knife-edge balance keenly when she crossed the bridge. Beneath her lay a chasm, sharp-rocked. The bridge itself was a fragile weft, rocking alarmingly with the motion of their bodies crossing its surface.

Once they were across, Aditya fell into step beside her. "The garden was carved—built—according to the vision of the first Srugani priest of the nameless. He was told to 'go to the valley of the lotus, and build within its heart a palace to me, a place of lac.' So he did."

Aditya took her hand. He led her to the fine, gem-hung trees surrounding the entrance to the monastery. Placed her hand against the surface of the bark.

Lac. Lacquer. Sweet, resinous.

Not simply a name after all.

She drew back her hand.

"Anyone," she said, "could burn this place to the ground, by error or design. You know that, don't you? It would take barely a spark."

"No more than one candle," a new voice agreed. A priest approached them, clad in the blue robes of the nameless, his voice and his expression tranquil. "But we are priests of the nameless, princess, and we surrender ourselves to fate. It is our calling."

"Come," Aditya said, gently urging her forward. "Let me show you your new chambers."

A simple room. A bed. These luxuries, after so long, should have overwhelmed her.

She sat on the ground and quite carefully resisted the urge to scream.

They lived willingly within an unlit pyre, the fools. She felt the knowledge close over her skull like a vise.

Fire. Burning. It was lucky she did not believe in fate, because these things seemed to be following her. Waiting for her.

"Princess Malini," said a voice. It was quiet but warm. "I am so glad you live."

She turned her head to the door. Her old teacher's favorite disciple stood before her. Like all sages, Lata was austere. She wore her hair in tight braids, bound in a corona against her skull. Her sari, covered by a gray shawl, was pristine.

"Lata! I did not expect to see you," said Malini in surprise.

"I accompanied the Aloran prince," murmured Lata. "As you asked me to."

Malini was lucky some of her many messages, sent during her confinement before she was meant to burn, or hastily written and paid for with bribes of jewels before her imprisonment in Ahiranya, had reached their targets after all.

"I am so very glad you did," said Malini warmly, though her heart felt cold. "Please. Come and sit."

Lata sat down by her side.

"How shall I begin, princess?" Lata said, cocking her head to one side. Those were the words of a sage—a kind of rote offering. "What knowledge do you seek?"

"Everything," she said. "Tell me everything."

According to Lata, the large bulk of the forces seeking to overthrow Chandra were based in Srugna and upon the road to Dwarali. There was no place for them in the monastery, confined and dangerous as it was. Only lords and princes interested in politicking, or who sought the measure of Aditya, had chosen to come to the lacquer gardens.

"Well," murmured Malini, when Lata was done. "If the highborn men want politicking..." She stood. "You'll have to act as chaperone and as one of my ladies," she said. "Can you do so?"

"I'm sure I can manage," Lata said.

"Then first," said Malini, "I need to bathe."

She bathed in cold water, and tried not to think of Priya offering her a ladle of cold water in the Hirana; Priya kneeling, gazing at her. Her hair was combed as best as it could be, after its long mistreatment. Lata gave Malini one of her own saris. The blouse was so loose that it gaped—but it would be hidden beneath cloth, so would have to do. Malini had no jewels. No marks of status. Nothing to signify her worth.

Then she looked up, at the window.

Of course.

With Lata's help, she bound her hair into a knot, and carefully pinned in place a crescent of freshly plucked lacquer flowers.

The men quieted abruptly when she entered the rooms. There was no sign of Aditya, and no sign of Rao either.

She'd interrupted a game of catur. But she understood that games of dice and strategy were not simply an amusement to highborn men. She inclined her head—a graceful motion she knew emphasized the vulnerability of her neck and the regality of her bearing—and said, "I fear I'm interrupting."

"Princess." The men did not stand, but they inclined their heads in equal respect. It was enough. "No apologies are necessary. Are you searching for someone?"

"Lord Narayan," she said, finding his face among the lords present. "I am so sorry for your loss. Prince Prem was a great friend to my brother Aditya. I greatly admired him."

"Thank you, princess," the young man said, suddenly somber. "It is a great sorrow to us to lose him."

"I grieve with you," Malini murmured. She crossed the room toward him, each step slow and deliberate.

As she did, she looked at each of them in turn. "You seem ill at ease, my lords."

The Dwarali lord was the one who spoke first. "We thought Emperor Aditya would return with an army." His mouth was unsmiling. "But it is not to be, I see."

Malini shook her head. "I could not bring him an army," she said. "Only myself. But I will do all I can, my lords, to see him upon his throne."

"Perhaps now," one of the Srugani lords murmured, ire in his voice, "he'll consider giving us the war we came for."

She exhaled a breath. Turn of the neck, just so, to emphasize the flowers of lac bound in her hair. She was an imperial princess of Parijat. That carried weight.

"Believe me, good lords," Malini said, with a demure lowering of her lashes, even as she kept her spine straight, her shoulders a firm line. "My brother Aditya will see your old glory restored. You will have what you once had. Control of your own kingdoms. Places of authority and respect in the imperial court. The glory of the empire, molded by loyalty, will be as it once was."

And that was why they were here, wasn't it? They were bound to belong to Chandra's remade, twisted Parijatdvipa—bound by the same oaths their ancestors had taken to repay the bloody, terrible sacrifice of the mothers who had formed Parijatdvipa in the first place. The sacredness of that promise still echoed through Parijatdvipa from those ancient deaths. They wanted only what they had always had—equality, clout, and prosperity—and Malini could ensure that Aditya provided that.

Better a weak emperor, they no doubt thought. *Better a reticent emperor who wishes to be a priest than a zealot who will take what is ours and make it his own.*

"And when," said the same Srugani lord, "will we have all we've been promised?"

"The hour is late," said the Dwarali lord who had first spoken, rising to his feet. "May I guide you back to your room, Princess Malini?"

"I'm not sure that would be wise," murmured Lata.

But Malini only smiled, and said, "By all means, my lord. Accompany me."

"You are Lord Khalil," she said, as they stepped out into the velvet dark, Lata trailing after them. "Lord of the Lal Qila, are you not?"

"I am," the lord acknowledged.

"Your wife thinks very highly of you, Lord Khalil," said Malini. "She described your defense of your fortress against the Jagatay with great admiration."

"And great detail, no doubt. That woman has an unhealthy interest in military strategy." He gave her a sidelong look. "I know you wrote to Raziya, Princess Malini. She shared many of your letters with me. I was—intrigued."

"I thought perhaps you had been," she said. "You're here, after all."

Lord Khalil gave a rumbling laugh that was not entirely full of good humor.

"A choice I am beginning to strongly regret. I miss my home. My horses. And this place..." He looked around with distaste. "I would not allow my best horsemen to enter this place," he said. "We're hemmed in on all sides. What good are horses on terrain like this?" He waved a hand, in obvious disgust at the profusion of glossy flowers hanging from the rockery. "I wait here at the emperor's pleasure. But I fear his pleasure is to remain here and meditate."

"He was kind to wait for me," said Malini. "Kind and noble, like a highborn of old."

The lord snorted derisively. "I have little patience for his form of nobility."

"I appreciate your frankness," said Malini.

"My apologies. We do not have time for flowery words in Dwarali."

Malini, who had read his wife's elegant missives and had once enjoyed Dwarali poetry, refrained from commenting upon this claim.

"How many advisors from Dwarali have been sent home in disgrace?" Malini asked mildly. "And how many executed? To be frank in return, Lord Khalil: Chandra's form of highborn honor will not favor you. Not as Aditya's will."

"Or as yours will," the lord said. "But you have a point. The burning of women—that was not well liked, I'll tell you that, princess. But raising your fire priests above the kings and lords who've given Parijatdvipa its greatness..." He clucked his tongue against the roof of his mouth. "That was ill thought-out."

"I warned you he would do as much," Malini reminded him.

"That you did," Khalil acknowledged. "You worked very hard to seed ill will toward the false emperor in your missives," Khalil said. "This, my wife told me too."

"Your wife is a canny woman."

"That she is."

They walked for a moment in silence. Birds fluttered above them. The sky was bright with stars, the lacquer garden gleaming strangely.

"A cruel emperor is unpleasant," Khalil said. His tone was light, almost conversational. "But if he protects the interests of those close to him, he can be forgiven a great deal."

"Chandra does not even protect the interests of his own family," Malini said. And ah, that was more honesty than she should have given.

"And that is the crux, is it not?"

Malini walked on. Steady, sure. "Aditya will always protect the interests of those loyal to him," she said. "I can promise you that, my lord."

"Aditya will indeed," Khalil murmured, gazing at her with shrewd eyes. It was not Aditya, his eyes seemed to say, that would protect his interests.

But that was all right. Malini's interests were aligned with Aditya's own, after all.

"I leave you here, princess," said Khalil, bowing his head.

"My thanks," murmured Malini.

She and Lata waited as he walked away.

"They are kinder to their women in Dwarali," said Malini to Lata, when he was long gone. "I took a risk."

Then, to herself, she muttered: "Someone has to."

61

RAO

More than a dozen men saw it when the messenger—not one of Prem's, but a Saketan in deep green, his braided hair half-unfurled and slick with blood—fell from his horse and collapsed at the far end of the bridge. He was already beginning to crawl his way across when the men reached him, helped him.

"Soldiers from Parijat," the messenger gasped, once he was on monastery soil. "They're—they're coming. One battalion only, mothers be praised."

"Do they know he's here?" Narayan asked urgently.

"I don't know," the messenger gasped. "I don't know, I—*ah!*" And with that gasp of pain, the soldiers and priests alike were upon him, flocking around him and lifting him up to get him to safety. One Dwarali man drew off his own sash, holding it to a wound in the messenger's side.

Rao's mind raced. Had one of Santosh's men managed to escape their encounter? Or had a contingent been left behind in Hiranaprastha, to seek help if Santosh did not return? There was no way to know.

Rao saw a flicker of movement from the monastery doors. A flash of blue, as a watcher vanished into the interior.

It could have been any of the priests. But Rao knew it was Aditya.

Rao stared at the door for a long moment, a kernel of bitterness and regret blooming in his stomach.

Aditya had listened. And then he had run.

Once, Rao had admired Aditya's stillness.

The man had never been rash or quick to anger. He had been scolded for his slow reflexes when they practiced with sabers, but the sages and the military leaders who had educated him in the rules of honorable warfare, in ancient and modern military strategy, had admired his careful consideration of all factors. Aditya was a thinker. Aditya had always been a thinker.

Aditya had always wanted to do what was right.

He had spent hours poring over texts, weighing up military strategies and gambits, mulling over the ethics of warfare, puzzling out the best choices, the stratagems that would provide the perfect balance: low cost to human life, a swift victory, an honorable battle.

He rarely found that he could achieve them all.

"It will not be this easy in the real world," Aditya had once said as they played catur, eyes fixed upon the board. His hand kept moving, hovering first over the little carved elephant, the charioteer, the infantryman, the minister. The king. "Here I can choose to sacrifice whoever I must to win." His voice, his expression—both were oddly subdued. "In our lessons, we're taught that we must. But sometimes I think, if there were no war at all—that would be easier."

"It would be," Rao had agreed, mystified. "But war happens."

"Does it have to?"

"I don't know," Rao had said. "I think it's just the way the world is."

Aditya had frowned. Stared at the board. Then he had picked up the piece that symbolized the king and placed it beyond the board, on the edge of the table.

"There," he said, smiling back at Rao. "Now the king can contemplate the distant horizon. Much more fun than war, I think."

"Pretty sure that's against the rules," Rao had teased.

"That's all right," Aditya had replied. "I don't care for catur anyway."

And Rao had laughed, and clapped him on the back, and said, "If you're that tired, then come and have a drink with me instead."

He'd believed, then, that there would be time for Aditya to grow into a good emperor.

He should have known, as a devotee of the nameless, that the king standing beyond the edge of the board had *meant* something. That a man can sometimes see his true fate unwittingly.

"A prophetic name is not always something whispered by a priest at a child's birth," a priest of the nameless had said, when Rao had asked why he had to be burdened with such a name, why *him*. "Even beyond our faith, there are people who discover their fates by chance. Their fate finds them—in dreams, in stories, in happenstance. Often they do not recognize truth when it graces them, and the knowledge of the prophecy passes them by. But your fate would have found you, young prince, whether you had been Aloran or no. Be glad that your faith leaves you forewarned of what is to come."

"It must be strange," Rao had murmured. "Not to know your fate, even when you see it."

"Perhaps," the priest had said, smiling benevolently. "But you are of the faith of the nameless, prince of Alor. You will recognize exactly such a prophecy when you see one. You may save another man from walking his path in ignorance one day."

Rao had not.

Rao found Aditya in a small garden replete with songbirds. Aditya did not turn, so Rao turned him, making the man meet his eyes.

"Your brother is coming for you," Rao said raggedly, his hands on Aditya's shoulders. "My prince, my emperor—my *friend*. Chandra has sent his men here. He will kill you. We need to flee."

"Just a little longer," Aditya murmured, looking away from Rao, out at the birds, the sky. Rao wondered what factors he was weighing up in that skull of his: how justice measured against ethics and against strategy, amounting to nothing but the stillness of his body, his distant eyes. "Just a little longer, and I will know what needs to be done."

"There is no more time! There has never been time."

Aditya closed his eyes. He looked like a terrible weight lay upon him—a crushing weight that bowed his shoulders as no court politics, no war, no thing they had experienced together as princes in Parijat ever had.

"You don't understand," Aditya whispered.

"I do. *I do.* I've kept to the tenets of this faith my whole life, Aditya. My sister died for it. But I can't allow you to do this."

Aditya met his eyes, finally. Dark eyes. Severe brows.

"If I am your emperor, you must give me the time I require. My word is, after all, law." His voice was sudden iron. "And if I am not your emperor, then go and fight your war without me. It's simple enough."

Rao thought of that long-ago catur board; of Aditya's frown, of the desire to step off the board. But there was no leaving this game. Aditya was a piece that had to move, if anything was to be won or lost.

"No," Rao said firmly. "I won't make this choice for you. This is your task, Aditya. Not mine. If you're to be emperor, if you're to lead us—you have to take the first step. You have to decide. I won't choose for you."

Aditya slipped from his grasp. Turned and walked away. And Rao bowed his head, thinking of his sister, who had burned, and the terrible weight of his own name. The hope of it.

The reality of Aditya, bound by a vision. Unwilling to rise.

62

MALINI

It took one of the Srugani lords and all his associated followers—a not insignificant number of men—abandoning the monastery for Malini to learn the full truth.

"The messenger dragged himself from his dead horse," Lord Narayan proclaimed, pacing. "Risked his life to bring this to us. And now—nothing. Where is Emperor Aditya? Prince Rao, do you know?"

Rao shook his head. Said nothing.

"Chandra cannot be sure that Aditya is here, or he would have sent far more men," said another lord.

"He may be targeting every monastery to the nameless," Rao said. "Or we were followed, on the seeker's path."

"Targeting every monastery would be foolish at best, an affront to the faith at worst," another voice said, appalled. "No sane man would do it."

Rao's laugh was bitter. "Chandra would."

"The soldiers will arrive here by tonight," said another.

"Are you sure?"

"If they're traveling inconspicuously, they won't have horses, or any possibility of arriving sooner. But the messenger was sure."

"And Emperor Aditya...?"

"Was told as soon as the report arrived," said Lord Khalil, gaze hooded. He watched the others as if over the catur table, weighing up his next move, and weighing them up too.

"And his plans?" Lata asked, from the corner of the room.

"He hasn't seen fit to enlighten us," Khalil said levelly. "But I'm sure he will speak to his beloved sister."

"I am sure he will," Malini replied, with just as much evenness. Her blood sang in her ears.

"There will be many battles and many wars, if Prince Aditya intends to take back the throne."

"*And he will,*" Malini said firmly.

Khalil made a noise. It was not quite agreement.

"Would he have us run, like cowards, ill-befitting our status?" Narayan asked.

Malini did not think survival was cowardly but refrained from saying so.

"We are warriors, my lords," said Rao, surprising her. "We do not run from battle. But we may at least use this time to strategize. If you will join me..."

Malini did not stay.

She went to walk through the gardens. Careful footsteps, passing priests at meditation, or painting lacquer upon leaves.

"Lata," said Malini, to her ever-present shadow. "Military history."

"My teacher was the one who knew her history best."

"If she were here, I'd gladly take her counsel. But you're her disciple. Tell me what you know."

"I know this, princess: You use any tools you have available to you. Take stock—what do you have?"

Malini looked around herself. The gardens. The unnatural trees; the leaves and fruit that would never rot that hung about them. A dark foreboding crept up her spine.

"I cannot use what I have."

"Why not?" Lata asked simply.

Because it's wrong. But no. That did not matter to her. Not truly.

Because it would be monstrous.

Even that. Even that did not matter as much as it should have.

"Because I may lose Aditya's followers. Or..." She paused. "Or I may gain him more," she murmured. "They think he does not have the capacity to be ruthless. They think..."

Lata's face was suddenly gray. She knew exactly what Malini intended to do. "I did not mean..."

"Did you not?" Malini did not smile at her. She did not feel joyful. "Thank you," she said instead.

"Don't thank me," Lata said. "Please."

Finally, thought Malini. *She understands the bitterness of knowledge.*

Malini found Aditya meditating in his room, cross-legged on the floor. She watched him for a long moment, waiting for him to notice her and raise his head. When he did not, she kneeled down beside him regardless.

"My brother," she said. She spoke in a low, gentle voice. The kind their mother had once used. "I need you to lead your men. We cannot remain here any longer."

There was a long moment where he said nothing.

"Did Rao send you?" he said finally.

"No." She did not need Rao to direct her on what was needful. Aditya should have known that.

"Strange. And yet you both want the same thing from me." There was a joyless smile on his mouth. "You want me to kill for the throne. Murder for it."

"You must kill for the throne," Malini said. She forced her voice to remain calm, kind. "That is what war is. And it isn't simply Rao and I who want you to take the throne. Aditya, you *know* this. You know all those men wait for you to guide them because Chandra must be stopped, and there is no one but you to do it. Why won't you act?"

Her brother's eyes were dark-ringed, but his expression underneath the hardness of his smile was determined.

"Come with me," he said. "I have something to show you."

He led her to a garden. Within it stood a basin of water upon a plinth. She followed him to it; placed her hands upon it, at his urging.

"You always want knowledge," he said. "Now you can receive it."

"I have plenty of books," said Malini, looking at her brother's face, and not at the water. "Or I did once. And now I have Lata to continue my education."

"You want to understand why I resist the path you think I must follow. To understand that, you must understand the knowledge the nameless granted me," said Aditya. He hesitated. Then spoke again. "Malini, in truth, I need you. I need your insight."

"You already have my guidance," she said. "You know exactly what I think is best."

"No," he said. "I need you to *see*. I need you to understand what holds me here, and why I cannot leave until I know what I must do. When you see, you will."

"I told Rao once long ago," said Malini. "I don't believe in fate."

"And yet there are forces greater than us," Aditya said. "Forces we cannot control, that carry us whether we will it or no. The greatest lesson the nameless has taught me is the strength it takes to recognize when there is no fight to be won, when there is no war of equals. Only the possibility of surrender."

Surrender. It was an ugly word, a burning word. She jerked her hands from the basin's edge.

"I don't accept that," Malini said sharply. "That isn't my way." She took a step back.

"Malini," said Aditya. "Please. If you don't look, you will never know why I struggle."

"Tell me, then," she said. "Tell me, so we may move beyond your struggle and return to the real world."

"You think I can reduce a vision of the nameless to words you'll understand?" He laughed, a tired laugh. "Malini, be reasonable."

She had been reasonable. She'd been more than reasonable. He had left his crown, his empire, for the sake of serving his new faith. And she had, very reasonably, begged him to return. Now she was here before him, with blood on the monastery's doorstep, reasonably asking him to act.

No more.

She couldn't look away from him, this brother she loved, who had rejected all the privileges life had given him, walking a path she could not understand. She let something rise inside herself then—something iron hard and angry.

"I am not asking for anything unreasonable," Malini retorted. "I never have. But if you will not explain yourself, let me explain something to you: You and Chandra both believe the right to rule is something that must be given to you, by the mothers of flame, by blood, by the nameless. I'm no such fool. I know there is no higher power that sanctions a king or emperor. There is only the moment when power is placed in your hands, and there is one truth: Either you take the power and wield it, or someone else will. And perhaps they will not be as kind to you and yours." She leaned forward. "You had your choice, Aditya. And when you relinquished power, Chandra turned on me and my women. Alori's death. Narina's death. Every single moment of suffering I have faced—they all lie on your shoulders. You *must* do better now."

He flinched. She forced more words from her throat, more poison and truth, pressing her advantage as his stubborn passivity began to crumble.

"If I had the ability, I would obliterate Chandra," she said slowly, deliberately. "I would cut off the trade routes that carry him rice and grain. I would burn his fields and destroy his mines. I would take every ally from him—by bribe or violence. And I would kill him. Slowly, and dishonorably. That is what I would do if I were lucky enough to be you, Aditya. To have your privileges. But I would never *be* you because I would never have rejected my birthright as you did."

"You, my own gentle flower of a sister, dreaming of war," he murmured. "I thought you of all people would understand my need to be free of such things. You were the most spiritual of the three of us as a girl. Do you remember that? No devotee of the nameless, certainly. But you used to make me take you to the mothers' shrine so you could lay jasmine blossoms and kiss their feet."

"That was before the first time Chandra hurt me," Malini said crisply. "That ended my childhood fancies abruptly."

He stared at her, uncomprehending. "When," he said, "did he hurt you, as a child?"

She sucked in a breath. He didn't remember.

She wanted to lift her hair and bare her neck. She wanted to show him how she had been hurt; to show him not simply the physical scar but the way Chandra's cruelties large and small had flayed her sense of self, until she was raw, a furious tangle of nerves, until she was forced to build herself armor, jagged and cruel, to be able to survive.

But he would not understand. He had never understood. Her hurts and her terrors, which had consumed her all her life, had always been small to him. He had either never truly seen them or simply, easily forgotten them.

So instead, she walked away from the plinth and touched her fingertips to one of the leaves in the garden. Rubbed her fingers back and forth over the surface, feeling the slick strangeness of it. Lac. Sweet lac.

"There are sewers beneath the gardens, are there not? To carry the waters away and feed the fruit orchard." She had seen the grates; heard the echo of them. "How deep are they? Large enough for men to walk through them?"

"I believe so," Aditya said, clearly perplexed by her change in conversation.

"Can they be used to leave the gardens discreetly?"

"Perhaps," Aditya said cautiously.

Malini thought of the oil that had been rubbed into Narina's hair, and Alori's, the day they burned. The wax stitched in small weights into their skirts.

She felt nauseous.

And exultant.

"I have a plan," said Malini. "To ensure that we survive, and are able to leave this place, and seek out your army—and we must hope, by the mothers, that they're still waiting for you."

She told him each detail, carefully delineated, deliberate. She watched the horror on his face grow.

"I won't do it," said Aditya. "I won't *allow* it."

"You will," said Malini. "You will. Or we will all die. Perhaps we could have fought them, but thanks to your unwillingness to act your numbers are depleted. This valley is a prison." The only stroke of luck was the narrowness of the entry to the monastery gardens. "Ask your nameless for guidance if you like, Aditya, but it's this plan that we will enact."

"And if I will not?" he said softly.

She could have threatened him. The lords were frightened and angry and restless, and she knew how to weave pretty words and wear a pretty face while doing it. It would take so little to turn them against him. Or she could have wept or pleaded with her brother, wearing her wounded heart on her skin.

But she was tired of all of it.

But she needed him, still.

"Look at the world, not at the water," said Malini. "Look at your sister. You know this is what must be done."

The lords were still bickering when she returned. She went to stand by Rao's side. Waited, until their noise lulled for a moment.

"My lords and princes," she said. "May I speak?"

They fell utterly silent.

"My brother Chandra always told me I did not obey the priests or the mothers as I should," said Malini. "He told me I should listen to the voice of the mothers in my heart. But when I listened, I heard nothing. And I knew he heard nothing, too."

Truth and lie. She wound them together, a weaving so fine that it had the look of one singular flesh. "Then he sought to burn me. And I finally heard the mothers. And I remembered one fact we have all forgotten, my lords."

She had them. Held them bound with her words, winding and winding.

"The first of the mothers, who founded our line and the empire, was a devotee of the nameless god, as the Alorans and Srugani are. In his faith and his nature, Aditya is closer to her than any scion of her line has ever been. He does not forget that Parijatdvipa is bound together for a reason. The mothers chose to ascend in fire to gain the power to protect their people. *Our* people, for we are one empire."

There was a noise from behind her. Malini did not turn as the men bowed; as Aditya approached, dressed in his soft priestly robes, his head held as high as an emperor's.

Aditya took a deep breath. Moved forward to stand before her.

"There is nothing to fear," he said, in that measured, resonant cadence of his, the one that had always quelled even the fiercest men to quiet. "My sister speaks true. I have never forgotten the bonds between us, my brothers. And I know how to ensure not only our survival, but our victory."

63

PRIYA

They traveled from Srugna back along the seeker's path. The people of the mahal and the rebels made uneasy company. The rebels kept trying to take the lead and the maidservants and men of the mahal looked like they were seriously considering gutting the lot of them in the dark of the night.

By necessity, they moved slowly. Bhumika could only travel in her palanquin. The rebels had also put together a makeshift palanquin for Ashok, a canvas held up by canes, more a hammock than anything else. Kritika walked beside him. Priya wondered how he fared. Could he still talk? Was he in pain?

She didn't approach him, though. She didn't know what to say to him. Once they were in Hiranaprastha, and he had passed through the deathless waters and was well again, they would talk.

She walked by Sima instead. At the moment, Sima held baby Padma in her arms, carefully bound to her chest with a sling made of ripped cloth, to allow Bhumika some time to sleep. Priya nudged close as they walked, peering down at Padma's scrunched face.

"She looks like an old lady, don't you think?" Priya observed.

"Babies always do, Pri. She'll get prettier." Sima looked down, and added dubiously, "Probably."

There was a noise ahead of them. One of the rebel men crumpled to the ground, and his fellows—their faces simultaneously horrified and resigned—hefted him to his feet. His face was wet with an outpouring of blood. He wasn't breathing.

That was another one lost, then.

"I don't know anything about politics, but I think people who kill innocents and burn a city should be killed themselves," Sima muttered.

"That's why we let Lady Bhumika do the politics," Priya replied.

"You seem to be going along with it happily enough," said Sima. And there was real accusation in her voice—and real hurt.

They'd not spoken of Priya's true nature since they'd first reunited in the forest. Then, relief had overwhelmed any hurt. But oh, the pain was there now, glinting in Sima's eyes.

Priya sighed. "It wasn't just my secret," she said. "What I am. And I...Sima. I didn't think I would ever be a temple child again. I thought I'd be a maidservant forever."

"Really?" Sima's voice was guarded.

"Really. I don't like any of this. The compromising with murderers, or the murders happening at all. The...all of this." She waved a hand at the crowd around them. "I wish things could be like they used to be."

"Do you really wish that?"

Did she? Priya let herself think of it, just for a moment. Did she want to be a maidservant again, drinking in the orchard, laughing and joking with Sima? Moving around Bhumika in guarded circles? Staring up at the Hirana and yearning for something she barely had—something lost and wanted—the possibility of *more* always beyond her, drawing her on like a song?

Did she wish she had never met Malini—never kissed her? Never left her behind?

"Of course," she lied. "Of course I do."

"Lady Bhumika," someone called out. It was Billu who'd spoken; who crouched now beside Bhumika's palanquin, as the two men holding it up lowered it to let her out. "One of our own is sick. The boy—he's getting worse."

Priya hurried forward. "What's the matter with Rukh? Billu, where is he?"

Bhumika looked up at her, dark circles shadowing her eyes. "I'll leave it to you, Priya?" she asked tiredly.

Priya gave her a nod. "Rest again if you can," Priya said, and left.

Billu took Priya to Rukh, who was curled up on his side against a tree. He was in obvious pain, hunched forward, clutching his arm against his chest.

"Hurts," he rasped, when Priya kneeled down to check on him. She took his hand away from his stomach. Shoots of wood had forced their way through his skin, from his fingers to his elbow. The flesh around them was mottled with blood, unnaturally pearly.

"Oh, Rukh," she said softly. Looking up at Billu, she said, "Does anyone have something for the pain?"

He shook his head. "The rebels have used up their own stock. We have nothing."

Priya lifted Rukh up. He gave a groan, and she bit her lip to stop herself swearing or crying or both.

"On my back," she said. "There you go."

She heard the crunch of the undergrowth, and Jeevan appeared.

"You need to be able to defend us," he said, looking between her and Billu and Rukh with narrow eyes. "Lady Bhumika cannot. You too, Billu."

"Oh, you don't need me," said Billu.

"You're strong," Jeevan said. "We don't know what we're going to come across."

"What do you expect us to do, then?" Priya snapped. "Leave him here?"

Rukh made a miserable sound, and Priya immediately felt like an awful human being. Billu gave her a helpless look.

"I'll do it." It was one of the rebels—a man called Ganam. "I can't fight," he added with a tight, wary smile of his own. "I could get sicker at any moment. But I'm healthier than most of those who drank the vial waters, and I could manage Ashok's weight. I can hold a child up."

Priya did not want to give him Rukh. But Jeevan was looking back at Bhumika's palanquin restlessly, and they couldn't afford to pause here for long.

"Fine," Priya said. "But—be gentle with him."

Ganam took Rukh from her arms. Rukh's eyes were squeezed shut, his breath short.

"He's not just one of yours," Ganam said, easily adjusting his weight. "He's ours too. Spied for us. Served our cause. Maybe freedom will mean being able to protect our children instead of using them," he added, brushing Rukh's leaf-strewn hair back from his forehead. "I'd like to believe that."

Priya looked at Rukh, pressing his head against Ganam's shoulder. At Ganam's guarded but tender expression. The crowd of people around them, and the anger in them, and the hunger too. For something better. For a future.

"I'd like that too," Priya said.

From across the path, Kritika was looking at her, a thoughtful expression on her face. She nodded to Priya. After a moment, Priya nodded in return.

They kept on walking.

64

BHUMIKA

Even with the use of a palanquin, she was exhausted by the time they reached the bower of bones. Labor had left her body changed and depleted, and the baby barely slept. Thank the spirits that she had Sima to give her advice on keeping the poor child alive.

This is no place for you, she thought, holding Padma close to her chest. They had made it to the bower of bones. There were fine, delicate profusions of bones upon the ground. Clinking in the leaves above them. *No place for any of us.*

As Khalida kept watch, she rested her back against a tree and fed Padma. She was so tired that she could have wept.

"Not long now," she whispered to Padma, who was now only quietly fretful. "Soon, we'll be home."

"The city isn't safe," Khalida reported, later. She and Jeevan had entered Hiranaprastha, returning to the edge of the forest, where the others waited, with what news they were able to gather. "People are protecting their own homes as best as they can, but guards and soldiers without masters are causing plenty of havoc. We could be in trouble if we enter the city as we are."

Bhumika nodded in acknowledgment, unsurprised. Her mind was overfull of possibilities and concerns—the likely distance of any imperial forces, sent to quell unrest or provide the regent aid; the quantity and strength of the soldiers she and the others would have to face; whether they would end up caught between multiple forces, in a melee of blood...

"We don't have to fight," Priya said suddenly. "There's a way to move through the city without upsetting anyone until we're ready and able to deal with them."

Priya's plan was neat and simple, and Bhumika couldn't keep an approving look from crossing her face.

"See," Priya said, with a smile. "I am clever. Shows you."

"I've never said that you're not clever."

"You call me a fool all the time."

Bhumika wrinkled her nose and looked away. *Sisters*.

"We're prepared," one rebel said, soon after. The vial-cursed stood in a circle around them. Ashok was lying near them, wrapped in a shawl, Padma fussing in her blanket next to him.

Priya met Bhumika's eyes. Bhumika nodded.

A slow, shared exhale of breath and the ground around them bloomed with sharp flowers, stormy purples and bitter yellows. The rebels breathed with them, sharing strength.

The flowers began to rise up the rebels' feet. Bhumika looked down and watched them curl around her own ankles. Moving across her like new flesh.

The city was broken: buildings burnt and smoldering, the few that stood shuttered and boarded. There were figures moving in the distance, groups of men with axes or maces, faces swathed in cloth. But they didn't approach the rebels or the people of the mahal.

Even from a distance, the leaves and flowers rising from their skin were visible. They looked like a huddle of rot sufferers, stumbling wide-eyed through a city that had no place for them. They were given a wide berth.

Bhumika held Padma—who was, blessedly, sleeping—against herself as they crossed Hiranaprastha, and gazed at the mahal. Its outer walls were shattered, where the rebels had broken the stone with vine, and shifted the foundations by moving soil and root with their vial-cursed strength. But as Bhumika looked, she saw a light flickering from deep within the mahal.

A woman on the walls, an arrow nocked upon her bow.

Bhumika shouldered to the front, head held high. When the woman on the walls saw her, she lowered her bow. Gave a shout. And with relief, Bhumika realized her people had held the rose palace after all.

"The thorns kept the worst out," the maidservant Gauri said gruffly. She walked with obvious pain, but there was a steel to her that told Bhumika she'd held her own well since Bhumika's departure. "Those are vicious, my lady. We were glad of them."

A handful of exhausted Parijati and Ahiranyi soldiers, the armed maids, the orphans—these were the people who had held the mahal since Bhumika's departure.

The servants looked uneasily at the rebels but said nothing. It was a relief, at least, that the rebels possessed the good sense not to wear their masks. But Bhumika had no desire to test her servants-turned-soldiers, or the fragile, uneasy truce that had grown between her retinue and Ashok's. It would not take much, she knew, to destroy it.

"Take her," she said, turning to Jeevan and handing him her sleeping daughter. "If I don't return, she'll need a wet nurse. Speak to the maids. They'll arrange it."

He stared at her, stricken.

"I must go to the Hirana," she said. "I must gain the strength we need to keep this country safe."

He looked as if he were struggling for words.

"Speak up," she said to him.

"She will have no one," he said finally. "My lady."

"If I die, then she's no one's child," Bhumika said. "And that would be fitting, I suppose. It was my fate once, and I refused it." But she touched her own face to Padma's regardless, and breathed her in, and kissed her forehead before straightening up.

Jeevan bowed his head to her. Said nothing more, as she left, his hands gently clasped around the small bundle.

Together, they began the walk to the Hirana. The rebels. Her siblings. Priya, expression determined. Ashok, half-conscious, blood trickling from his nose.

"Lean on me," said Priya.

Ashok shook his head, exhausted.

"I can carry you," said Priya, taking his arm.

65

RAO

If the rain came, the plan would fail.

As it was, the waters in the tunnel beneath the lacquer gardens were swollen, a reservoir that rose to the chests of the men who lowered themselves down first into the dark. For all that Malini was a tall woman, Rao feared she would not be able to stand in it.

But she lowered herself down anyway. It touched her chin.

The warriors who led the way held their wrapped weapons above them, covered in sacking to protect them from water damage. The water was fetid and stank, and Rao had to resist the urge to gag.

Be thankful, he told himself, *that it has not recently rained. Be thankful we're not drowning here.*

Be thankful there's a way out at all.

He steeled himself, moving forward in the dark.

They had left men and women in the lacquer gardens. They'd had to. "If there are soldiers coming here, they'll see clear as day if the place is empty," the Dwarali lord had said. "So I'll leave a boy or two, and I'll ask the rest of you fine men to do the same."

The other princes and lords had agreed, and done so. And Rao had not looked at Malini. He hadn't needed to. He knew how carefully she spun her webs. Her silence, when the men spoke, meant nothing at all.

The priests of the nameless had elected to remain. "This is our place, and the site of our service and duty," one man had said, tranquil as he kneeled in a copse of lacquer trees, beneath the pearly sheen of their leaves and the slick, shimmering oil of their bark. "The nameless will decide what becomes of us."

"Likely nothing will come of this," Mahesh, a Parijati lord who'd been thoroughly loyal to Aditya from the start, had responded gruffly. "But we thank you for your bravery."

"It isn't bravery," Aditya had murmured to Rao later, as the men packed their gear and their weapons—as Malini watched from beneath the shade of the monastery's veranda, her pallu drawn over her face. "It's merely our calling. Acceptance of the winds of fate."

"I think acceptance of your fate can be brave," Rao had said in response, thinking of Alori. "To face your death calmly . . . it can be brave."

Aditya must have thought of her then, too. He looked suddenly stricken.

"Rao, I didn't mean—"

"It's nothing," Rao had cut in. And it was nothing. It had to be nothing. But he could not have borne Aditya's apologies. "We'd best prepare to go."

Now they moved farther and farther through the tunnels of water, great stone-lined hollows, with the darkness growing steadily thicker, closing in upon them. No lanterns. No fire. There could not be fire here. Not yet, and hopefully not ever. He looked back once more at Malini. She was almost invisible, but he could see her eyes, the whites of them a gleam against water.

"Prince Rao," one of Prem's men said in a low voice. "We're nearing the end."

A grate above them. Thin segments of moonlight. Three men reached up to heave the thing aside. Rao only had a moment to fear ambush—a canny strategist with a mere handful of men could pick them off one by one here—but they managed to worm their way through the grate without issue. When Malini was dragged out of the water, Aditya immediately wrapped her in the sacking that had been removed from one of the weapons. Malini whispered her thanks, clinching the wrapping around her as if it were the finest Dwarali shawl.

They moved quietly into the cover of trees—fresh, unlacquered, sweet with the scent of sap and soil. No lights between them, as bows were strung, their weight tested. Behind the cover of trees lay the great reservoir dam of Srugna, held back by a cunning artifice of stone the likes of which Rao had never seen before. He would have liked to admire it, to study it, once. Not today.

Malini came to stand near him. She was shivering faintly, but her eyes were sharp, fixed on the monastery below them.

"All's quiet," said Malini.

"Did your Dwarali lord tell you so?"

"Lord Khalil did, yes," said Malini. "And he is not mine, Rao. Don't be petty. His first loyalty is to his emperor."

"His first loyalty is to Dwarali's interests."

"Lucky, then, that Aditya's interests and Dwarali's align." Her voice, her expression, were impassive. "I have the impression you're angry at me, Rao."

He was silent for a moment. Then he said, "This plan."

"Yes?"

"It's foolish. I don't know how you convinced Aditya to support it, but I fear it."

Malini did not even pretend it had not been her plan. "I didn't convince him of anything. I merely made a suggestion. And Emperor Aditya gave it due consideration."

"Due consideration," Rao repeated. "What did you say to him?"

"The truth," Malini said simply.

"This plan is..." He hesitated.

"Say it, Rao."

"Cold," he said. "Cruel. Unlike you."

"You sound a little like Aditya did," she said, after a pause that stretched the air between them thin. "But I suppose you've long been friends for a reason. You both have a weakness in you that I don't understand."

"Morality isn't weakness."

"It is if it will see us all dead. Rao, we have men, but only so many men, and so many weapons," said Malini. "The monastery is in a valley. Vulnerable, for all that it has only one known entrance. All that, you know. If we remained there, we would be rounded up with ease. Or slaughtered. Perhaps they would burn us. It would be so easy." Her voice shifted, like fingers upon a sitar's strings, from softness to thrumming savagery. "And I will not burn, Rao."

"Malini."

"What? What will you have of me? If Lord Khalil or Mahesh or Narayan had come up with the idea, you would not react so. If Aditya had done it, you would have obeyed with a heavy heart, but you would not have talked to him as you do to me. Why is that?"

"You believe I think less of you than I do of these men," Rao said, incredulous.

She gave him a look that held nothing in it. Not even judgment. "I don't know what you see when you look at me. But if you think it is too cold for me, or too cruel..." She shrugged. "I have never lied to you, Rao. If you don't know me, if you fail to understand what I want to achieve, you alone are responsible for that."

Rao held his tongue at that.

Perhaps this was the moment. Perhaps it was time for him to tell her the truth. The secret of his name, wrapped like a dark gift, waiting to be spoken. He had always believed he would know when the time was right—had always been told he would know when the name needed to be uttered. But he didn't feel that weight of rightness in his bones now. Only the creeping damp of his stinking wet clothes, and the eerie stillness of the air, as warriors crouched around him in the darkness.

He almost said it anyway. Almost turned to Malini, shaping his mouth around the words. *My name, the name the priests whispered in my ear at birth. Malini, my name is—*

"They're here." A murmur, passed from warrior to warrior, reached the place where Malini and Rao stood. Rao's body went numb.

Below them, snaking through the one pass that allowed direct entry into the lacquer gardens, was a procession of warriors. Not Chandra's full forces by any means, no, but Parijati royal warriors all the same. They were moving silently, swiftly, but Rao recognized them regardless. There was something about the way they moved. And of course, those weapons, great gleaming sabers, the glint of a sharp-edged discus at another man's belt.

A retinue sent to kill a man in his bed. They did not know, he suspected, that Aditya had any followers congregating in his service. If they had, they would not have come in such small numbers. They would have brought greater weapons of war.

Nonetheless, if Aditya's followers had not left the lacquer gardens as the scout had warned them to; if they had remained and followed the way of the priesthood, allowing the tide of fate to wash over them...

Rao looked at Malini. She did not look back.

Kneeling at their feet, the warrior who'd spoken was making slow, deliberate motions: reaching for his flint, for the arrow, for the basic preparation of oil and ghee that had been hastily bottled before their descent. The others were doing the same. In the tense silence, Aditya made his way free from the crowd. He had a bow in his hands, and a quiver of arrows at his back.

It was a relief to see him stand forward so, with his shoulders straight and his head raised, his eyes narrowed as he stared through the night gloom at the monastery below them.

He held his hand up, making an unmistakable gesture. *Hold fast.*

They waited. Below there were cries, and the clash of swords. As planned, the few soldiers who remained below turned on Chandra's men. It was a lure. Let the warriors of Parijat think they had come upon the monastery unaware. Let them think they would overcome Aditya, and send him to his slaughter.

Let them flood deeper into the lacquer gardens.

Aditya's hand remained up. *Hold fast*. And Rao, who held no bow, held nothing fast but his breath inside his throat. Even his heart was frozen inside him, waiting for the inevitable cue.

Light the arrows. Set the monastery ablaze. Ensure that all of Chandra's men—and all the poor, priestly sacrifices who'd remained behind—burned.

Hold fast.

He waited. Aditya did not lower his hand.

There was a rustle of unease. The noise below was growing fiercer.

Any moment, they were going to be spotted. The Parijati warriors would see them and turn their weapons upward, catching their men with arrows through the throat, the belly. The Parijati had the disadvantage, low in the valley as they were, but Rao still came out in a cold sweat at the thought.

One of the lords muttered an oath, moving as if to lower Aditya's hand for him, to make the motion that commanded death—but Aditya said, in a voice like the coldest rain, "Would you burn priests? Hold, brother."

The lord flinched. Stopped.

Aditya was imposing, in profile. Gaze like ice, his jaw a sharp line, austere and remote. He looked more like himself—like the Aditya Rao had grown up alongside, a prince of Parijat, a man who had never been anything but unfailingly honest, a scrupulous follower of honor and the noble code—than he had since the night he had heard the nameless speak.

Rao knew Aditya, *this* Aditya, well enough to know what would come next. They were well placed here, to race down the valley, to slaughter warriors aplenty. It would be a purer path than the one planned. It would result in the deaths of many of their own men whom they could ill afford to lose. And yet the thought of it was a relief. It was a noble kind of war, and Aditya was a noble kind of emperor-in-waiting.

Rao was already reaching for his sword when Malini stepped forward. She had dropped the sacking and stood in nothing but her damp sari, her braid a black snake coiled at her throat. She strode forward as ugly cries intensified below them—the bellows of men murdering and men dying. Aditya went utterly still. Whatever he saw in his sister's face held him fast.

"No man wants to kill his kin," Malini said gently. "I understand that."

She took Aditya's bow from him. It was overlarge for her, but she held it steady.

"The priests of the nameless believe in fate," she said, in clear common Zaban—loud enough for their men to hear her. Loud enough, Rao feared, for the men below to hear her too. But she did not flinch, and she did not protect herself. She stood tall. "The priests of the nameless built their garden of lac and resin. They knew this day would come to pass. Is that not so, Prince Rao? Do your priests know the path of fate?"

"They do," he heard himself say, and knew he had condemned them.

"You will, perhaps, not wish to listen to the entreaties of a mere woman," she said, in a voice that was even and calm and had no humility in it at all. "But I am a daughter of Parijatdvipa's oldest line. A princess of Parijat. I am descended from the first mother of flame. My brother, the false emperor, tried to burn me alive, but I lived. I know the judgment of fire, and the price it demands. And here, in this dark, I hear the mothers. And I know it is my duty to ensure that fate is done." She sucked in a deep breath, as if fortifying herself, as if she carried a burden of unfathomable weight—and turned and looked at the kneeling warrior, who stared up at her, silent and rapt. "Light my arrow," she said.

He dipped an arrow in ghee. Held up his flint. Lit a spark.

The priests of the nameless built their garden of lac and resin. They knew this day would come to pass.

Rao watched the burning point of flame as Malini raised and nocked the arrow with a face like stone. He thought of the priests who'd remained behind and their own calm eyes. He thought of the way fate moved like a winding noose, a thing of silk, waiting until the time came to tighten its grip.

They knew this day would come to pass. It felt right. Ah, damn her, it felt true.

Behind her—around her—a dozen new points of flame appeared. A dozen more. Arrows were drawn. Spears held high.

Malini released her arrow, and the fire followed the arc of her loosed flame.

For a moment there was nothing more than the tips of those burning arrows in the dark, small motes lighting like falling stars.

And then the lacquer garden began to burn.

Through the crackle of the flames, Rao heard screams. Malini stood, for a brief moment, limned in light, the bow still in her hands. The smoke rose up behind her, a great cloud of it, curling gray into the night, its edges faded gold. He swallowed, staring at her and staring at her, until the smoke and the fire made his eyes tear and burn. Such was the way of fate.

He should have known this day would come to pass, too.

66

PRIYA

It was no burden to carry Ashok's weight, even though he seemed convinced that it was. She could feel the fragility of his body: the in and out of his breath rattling his ribs, the wetness in his lungs.

"You'll fall under my weight," Ashok said to Priya, his voice uneven. There was blood on his lips, falling like tears from his eyes.

"Don't lean on me entirely, and we'll be fine, then," she said.

They walked forward in silence for a moment. Then he said, "Kritika carries a crown mask with her. When we're thrice-born—one of us should wear it."

"We don't need crowns or masks," said Bhumika tiredly.

"But we do need power," Ashok responded. Doubled over with coughing. Bhumika looked away from them, her face a mask of its own kind, and kept on walking. But Priya stopped, allowing him to breathe, still holding him up.

He was going to be fine, she reminded herself. Once they had passed through the deathless waters, his strength would return to him.

"Priya," he said, after a moment. "Priya. You—you need to know."

"What?"

"I killed Chandni. Or as good as killed her. I left her tied to the rot-riven tree. And Sendhil." A heaved breath. "The elders are all gone. We're all that remains."

Dead. Chandni dead.

The words rung in Priya's head like a bell. *I killed her. I left her tied to the rot-riven tree. I killed her.*

She couldn't speak for a long moment. Then she forced her tongue, her lips to move, even though they felt leaden.

"Why are you telling me this? Do you want me to be happy about it?"

"I just wanted you to know," Ashok murmured.

"By soil and sky, *why*?"

"It's your right to know," he said. "Consider it my deathbed confession."

He did not sound guilty. She wasn't sure if she wanted him to. She only knew that the knowledge felt like a blow to the skull; it rang in her ears still. She couldn't think around it, and yet she tried. What was the last thing she had said to Chandni? How had Chandni looked at Priya when Priya had left her? She couldn't recall it. She hadn't thought she would want to.

"She was an old woman who was dying anyway. And you're not afraid of killing. I should have expected it. And I shouldn't care." Priya's throat felt thick. It was hard to force the words out. "And I wish I could say that I don't know why you're like this— why you always gut the heart out of me, over and over—but I know why. I lived through our childhood too." She looked away from him. "We're here."

They stood at the base of the Hirana.

Bhumika gave Priya a level look, and Priya shook her head. "We don't need to climb," Priya said swiftly. "The Hirana knows me. And I know it. It will let us in."

Bhumika didn't argue when Priya passed the weight of Ashok over. He rested on Bhumika's shoulder as Priya pressed a hand to the Hirana's deep gray stone, awash with mosaics of moss. The Hirana felt her. Welcomed her.

The way opened.

It was a tunnel. Lightless, dark, but a way through all the same. "All of you," said Priya. "Follow me."

They walked together into the darkness. Priya could smell the deathless waters growing closer, fresh and sharp as a cold night. The liquid cosmos of them, almost within their reach.

And then, quite suddenly, there they were.

The deathless waters lay before them, incandescent blue in the darkness of the hollow temple. Priya took Ashok from Bhumika's grip; guided Ashok to the edge and released him. He kneeled down by the water, palms flat to the ground. He breathed, long ragged breaths, heavy with blood, and touched his forehead to the soil.

Next to Priya, Bhumika was staring at the pool, her hands in fists at her sides. The rebels milled behind them, terror and wonder on their faces.

"Should we be saying some special words?" Priya muttered to Bhumika. "To make them feel better?"

Bhumika sighed, tipping her head back as if to say, *Spirits save me*, then said, "Or we can enter the water and be done with this."

But some of the tension had unfurled from her hands. When Priya reached for her, Bhumika laced their fingers together. Squeezed, once.

"Come forward," gasped Ashok, and the other vial-poisoned rebels stepped forward, standing at the edge of the water. "We enter the water," he said. "If we're lucky, we emerge. And then we protect Ahiranya. We do our duty."

There was a murmur of agreement. Ashok looked up at Priya. His eyes were wet.

Priya looked at him in return and chose not to think of all he had done. She thought instead of the fact that she and Ashok and Bhumika were the last survivors of their family, a family not of blood but of history and suffering, love and the kind of hurt that only love can breed.

She held her hand out to him. He took it and stood with care. She looked at the water ahead of her. Forced herself not to think of anything, not to hope for anything, as she clutched her siblings' hands tightly, and entered.

And sank.

Falling and rising are alike, in water, when you're deep enough, and the deathless waters were a thing without ending. They were a cold, brilliant blue—the blue of the universe. The blue of stars enfolded in skeins of sky that contained all things. Priya was deep within them, eyes open, lungs burning. She wondered if she would drown.

She could not remember this. Had this happened the last time she entered? Had it happened the first? She kicked her feet and did not know if she was rising to the surface or dragging herself deeper.

She raised her arms in front of her. In the wavering water, to her panicked eyes, her skin was like shadow—the shade thrown between great trees, deep darkness blurred to the charcoal of light beneath dappled leaves.

She couldn't breathe. She kept kicking, kept struggling to rise when she didn't know what rising was. But eventually she could hold out no longer. She opened her mouth, and sucked in a burning breath, and drank in the waters. Drank, and was consumed.

She lifted her head, gasping for air. It took her a moment to realize her lungs were not burning. The water around her was dark, but within it floated the roots of lotus flowers, swirling and twining. Within them were bodies.

And there, before her once more, was the yaksa.

It did not wear her face this time.

"Ah, sapling." It sounded fond. "You like this face better. I knew you would."

"You're not her," whispered Priya. "Please. Don't be her. That isn't what I want."

The yaksa shook its head. Malini's dark curls floated loose around its face, with its elegant bones and fathomless eyes.

"But you do," the yaksa said. It touched her cheek once more. Drew its fingers back, and wound about the tip Priya saw a thread or a root—a thing of blood and green twined. "I know you. We're bound, you and I. So I know."

"Please," Priya said again.

The yaksa shook its head once more, and Malini's curls blurred into a halo, and the yaksa...changed.

Deep marigold eyes. Hair of coiling vines. Rose-red mouth. A smile that was all thorns, sharp as points of light.

It was both beautiful and like a woman deep in the throes of rot. Its head was tilted, gold-petaled eyes fixed upon her chest.

"What is worship?" the yaksa asked.

She knew this.

"Hollowing," she said. "It is..." And she trailed off, looking down at where the yaksa gazed. Her shadowy chest was a cavity, a blown-open wound. The wound was covered in a profusion of petals; the bones were angular striations of wood, the blood a clean and sweet sap of leaf. Within it lay a pulsing heart of... flowers.

She looked at what had been her heart. Thought of Ashok's words, when he had called the yaksa a cuckoo in the body. She remembered the tree behind Chandni's hermitage.

The yaksa raised a hand. Neatly, it snapped a finger free and breathed upon it. The finger was wood, and it curved and sharpened, neatly carved by the yaksa's breath. Even before the yaksa held the knife out to her, Priya knew it was sacred wood, a thing born from the sacrifice of a yaksa's flesh and blood. And she knew—with a horror and hunger that shook her—what she was expected to do.

"Hollow yourself," the yaksa said.

"I can't," she said. "How can I?"

"Every time you come here, you do this," it said, in a voice both gentle and unutterably cruel. "Every time, the water fills you from head to toe, and you ask yourself the question: Shall I allow the water to obliterate and remake me, or shall I hold all my mortal flesh tight? Shall I keep this soul contained, in the vial of my flesh, this poisonous body bound to death, or become one with the waters of the universe?"

Was this why the others had died? Because they'd been unwilling to make the sacrifice—to be less or more than human?

She'd fought to be here, over and over, and now she was. And yet her shadow of a hand trembled, as she reached for the knife. As she placed her fingertips upon it, they burned.

"This is the only way I can be strong enough to save Ahiranya," she whispered. "This is the only way I can save my family."

The yaksa said nothing.

Priya took the blade. Held it against her own skin of shadow, her skin of soul. And cut a place for the magic.

There was no pain. Only a feeling like air leaving her lungs, like water rushing in, and then fire, and then a clear light, green and pure.

In her throat, something caught. Something of the mortal soul. Something of lifeblood.

The flower she'd given Malini. A needle-flower.

She'd placed a bit of her heart inside that.

"I can't give you everything," she gasped out around the drawing wound of it. "I don't have it any longer."

"No matter," the yaksa said gently. "No matter, sapling. We have enough."

She thought of heart's blood, of love and fury and the sweet place in between, where thoughts of Malini dwelled. And the bloom—the sapling—that was her own magic grew and grew, until she knew she was not exactly Priya anymore. Perhaps she never had been. Perhaps from the moment she'd arrived on the Hirana as an infant, the deathless waters had been remolding her from within, making her a vessel for their magic and their voices, discarding all the parts of her that made her a mortal woman with a simple mortal heart.

"This too," she heard the yaksa say, "can be hollowed away in time."

And then Priya was in the water once more, cold and brilliant and blue, and she was kicking her feet. She knew the way now. She was remade and whole, and she knew how to rise.

She rose, heaving for breath, coughing water from her lungs even as she struggled to stay on the surface, legs kicking through heavy nothing. She swam to the shore and dragged herself up, up.

Bhumika was already there, her hair sodden, her face mottled with cold and relief.

"Yaksa," Priya gasped out, and Bhumika turned her head with firm hands. Another rebel—a fellow temple child, now—thumped her back hard once, twice, and then Priya was vomiting water on the stone, no more words spoken.

She couldn't remember what she intended to say. But her cheek burned with a cool fire and she could not forget the feeling of roots and flowers rising up where her heart should have been, unfurling their way to her soul. A hollowing.

But it had felt right. It had felt glorious. And she had learned something, in that moment of change; something about what it meant to be a temple elder. Something about what it meant to serve the yaksa.

Something that was already fading.

She clung to it tight, and felt a pain, sharp, in her cheek where the yaksa had drawn its nail across her flesh. The pain held fragments of the memory down, like a stitch through cloth.

"I thought you wouldn't rise," Bhumika said through chattering teeth. "Priya, you took so long. So…" And then to Priya's shock, Bhumika was embracing her, breathing hard, unsteady breaths against Priya's wet hair. Priya clung back reflexively.

"Ashok," she whispered. "Where is Ashok?"

Bhumika said nothing. One of the rebels was wailing, a low keening cry.

"You can't go back in, Priya," Bhumika said finally. "You can't."

Priya shook her off. Turned, back toward the water, still on her knees. And Bhumika was tackling her to the ground, but Priya was stronger, she could throw Bhumika off without even trying—

"Stop," said Bhumika. "Stop, stop, please stop. Pri. Priya." She pressed her cheek to Priya's own. Her skin was wet, with water and tears. "He's gone, Priya."

"No. No, he's not."

"He's gone," Bhumika said again, and Priya knew she was right. She could feel the absence of him. The silence in the sangam. "He's gone."

67

MALINI

The fires didn't gutter until late morning.

When they finally died, the warriors made their way down to the remains of the monastery.

"You shouldn't come, princess," one warrior said. He had the length of his own shawl knotted around his face, leaving nothing but his eyes and the furrow of his brow visible. "The air is poisonous."

She knew that. She could smell it, feel it, even from here.

"I must," she said, and wrapped the long edge of her own sari around her mouth. The cloth was still faintly damp from the waters beneath the gardens—a green, ugly dampness. "But I will accept you as my guard, if you will accompany me."

There were no priests or Parijati soldiers left alive. A few royal warriors had run for their lives, when the flames had begun. Many had been burned too badly to make it far, and Aditya's men had found what remained of them at the edge of what remained of the bridge.

Some of the lords were already beginning to work out how a makeshift bridge would be built. There was precious little left in the lacquer gardens of use, but at least a handful of their own men were from Dwarali and knew how to climb perilous rock faces. Three offered to make the way down, with only rope to hold them steady, and seek a safe route or supplies.

As they discussed what options were available to them, Malini kneeled down upon the charred ground. The sun was warm upon her back. Over the grate that led to the water were panels of thick wood, nailed in place. They were scorched or burned beyond recognition, but Malini could see marks upon them, like those made by scrabbling animals upon the trunks of trees.

Nail marks. Someone had clawed at the cover of the entrances to the water. Someone had fought to survive. But Aditya's men had sealed the exits carefully. The bridge had burned. They had died in terror and in pain.

She looked and felt... nothing. The nothing was so solid, so complete, that she knew it wasn't true emptiness or true neutrality. It was a feeling like a fist around a throat.

"Princess," the warrior said again. He sounded anxious. "Please."

She took his offer of a hand and walked away from the dead.

And that night, after the Dwarali soldiers had long since departed, she dreamt. Narina and Alori sat at the end of her bed, their hands clasped, their hair haloed with crowns of silent flame.

"You are not real," she told them. "I am done with the needle-flower."

"But it isn't done with you," Narina said pityingly. "I am sorry for it, Malini. But here we are."

"Malini," Alori said. "Malini. What do you think your name would be, if you'd been born like me, a royal of the nameless faith? What do you think the priest would have whispered in your ear?"

Fate had not named her. But the choices men had made, and the choices she had made—when her brother had pressed a knife to her neck, when her brother had tried to see her burn—had shaped her and given her a purpose.

"I don't think of it," she said. "I don't believe in it."

"And yet the nameless thinks of you," said Narina. "The spirits think of you. The mothers think of you."

"I do not believe in the mothers any longer," whispered Malini.

"I do not believe that what Chandra did made anything more of you."

"The universe is vaster and stranger than you know," Alori said sorrowfully. "But, Malini..."

Her voice faded. Odd. She had not thought a vision could weep.

"When you murder your brothers, remember that we loved you once, heart sister," Narina finished. "Remember that we love you still, no matter what you become."

Malini closed her eyes, which burned with tears. She closed her eyes against the vision of them, and the grief. When she opened them, Narina and Alori were gone.

At dawn, one of the Dwarali soldiers returned. He came with more rope and a plan to make their laborious way down the cliff face, with the security of rope and a winch to guide them all down.

Malini thought of her treacherous descent of the Hirana and nearly laughed. Oh, if only Priya were here.

"Can you do this?" Rao asked.

"I can do whatever is needful," she said.

They made their way down, Malini seated upon a sling of rope. She held it tightly and gazed at the drop beneath her—a great endless sweep of air, ending in jagged rocks. When she found her feet once more on steady ground, she did her best to hide her relief.

They began their journey. There could be no more dallying. They would need to meet their strongest forces, waiting upon the road to Dwarali, and pray that Chandra's men had not come across them yet. They would follow the coast as much as possible. The lands there were beyond Parijatdvipa's borders, and accordingly likely to be safer from Chandra's spies or soldiers. Khalil relayed all of this, as Rao stood stiff and grief-stricken at Malini's side, as Lata held her arm—as Aditya stood at the head of them all, quiet as a ghost.

"It will be a long journey," the Dwarali lord said gruffly. "But we'll rig a chariot for you, princess. Something suitable."

"Dwarali women ride, don't they?"

"We all ride," he told her. "Man, woman, or any soul between."

"It is a shame I do not have their skill," she said. "This skill your Dwarali women possess."

"Skills are learned, princess," he said. "I think you will gain them swiftly enough."

He spoke with a respect that verged on reverence. Malini simply nodded, eyes fixed on the distance, and kept on walking.

They had been traveling for days. Days. They were nowhere of consequence, a dirt track, surrounded by dust burnished bronze in the light of the setting sun, when Rao turned.

Lata's grip tightened upon her arm. "Prince," Lata said, voice firm. "Is it time?"

Rao's expression—she had never seen the like of it. He looked determined and terrified all at once, staring at her, through her, his eyes blazing.

"It is time," he said.

Lata exhaled. Her grip on Malini's arm released. She stepped back, leaving Malini alone.

Rao took a step closer to Malini.

"Rao," she said, suddenly frightened. "What is it?"

"You may mock our fates," said Rao, "but you understand. We'd run from them if we could. To know your greatest purpose in life, or your inevitable end—it's a terrible burden.

"I didn't envy my sister her name," Rao went on. "Not once I knew it. But even then, I believed my fate would be easier to bear. Now, I'm not so sure."

Rao kneeled down before her. He did not kneel like a man overcome by grief, or as men in tales kneel before women they loved. He did not even kneel as he had when his sister had burned upon the pyre, with his face blank and his hands in fists, too devastated to move or breathe.

He kneeled and lowered his head. Touched his fingertips to the ground before her feet.

He kneeled as a man kneels before a king. An emperor.

"It's time," he said, in a clear voice, to Malini and all the assembled highborn of Parijatdvipa, "to tell you my name."

68

BHUMIKA

They didn't call it a coronation, but that was exactly what it was.

There was a throne room for the regent, half-burned and ransacked, in the mahal. Soon, they would have to make use of it. But they were Ahiranyi. So they went first to the triveni. To its plinth. There were only two of them there, thrice-born upon the Hirana. But behind them were the new once-borns who had been rebels and had been Ashok's. At their back rose the servants of the mahal. This was a portentous day, and everyone wanted to be present.

Some of the servants had asked to follow their footsteps. To enter the waters, now that they had seen the change it had wrought in the surviving rebels, in Bhumika and Priya. But Bhumika had refused.

"Not yet," she said. "The waters demand a price. Let the ones of us who must go survive it first and learn its strength. And then we'll see."

They had waited a single night. Waited, and no one had sickened and died. Maybe fever would come for them and kill them. But Bhumika had hope.

She carried Padma against her chest, bound to her in a sling of cloth. One of the men had tried to argue with her, saying the Hirana was no place for a child. But Bhumika had raised an eyebrow and said, "Is there anywhere safer in Ahiranya than at the side of a thrice-born?" And he had fallen silent.

Priya's face was drawn, her eyes red. She had not mentioned Ashok since his death in the waters, but Bhumika knew she thought of him constantly.

"Come," said Bhumika. Held out a hand. "We go together."

Priya took it.

Once, long ago, a new elder would be initiated in fine clothes—robes of silk, their hair a loose river perfumed with oil, jewels and gold upon their throats and wrists. There would have been hymns sung, and offerings made to the yaksa. Pilgrims, risen to the Hirana, would have been given flowers and fruit and vials of deathless water, bound with ribbons of silver.

This rising was performed with ramshackle reverence.

They crossed the triveni.

Bhumika rose, with due gravity, to the zenith of the plinth. Priya rose with her. They stood, the two of them, beneath an opening that let in the sky, and looked at one another.

Kritika crossed the room. Bowed her head.

"Elders," she said. "It's time."

In her hands, on a bed of cloth, lay a crown mask.

Priya reached down. Touched it, bare-fingered.

"It doesn't burn," she murmured.

Good, thought Bhumika, with some relief, as Priya lifted the crown mask and held it. She met Bhumika's eyes.

They had spoken of this before rising. Spoken of how the elders had always been led by one of their own—the strongest, the wisest, the oldest of them. They were only two now. Only two.

But Bhumika would not underestimate herself again.

She gave Priya a nod. Drew the sling, gently, to shroud Padma's face, as Priya nodded in return, a slight twist of grief to her lips.

"You were always meant to rule," Priya said. And she placed the mask upon Bhumika's face.

It should have burned her. Should have shorn away her skin. But she was thrice-born, blessed soul-deep with the power of the waters, and she felt the strength of it fill her like a glowing light—bright and powerful and beautiful.

They held hands with one another. And in that moment, they were in the sangam and on the triveni at the same time. Bhumika could feel all Ahiranya gleaming inside her, every river and pool of water, every root of every tree. She could see Priya in the sangam, a thing not of shadow now, but of bark and leaf and winding flowers, dark as night.

"Ready?" Bhumika asked. Her voice was a rasp.

"Yes." Priya's voice was full of determination—and wonder. "I am."

They breathed in. Out.

And felt everything.

They felt Ahiranya, from end to end. They felt the forest, the branches of those great trees, the green sentience of the soil, the power of venomous crop, of leaf, of vine.

They reached farther than they ever had, and knew that if any army invaded Ahiranya they could splinter it upon their thorns.

Their hands separated, but the knowledge and the power remained between them still, in the waters that fed both of their strengths.

"Bhumika, Elder of Ahiranya," said a voice. Another. A song of voices. An exultation.

"Priya, Elder of Ahiranya."

"Elders. Elders of Ahiranya!"

Bhumika removed the crown mask from her face and realized she was weeping. And smiling. And that Priya's face was a reflection of her own.

69

MALINI

The true name of an Aloran prince was no small thing. She did not think any highborn present failed to understand the importance of what was happening before them. Even the soldiers had fallen deathly silent.

"What," she said, "has your name to do with me?"

He released a breath, as if she had struck him.

"Everything, Princess Malini," he said. "Everything."

He stared at the ground. Closed his eyes in pain and reverence, and when he spoke, it was in Aloran. Ancient, archaic Aloran, a melodic language that even Malini had never learned. But Aditya knew it, and she judged the weight of the prophecy by the way her brother's face paled, and his eyes closed, and his head tipped back to the bleeding dusk.

"When she is crowned in jasmine, in needle-flower, in smoke and in fire, he will kneel before her and name her," repeated Rao, in common Zaban. And suddenly Malini was shivering, every inch of her afire with a mad elation that rose up, up in her blood. "He will give the princess of Parijat her fate: He will say..." He swallowed. Raised his eyes, which were fierce and wet. "Name who shall sit upon the throne, princess. Name the flower of empire. Name the head that shall reign beneath a crown of poison. Name the hand that lit the pyre." The silence was deep; a drumming tense silence, drawn taught as a bowstring. "He will name her thus," finished Rao. "And she will know."

Malini could not feel her feet beneath her. It was as if she were floating in her own skin, on a wave of something that wasn't quite fear or quite joy but burned in her, headier than liquor, more potent than needle-flower.

"I lit the pyre," Malini said jerkily. "I lit the monastery. It was me."

She saw in his face then, that he had realized the same thing.

"Yes," he said.

The moment was on a knife edge. How easily it could turn.

Malini looked once more at Aditya.

Aditya, who had rejected the throne over and over again. She had given him the tools to become emperor and he had discarded or lowered them, over and over again. She had told him the way power worked, and the price it demanded. He had not given power its due. When power had come, he had turned away from it.

But she had taken the arrow. She had set the monastery aflame.

And here—here was her chance to take power for herself. A terrible chance. If she took the crown Rao had placed in her hands, if she turned the noose of his words into a weapon...

It would be foolish to try to take what was not hers to take. Royal sons were the ones who wore the crown. Royal women were...

Well.

She thought of her fellow princess Alori, and of highborn Narina, and how they had screamed when the flames had touched them. How they had smelled as they burned, as their crowns of stars splintered around their skulls, as even the sweetness of perfume and flowers could not blot out the acrid scent of burnt hair and silk, or the smell of flesh, fat, marrow burning and burning and burning.

Royal women are only crowned in death, Malini thought furiously.

She did not want to die. She wanted her crown *now*. She had politicked for it; played for it and lost for it and nearly died for it. And yet here she was. Alive.

And here was Rao, an unnamed prince of Alor, his birth name a prophecy whispered in his mother's ear. Here was the prince who had given her a crown and a throne and told her she had the right to grant them where she would.

Here he was. Kneeling before her.

It could not be done. She knew it could not be done. Her whole life, she had been told it could not.

But she had seen the look of hope and loyalty in the eyes of the men when she'd ordered them to battle. She had seen the way their faces changed when she had told them she was a mother of flame made flesh—a lie like a lever, a chain for their throat, a hand curled around the sinew and thick blood of their beating hearts.

She had Alor. She had a pact with the usurpers of Ahiranya. She had herself.

Fate was closing around her. False, false fate. And yet she gloried in it, because this—this was an opportunity to be seized. And Malini was not fool enough to let it slip by.

The men were watching her. Her Aloran prince. Lords of Saketa and Dwarali, Srugna and Parijat.

Her brother, grief in his eyes.

She waited for him to speak. She gave him one heartbeat, and another, and watched him lower his eyes without a word.

"It would be a great sacrifice on my part, to rule this land," Malini said, slow and solemn, as if her heart were not a burning coal, a thing of joy and rage. "I am only a woman, with brothers still living. If I am to rule...my lords, I must rule in the name of the mothers. I must rule as a mother of Parijatdvipa.

"I have not burned, as the mothers burned," she continued. "I know it isn't their will. But I burned my goodness upon the monastery's flames. I burned my gentleness. I made a fitting empress of myself. My lords, if it is the will of the mothers and the nameless both, then I will take the throne of Parijatdvipa for the good of all of us. I will do it, as the prophecy demands."

Silence. And then, a roar. An exultation.

Rao, shoulders trembling, did not rise.

"My empress," he said. And his voice was not exultant, but empty.

She touched her knuckles to her chest.

The flower bloomed still, as if no water could kill it, no fire could burn it. Her needle-flower.

Priya's face against Malini's palm. The steady, piercing light of her eyes.

I know you. I know exactly who you are.

She let her hand lower.

She knew herself. She knew what she was beneath the artifice. But these men did not know her. They looked at her and saw the mother of flame she claimed to be. Some looked at her with calculation, considering her worth and her biddability, the potential benefit of rule beneath a woman of Parijat instead of an imperial son.

Some looked at her with real faith burning in their eyes.

Others—like the archers she had stood beside when she had loosed her own arrow and burned the monastery down—looked at her with something akin to respect.

All that, she could use.

She saw Aditya watching her. There was a bleak, accepting look on his face. No joy. He looked at her as if he saw her death upon her.

Well, let him. Let him. She would not grieve.

She could make something new of Parijatdvipa.

She could make herself something monstrous. She could be a creature born of poison and pyre, flame and blood. She had told Aditya that when the opportunity to seize power came—to wield it—the opportunity had to be taken and held and used. If he would not wield it, she would.

If he would not take their brother's throne, in that room of sweet falling jasmine where the sisters of her heart had burned, then she would do it.

She was going to build a new world.

All this she would do, when she sat on Parijatdvipa's throne.

But first, she thought quietly, savagely, to herself, as the men around her kneeled and shouted her name. Malini. Malini. Mother Malini. Empress Malini. *I am going to find my emperor brother. I am going to make Chandra kneel before his peers, humiliated and broken. And I am going to watch him burn.*

70

PRIYA

After the coronation, Priya went to Rukh.

There was a makeshift sickroom, for all the people who had been injured protecting the mahal. Rukh had his own bed. It was by the window, under a fall of sunlight. He was lying on his side, and the leaves of his hair had all turned, seeking the sun.

She had waited until she was sure she would live—that the waters wouldn't take her life. She had waited until she felt like the magic had settled in her blood, steady and strong. To delay any longer would just be cowardice.

She didn't want him to know that she was afraid.

"Rukh," she said. "Are you awake?"

When he raised his head, the leaves of his hair moved. The spines of wood on his hands shifted, moving with the fine bones of his fingers, as he turned his body to look at her.

"Priya?"

"That's me," she said with a smile. "Is there room for me?"

He shuffled over. She sat on the bed beside him.

"I want to try something, if you'll let me," she said. She cupped his hand between two of her own. "I want to try to help the rot."

"I don't want to wear any more beads," he said, resigned.

"No," she said. "Not that. I want to try something magical. Will you let me try, Rukh?"

He was silent for a moment.

"I'm so tired," Rukh said in a small voice.

"I know," she said. She rubbed her thumb over his fingers, careful to avoid the broken skin around the green. "I know, Rukh."

He looked down at her hand on his.

"Will it...will it hurt?" he asked.

"I don't know," she said quietly. "I don't know. But if it does, you tell me, and I'll stop."

"Okay," he said. He opened his fingers, with an audible snap of joints. "Okay," he repeated. "I trust you."

Priya tried to project confidence as she held his hand tighter. Breathed deep. Closed her eyes.

All she had was Ashok's words—his memory that the thrice-born had once been able to manipulate the rot. All she had was her own hope, that what she was could be used for something good.

She let the magic rise in her. Pour out of her.

As she held his hand, she felt the rot within him, a living, magical sentience—the same green life that lived in the forest, in its trees and its earth—and felt it respond to her.

Slow, deep breaths. That was what it took, to move her magic gently, to bid the rot as she would any other green and living thing. *Do not grow*, she told it. *Do not spread*. She tried to draw it back, wither it into nothingness, but it had made a place in Rukh; hollowed itself a home, and without it he would die.

She did what she could. Only that.

Then she opened her eyes once more, and smiled at him.

"Priya," he breathed deeply, as if he hadn't breathed fully in a long time. "I...Priya, what did you do?"

"You're not going to die," said Priya. "I've made sure you won't die. The rot won't hurt you anymore."

He looked wildly at his hands, which were still bark-whorled, still strange.

"But you can't fix me? I'm...not going to change back?"

"I can't make you like you were before," Priya said slowly, looking at the roots curling around his ears; the lines of sap, like veins,

that showed through at his throat and in the shaded whites of his
eyes. "But you're okay, Rukh," she said gently. "You're okay."

Rukh nodded solemnly. Then his lip trembled, and he placed
his forehead against her shoulder, and she felt big, racking sobs
break out of him. She clambered further onto the bed with him,
holding him tight. She pressed her face to his hair, her own eyes
wet, and was so horribly, brilliantly glad that she hadn't lost
him too.

"It's all right," she whispered. "Rukh. It's all right. It's all right."

Bhumika was alone, waiting for her, standing at a broken window
of the great mahal. Staring at the Hirana. She was drinking from
a bottle of wine. One of the regent's own stores that had, miracu-
lously, survived the carnage.

"Where's Padma?" Priya asked.

"Sleeping," said Bhumika. "Khalida is with her. You think I'd
leave my newborn infant alone?"

"I was just asking," said Priya. "Besides, you can leave babies
alone to sleep. Can't you?"

Bhumika muttered something unsavory under her breath and
nudged the bottle of wine toward Priya. Priya took it and drank.

"So," Bhumika said. "What will you do?"

Priya lowered the bottle.

"What do you mean?"

"I know you want to leave, Priya."

Priya swallowed. Stared out at the Hirana, broken but standing,
a light flickering upon the triveni, where some of the once-born
remained. "I never said that."

"You didn't have to, Pri." When Priya remained quiet, Bhumika said, "All I ask is that you . . . don't simply go. Talk to me.
There's so much I need you for here. Unrest. Trying to ensure
that the rebels and our own people don't tear out one another's
throats. The threat of Parijatdvipa at our borders. The need for
allies to trade with."

"That is a lot, isn't it?" Priya sighed, and rolled her shoulders, straightening her spine. "I'd like to help keep us safe. Though I don't think Jeevan would be happy about that. He wasn't well pleased when I cracked a soldier's head with a branch."

"He'd cope," Bhumika said dryly.

"As for the rest—the truth is, I'm not a politician," said Priya. "I'm not a warrior. I'm not even a maidservant anymore. I am..."

She thought of the feel of Ahiranya unfurling in her mind. Of power in her blood. Of what it meant to be touched by spirits—to be a temple child, a keeper of faith.

To be...elemental.

Bhumika was still watching her.

"Not very much at all," finished Priya. "I'm not very much at all."

"You're an elder, now."

"Come on. We both know you're the only true elder here."

Bhumika shook her head. "That's not true, Priya," she said. "Maybe you'll see that one day."

"I do want to leave," Priya admitted. "I suppose I always want to do the wrong thing. But I promise you, I won't go. I won't leave you to suffer dealing with this work alone."

Bhumika shook her head. "That isn't what I want."

"What do you want, then?"

"Tell me what *you* want to do," Bhumika said. "That's all I want to know."

She wanted to sink beneath the waters again.

She wanted Ashok to be alive.

She wanted Malini. She wanted the woman who had held a knife to her heart. She wanted only things that would destroy her, and what good would that do anyone?

"So many things," said Priya, finally. "They don't matter."

Bhumika waited. Then drew the bottle toward herself. "This is a very fine Saketan vintage," Bhumika said, looking down at the bottle. "Vikram was fond of good wine. Once, I arranged for a cask to be brought from the Sonali stores. An old vintage, beloved of my uncle. He didn't even touch it. And yet sometimes,

I thought he valued me." She raised her head. "Do you love her more than your own family?"

Of course Bhumika knew. Priya had never been good at hiding her feelings.

"We're not a very good family," Priya said. "We never have been. But she...she isn't very good either."

"Ah, Priya. That isn't an answer."

"Here's my answer, then. I chose you. I chose—Ashok." Her voice broke a little. She swallowed. "I choose Ahiranya first. I have to. It lives inside me."

"One day you'll leave," said Bhumika. "I know you will. But I need you to make me a promise you won't break." Bhumika turned to look at her. "Make an ally of her," she said. "A sweetheart, if you like, but an ally. If you cannot do that—if she will be a threat to our country—then I need you to remove her. Do you understand?"

Silence.

"You want me to kill her," Priya said.

"I want you to use your closeness to her, if Ahiranya requires it," Bhumika said calmly. "I want you to remember, always, where your loyalties lie."

"Here?"

"Yes, Priya. Here."

Priya shook her head.

"You think strangely," she said.

"I think like a ruler," Bhumika said, resignation in her tone. "I have to, now."

"I may never seek her out. I may..." Priya shrugged, helpless beneath the weight of want and duty both. "She may not want anything to do with me. But if I go to her, if she does..."

"You shouldn't lie to yourself," Bhumika said gently. "Believe me. It does no good."

Priya nodded. Pressed her knuckles lightly to her ribs, where Malini's knife had touched her.

"You're right," Priya admitted. "I will go to her. But not right now. Perhaps not for a very long time. And if I do—if she will see me, if she..." Priya paused. Swallowed. Said carefully, "I won't forget where my loyalties lie."

"Thank you," said Bhumika. She touched her shoulder to Priya's. "More wine?"

"Absolutely."

Priya drank, one deep swig, and lowered the bottle again. "I meant it, when I said I'm no politician and no warrior."

"I know that, Pri."

"But there is something I can do," she said. "Something useful. Something good."

"What is that?" Bhumika asked.

Priya looked out at the Hirana again. She thought of how long she had kneeled on the bed with Rukh. Rukh crying, devastated and full of hope.

She and Bhumika were finally the cure they were always intended to be. The destiny they deserved lay inside them, belonged to them alone.

A cure. The thought made her skin burn.

She touched a hand to her cheek, feeling the line of warmth that lay there, a stitch of throbbing fire. She breathed through the hope and her chest took in air, hollow to it like a thing carved open. For a second, one dizzying second, she felt as if she lay under water still, something growing in her lungs, her heart, something blooming, something she had *forgotten*—

Then the moment passed, and she lowered her hand. She was Priya again, and she knew what she needed to do.

"The rot," she said. "I'm going to destroy the rot."

EPILOGUE

Chandra kneeled in the ruins of his mother's garden. Around him the flowers lay in rotten heaps, their roots exposed, the flies and ants climbing over their remains. When Chandra had ordered that the garden be prepared for his use, a mere handful of weeks ago, he had made it clear that the flowers were to be left here to die.

There was a sweetness to the scent of dying vegetation that soothed him.

His mother had loved her Dwarali birch trees—the pale bark, the proud spires of the branches, laden with leaves.

Servants had cut down all the trees in one morning, years of growth instantly obliterated. The roots had been levered out of the soil, the wood dried, then axed and carefully arranged into individual pyres. Women had been led to the pyres; the pyres had been lit; the ash had been cleared and piled high again, until all the wood was gone, put to good use in service of a higher purpose.

Chandra had watched it all.

Today, only one pyre still burned. Its fire had reduced to glowing embers, pulsing under the blackened weight of the wood. The woman upon it had long since died, and the garden was blissfully quiet once more. A maidservant had brought Chandra refreshments: sherbet laden with crushed blossoms and pearly basil seeds, pink and white. A clay cup of tea, covered with a cloth to maintain its heat. She had arranged these neatly on the low table beside him, bowed, and departed, her pallu drawn over her mouth and nose, her eyes red from the miasma of smoke.

The light of the embers faded further, choked by the weight of burnt wood. Chandra looked closer, through ash white and black, through birch and bone. And there it was.

One ember—only one—had brightened. Grown. It lay in the dark, pulsing like a heartbeat. The small fist of light shuddered before Chandra's astonished, hopeful eyes, and began to uncurl. A molten gold bud blooming into a flower of fire.

Chandra breathed in, a deep breath to give him the air for the joyous laugh that left him then. His mouth was full of the smoke of human char; the sickly perfume of dead jasmine. He had never tasted anything so sweet.

He sat and watched the fire burn. And he thought of his sister with a smile on his lips.

The story continues in ...

BOOK TWO OF
THE BURNING KINGDOMS

ACKNOWLEDGMENTS

A new series is always like an adventure into the dangerous unknown: terrifying and exciting, and much better with company. I'm grateful to all the people who took this journey with me.

Thank you, first and foremost, to every single reader of this book. Books are nothing without their readers, and this author is very thankful to have you here. Special love and thanks go to my sapphic desi readers. I hope this book made you feel seen, at least a little.

Thank you to my agent, Laura Crockett, who has consistently given me the chance to write the books of my dreams. Thank you, also, to everyone at Triada US Literary Agency, especially Uwe Stender.

Huge thanks to everyone at Orbit: Priyanka Krishnan, my brilliant editor who made this book bigger and better and significantly more romantic—this book wouldn't be half as good without you, and I'm so grateful for your guidance. Hillary Sames, for combing through draft after draft and making this book shine. My UK editor, Jenni Hill, and my UK publicist, Nazia Khatun, for guiding *The Jasmine Throne* into the world closer to home. Lauren Panepinto and Micah Epstein, for the beautiful cover. Ellen Wright and Paola Crespo, for their amazing marketing and publicity and support. Anna Jackson and Tim Holman, for running the ship. Thank you to Bryn A. McDonald and Amy J. Schneider, for being wizards (copy editors are absolutely wizards). And finally, veering gently away from Orbit: Thank you to Sarah Guan, who planted the seed that grew into this book.

Kat, Kate, Daphne, Tori, Lesedi, Shuo—in these extremely weird times, you've kept me grounded. Love you. And thank you to all the friends I haven't mentioned here by name, who've supported me in ways large and small and deserved better than this vague mention.

Big thanks to every fellow author who has supported me as I rambled about this book in our chats. One day I hope to see you all at a convention again so I can thank you properly over a cup of tea (or a whiskey, if you so prefer). Devin Madson, Rowenna Miller, Anna Stephens—thank you especially for reading early drafts of this book. And thank you to Natasha Ngan, for telling me to write the sapphic book I was afraid to.

Lan Zhan bunny, Wei Ying bunny, and Asami—you can't read because you're animals, but thank you all the same for supporting me by being fluffy and cute, I guess.

I wouldn't have been able to do any of this without the loving, patient support of my family. Special thanks to my mum, Anita Suri, for keeping me fed and being an absolute rock (and a powerhouse).

And finally, Carly: I love you. None of this would have been possible without you. This one is for you.

CAST OF CHARACTERS

Ahiranyi

Ashok—Rebel against Parijatdvipan rule, temple son
Bhumika—Wife of the regent of Ahiranya, temple daughter
Billu—Cook in the household of the regent of Ahiranya
Bojal—Temple elder, deceased
Chandni—Temple elder
Ganam—Rebel against Parijatdvipan rule
Gauri—Senior maidservant in the household of the regent of Ahiranya
Gautam—Dealer of Ahiranyi medicines
Govind—Highborn lord, uncle of Bhumika
Jeevan—Captain of the guard to the regent of Ahiranya
Jitesh—Guard in the household of Lord Iskar
Khalida—Maidservant to Lady Bhumika
Kritika—Rebel against Parijatdvipan rule
Meena—Rebel against Parijatdvipan rule
Mithunan—Guard in the household of the regent of Ahiranya
Nandi—Temple son, deceased
Nikhil—Guard in the household of Lord Iskar
Priya—Maidservant in the household of the regent of Ahiranya, temple
    daughter
Rukh—Young servant in the household of the regent of Ahiranya, rot
    sufferer
Sanjana—Temple daughter, deceased
Sarita—Ahiranyi rebel
Sendhil—Temple elder
Sima—Maidservant in the household of the regent of Ahiranya

Aloran

Alori—Princess of Alor, attendant of Princess Malini, deceased
Rao—Prince of Alor
Viraj—King of Alor

Dwarali

Khalil—Lord of the Lal Qila
Raziya—Highborn lady, wife of Lord Khalil

Parijati

Aditya—Ex-crown prince of Parijatdvipa; priest of the nameless
Chandra—Emperor of Parijatdvipa
Divyanshi—First mother of flame, founder of Parijatdvipa, deceased
Iskar—Advisor to the regent of Ahiranya
Lata—Sage
Mahesh—Highborn lord, loyal to Prince Aditya
Malini—Princess of Parijat
Narina—Noble attendant of Princess Malini, deceased
Pramila—Highborn lady, jailer of Malini
Santosh—Highborn lord, loyal to Emperor Chandra
Sikander—Previous emperor of Parijatdvipa, deceased
Vikram—Regent of Ahiranya

Saketan

Narayan—Highborn lord
Prem—Low prince of Saketa

extras

orbitbooks.net

about the author

Tasha Suri was born in London to Punjabi parents. She studied English and creative writing at Warwick University and is now a cat-owning librarian in London. A love of period Bollywood films, history, and mythology led her to write South Asian-influenced fantasy. Find her on Twitter @tashadrinkstea.

Find out more about Tasha Suri and other Orbit authors by registering for the free monthly newsletter at orbitbooks.net.

if you enjoyed
THE JASMINE THRONE

look out for

THE MASK OF MIRRORS

Rook & Rose: Book One

by

M. A. Carrick

Nightmares are creeping through the city of dreams ...

*Renata Virdaux is a con artist who has come to the sparkling city of
Nadezra — the city of dreams — with one goal: to trick her way into a
noble house and secure her fortune and her sister's future.*

*But as she's drawn into the aristocratic world of House Traementis,
she realises her masquerade is just one of many surrounding her.
And as corrupted magic begins to weave its way through Nadezra,
the poisonous feuds of its aristocrats and the shadowy dangers of its
impoverished underbelly become tangled — with Ren at their heart.*

The Mask of Mirrors

Isla Traementis, the Pearls: Suilun 1

After fifteen years of handling the Traementis house charters, Donaia Traementis knew that a deal which looked too good to be true probably was. The proposal currently on her desk stretched the boundaries of belief.

"He could at least try to make it look legitimate," she muttered. Did Mettore Indestor think her an utter fool?

He thinks you desperate. And he's right.

She burrowed her stockinged toes under the great lump of a hound sleeping beneath her desk and pressed cold fingers to her brow. She'd removed her gloves to avoid ink stains and left the hearth in her study unlit to save the cost of fuel. Besides Meatball, the only warmth was from the beeswax candles—an expense she couldn't scrimp on unless she wanted to lose what eyesight she had left.

Adjusting her spectacles, she scanned the proposal again, scratching angry notes between the lines.

She remembered a time when House Traementis had been as powerful as the Indestor family. They had held a seat in the Cinquerat, the five-person council that ruled Nadežra, and charters that allowed them to conduct trade, contract mercenaries, control guilds. Every variety of wealth, power, and prestige in Nadežra had been theirs. Now, despite Donaia's best efforts and her late husband's before her, it had come to this: scrabbling at one Dusk Road trade charter as though she could milk enough blood from that stone to pay off all the Traementis debts.

Debts almost entirely owned by Mettore Indestor.

"And you expect me to trust my caravan to guards you provide?" she growled at the proposal, her pen nib digging in hard enough to tear the paper. "Ha! Who's going to protect it from them? Will they even wait for bandits, or just sack the wagons themselves?"

Leaving Donaia with the loss, a pack of angry investors, and debts she could no longer cover. Then Mettore would swoop in like one of his thrice-damned hawks to swallow whole what remained of House Traementis.

Try as she might, though, she couldn't see another option. She couldn't send the caravan out unguarded—Vraszenian bandits were a legitimate concern—but the Indestor family held the Caerulet seat in the Cinquerat, which gave Mettore authority over military and mercenary affairs. Nobody would risk working with a house Indestor had a grudge against—not when it would mean losing a charter, or worse.

Meatball's head rose with a sudden whine. A moment later a knock came at the study door, followed by Donaia's majordomo. Colbrin knew better than to interrupt her when she was wrestling with business, which meant he judged this interruption important.

He bowed and handed her a card. "Alta Renata Viraudax?" Donaia asked, shoving Meatball's wet snout out of her lap when he sniffed at the card. She flipped it as if the back would provide some clue to the visitor's purpose. Viraudax wasn't a local noble house. Some traveler to Nadežra?

"A young woman, Era Traementis," her majordomo said. "Well-mannered. Well-dressed. She said it concerned an important private matter."

The card fluttered to the floor. Donaia's duties as head of House Traementis kept her from having much of a social life, but the same could not be said for her son, and lately Leato had been behaving more and more like his father. Ninat take him—if her son had racked up some gambling debt with a foreign visitor...

Colbrin retrieved the card before the dog could eat it, and handed it back to her. "Should I tell her you are not at home?"

"No. Show her in." If her son's dive into the seedier side of Nadežra had resulted in trouble, she would at least rectify his errors before stringing him up.

Somehow. With money she didn't have.

She could start by not conducting the meeting in a freezing study. "Wait," she said before Colbrin could leave. "Show her to the salon. And bring tea."

Donaia cleaned the ink from her pen and made a futile attempt to brush away the brindled dog hairs matting her surcoat. Giving that up as a lost cause, she tugged on her gloves and straightened the papers on her desk, collecting herself by collecting her surroundings. Looking down at her clothing—the faded blue surcoat over trousers and house scuffs—she weighed the value of changing over the cost of making a potential problem wait.

Everything is a tallied cost these days, she thought grimly.

"Meatball. Stay," she commanded when the hound would have followed, and headed directly to the salon.

The young woman waiting there could not have fit the setting more perfectly if she had planned it. Her rose-gold underdress and cream surcoat harmonized beautifully with the gold-shot peach silk of the couch and chairs, and the thick curl trailing from her upswept hair echoed the rich wood of the wall paneling. The curl should have looked like an accident, an errant strand slipping loose—but everything else about the visitor was so elegant it was clearly a deliberate touch of style.

She was studying the row of books on their glass-fronted shelf. When Donaia closed the door, she turned and dipped low. "Era Traementis. Thank you for seeing me."

Her curtsy was as Seterin as her clipped accent, one hand sweeping elegantly up to the opposite shoulder. Donaia's misgivings deepened at the sight of her. Close to her son's age, and beautiful as a portrait by Creciasto, with fine-boned features and flawless skin. Easy to imagine Leato losing his head over a hand of cards with such a girl. And her ensemble did nothing to comfort Donaia's fears—the richly embroidered brocade, the sleeves an elegant fall of sheer silk. Here was someone who could afford to bet and lose a fortune.

That sort was more likely to forgive or forget a debt than come collecting...unless the debt was meant as leverage for something else.

"Alta Renata. I hope you will forgive my informality." She brushed a hand down her simple attire. "I did not expect visitors, but it sounded like your matter was of some urgency. Please, do be seated."

The young woman lowered herself into the chair as lightly as mist on the river. Seeing her, it was easy to understand why the people of Nadežra looked to Seteris as the source of all that was stylish and elegant. Fashion was born in Seteris. By the time it traveled south to Seteris's protectorate, Seste Ligante, then farther south still, across the sea to Nadežra, it was old and stale, and Seteris had moved on.

Most Seterin visitors behaved as though Nadežra was nothing more than Seste Ligante's backwater colonial foothold on the Vraszenian continent and merely setting foot on the streets would foul them with the mud of the River Dežera. But Renata's delicacy looked like hesitation, not condescension. She said, "Not urgent, no—I do apologize if I gave that impression. I confess, I'm not certain how to even begin this conversation."

She paused, hazel eyes searching Donaia's face. "You don't recognize my family name, do you?"

That had an ominous sound. Seteris might be on the other side of the sea, but the truly powerful families could influence trade anywhere in the known world. If House Traementis had somehow crossed one of them...

Donaia kept her fear from her face and her voice. "I am afraid I haven't had many dealings with the great houses of Seteris."

A soft breath flowed out of the girl. "As I suspected. I thought she might have written to you at least once, but apparently not. I . . . am Letilia's daughter."

She could have announced she was descended from the Vraszenian goddess Ažerais herself, and it wouldn't have taken Donaia more by surprise.

Disbelief clashed with relief and apprehension both: not a creditor, not an offended daughter of some foreign power. Family—after a fashion.

Lost for words, Donaia reassessed the young woman sitting across from her. Straight back, straight shoulders, straight neck, and the same fine, narrow nose that made everyone in Nadežra hail Letilia Traementis as the great beauty of her day.

Yes, she could be Letilia's daughter. Donaia's niece by marriage.

"Letilia never wrote after she left." It was the only consideration the spoiled brat had ever shown her family. The first several years, every day they'd expected a letter telling them she was stranded in Seteris, begging for funds. Instead they never heard from her again.

Dread sank into Donaia's bones. "Is Letilia here?"

The door swung open, and for one dreadful instant Donaia expected a familiar squall of petulance and privilege to sweep inside. But it was only Colbrin, bearing a tray. To her dismay, Donaia saw two pots on it, one short and rounded for tea, the other taller. Of course: He'd heard their guest's Seterin accent, and naturally assumed Donaia would also want to serve coffee.

We haven't yet fallen so far that I can't afford proper hospitality. But Donaia's voice was still sharp as he set the tray between the two of them. "Thank you, Colbrin. That will be all."

"No," Renata said as the majordomo bowed and departed. "No, Mother is happily ensconced in Seteris."

It seemed luck hadn't *entirely* abandoned House Traementis. "Tea?" Donaia said, a little too bright with relief. "Or would you prefer coffee?"

"Coffee, thank you." Renata accepted the cup and saucer with a graceful hand. Everything about her was graceful—but not the artificial, forced elegance Donaia remembered Letilia practicing so assiduously.

Renata sipped the coffee and made a small, appreciative noise. "I must admit, I was wondering if I would even be able to find coffee here."

Ah. *There* was the echo of Letilia, the little sneer that took what should be a compliment and transformed it into an insult.

We have wooden floors and chairs with backs, too. Donaia swallowed down the snappish response. But the bitter taste in her mouth nudged her into pouring coffee for herself, even though she disliked it. She wouldn't let this girl make her feel like a delta rustic simply because Donaia had lived all her life in Nadežra.

"So you are here, but Letilia is not. May I ask why?"

The girl's chin dropped, and she rotated her coffee cup as though its precise alignment against the saucer were vitally important. "I've spent days imagining how best to approach you, but—well." There was a ripple of nervousness in her laugh. "There's no way to say this without first admitting I'm Letilia's daughter...and yet by admitting that, I know I've already gotten off on the wrong foot. Still, there's nothing for it."

Renata inhaled like someone preparing for battle, then met Donaia's gaze. "I'm here to see if I can possibly reconcile my mother with her family."

It took all Donaia's self-control not to laugh. Reconcile? She would sooner reconcile with the drugs that had overtaken her husband Gianco's good sense in his final years. If Gianco's darker comments were to be believed, Letilia had done as much to destroy House Traementis as aža had.

Fortunately, custom and law offered her a more dispassionate response. "Letilia is no part of this family. My husband's father struck her name from our register after she left."

At least Renata was smart enough not to be surprised. "I can hardly blame my gra—your father-in-law," she said. "I've only my mother's version of the tale, but I also know *her*. I can guess the part she played in that estrangement."

Donaia could just imagine what poison Letilia's version had contained. "It is more than estrangement," she said brusquely, rising to her feet. "I am sorry you crossed the sea for nothing, but I'm afraid that what you're asking for is impossible. Even if I believed that your mother wanted to reconcile—which I do not—I have no interest in doing so."

A treacherous worm within her whispered, *Even if that might offer a new business opportunity? Some way out of Indestor's trap?*

Even then. Donaia would burn Traementis Manor to the ground before she accepted help from Letilia's hand.

The salon door opened again. But this time, the interruption wasn't her majordomo.

"Mother, Egliadas has invited me to go sailing on the river." Leato was tugging on his gloves, as if he couldn't be bothered to finish dressing before leaving his rooms. But he stopped, one hand still caught in the tight cuff, when he saw their visitor.

Renata rose like a flower bud unfurling, and Donaia cursed silently. Why, today of all days, had Leato chosen to wake early? Not that fourth sun was early by most people's standards, but for him midmorning might as well be dawn.

Reflex forced the courtesies out of her mouth, even though she wanted nothing more than to hurry the girl away. "Leato, you recall stories of your aunt Letilia? This is her daughter, Alta Renata Viraudax of Seteris. Alta Renata, my son and heir, Leato Traementis."

Leato captured Renata's hand before she could touch it to her shoulder again and kissed her gloved fingertips. When she saw them together, Donaia's heart sank like a stone. She was used to thinking of her son as an adolescent scamp, or an intermittent source of headaches. But he was a man grown, with beauty to match Renata's: his hair like antique gold, fashionably mussed on top; his ivory skin and finely carved features, the hallmark of House Traementis; the elegant cut of his waistcoat and fitted tailoring of the full-skirted coat over it in the platinum shimmer of delta grasses in autumn.

And the two of them were smiling at one another like the sun had just risen in the salon.

"Letilia's daughter?" Leato said, releasing Renata's hand before the touch could grow awkward. "I thought she hated us."

Donaia bit down the impulse to chide him. It would sound like she was defending Renata, which was the last thing she wanted to do.

The girl's smile was brief and rueful. "I may have inherited her nose, but I've tried not to inherit *everything* else."

"You mean, not her personality? I'll offer thanks to Katus." Leato winced. "I'm sorry, I shouldn't insult your mother—"

"No insult taken," Renata said dryly. "I'm sure the stories you know of her are dreadful, and with good cause."

They had the river's current beneath them and were flowing onward; Donaia had to stop it before they went too far. When Leato asked what brought Renata to the city, Donaia lunged in, social grace be damned. "She just—"

But Renata spoke over her, as smooth as silk. "I was hoping to meet your grandfather and father. Foolish of me, really; since Mother hasn't been in contact, I didn't know they'd both passed away until I arrived. And now I understand she's no longer in the register, so there's no bond between us—I'm just a stranger, intruding."

"Oh, not at all!" Leato turned to his mother for confirmation.

For the first time, Donaia felt a touch of gratitude toward Renata. Leato had never known Letilia; he hadn't even been born when she ran away. He'd heard the tales, but no doubt he marked at least some of them as exaggeration. If Renata had mentioned a reconciliation outright, he probably would have supported her.

"We're touched by your visit," Donaia said, offering the girl a courteous nod. "I'm only sorry the others never had a chance to meet you."

"Your visit?" Leato scoffed. "No, this can't be all. You're my cousin, after all—oh, not under the law, I know. But blood counts for a lot here."

"We're Nadežran, Leato, not Vraszenian," Donaia said reprovingly, lest Renata think they'd been completely swallowed by delta ways.

He went on as though he hadn't heard her. "My long-lost cousin shows up from across the sea, greets us for a few minutes, then vanishes? Unacceptable. Giuna hasn't even met you—she's my younger sister. Why don't you stay with us for a few days?"

Donaia couldn't stop a muffled sound from escaping her. However much he seemed determined to ignore them, Leato knew about House Traementis's financial troubles. A houseguest was the last thing they could afford.

But Renata demurred with a light shake of her head. "No, no—I couldn't impose like that. I'll be in Nadežra for some time, though. Perhaps you'll allow me the chance to show I'm not my mother."

Preparatory to pushing for reconciliation, no doubt. But although Renata was older and more self-possessed, something about her downcast gaze reminded Donaia of Giuna. She could all too easily imagine Giuna seeking Letilia out in Seteris with the same impossible dream.

If House Traementis could afford the sea passage, which they could not. And if Donaia would allow her to go, which she would not. But if that impossible situation happened...she bristled at the thought of Letilia rebuffing Giuna entirely, treating her with such cold hostility that she refused to see the girl at all.

So Donaia said, as warmly as she could, "Of course we know you aren't your mother. And you shouldn't be forced to carry the burden of her past." She let a smile crack her mask. "I'm certain from the caterpillars dancing on my son's brow that he'd like to know more about you, and I imagine Giuna would feel the same."

"Thank you," Renata said with a curtsy. "But not now, I think. My apologies, Altan Leato." Her words silenced his protest before he could voice it, and with faultless formality. "My maid intends to fit me for a new dress this afternoon, and she'll stick me with pins if I'm late."

That was as unlike Letilia as it was possible to be. Not the concern for her clothing—Letilia was the same, only with less tasteful results—but the graceful withdrawal, cooperating with Donaia's wish to get her out of the house.

Leato did manage to get one more question out, though. "Where can we reach you?"

"On the Isla Prišta, Via Brelkoja, number four," Renata said. Donaia's lips tightened. For a stay of a few weeks, even a month or two, a hotel would have sufficed. Renting a house suggested the girl intended to remain for quite some time.

But that was a matter for later. Donaia reached for the bell. "Colbrin will see you out."

"No need," Leato said, offering Renata his hand. When she glanced at Donaia instead of taking it, Leato said, "Mother, you won't begrudge me a few moments of gossip with my new cousin?"

That was Leato, always asking for forgiveness rather than permission. But Renata's minute smile silently promised not to encourage him. At Donaia's forbearing nod, she accepted his escort from the room.

Once they were gone, Donaia rang for Colbrin. "I'll be in my study. No more interruptions barring flood or fire, please."

Colbrin's acknowledgment trailed after her as she went upstairs. When she entered the room, Meatball roused with a whine-snap of a yawn and a hopeful look, but settled again once he realized no treats were forthcoming.

The space seemed chillier than when she'd left it, and darker. She thought of Alta Renata's fine manners and finer clothes. Of course Letilia's daughter would be dressed in designs so new they hadn't yet made their way from Seteris to Nadežra. Of course she would have enough wealth to rent a house in Westbridge for herself alone and think nothing of it. Hadn't Gianco always said that Letilia took House Traementis's luck with her when she left?

In a fit of pique, Donaia lit the hearthfire, and damn the cost. Once its warmth was blazing through the study, she returned to her desk. She buried her toes under the dog again, mentally composing her message as she sharpened her nib and filled her ink tray.

House Traementis might be neck-deep in debt and sinking, but they still had the rights granted by their ennoblement charter. And Donaia wasn't such a fool that she would bite a hook before examining it from all sides first.

Bending her head, Donaia began penning a letter to Commander Cercel of the Vigil.

Upper and Lower Bank: Suilun 1

Renata expected Leato Traementis to see her out the front door, but he escorted her all the way to the bottom of the steps, and kept her hand even when they stopped. "I hope you're not too offended by Mother's reserve," he said. A breeze ruffled his burnished hair and carried the scent of caramel and almonds to her nose. A rich scent, matching his clothes and his carriage, and the thin lines of gold paint limning his eyelashes. "A lot of dead branches have been pruned from the Traementis register since my father—and your mother— were children. Now there's only Mother, Giuna, and myself. She gets protective."

"I take no offense at all," Renata said, smiling up at him. "I'm not so much of a fool that I expect to be welcomed with open arms. And I'm willing to be patient."

The breeze sharpened, and she shivered. Leato stepped between her and the wind. "You'd think Nadežra would be warmer than Seteris, wouldn't you?" he said with a sympathetic grimace. "It's all the water. We almost never get snow here, but the winters are so damp, the cold cuts right to your bones."

"I should have thought to wear a cloak. But since I can't pluck one from thin air, I hope you won't take offense if I hurry home."

"Of course not. Let me get you a sedan chair." Leato raised a hand to catch the eye of some men idling on the far side of the square and paid the bearers before Renata could even reach for her purse. "To soothe any lingering sting," he said with a smile.

She thanked him with another curtsy. "I hope I'll see you soon."

"As do I." Leato helped her into the sedan chair and closed the door once her skirts were safely out of the way.

As the bearers headed for the narrow exit from the square,

Renata drew the curtains shut. Traementis Manor was in the Pearls, a cluster of islets strung along the Upper Bank of the River Dežera. The river here ran pure and clear thanks to the numinat that protected the East Channel, and the narrow streets and bridges were clean; whichever families held the charters to keep the streets clear of refuse wouldn't dream of letting it accumulate near the houses of the rich and powerful.

But the rocky wedge that broke the Dežera into east and west channels was a different matter. For all that it held two of Nadežra's major institutions—the Charterhouse in Dawngate, which was the seat of government, and the Aerie in Duskgate, home to the Vigil, which maintained order—the Old Island was also crowded with the poor and the shabby-genteel. Anyone riding in a sedan chair was just asking for beggars to crowd at their windows.

Which still made it better than half of the Lower Bank, where a sedan chair risked being knocked to the ground and the passenger robbed.

Luckily, her rented house was on Isla Prišta in Westbridge—technically on the Lower Bank, and far from a fashionable district, but it was a respectable neighborhood on the rise. In fact, the buildings on the Via Brelkoja were so newly renovated the mortar hadn't had time to moss over in the damp air. The freshly painted door to number four opened just as Renata's foot touched the first step.

Tess made a severe-looking sight in the crisp grey-and-white surcoat and underskirt of a Nadežran housemaid, but her copper Ganllechyn curls and freckles were a warm beacon welcoming Renata home. She bobbed a curtsy and murmured a lilting "alta" as Renata passed across the threshold, accepting the gloves and purse Renata held out.

"Downstairs," Ren murmured as the door snicked shut, sinking them into the dimness of the front hall.

Tess nodded, swallowing her question before she could speak it. Together they headed into the half-sunken chambers of the cellar, which held the service rooms. Only once they were safely in the kitchen did Tess say, "Well? How did it go?"

Ren let her posture drop and her voice relax into the throaty tones of her natural accent. "For me, as well as I could hope. Donaia refused reconciliation out of hand—"

"Thank the Mother," Tess breathed. If Donaia contacted Letilia, their entire plan would fall apart before it started.

Ren nodded. "Faced with the prospect of talking to her former sister-in-law, she barely even noticed me getting my foot in the door."

"That's a start, then. Here, off with this, and wrap up before you take a chill." Tess passed Ren a thick cloak of rough-spun wool lined with raw fleece, then turned her around like a dressmaker's doll so she could remove the beautifully embroidered surcoat.

"I saw the sedan chair," Tess said as she tugged at the side ties. "You didn't take that all the way from Isla Traementis, did you? If you're going to be riding about in chairs, I'll have to revise the budget. And here I'd had my eye on a lovely bit of lace at the remnants stall." Tess sighed mournfully, like she was saying farewell to a sweetheart. "I'll just have to tat some myself."

"In your endless spare time?" Ren said sardonically. The surcoat came loose, and she swung the cloak around her shoulders in its place. "Anyway, the son paid for the chair." She dropped onto the kitchen bench and eased her shoes off with a silent curse. Fashionable shoes were *not* comfortable. The hardest part of this con was going to be pretending her feet didn't hurt all day long.

Although choking down coffee ran a close second.

"Did he, now?" Tess settled on the bench next to Ren, close enough that they could share warmth beneath the cloak. Apart from the kitchen and the front salon, protective sheets still covered the furniture in every other room. The hearths were cold, their meals were simple, and they slept together on a kitchen floor pallet so they would only have to heat one room of the house.

Because she was not Alta Renata Viraudax, daughter of Letilia Traementis. She was Arenza Lenskaya, half-Vraszenian river rat, and even with a forged letter of credit to help, pretending to be a Seterin noblewoman wasn't cheap.

Pulling out a thumbnail blade, Tess began ripping the seams of Ren's beautiful surcoat, preparatory to alteration. "Was it just idle flirtation?"

The speculative uptick in Tess's question said she didn't believe any flirtation Ren encountered was idle. But whether Leato's flirtation had been idle or not, Ren had lines she would not cross, and whoring herself out was one of them.

It would have been the easier route. Dress herself up fine enough to catch the eye of some delta gentry son, or even a noble, and marry her way into money. She wouldn't be the first person in Nadežra to do it.

But she'd spent five years in Ganllech—five years as a maid under Letilia's thumb, listening to her complain about her dreadful family and how much she dreamed of life in Seteris, the promised land she'd never managed to reach. So when Ren and Tess found themselves back in Nadežra, Ren had been resolved. No whoring, and no killing. Instead she set her sights on a higher target: use what she'd learned to gain acceptance into House Traementis as their long-lost kin...with all the wealth and social benefit that brought.

"Leato is friendly," she allowed, picking up the far end of the dress and starting on the seam with her own knife. Tess didn't trust her to sew anything more complicated than a hem, but ripping stitches? That, she was qualified for. "And he helped shame Donaia into agreeing to see me again. But *she* is every bit as bad as Letilia claimed. You should have seen what she wore. Ratty old clothes, covered in dog hair. Like it's a moral flaw to let a single centira slip through her fingers."

"But the son isn't so bad?" Tess rocked on the bench, nudging Ren's hip with her own. "Maybe he's a bastard."

Ren snorted. "Not likely. Donaia would give him the moon if he asked, and he looks as Traementis as I." Only he didn't need makeup to achieve the effect.

Her hands trembled as she worked. Those five years in Ganllech were also five years out of practice. And all her previous cons had been short touches—never anything on this scale. When she got caught before, the hawks slung her in jail for a few days.

If she got caught now, impersonating a noblewoman . . .

Tess laid a hand over Ren's, stopping her before she could nick herself with the knife. "It's never too late to do something else."

Ren managed a smile. "Buy piles of fabric, then run away and set up as dressmakers? You, anyway. I would be your tailor's dummy."

"You'd model and sell them," Tess said stoutly. "If you want."

Tess would be happy in that life. But Ren wanted more.

This city *owed* her more. It had taken everything: her mother, her childhood, Sedge. The rich cuffs of Nadežra got whatever they wanted, then squabbled over what their rivals had, grinding everyone else underfoot. In all her days among the Fingers, Ren had never been able to take more than the smallest shreds from the hems of their cloaks.

But now, thanks to Letilia, she was in a position to take more.

The Traementis made the perfect target. Small enough these days that only Donaia stood any chance of spotting Renata as an imposter, and isolated enough that they would be grateful for any addition to their register. In the glory days of their power and graft, they'd been notorious for their insular ways, refusing to aid their fellow nobles in times of need. Since they lost their seat in the Cinquerat, everyone else had gladly returned the favor.

Ren put down the knife and squeezed Tess's hand. "No. It is nerves only, and they will pass. We go forward."

"Forward it is." Tess squeezed back, then returned to work. "Next we're to make a splash somewhere public, yes? I'll need to know where and when if I'm to outfit you proper." The sides of the surcoat parted, and she started on the bandeau at the top of the bodice. "The sleeves are the key, have you noticed? Everyone is so on about their sleeves. But I've a thought for that . . . if you're ready for Alta Renata to set fashion instead of following."

Ren glanced sideways, her wariness only half-feigned. "What have you in mind?"

"Hmm. Stand up, and off with the rest of it." Once she had Ren stripped to her chemise, Tess played with different gathers and drapes until Ren's arms started to ache from being held out for so long. But she didn't complain. Tess's eye for fashion, her knack for imbuing, and her ability to rework the pieces of three outfits into nine were as vital to this con as Ren's skill at manipulation.

She closed her eyes and cast her thoughts over what she knew about the city. Where could she go, what could she do, to attract the kind of admiration that would help her gain the foothold she needed?

A slow smile spread across her face.

"Tess," she said, "I have the perfect idea. And you will love it."

The Aerie and Isla Traementis: Suilun 1

"Serrado! Get in here. I have a job for you."

Commander Cercel's voice cut sharply through the din of the Aerie. Waving at his constables to take their prisoner to the stockade, Captain Grey Serrado turned and threaded his way through the chaos to his commander's office. He ignored the sidelong smirks and snide whispers of his fellow officers: Unlike them, he didn't have the luxury of lounging about drinking coffee, managing his constables from the comfort of the Aerie.

"Commander Cercel?" He snapped the heels of his boots together and gave her his crispest salute—a salute he'd perfected during hours of standing at attention in the sun, the rain, the wind, while other lieutenants were at mess or in the barracks. Cercel wasn't the stickler for discipline his previous superiors had been, but she was the reason he wore a captain's double-lined hexagram pin, and he didn't want to reflect badly on her.

She was studying a letter, but when she brought her head up to reply, her eyes widened. "What does the *other* guy look like?"

Taking the casual question as permission to drop into rest, Grey spared a glance for his uniform. His patrol slops were spattered with muck from heel to shoulder, and blood was drying on the knuckles of his leather gloves. Some of the canal mud on his boots had flaked off when he saluted, powdering Cercel's carpet with the filth of the Kingfisher slums.

"Dazed but breathing. Ranieri's taking him to the stockade now." Her question invited banter, but the door to her office was open, and it wouldn't do him any good to be marked as a smart-ass.

She responded to his businesslike answer with an equally brisk nod. "Well, get cleaned up. I've received a letter from one of the noble houses, requesting Vigil assistance. I'm sending you."

Grey's jaw tensed as he waited for several gut responses to subside. It was possible the request was a legitimate call for aid. "What crime has been committed?"

Cercel's level gaze said, *You know better than that.* "One of the noble houses has requested Vigil assistance," she repeated, enunciating each word with cut-glass clarity. "I'm sure they wouldn't do that without good cause."

No doubt whoever sent the letter thought the cause was good. People from the great houses always did.

But Grey had a desk full of real problems. "More children have gone missing. That's eleven verified this month."

They'd had this conversation several times over the past few weeks. Cercel sighed. "We haven't had any reports—"

"Because they're all river rats so far. Who's going to care enough to report that? But the man I just brought in might know something about it; he's been promising Kingfisher kids good pay for an unspecified job. I got him on defacing public property, but he'll be free again by tonight." Pissing in public wasn't an offense the Vigil usually cracked down on, unless it suited them. "Am I to assume this noble's 'good cause' takes precedence over finding out what's happening to those kids?"

Cercel breathed out hard through her nose, and he tensed. Had he pushed her patience too far?

No. "Your man is on his way to the stockade," she said. "Have Kaineto process him—you're always complaining he's as slow as river mud. By the time you get back, he'll be ready to talk. Meanwhile, send Ranieri to ask questions around Kingfisher, see if he can find any of the man's associates." She set the letter aside and drew another from her stack, a clear prelude to dismissing him. "You know the deal, Serrado."

The first few times, he'd played dense to make her spell it out in unambiguous terms. The last thing he could afford back then was to mistake a senior officer's meaning.

But they were past those games now. As long as he knuckled under and did whatever this noble wanted of him, Cercel wouldn't question him using Vigil time and resources for his own investigations.

"Yes, Commander." He saluted and heel-knocked another layer of delta silt onto her carpet. "Which house has called for aid?"

"Traementis."

If he'd been less careful of his manners, he would have thrown her a dirty look. *She could have* led *with that.* But Cercel wanted him to understand that answering these calls was part of his duty, and made him bend his neck before she revealed the silver lining. "Understood. I'll head to the Pearls at once."

Her final command followed him out of the office. "Don't you dare show up at Era Traementis's door looking like that!"

Groaning, Grey changed his path. He snagged a pitcher of water and a messenger, sending the latter to Ranieri with the new orders.

There was a bathing room in the Aerie, but he didn't want to waste time on that. A sniff test sent every piece of his patrol uniform into the laundry bag; aside from the coffee, that was one of the few perks of his rank he didn't mind taking shameless advantage of. If he was wading through canals for the job, the least the Vigil could do was ensure he didn't smell like one. A quick pitcher bath in his tiny office took care of the scents still clinging to his skin and hair before he shrugged into his dress vigils.

He had to admit the force's tailors were good. The tan breeches were Liganti-cut, snug as they could be around his thighs and hips without impeding movement. Both the brocade waistcoat and the coat of sapphire wool were tailored like a second skin, before the latter flared to full skirts that kissed the tops of his polished, knee-high boots. On his patrol slops, the diving hawk across the back of his shoulders was mere patchwork; here it was embroidered in golds and browns.

Grey didn't have much use for vanity, but he did love his dress vigils. They were an inarguable reminder that he'd climbed to a place few Vraszenians could even imagine reaching. His brother, Kolya, had been so proud the day Grey came home in them.

The sudden trembling of his hands stabbed his collar pin into his thumb. Grey swallowed a curse and sucked the blood from the puncture, using a tiny hand mirror to make sure he hadn't gotten any on his collar. Luckily, it was clean, and he managed to finish dressing himself without further injury.

Once outside, he set off east from Duskgate with long, ground-eating strides. He could have taken a sedan chair and told the bearers to bill the Vigil; other officers did, knowing all the while that no such bill would ever be paid. But along with stiffing the bearers, that meant they didn't see the city around them the way Grey did.

Not that most of them would. They were Liganti, or mixed enough in ancestry that they could claim the name; to them, Nadežra was an outpost of Seste Ligante, half tamed by the Liganti general Kaius Sifigno, who restyled himself Kaius Rex after conquering Vraszan two centuries past. Others called him the Tyrant, and when he died, the Vraszenian clans took back the rest of their conquered land. But every push to reclaim their holy city failed, until exhaustion on both sides led to the signing of the Accords. Those established Nadežra as an independent city-state—under the rule of its Liganti elite.

It was an uneasy balance at best, made less easy still by Vraszenian radical groups like the Stadnem Anduske, who wouldn't settle for anything less than the city back in Vraszenian hands. And every time they pushed, the Cinquerat pushed back even harder.

The busy markets of Suncross at the heart of the Old Island parted for Grey's bright blue coat and the tawny embroidered hawk, but not without glares. To the high and mighty, the Vigil was a tool; to the common Nadežran, the Vigil was the tool of the high and mighty. Not all of them—Grey wasn't the only hawk who cared about common folk—but enough that he couldn't blame people for their hostility. And some of the worst glares came from Vraszenians, who looked at him and saw a slip-knot: a man who had betrayed his people, siding with the invaders' descendants.

Grey was used to the glares. He kept an eye out for trouble as he passed market stalls on the stoops of decaying townhouses, and a bawdy puppet show where the only children in the crowd were the pickpockets. They trickled away like water before he could mark their faces. A few beggars eyed him warily, but Grey had no grudge against them; the more dangerous elements wouldn't come out until evening, when the feckless sons and daughters of the delta gentry prowled the streets in search of amusement. A pattern-reader had set up on a corner near the Charterhouse, ready to bilk people in exchange for a pretty lie. He gave her a wide berth, leather glove creaking into a fist as he resisted the urge to drag her back to the Aerie for graft.

Once he'd passed under the decaying bulk of the Dawngate and across the Sunrise Bridge, he turned north into the narrow islets of the Pearls, clogged with sedan chairs. Two elderly ladies impressed with their own importance blocked the Becchia Bridge entirely, squabbling like gulls over which one should yield. Grey marked the house sigil painted onto each chair's door in case complaints came to the Aerie later.

His shoulders itched as he crossed the lines of the complex mosaic in the center of Traementis Plaza. It was no mere tilework, but a numinat: geometric Liganti magic meant to keep the ground dry and solid, against the river's determination to sink everything into the mud. Useful . . . but the Tyrant had twisted numinatria into a weapon during his conquest, and mosaics like this one amounted to emblems of ongoing Liganti control.

On the steps of Traementis Manor, Grey gave his uniform a final smoothing and sounded the bell. Within moments, Colbrin opened the door and favored Grey with a rare smile.

"Young Master Serrado. How pleasant to see you; it's been far too long. I'm afraid Altan Leato is not here to receive you—"

"It's 'Captain' now," Grey said, touching the hexagram pin at his throat. The smile he dredged up felt tired from disuse. "And I'm not here for Leato. Era Traementis requested assistance from the Vigil."

"Ah, yes." Colbrin bowed him inside. "If you'll wait in the salon, I'll inform Era Traementis that you're here."

Grey wasn't surprised when Colbrin returned in a few moments and summoned him to the study. Whatever Donaia had written to the Vigil for, it was business, not a social call.

That room was much darker, with little in the way of bright silks to warm the space—but warmth came in many shapes. Donaia's grizzled wolfhound scrambled up from his place by her desk, claws ticking on wood as he trotted over for a greeting. "Hello, old man," Grey said, giving him a good tousling and a few barrel thumps on the side.

"Meatball. Heel." The dog returned to Donaia's side, looking up as she crossed the room to greet Grey.

"Era Traementis," Grey said, bowing over her hand. "I'm told you have need of assistance."

The silver threads lacing through her hair were gaining ground against the auburn, and she looked tired. "Yes. I need you to look into someone—a visitor to the city, recently arrived from Seteris. Renata Viraudax."

"Has she committed some crime against House Traementis?"

"No," Donaia said. "*She* hasn't."

Her words piqued his curiosity. "Era?"

A muscle tightened in Donaia's jaw. "My husband once had a sister named Letilia—Lecilla, really, but she was obsessed with Seteris and their high culture, so she badgered their father into changing it in the register. Twenty-three years ago, she decided she would rather be in Seteris than here . . . so she stole some money and jewelry and ran away."

Donaia gestured Grey to a chair in front of the hearth. The warmth of the fire enveloped him as he sat down. "Renata Viraudax is Letilia's daughter. She claims to be trying to mend bridges, but I have my doubts. I want you to find out what she's really doing in Nadežra."

As much as Grey loathed the right of the nobility to commandeer the Vigil for private use, he couldn't help feeling sympathy. When he was younger and less aware of the differences that made it impossible, he'd sometimes wished Donaia Traementis was his mother. She was stern, but fair. She loved her children, and was fiercely protective of her family. Unlike some, she never gave Leato and Giuna reason to doubt her love for them.

This Viraudax woman's mother had hurt her family, and the Traementis had a well-earned reputation for avenging their own.

"What can you tell me about her?" he asked. "Has she given you any reason to doubt her sincerity? Apart from being her mother's daughter."

Donaia's fingers drummed briefly against the arm of the chair, and her gaze settled on a corner of the fireplace and stayed there long enough that Grey knew she was struggling with some thought. He kept his silence.

Finally she said, "You and my son are friends, and moreover you aren't a fool. It can't have escaped your notice that House Traementis is not what it once was, in wealth, power, or numbers. We have many enemies eager to see us fall. Now this young woman shows up and tries to insinuate herself among us? Perhaps I'm jumping at shadows...but I must consider the possibility that this is a gambit intended to destroy us entirely." She gave a bitter laugh. "I can't even be certain this girl *is* Letilia's daughter."

She must be worried, if she was admitting so much. Yes, Grey had suspected—would have suspected even if Vigil gossip didn't sometimes speculate—that House Traementis was struggling more than they let on. But he never joined in the gossip, and he never asked Leato.

Leato...who was always in fashion, and according to that same gossip spent half his time frequenting aža parlours and gambling dens. *Does Leato know?* Grey swallowed the question. It wasn't his business, and it wasn't the business Donaia had called him for.

"That last shouldn't be too hard to determine," he said. "I assume you know where she's staying?" He paused when Donaia's lips flattened, but she only nodded. "Then talk to her. If she's truly Letilia's daughter, she should know details an imposter wouldn't easily be able to discover. If she gives you vague answers or takes offense, then you'll know something is wrong."

Grey paused again, wondering how much Donaia would let him pry. "You said you had enemies she might be working for. It would help me to know who they are and what they might want." At her sharply indrawn breath, he raised a hand in pledge. "I promise I'll say nothing of it—not even to Leato."

In a tone so dry it burned, Donaia began ticking possibilities off on her fingers. "Quientis took our seat in the Cinquerat. Kaineto are only delta gentry, but have made a point of blocking our attempts to contract out our charters. Essunta, likewise. Simendis, Destaelio, Novrus, Cleoter—Indestor—I'm afraid it's a crowded field."

That was the entire Cinquerat and others besides...but she'd only stumbled over one name.

"Indestor," Grey said. The house that held Caerulet, the military seat in the Cinquerat. The house in charge of the Vigil.

The house that would not look kindly upon being investigated by one of its own.

"Era Traementis...did you ask for any officer, or did you specifically request me?"

"You're Leato's friend," Donaia said, holding his gaze. "Far better to ask a friend for help than to confess our troubles to an enemy."

That startled a chuckle from Grey. At Donaia's furrowed brow, he said, "My brother was fond of a Vraszenian saying. 'A family covered in the same dirt washes in the same water.'"

And Kolya would have given Grey a good scolding for not jumping to help Donaia right away. She might not be kin, but she'd hired a young Vraszenian carpenter with a scrawny kid brother when nobody else would, and paid him the same as a Nadežran.

He stood and bowed with a fist to his shoulder. "I'll see what I can discover for you. Tell me where to find this Renata Viraudax."

The Face of Gold

Isla Prišta, Westbridge: Suilun 4

Some things were worth paying good money for. The materials for Ren's clothing, for example: Tess was a genius at sewing, but even she couldn't make cheap fabric hold up to close inspection.

The mirror Ren arranged next to an upstairs window was another one of her investments, as were the cosmetics she set in front of it. The one contribution her unknown father had made to her life was hair and skin a few shades lighter than her Vraszenian mother's—light enough to pass for Liganti or Seterin, with help. But making herself look plausibly like Letilia Traementis's daughter took extra effort and care.

Ren angled the silvered glass to take advantage of the natural light, then brushed powder across her face, making sure she blended it up into her hairline and down her throat. Years cooped up indoors as Letilia's maid had done a fair bit to lighten her complexion, and the oncoming winter wouldn't afford her many opportunities to be in the sun, but she would have to be careful when the warmer months came. Given half an excuse, her skin would eagerly tan.

But at least she didn't have to worry about the powder rubbing off. All her cosmetics were imbued by artisans like Tess, people who could infuse the things they made with their own spiritual force to make them work better. Imbued cosmetics might be more expensive, but they would stay in place, blend until their effects looked natural, and not even irritate her skin. Imbuing didn't receive the respect given to numinatria, but compared to the pastes and powders Ren had used back when she was a Finger, these seemed like a miracle.

Switching to a darker shade, she thinned the apparent shape of her nose and made her eyes seem more closely set, adding a few years to her age by contouring out the remaining softness of youth. Her cheekbones, her mouth—nothing remained untouched, until the woman in the mirror was Renata Viraudax instead of Ren.

Tess bustled in with an armful of fabric. She hung the underdress and surcoat from the empty canopy bars of the bed before flopping onto the dusty ropes that should have held a mattress.

"Whoof. Well, I can't speak to the state of my fingers or my eyesight, but the embroidery's done." She held her reddened fingers up to the light. "Wish I could just leave the insides a tangle, but it'd be Quarat's own ill luck if a gust of wind flipped your skirts and flashed your messy backing for the world to see." She stifled a giggle. "I meant your embroidery, not what's under your knickers."

A masquerade was more than just its physical trappings. "Tess."

The mere pitch of that word was enough to remind her. Renata's voice wasn't as high as Letilia's—that woman had cultivated a tone she referred to as "bell-like," and Ren thought of as "shrill"—but she spoke in a higher register than Ren. Now she said Tess's name in Renata's tone, and Tess sat up.

"Yes, alta. Sorry, alta." Tess swallowed a final hiccup of laughter. Her part required less acting, but she struggled harder to get into it. With her round cheeks and moss-soft eyes, she'd been one of the best pity-rustlers in the Fingers, but not much good at lying. She stood and bobbed a curtsy behind Renata, addressing her reflection. "What would the alta like done with her hair?"

It felt uncomfortable, having Tess address her with such deference. But this wasn't a short-term con, talking some shopkeeper into believing she was a rich customer long enough for her to pocket something while his back was turned; she would need to be Renata for hours at a time, for weeks and months to come. And she needed to associate every habit of manner and speech and thought with Renata's costumes, so they wouldn't slip at an inopportune moment.

"I believe you had some ribbon left over," Renata said. "I think it would look lovely threaded through my hair."

"Oooh, excellent idea! The alta has such a refined sense of style."

Tess had never been an alta's maid. While Ren had run herself ragged satisfying Letilia's petty demands, Tess had been sewing herself half-blind in the windowless back room of a grey-market shop. Still, she insisted that obsequiousness was part of the role, and no amount of correction from either Ren or Alta Renata could stamp it out. Sighing, Renata put in her earrings—formerly Letilia's— while Tess retrieved ribbon, brushes, needle, and thread, and set to work.

Tess's skill at imbuing went toward clothing, not hair, but by some undefinable magic she twisted the strands into a complicated knot, turning and tucking them so the outermost parts were the ones bleached lighter by sun and wind, and the darker sections were hidden away.

Just as Ren herself was hidden away. She breathed slowly and evenly, nerves beginning to thrum with familiar excitement.

By the end of today, the nobles of the city would know Renata Viraudax's name.

The Rotunda, Eastbridge: Suilun 4

The Rotunda, situated on the Upper Bank side of the Sunrise Bridge, was a marvel of beauty and magic. Under a vaulted glass dome etched with colored numinata that kept the interior cool in the day and lit at night, a wide marble plaza allowed for casual strolling and diverting entertainments. In the center, a small garden offered benches where patrons could rest their weary feet. Around the perimeter, shops presented the finest imbued wares for the delight of those who could afford them.

Twice a year, in the spring and the fall, merchants from Seste Ligante arrived bearing the newest fabrics and fashions, setting up displays of their wares in the Rotunda. And all the nobles and delta gentry of Nadežra flocked to the seasonal Gloria, to spend, to see, and to be seen.

Despite her resolve to think only Renata's thoughts, Ren couldn't keep her pulse from quickening as she passed through the Rotunda's grand archway with Tess in tow. She'd often peered at the riches beyond, but she'd been inside only once before—with Ondrakja, not long before everything fell apart.

The scheme had been an audacious one. Ondrakja came in first, dressed as a rich merchant from one of the upriver cities, and examined some jewelry. While the jeweler's back was turned, a sapphire bracelet vanished. The Vigil constables guarding the Rotunda searched Ondrakja from head to foot, but found no sign of the gems, and the only people near her when the bracelet disappeared were nobility they dared not accuse. The hawks threw her in jail for the night on principle, but the next day they let her go.

Half an hour after Ondrakja was quietly force-marched out of the Rotunda, a beautiful girl who presumably belonged to one of the delta houses came up and browsed the jeweler's wares. It had been laughably easy for Ren to remove the bracelet from the putty Ondrakja had stuck to the underside of the counter, then walk out with no one the wiser.

Ondrakja had been so pleased with her for that one. She'd bought Ren a bag of honey stones to suck on, and let her wear the bracelet for a whole day before it was fenced.

"May I help you find someone, alta?" a man asked, stepping too close to her side. "You seem lost."

Djek. A hawk!

"Just taking in the view," she said reflexively. Long hours of practice paid off; despite the skin-shock of fear, her words came out in the clipped, fronted vowels of Seteris.

She got a second shock when she looked properly at the man who'd addressed her. *Since when are they making Vigil officers out of Vraszenians?* His accent was cleanly Nadežran, but there was no mistaking him for anything other than full-blooded Vraszenian, with his thick, dark hair—trimmed short though it was—and sun-bronzed skin.

Yet he wore the double-lined hexagram pin of a captain.

Maybe they just thought he looked too good in dress vigils to pass up. He was tall and broad-shouldered, with the lean build of a duelist rather than a soldier, his eyes a deeper shade of his coat's sapphire. Apart from his heritage, he was exactly the kind of man Nadežra's elite would prop up in a corner as decoration at an event like this.

But she'd used her own pretty face as a tool too often to let someone else do the same to her.

He stepped closer to avoid a passing couple, and Renata found herself expertly edged aside from the traffic. "Your accent—you're from Seteris? Welcome to Nadežra. Is this your first visit to the Rotunda?"

"It is indeed." She let her gaze drift across the tables and mannequins displaying wares for this season's Gloria. "I must say, it is ... interesting, seeing what happens to Seterin fashion in its journey here."

Just a touch of condescension. To the Seterins and Liganti across the sea, Nadežra was a foreign backwater. Letilia had never hesitated to heap scorn on it, and her daughter wouldn't have shed those prejudices entirely.

The captain nodded amiably rather than taking offense. "The Rotunda can be distracting for those unused to it—and the pickpockets who manage to sneak in like to take advantage of that. Allow me to escort you until you get your bearings."

The worst thing she could do would be to hesitate. "I'd be grateful," she said, motioning for Tess to fall back a few steps. A Seterin woman who hadn't grown up among Nadežra's political tensions wouldn't turn her nose up at the escort of a handsome Vigil captain, even if he was Vraszenian. She laid gloved fingers on the sleeve of his coat. "Your uniform is that of this city's guard, I believe? No pickpocket will dare approach if I have you at my side."

"Captain Grey Serrado of the Vigil, yes. And I will make certain they do not, alta." He drew away from her touch, his smile betraying not a flicker of interest in her flirtation.

Serrado. She rolled the syllables around in her mind as she returned the introduction, comparing them against his appearance. *Szerado.* And "Grey" was hardly a Vraszenian name. So he was one of those types—the ones who tried to separate themselves from their origins, in hopes of currying favor with the Liganti.

Ren might play the role out of necessity. He was a slip-knot by choice.

She pushed the thought away. It wouldn't matter to Alta Renata. "This way looks more interesting," she said, glancing to the left when Serrado would have led her right—as though she didn't know the ebb and flow of the Gloria.

"The promenade progresses earthwise for the Autumn Gloria," Serrado explained, following the rest of the foot traffic that curved rightward from the entry. "In the spring, it circles sunwise. You'll find the newest and most expensive goods at the start, and the overlooked treasures near the end."

"Is that so." She stopped at a table of perfumes. The woman behind it sized her up in a blink and glided forward, inquiring whether the alta would like to sample any of the scents. Renata allowed her to unstopper a few bottles and wave their wands under her nose, then dab a touch of one to the inside of her wrist. It smelled of eucalyptus, mellowed by something earthier beneath, and the seller promised the scent was imbued to last all day. *Buy something now, to show that I don't care about cost?* she wondered. *Or demonstrate my taste and discretion by refraining?*

She was beginning to attract notice, and not just from the shopkeepers. Some of that was because she looked both noble and unfamiliar, but mostly it was due to her clothing.

Even amid the splendor of the Gloria, she stood out like the blue of autumn skies. Her underdress of gold-shot amber silk was simple almost to the point of austerity, but the azure surcoat showed Tess's fine hand at work. The bandeau was stitched with clever tucks, lifting her bosom rather than crushing it flat. The surcoat's bodice lacked the rigid stays meant to give it a straight shape; instead it was tailored almost like a man's waistcoat, tight through her waist and flaring over her hips before falling into the apron-like panels of the fore and back skirts. On those Tess had exercised restraint; the beauty of the embroidered leaf motif came from quality rather than quantity—turning their tight finances into a virtue. Subtle imbuing made the gold threads shift with the colors of the season. Nobody could look at such a dress and doubt that Alta Renata had paid a small fortune for such work.

And then there were the sleeves. Attached at the shoulder and wrist, they parted and draped in between, leaving the entirety of her arm exposed. She caught one grey-haired old trout frowning in disapproval and hid a smile. *Good. I have their attention.*

That was the goal of today's excursion. If Renata Viraudax sat quietly in her townhouse waiting for Donaia to acknowledge her, she'd be easy to ignore. But if she made herself a public sensation, the Traementis would have to respond.

Besides, it was *fun*. Strolling the Rotunda in beautiful clothing, perusing the wares like she could afford to buy this whole place . . . if only it met her exacting standards. After a life on the streets, even a sip of this wine tasted sweet.

Renata made unimpressed noises at the perfume and wandered onward, attracting more eyes as she went. No one approached her, though—perhaps put off by the fact that she seemed to have her own personal escorting hawk.

She did her best to shed him. But no matter how long she perused wares and vocally dithered over whether they were the best the Gloria had to offer, Captain Serrado didn't oblige her with his boredom so she could send him on his way. She was halfway around the Rotunda, contemplating increasingly absurd schemes for getting rid of him, when she caught sight of the next display.

Velvet panels formed a backdrop for beautiful, empty faces of filigree and stiffened silk. While the masks that rich Nadežrans wore when slumming on the Old Island and the Lower Bank mostly marked them out as targets for plucking, Ren had always loved the masks brought out during the Festival of Veiled Waters. When she was five, her mother had bought her one—just a cheap paper thing, but she'd treasured it like it was made of solid gold.

But Renata Viraudax knew nothing of Nadežran mask traditions. "How odd," she said, drifting toward the display as if it held no particular allure. "I've never seen anything like this in Seteris."

"That's because Seteris doesn't have Nadežra's long and storied history with masks."

The reply didn't come from Captain Serrado. Behind Renata, Tess whimpered.

Tess liked a handsome man as much as the next person, but what really made her go faint was good tailoring. And the clothes of the man who had spoken were *exquisite*—even Ren could see that. Not innovative in the ways Tess could achieve, but the green wool of his coat was as soft as a carpet of stone moss, cut flawlessly so it didn't wrinkle as he moved. His waistcoat was much darker than Liganti fashion favored, appearing black until it caught the light and flashed emerald, and his coat and collar points rose to his jaw without threatening to wilt. Renata's gaze passed over an odd, iridescent spider pin clasped to his lapel, then snagged on the jagged scar ripping up the side of his neck, too high for even fine linens and high collars to entirely hide.

Ignoring Tess and Captain Serrado, the man stepped into the gap next to Renata. It would have felt invasive if he'd been looking at her, but his gaze was on the array of wares. "Masks are worn for many Nadežran festivals, and sometimes ordinary occasions, to sweeten the air and protect the skin. The Tyrant became quite attached to them in the latter stages of his... illness." He gave a delicate shudder. "Even our most infamous outlaw, the Rook, is known for hiding his face. One can't visit our fair delta and not acquire a mask."

He plucked down one of lapis caught in stiffened gold lace,

similar to the embroidery on Renata's surcoat, and offered it to her. "Derossi Vargo. Apologies for my presumption, but I had to make the acquaintance of the most stylish woman to grace this year's Gloria."

The flattery was unsubtle, but delivered smoothly enough to charm, and Renata was just grateful someone had finally broken the hawk-shaped wall at her back.

Derossi Vargo. The name seemed nigglingly familiar, and it annoyed her that she couldn't place it. It wasn't a noble name, but he might be from one of the delta houses, the gentry of Nadežra.

She accepted the mask and held it against her face. "How is a visitor to know which one to buy?"

"Why, whichever one pleases you best and costs the most."

Before Vargo could fetch down another, the shopkeeper hurried over. "There's more than just beauty to be had here, alta," she said, selecting a few other styles that complemented Renata's coloring and ensemble. "My husband does the finest imbuing in Nadežra. Take this one." She held up two circles of overlapping silver and gold. "It'll keep your complexion dry in our humid air. Or here." Up came a midnight-blue domino decked with shimmering onyx. "This will hide you from prying eyes on your way to an assignation. I've masks that'll clear up your spots—not that you've any need for that—or that'll protect you from the sick fogs that roll up from the Lower Bank."

"Really," Vargo murmured, reaching for that last one. "It fends off disease?"

Renata drifted away as the shopkeeper made improbable promises. The display was small—most of the focus in the Rotunda was on imported goods, not local products—and her wandering gaze alighted on a mask tucked into a bottom corner, as if the shopkeeper knew nobody was likely to want it.

Where her childhood mask had been clumsily painted with a rainbow of colors, this one was hammered prismatium, shimmering like the tail of a dreamweaver bird. The mask-maker had sculpted the metal into gentle waves, ebbing and flowing like the

River Dežera. It wasn't anything Renata Viraudax needed…but Ren wanted it so badly it took all her will not to let the yearning show.

"What's caught your attention?" Vargo's question was warm, amused, like they were old friends rather than acquaintances of mere moments. He drew close, peering over her shoulder. "Ah. That's a very…Nadežran mask."

"Vraszenian, you mean," Captain Serrado muttered. He looked away when Vargo glanced over.

"I suppose you would know, Captain." Vargo's tone rippled like the prismatium of the mask, full of colors hidden just under the surface. The smile he turned on Renata was equally pleasant and enigmatic. "Do you like it?"

Just be Renata. It had sounded so easy when she was getting dressed this morning. In practice, keeping unwanted thoughts from welling up was proving far harder than she'd anticipated. "What makes it so Nadežran? Or Vraszenian—whichever." She dismissed the quibble over terminology with a flutter of one hand.

If she'd wanted to persuade them she'd never been to Nadežra in her life, she couldn't have chosen a better method. Both men bristled, brothers in indignation. Serrado might be a slip-knot, but his ancestry was as Vraszenian as they came, while Vargo looked like a typical Nadežran, mixed Vraszenian and Liganti blood—and neither of them appreciated being lumped in with the other.

Vargo's indignation broke first, into rueful chuckles. He lifted the mask and turned it to admire the prismatium. Faint etching and the shape of the edges gave it the appearance of feathers. "Nadežran because the dreamweaver bird is a symbol of the city. They flock here every spring to mate, when we celebrate the Festival of Veiled Waters. Vraszenian because the Vraszenian people say they're descended from those same birds, so they flock here as well."

A muscle jumped in Serrado's jaw, but he said nothing to correct the inaccuracy or half-veiled insult in Vargo's description. Vraszenians did not consider dreamweavers their ancestors, but the symbol of one: Ižranyi, the youngest and most favored daughter of Ažerais, the goddess of their people. She and her siblings had founded the seven Vraszenian clans.

The Ižranyi clan was lost now, slaughtered centuries ago in a divine cataclysm that left their entire city a haunted ruin. But their emblem was still honored.

Taking the mask from Vargo, Renata held it up, comparing it against him. "It almost matches your spider pin! But not your coat, I fear."

Fighting a smile, Vargo absently touched the pin as Renata settled the mask on her face and checked the shopkeeper's mirror.

It was a mistake. Seeing the mask's sculpted curve cradling the line of her jaw like a caress, Ren found herself completely unable to care about Tess's budget and the limits of her forged letter of credit.

Her reflection assured that her yearning remained hidden, but nevertheless Vargo nodded. "I'll buy it for you—if the alta will allow." He lifted the mask from Renata's face, his gloved fingers brushing her cheek in passing, and handed it to the shopkeeper for wrapping, along with the mask that kept away disease. "Call it a welcoming gift."

Well, that solves the budget problem. "You don't even know my name," she said, smiling.

There was another scar through his brow, smaller than the one on his neck, that became visible when he arched it. Whoever Derossi Vargo was, he flung money around like a cuff and had the marks of a Lower Bank rat. He handed her the wrapped mask with a flourish. "There's an obvious solution to that."

In response, Renata swept him the most elegant curtsy she could in the confines of the stall, giving her name in a voice that carried to the onlookers. Vargo cocked his head and said, "Viraud—Oh! Number four, Via Brelkoja."

A chill washed over her skin. How did he know her address?

"I believe I'm your new landlord," he said, with a small bow. "I hope you're finding the house suitable to your needs."

That niggling sense of recognition flashed into clarity, and a sense of relief. She knew his name because she'd seen it on the papers she'd signed to lease her townhouse. "Ah, of course! Please forgive me—I should have known." Passing the mask to Tess, she curtsied again. "Thank you, Master Vargo, for the gift. It seems I could have no more fitting memento of this city."

Serrado was radiating disapproval like a blazing hearth. And it seemed Tess agreed with him, because she intervened. "Oh, alta, it's that cold in here. I've your wrap for you." She bundled Renata in an artful drape of silk, conveniently stepping in front of Vargo. "Do you wish to go back? I can ask the captain to call a chair."

Go back? At this point that would be disastrous. Renata was here to make an impression on the great and powerful, and her first conversation of substance was with someone of no social standing, rich and charming though Vargo might be.

But she'd seen Letilia make enemies by giving people her back when she decided they weren't important enough to merit her time. "Nonsense, Tess. Seterin winters are much colder than this." She let the wrap slip down enough to show her bare shoulders—which had, after all, been Tess's idea in the first place. "I've barely seen half the Gloria yet."

As if sensing the dismissal, Vargo swept the skirts of his coat back and bowed to Renata. "I've taken up too much of your time. I hope our paths may cross again. Perhaps an occasion that allows you to wear your new mask? Alta." After a brief hesitation, he nodded at Serrado as well. "Captain."

A sigh escaped Tess as Vargo sauntered off, giving an excellent view of his broad shoulders and striking bootheels and swinging green coat.

Serrado, unfortunately, did not follow suit. He'd gotten his disapproval under control, his face once again a bland mask, avoiding the eye contact that would let Renata gracefully release him.

Sighing inwardly, she turned to face the remaining half circle of the Rotunda. She saw people murmuring behind their fans and gloves, trying with varying degrees of success to pretend they weren't gossiping about her... and among them, moving toward her, a recognizable golden head.